Lily the Thief

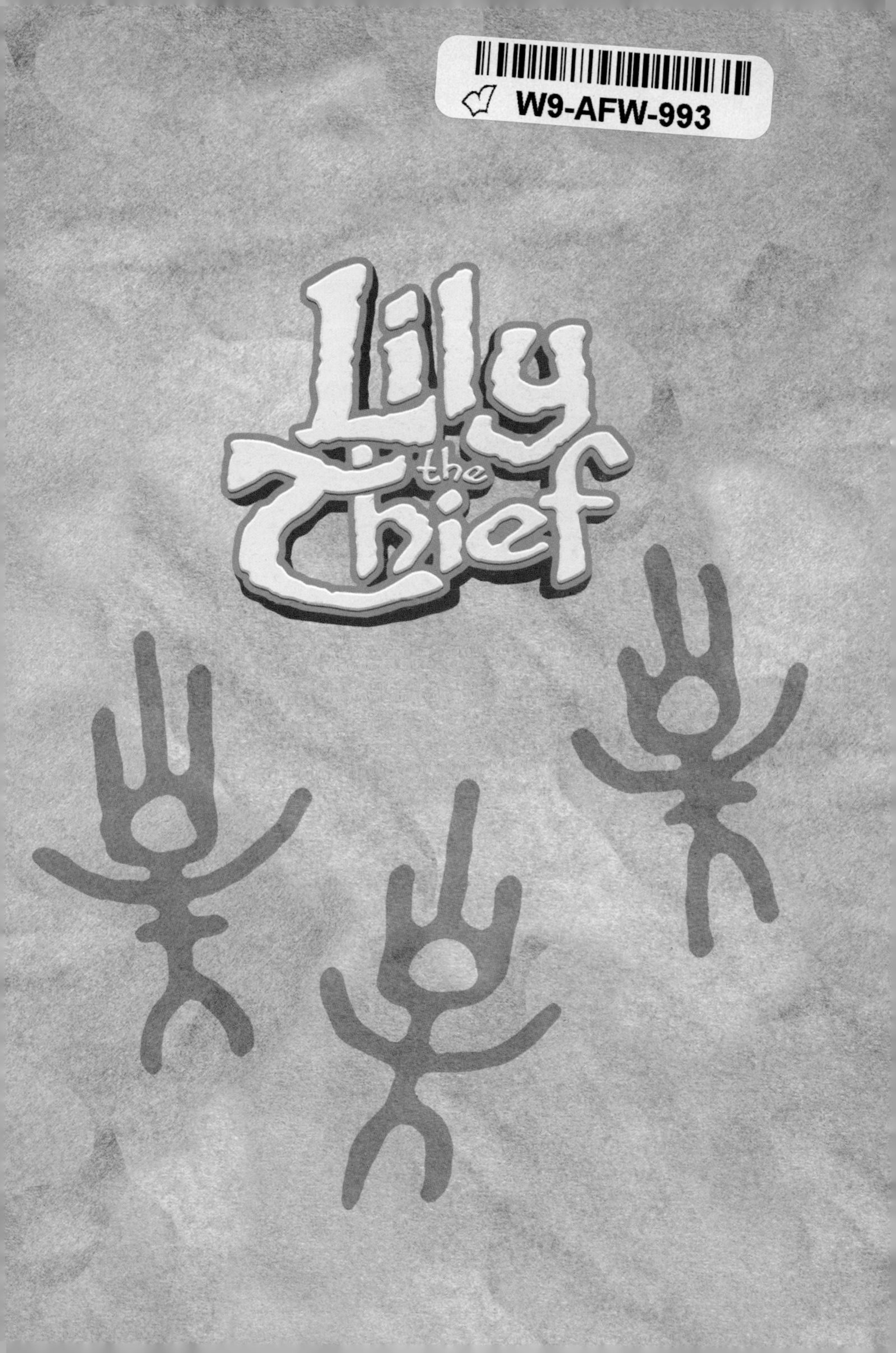

Lily the Thief

Janne Kukkonen

Color by
Kévin Bazot

:01
First Second
New York

On the dark day of rising,
From their lairs they'll come knocking,
Scratching a crack in the calm.
Beware, then, all that is bright,
Even the palest moon's light.

1

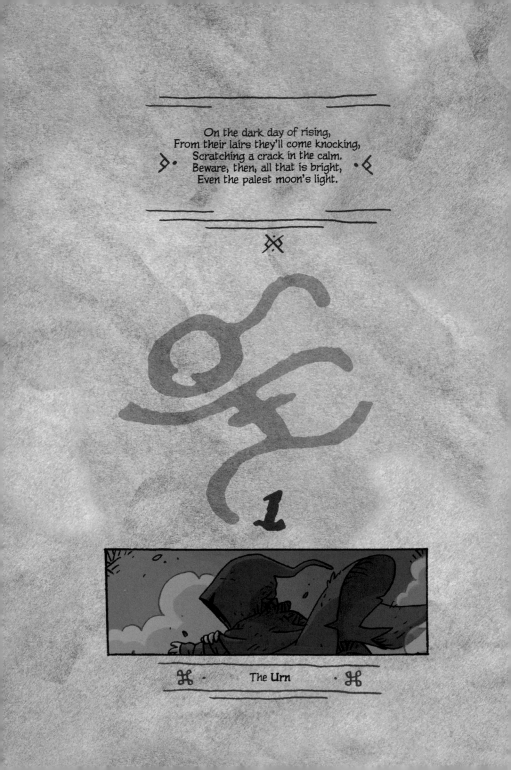

The Urn

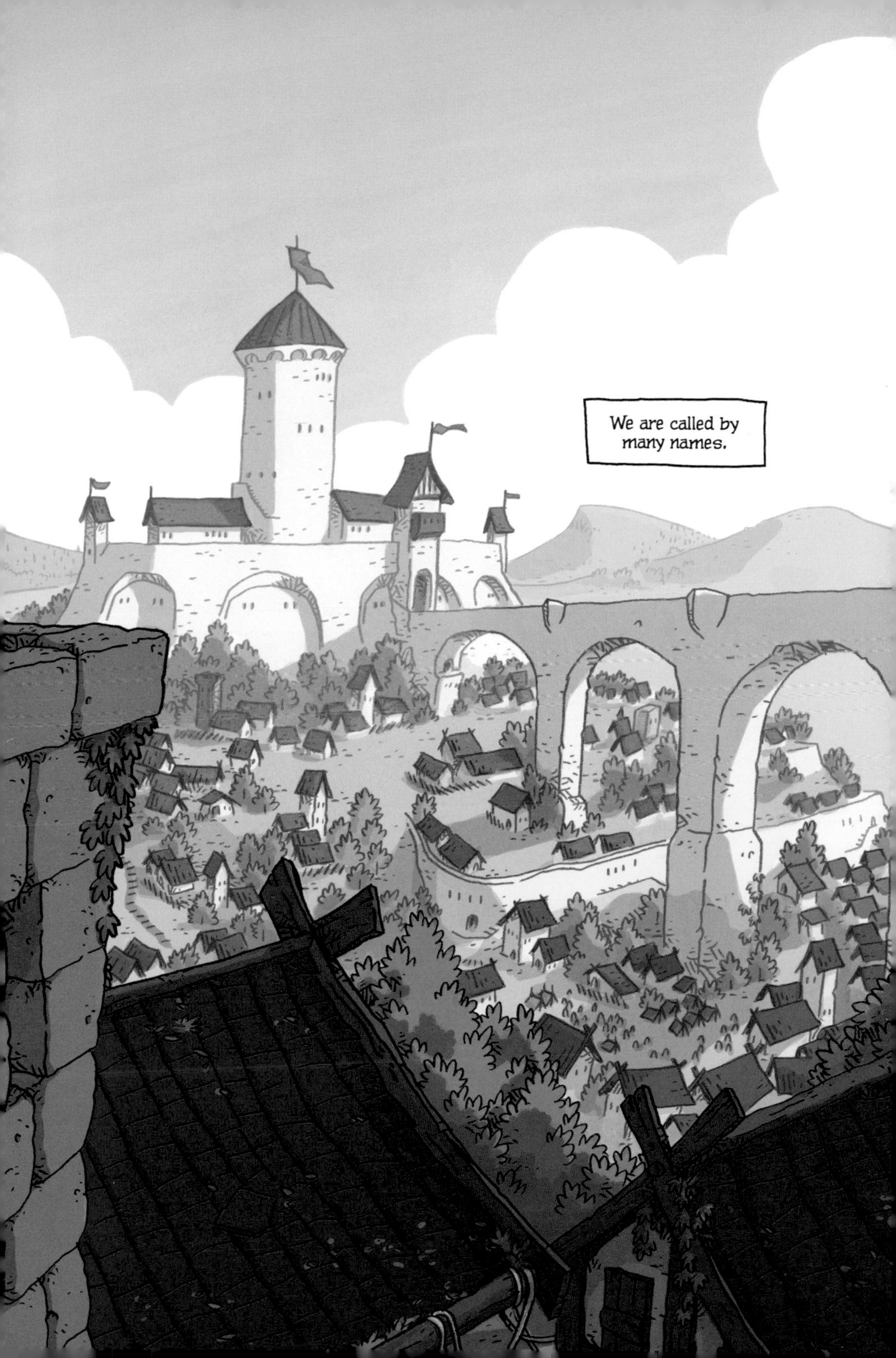
We are called by many names.

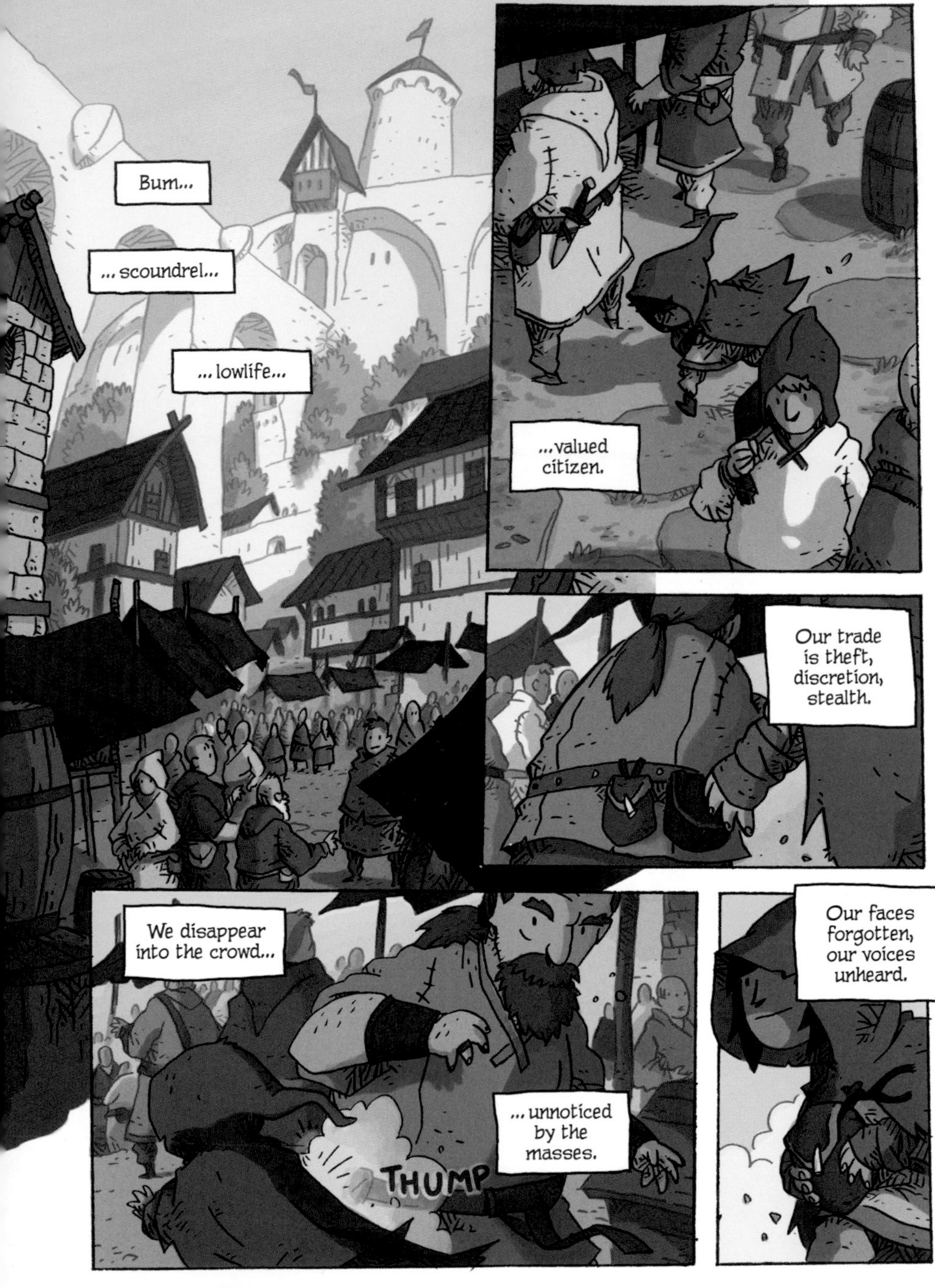

Bum...
...scoundrel...
...lowlife...
...valued citizen.
Our trade is theft, discretion, stealth.
We disappear into the crowd...
...unnoticed by the masses.
THUMP
Our faces forgotten, our voices unheard.

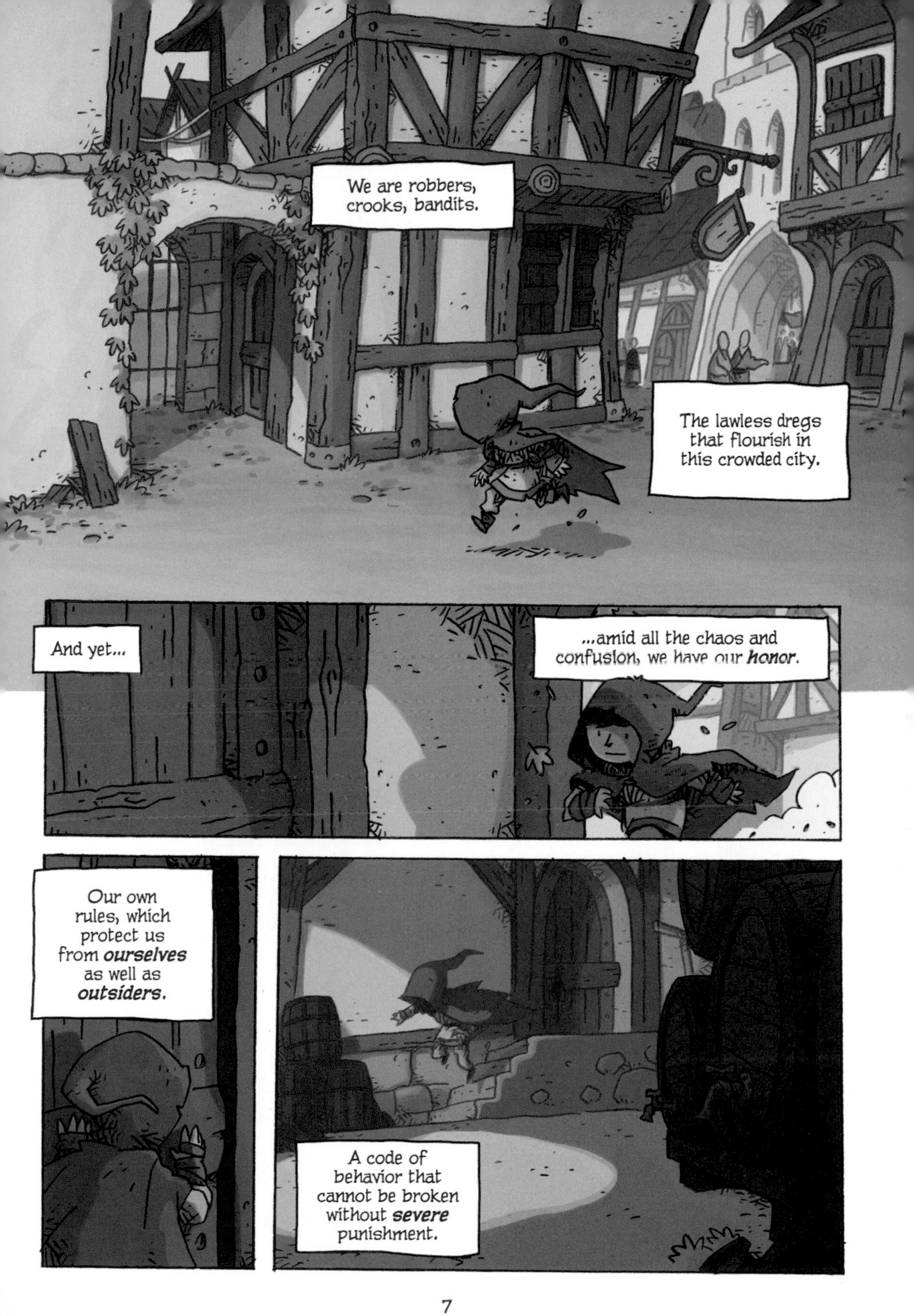
We are robbers, crooks, bandits.
The lawless dregs that flourish in this crowded city.
And yet...
...amid all the chaos and confusion, we have our ***honor***.
Our own rules, which protect us from ***ourselves*** as well as ***outsiders***.
A code of behavior that cannot be broken without ***severe*** punishment.

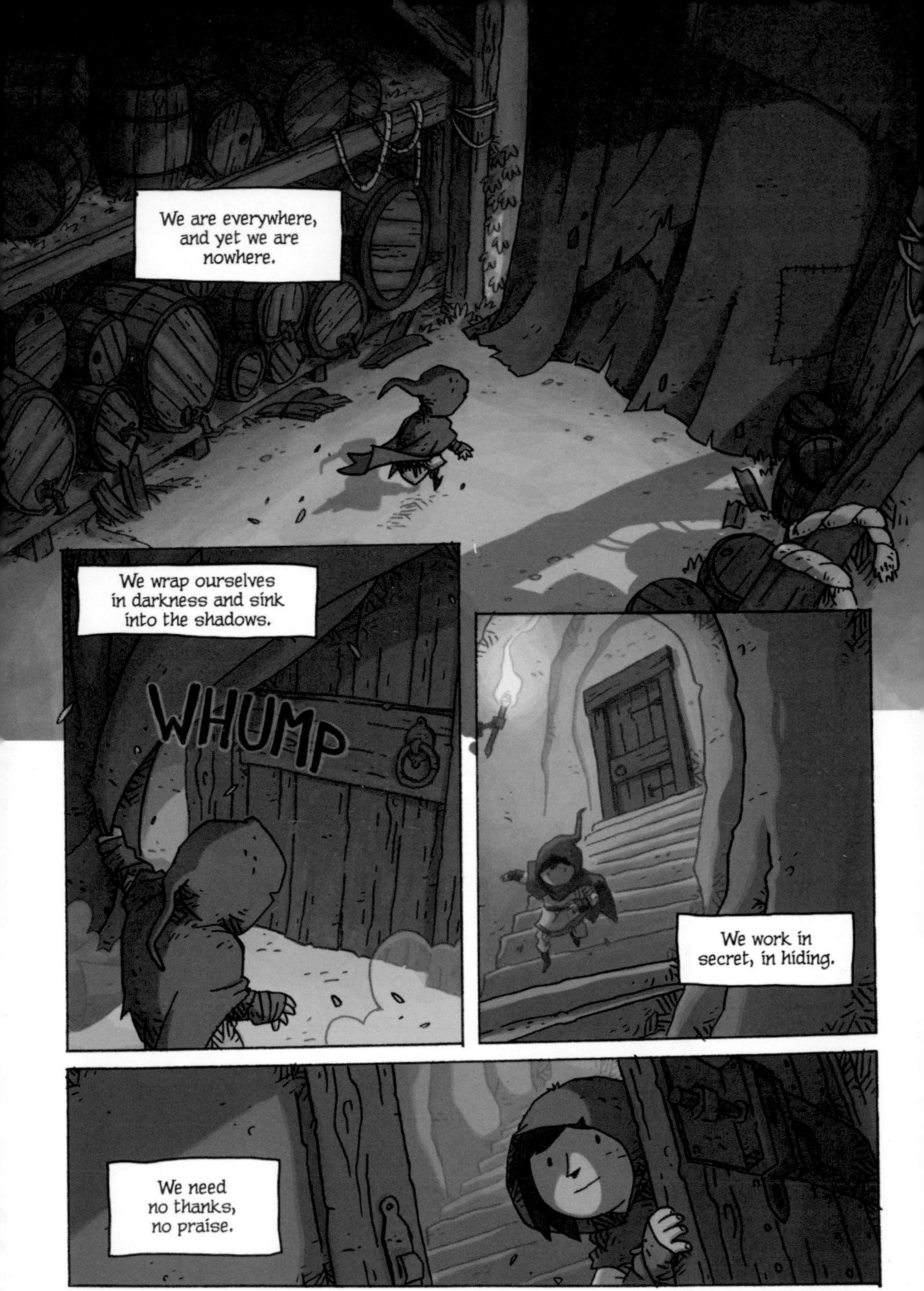
We are everywhere, and yet we are nowhere.
We wrap ourselves in darkness and sink into the shadows.
WHUMP
We work in secret, in hiding.
We need no thanks, no praise.

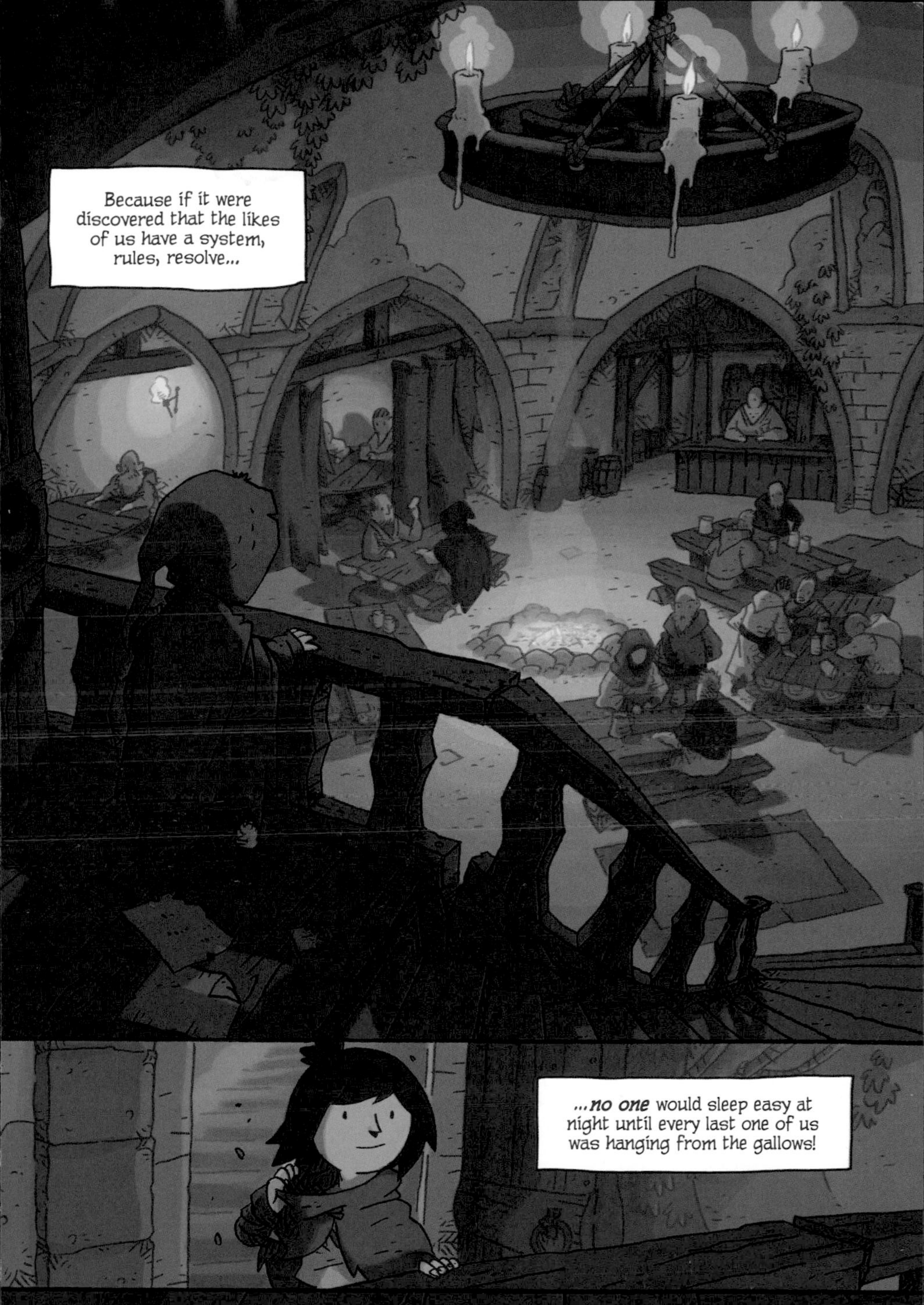
Because if it were discovered that the likes of us have a system, rules, resolve...
...**no one** would sleep easy at night until every last one of us was hanging from the gallows!

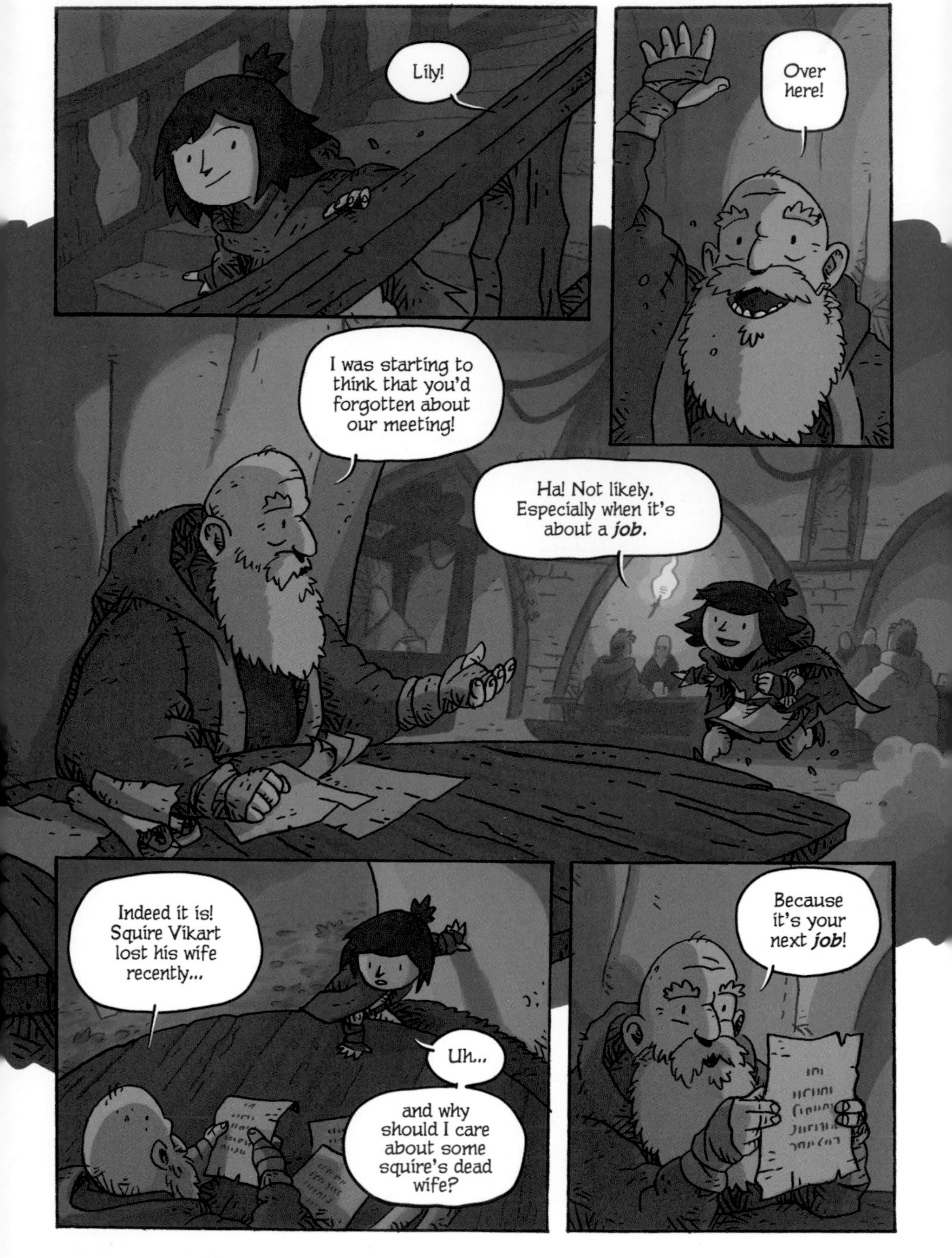

Lily!
Over here!
I was starting to think that you'd forgotten about our meeting!
Ha! Not likely. Especially when it's about a *job*.
Indeed it is! Squire Vikart lost his wife recently...
Uh...
and why should I care about some squire's dead wife?
Because it's your next *job*!

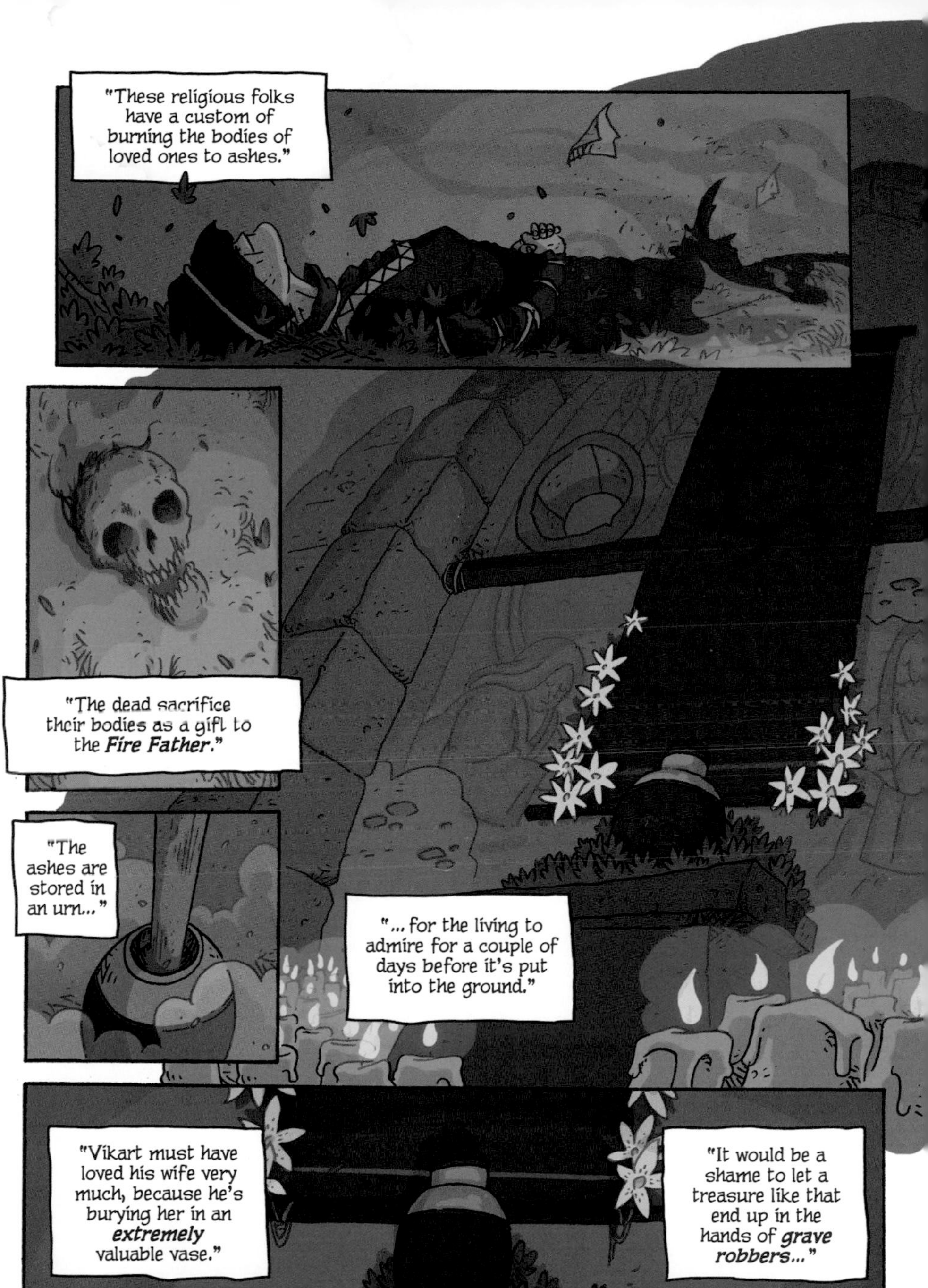
"These religious folks have a custom of burning the bodies of loved ones to ashes."
"The dead sacrifice their bodies as a gift to the *Fire Father*."
"The ashes are stored in an urn..."
"...for the living to admire for a couple of days before it's put into the ground."
"Vikart must have loved his wife very much, because he's burying her in an *extremely* valuable vase."
"It would be a shame to let a treasure like that end up in the hands of *grave robbers*..."

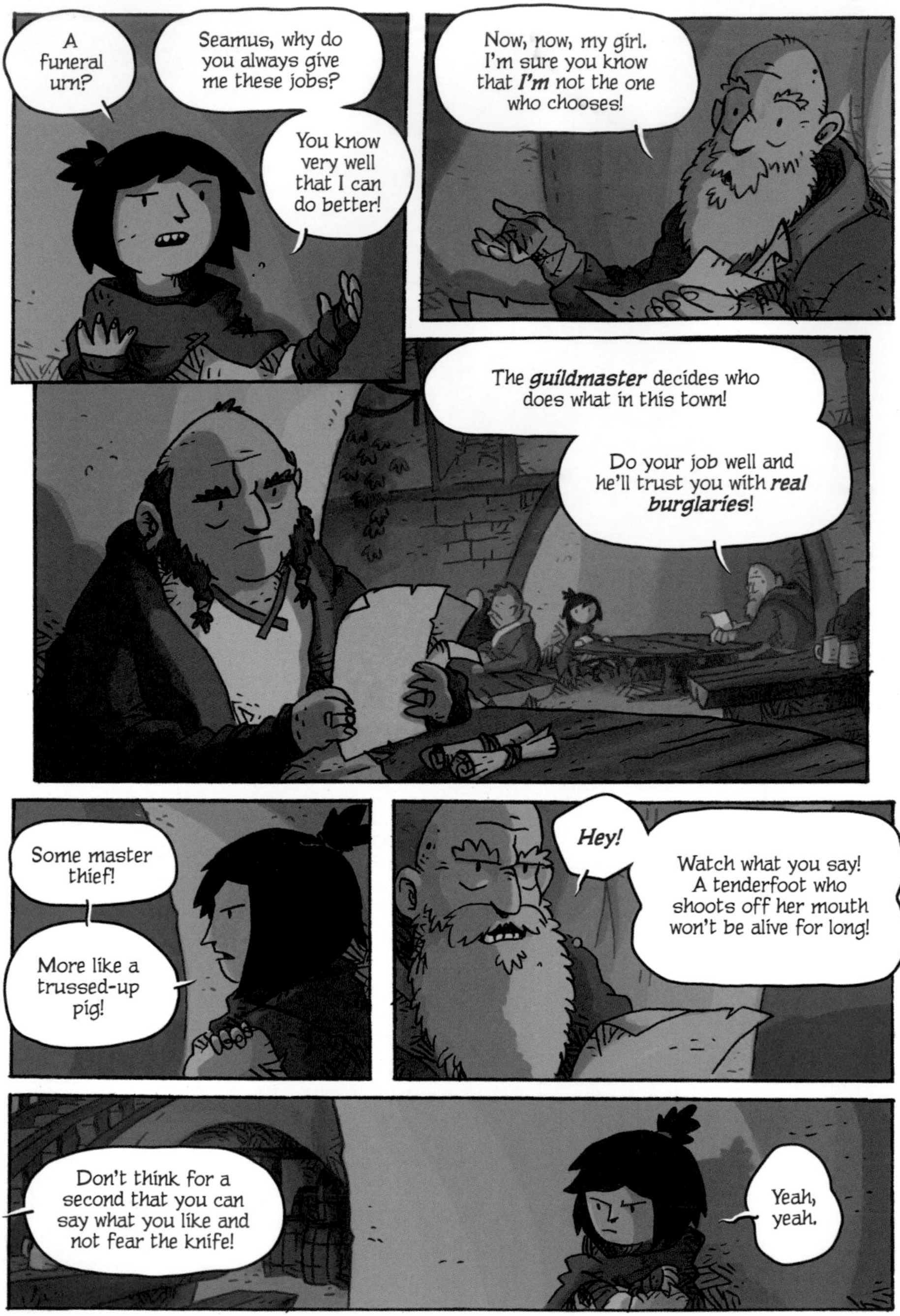
A funeral urn?
Seamus, why do you always give me these jobs?
You know very well that I can do better!
Now, now, my girl. I'm sure you know that ***I'm*** not the one who chooses!
The ***guildmaster*** decides who does what in this town!
Do your job well and he'll trust you with ***real burglaries***!
Some master thief!
More like a trussed-up pig!
Hey!
Watch what you say! A tenderfoot who shoots off her mouth won't be alive for long!
Don't think for a second that you can say what you like and not fear the knife!
Yeah, yeah.

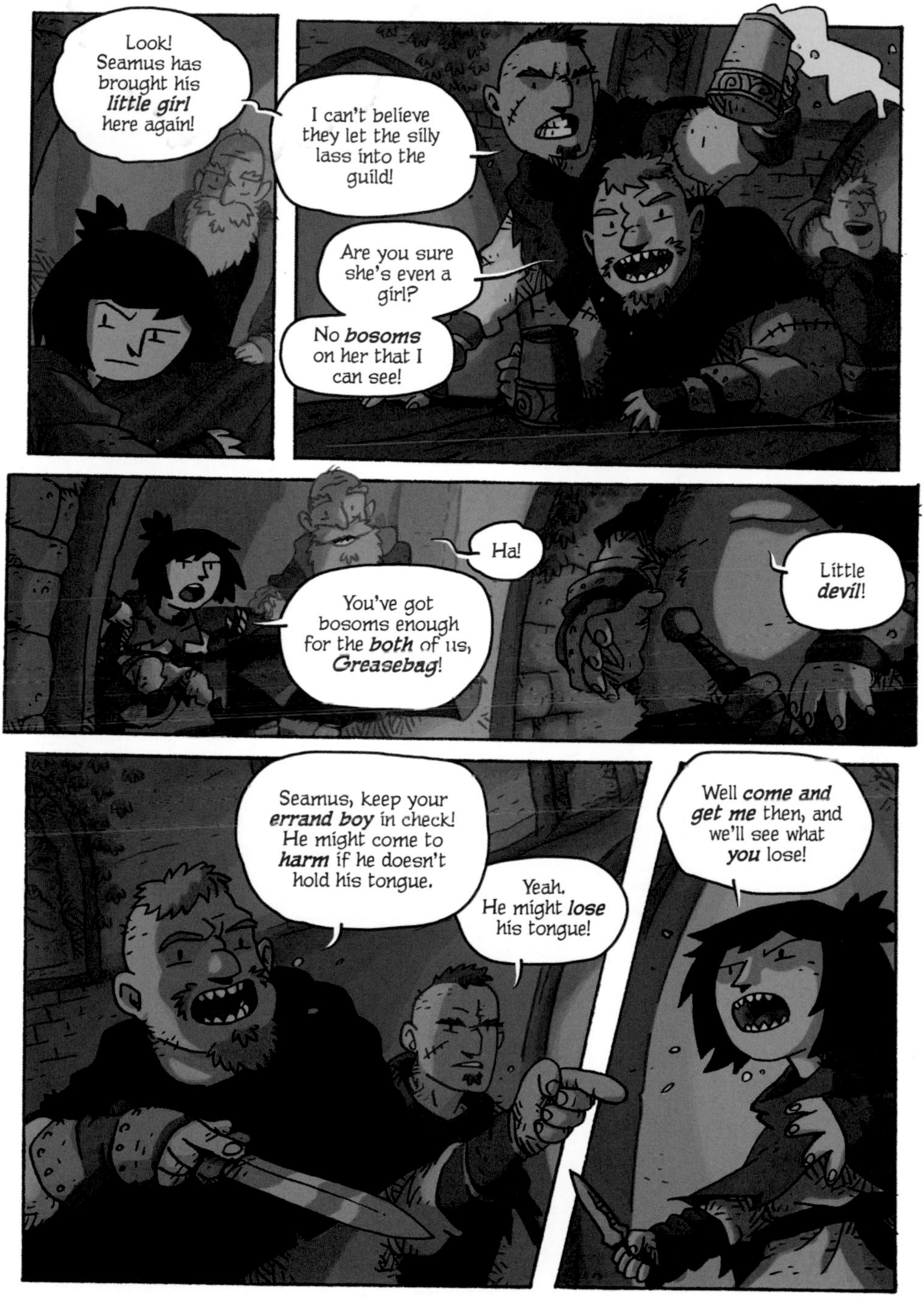
Look! Seamus has brought his *little girl* here again!
I can't believe they let the silly lass into the guild!
Are you sure she's even a girl?
No *bosoms* on her that I can see!
Ha!
You've got bosoms enough for the *both* of us, *Greasebag*!
Little *devil*!
Seamus, keep your *errand boy* in check! He might come to *harm* if he doesn't hold his tongue.
Yeah. He might *lose* his tongue!
Well *come and get me* then, and we'll see what *you* lose!

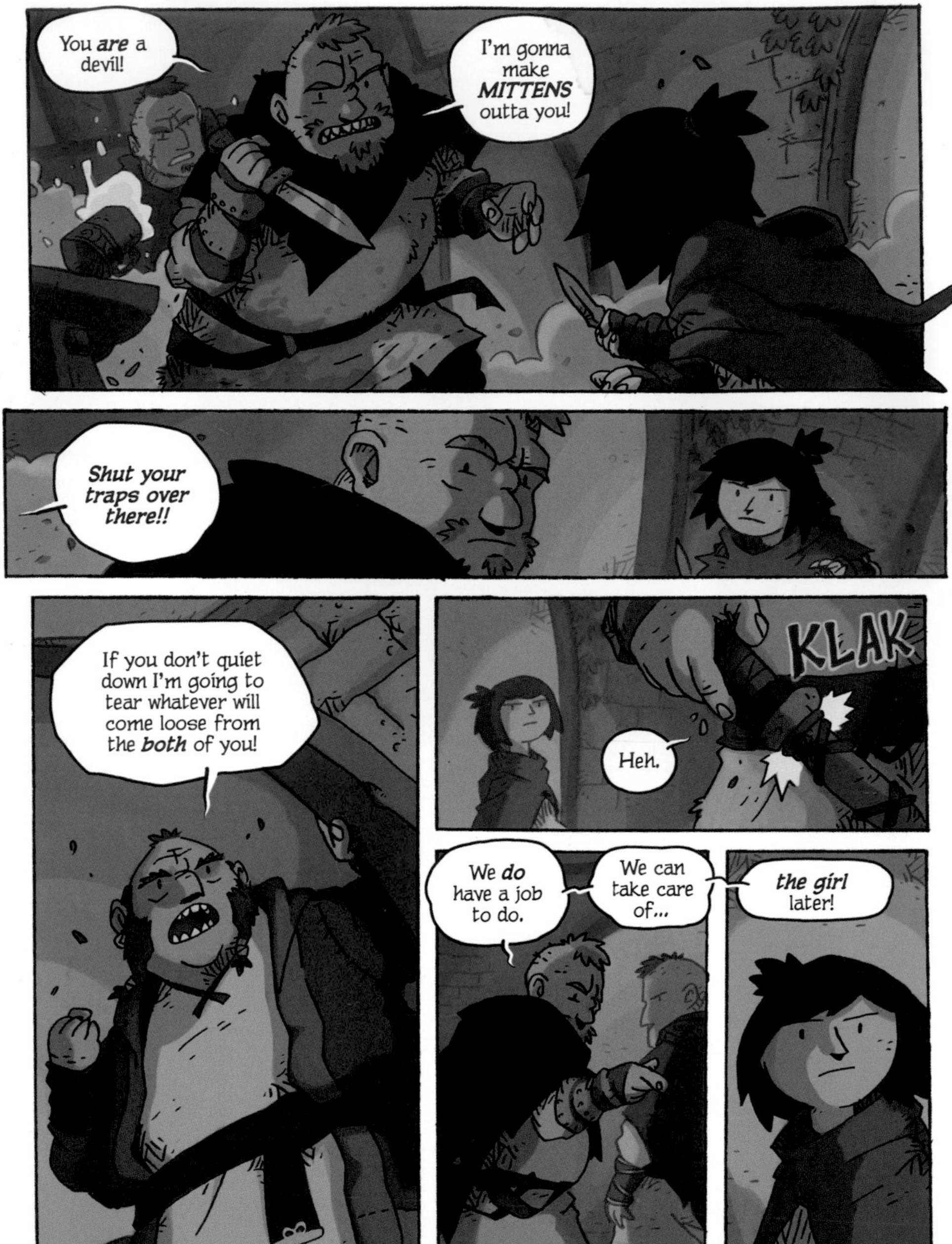
You *are* a devil!
I'm gonna make ***MITTENS*** outta you!
Shut your traps over there!!
If you don't quiet down I'm going to tear whatever will come loose from the ***both*** of you!
KLAK
Heh.
We ***do*** have a job to do.
We can take care of...
the girl later!

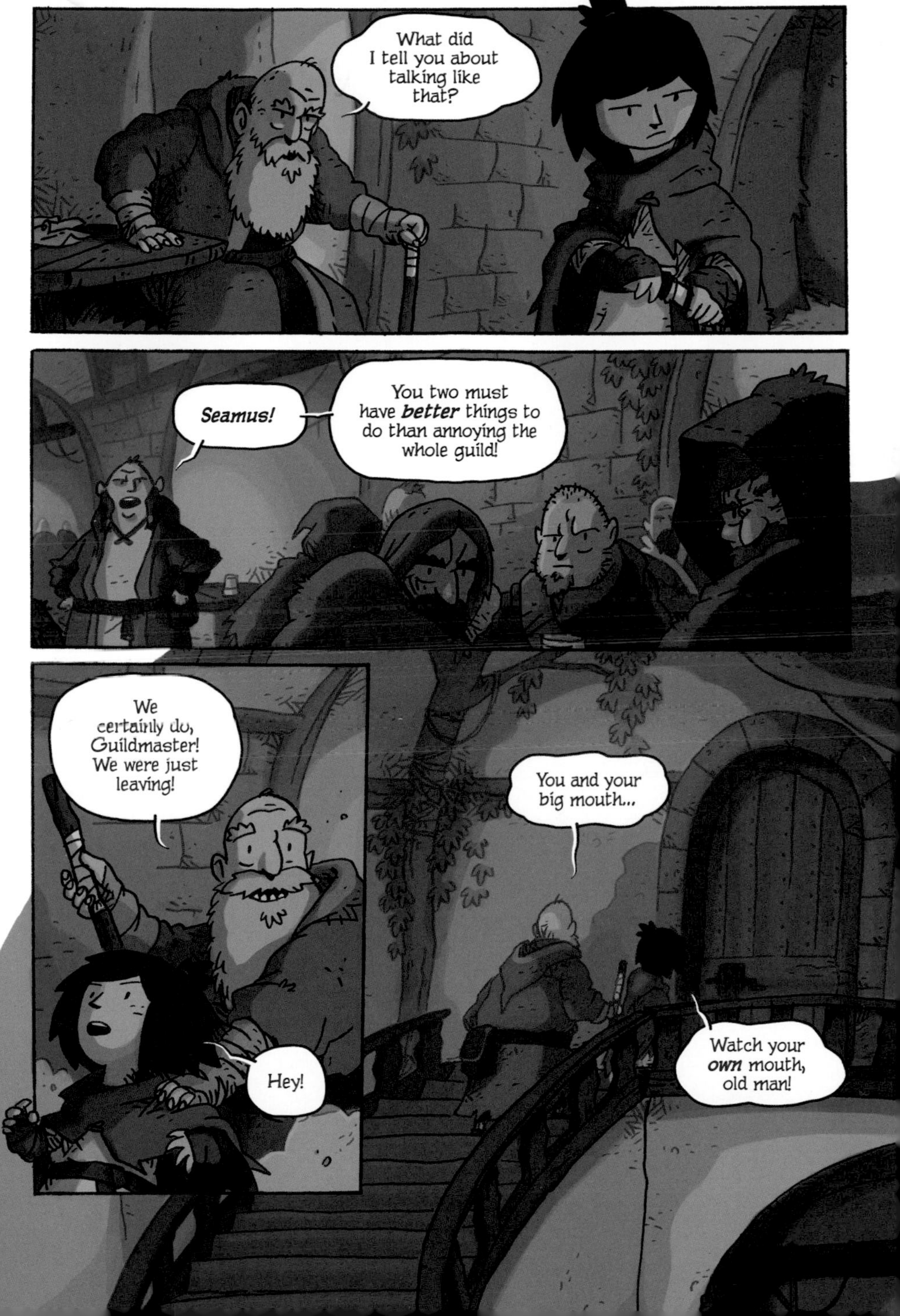
What did I tell you about talking like that?
Seamus!
You two must have *better* things to do than annoying the whole guild!
We certainly do, Guildmaster! We were just leaving!
Hey!
You and your big mouth...
Watch your *own* mouth, old man!

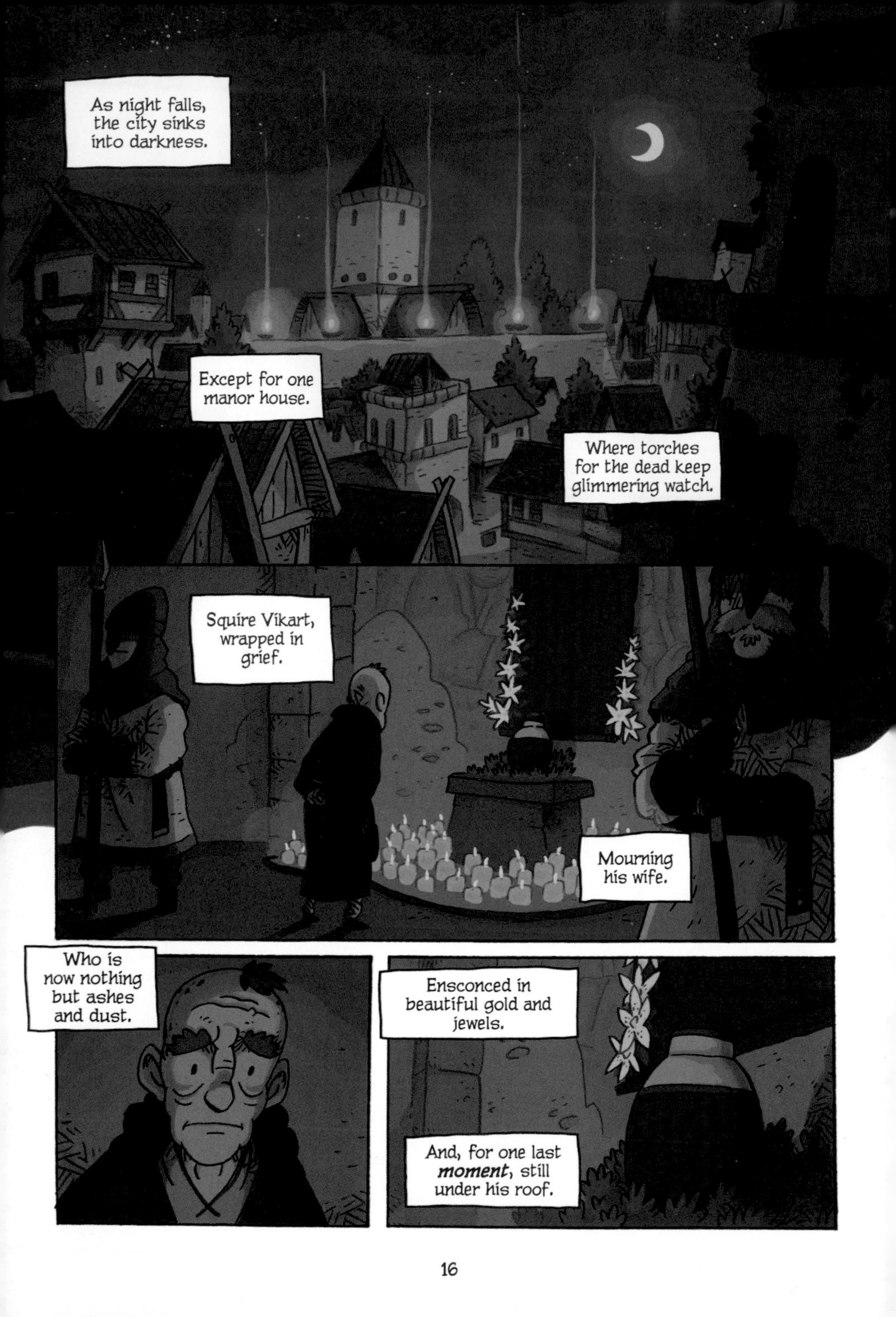
As night falls, the city sinks into darkness.
Except for one manor house.
Where torches for the dead keep glimmering watch.
Squire Vikart, wrapped in grief.
Mourning his wife.
Who is now nothing but ashes and dust.
Ensconced in beautiful gold and jewels.
And, for one last *moment*, still under his roof.

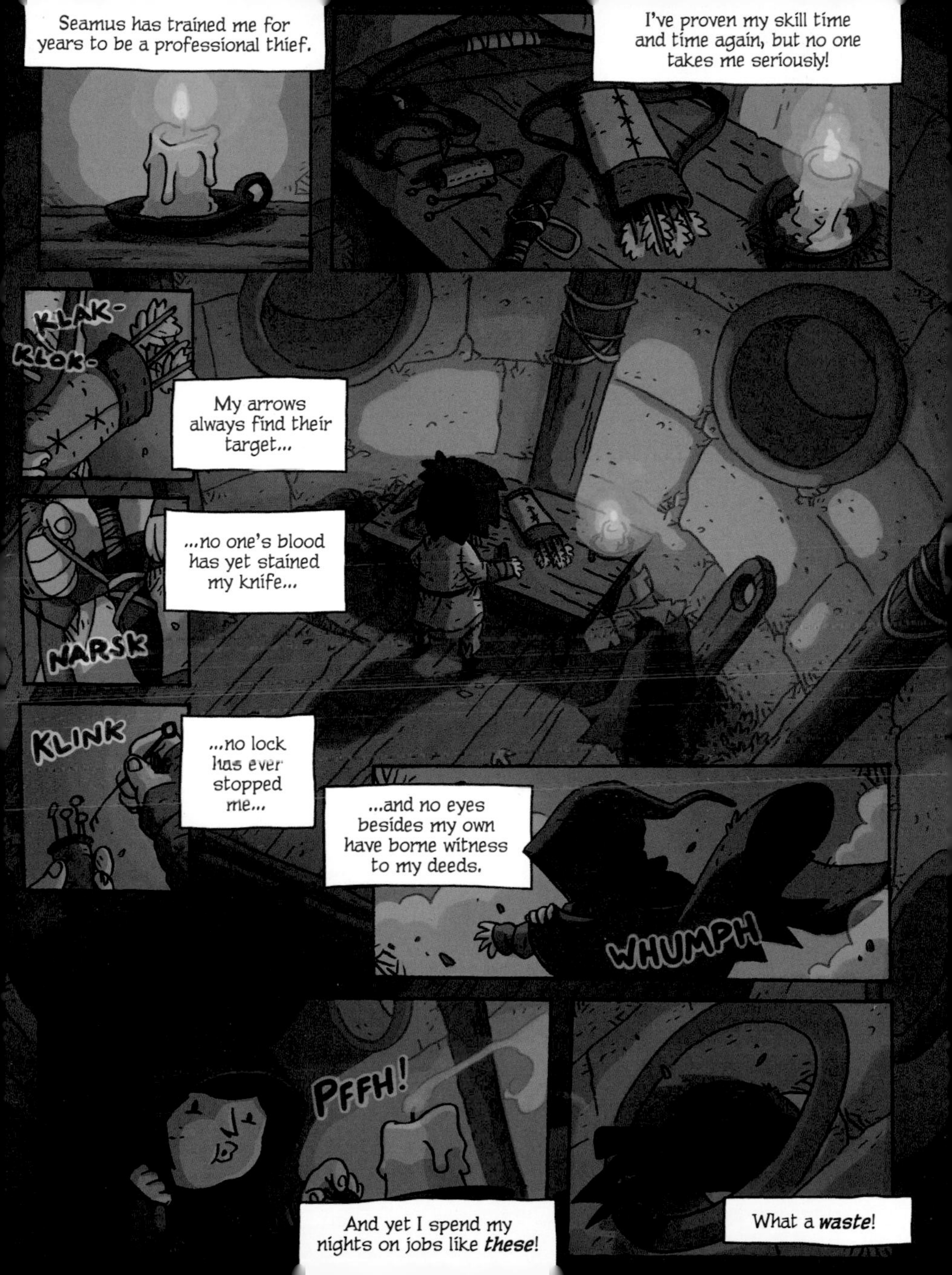
Seamus has trained me for years to be a professional thief.
I've proven my skill time and time again, but no one takes me seriously!
KLAK-
KLOK-
My arrows always find their target...
...no one's blood has yet stained my knife...
NARSK
KLINK
...no lock has ever stopped me...
...and no eyes besides my own have borne witness to my deeds.
WHUMPH
PFFH!
And yet I spend my nights on jobs like *these*!
What a *waste*!

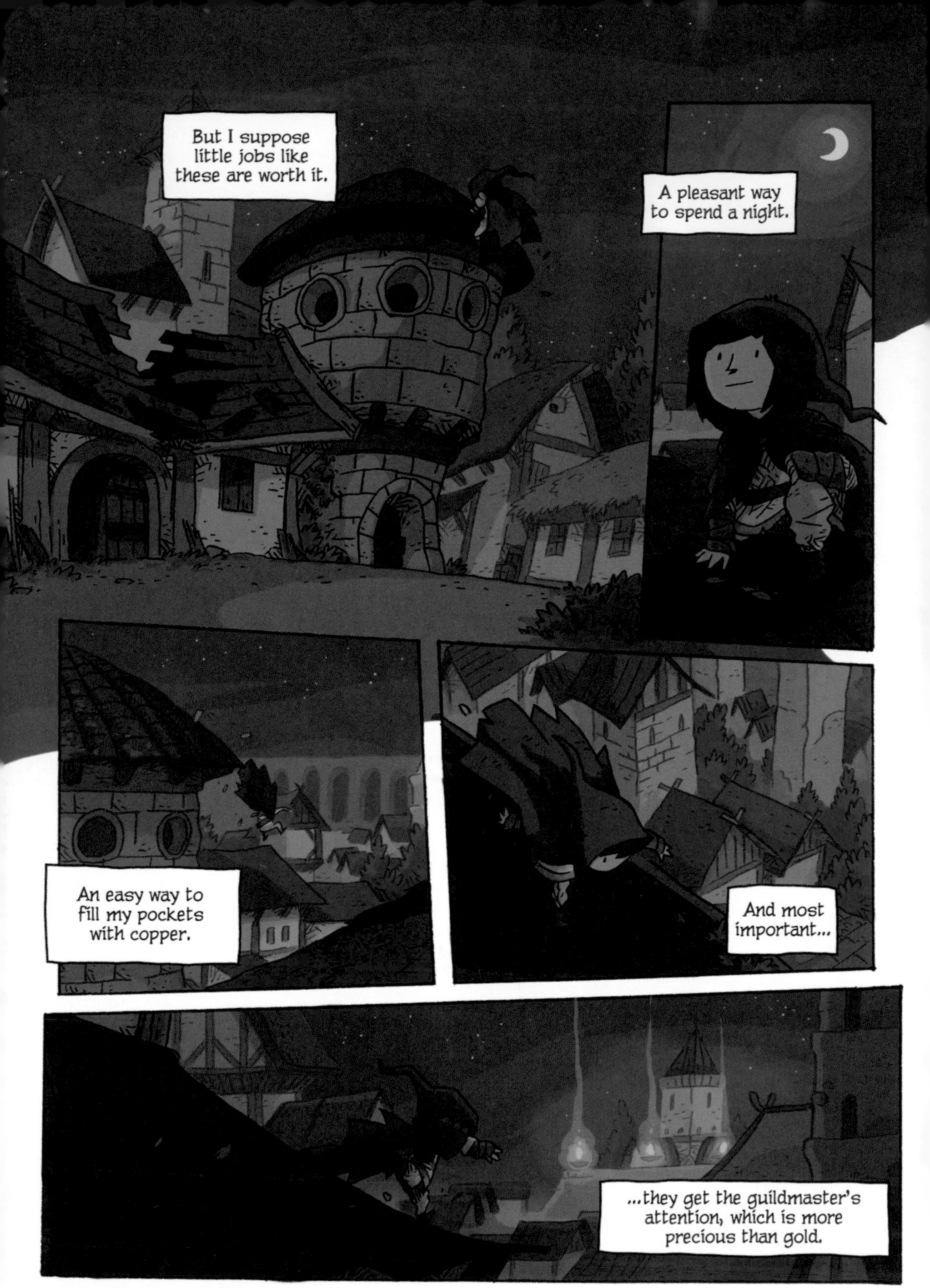
But I suppose little jobs like these are worth it.
A pleasant way to spend a night.
An easy way to fill my pockets with copper.
And most important...
...they get the guildmaster's attention, which is more precious than gold.

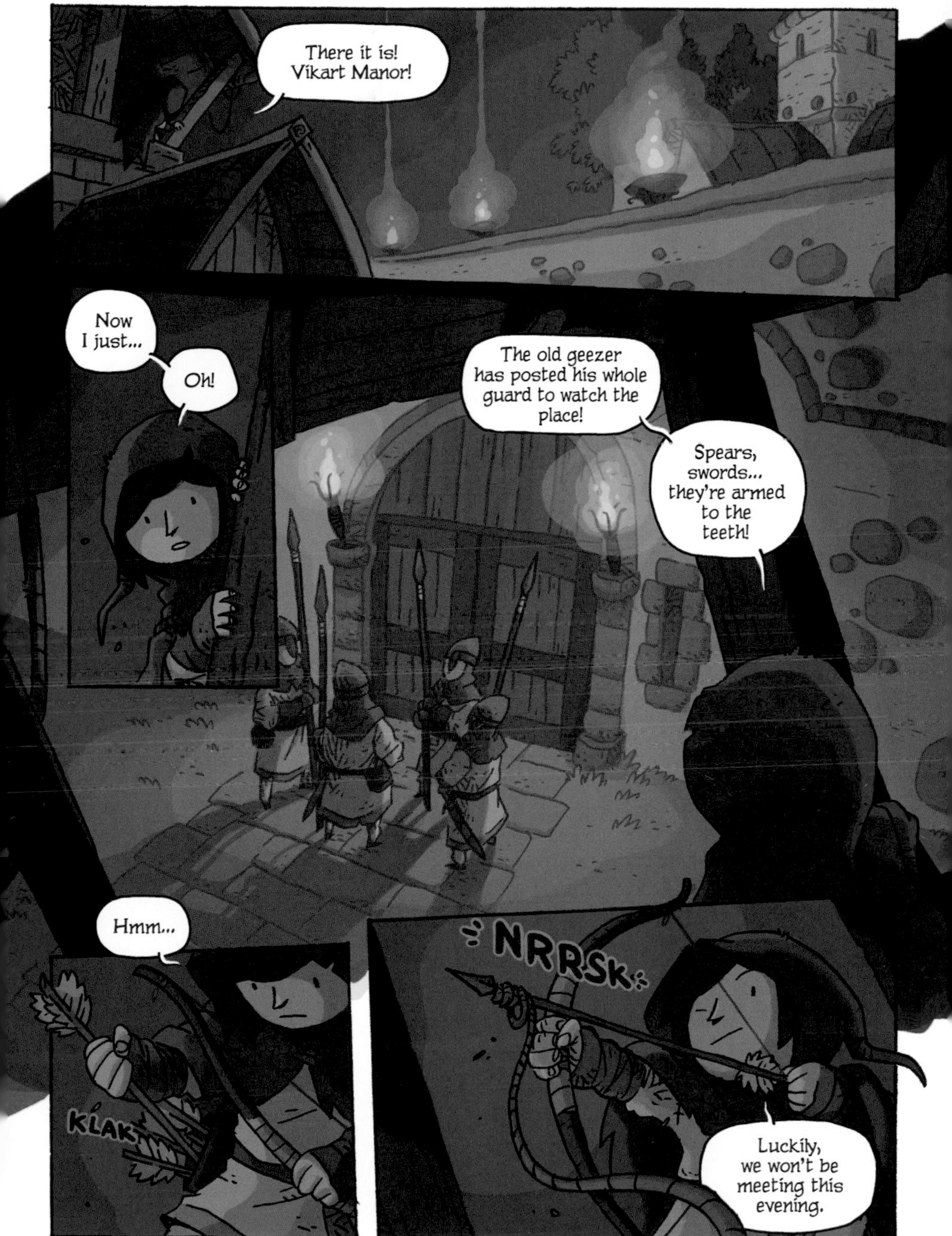
There it is! Vikart Manor!
Now I just...
Oh!
The old geezer has posted his whole guard to watch the place!
Spears, swords... they're armed to the teeth!
Hmm...
KLAK
NRRSK
Luckily, we won't be meeting this evening.

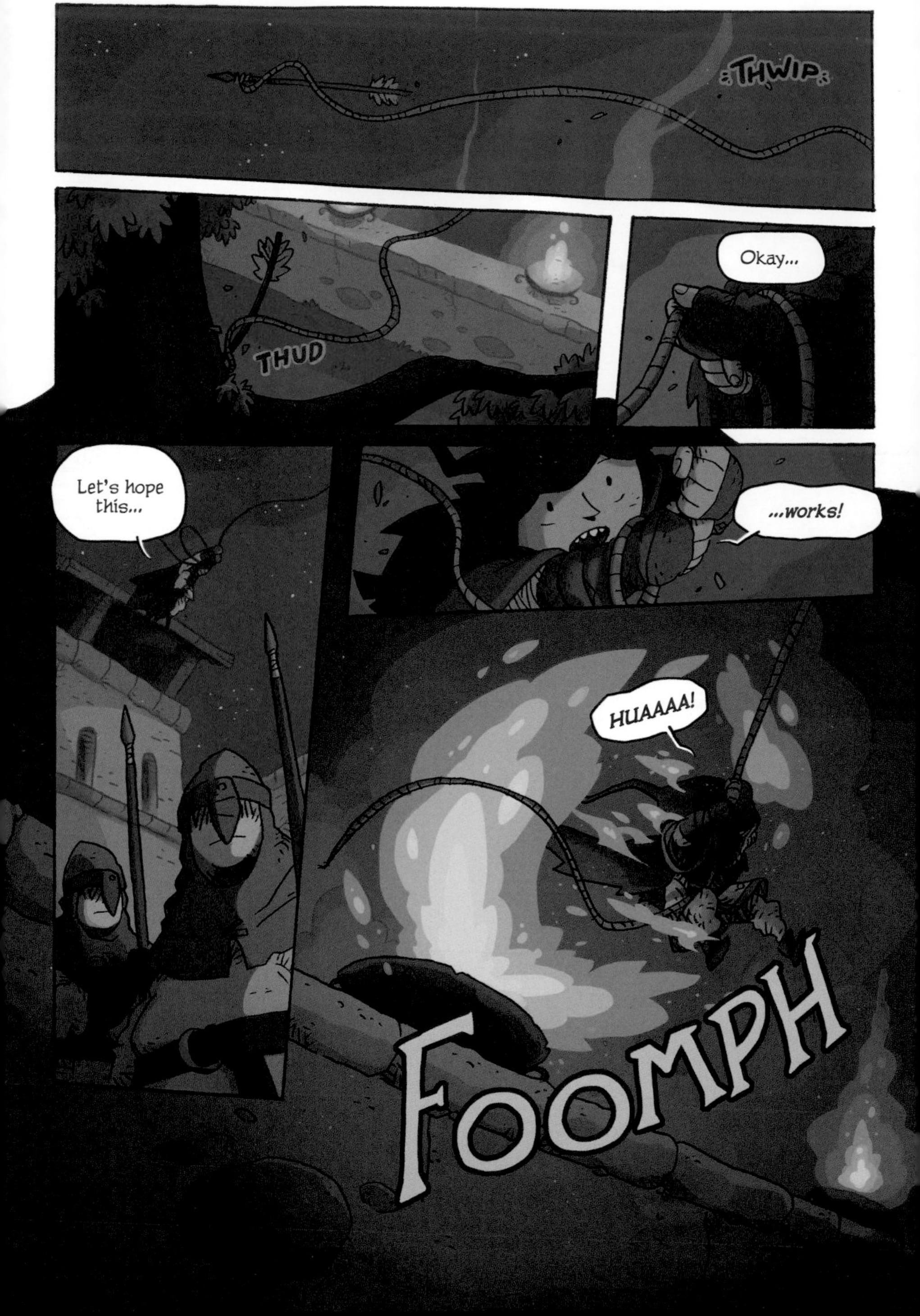
THWIP
THUD
Okay...
Let's hope this...
...works!
HUAAAA!
FOOMPH

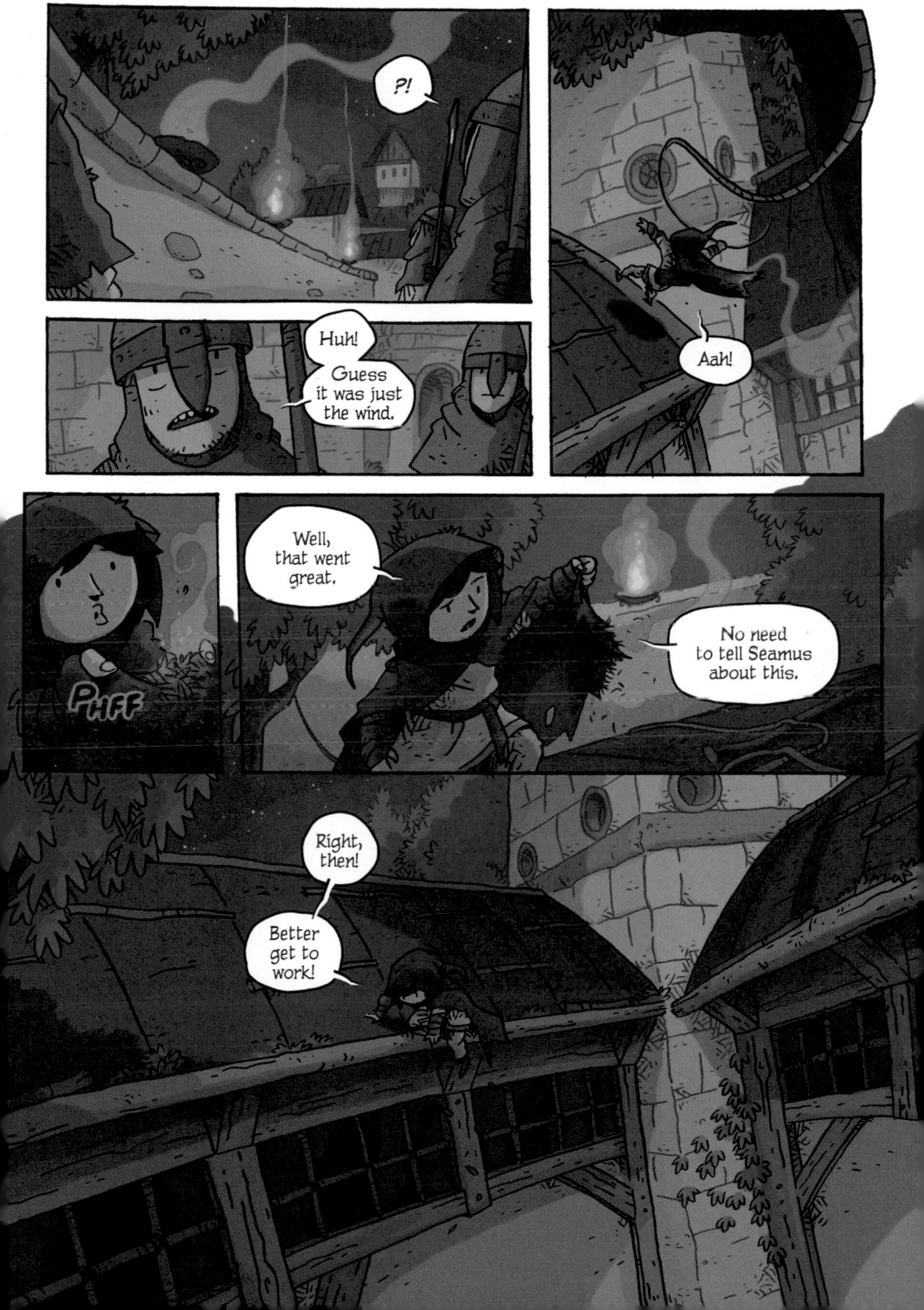

?!
Huh!
Guess it was just the wind.
Aah!
PHFF
Well, that went great.
No need to tell Seamus about this.
Right, then!
Better get to work!

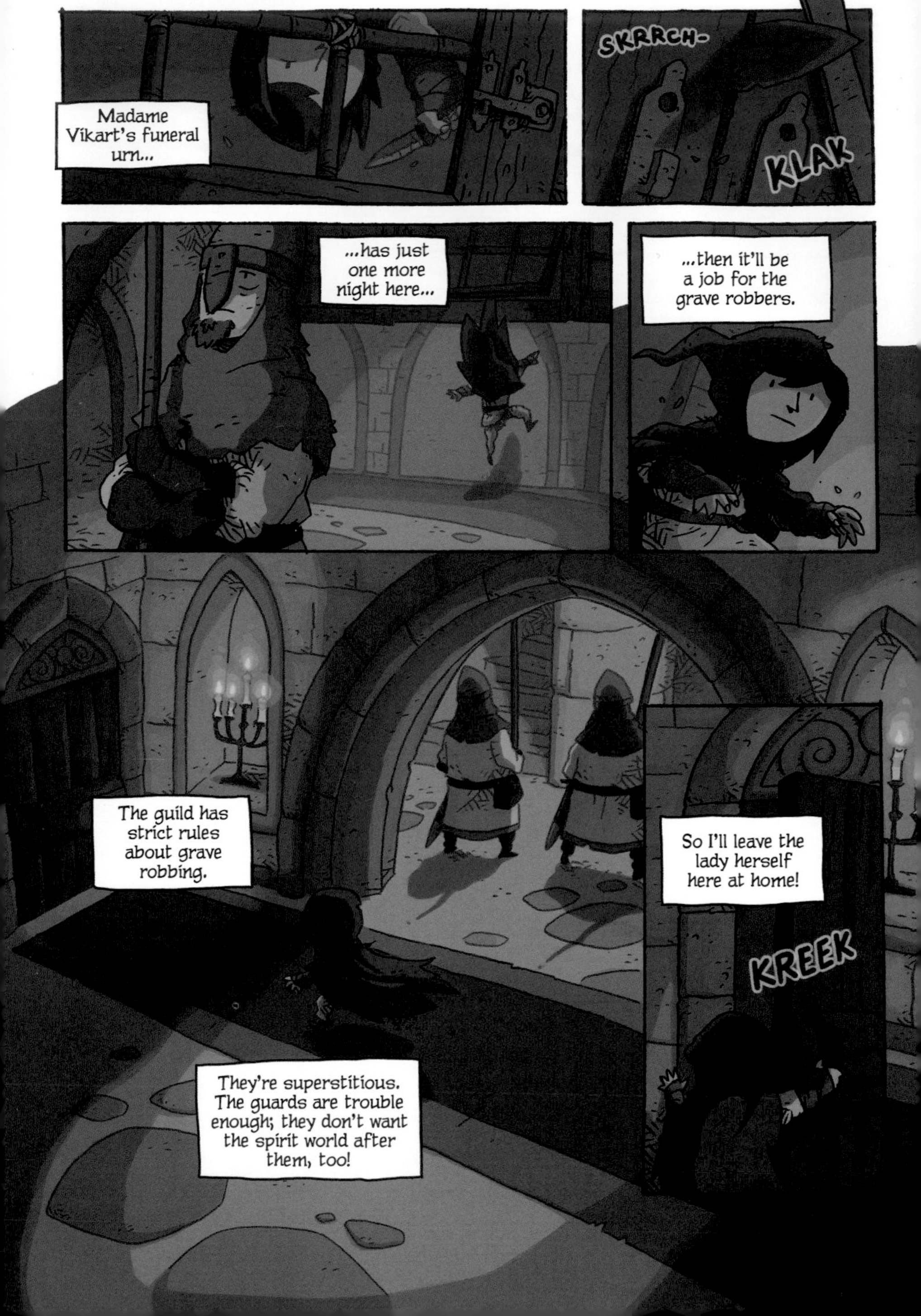
Madame Vikart's funeral urn...
SKRRCH-
KLAK
...has just one more night here...
...then it'll be a job for the grave robbers.
The guild has strict rules about grave robbing.
So I'll leave the lady herself here at home!
KREEK
They're superstitious. The guards are trouble enough; they don't want the spirit world after them, too!

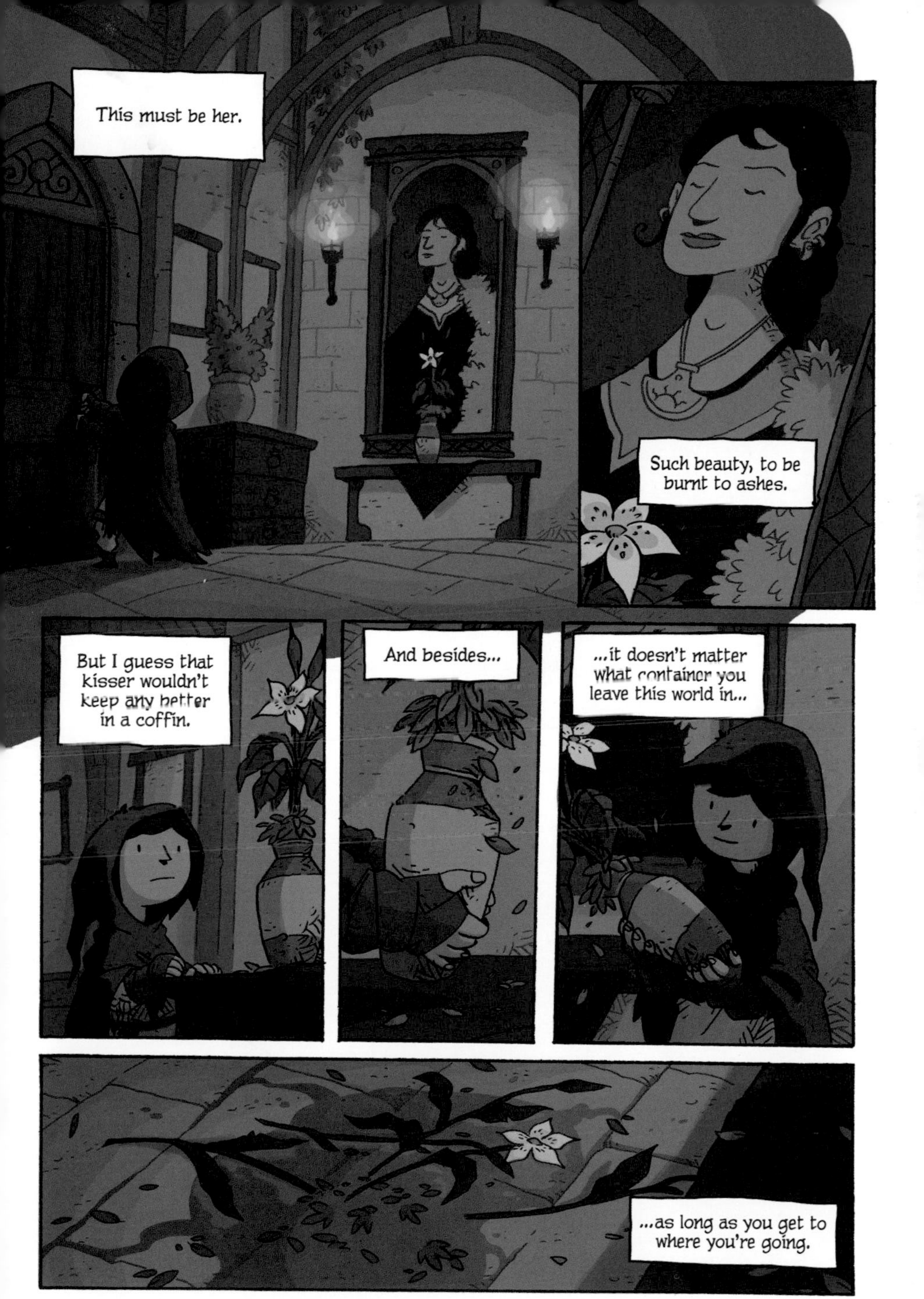
This must be her.
Such beauty, to be burnt to ashes.
But I guess that kisser wouldn't keep any better in a coffin.
And besides...
...it doesn't matter what container you leave this world in...
...as long as you get to where you're going.

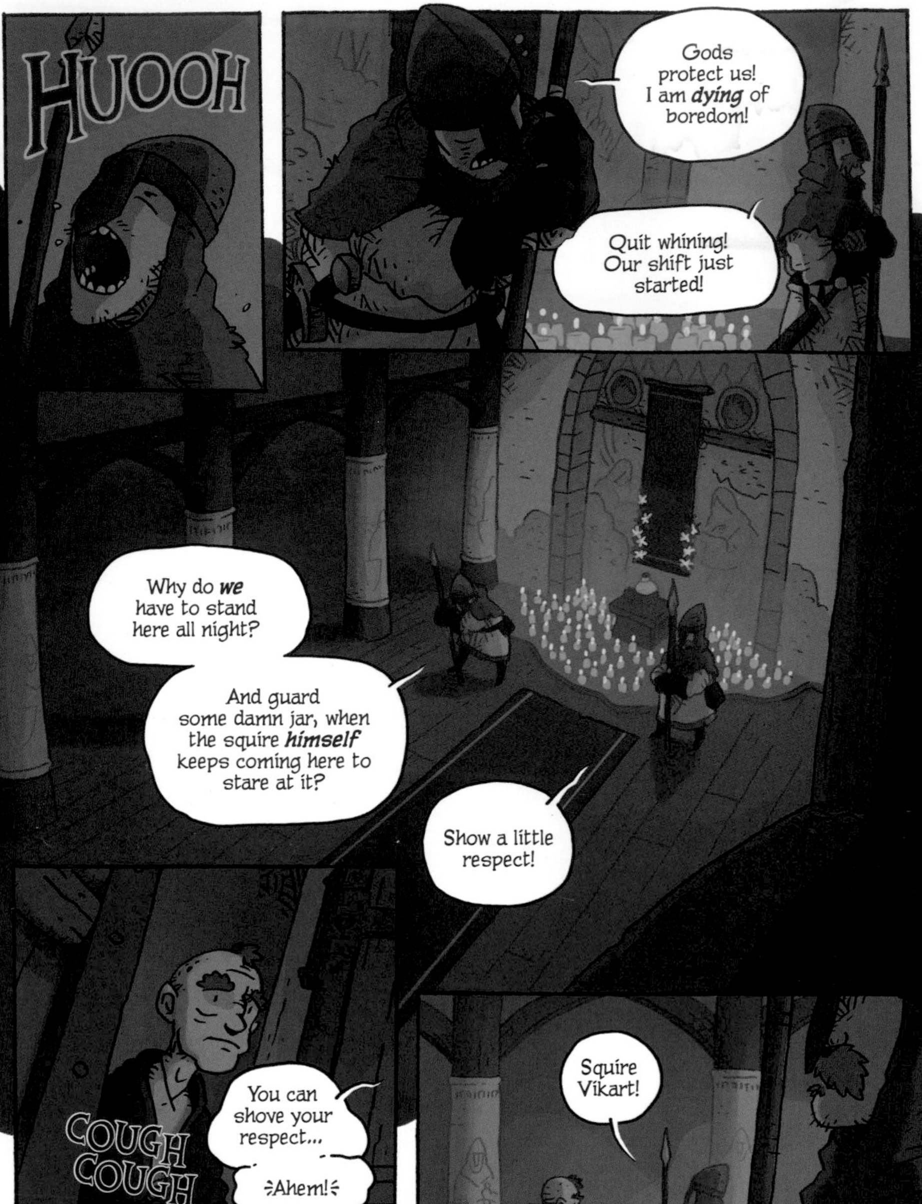
HUOOH
Gods protect us! I am *dying* of boredom!
Quit whining! Our shift just started!
Why do *we* have to stand here all night?
And guard some damn jar, when the squire *himself* keeps coming here to stare at it?
Show a little respect!
COUGH COUGH
You can shove your respect...
Ahem!
Squire Vikart!

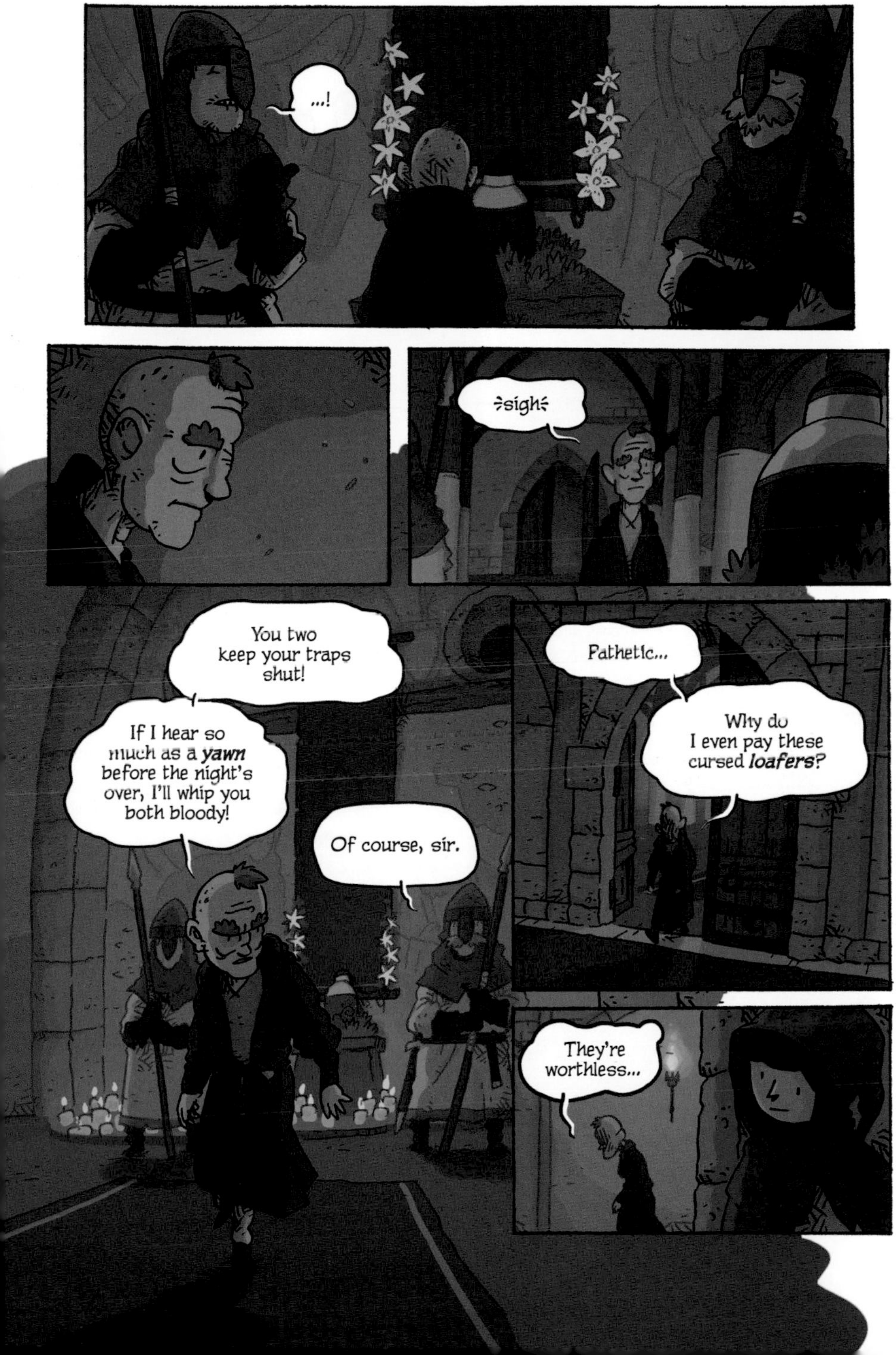
...!
⁼sigh⁼
You two keep your traps shut!
If I hear so much as a *yawn* before the night's over, I'll whip you both bloody!
Of course, sir.
Pathetic...
Why do I even pay these cursed *loafers*?
They're worthless...

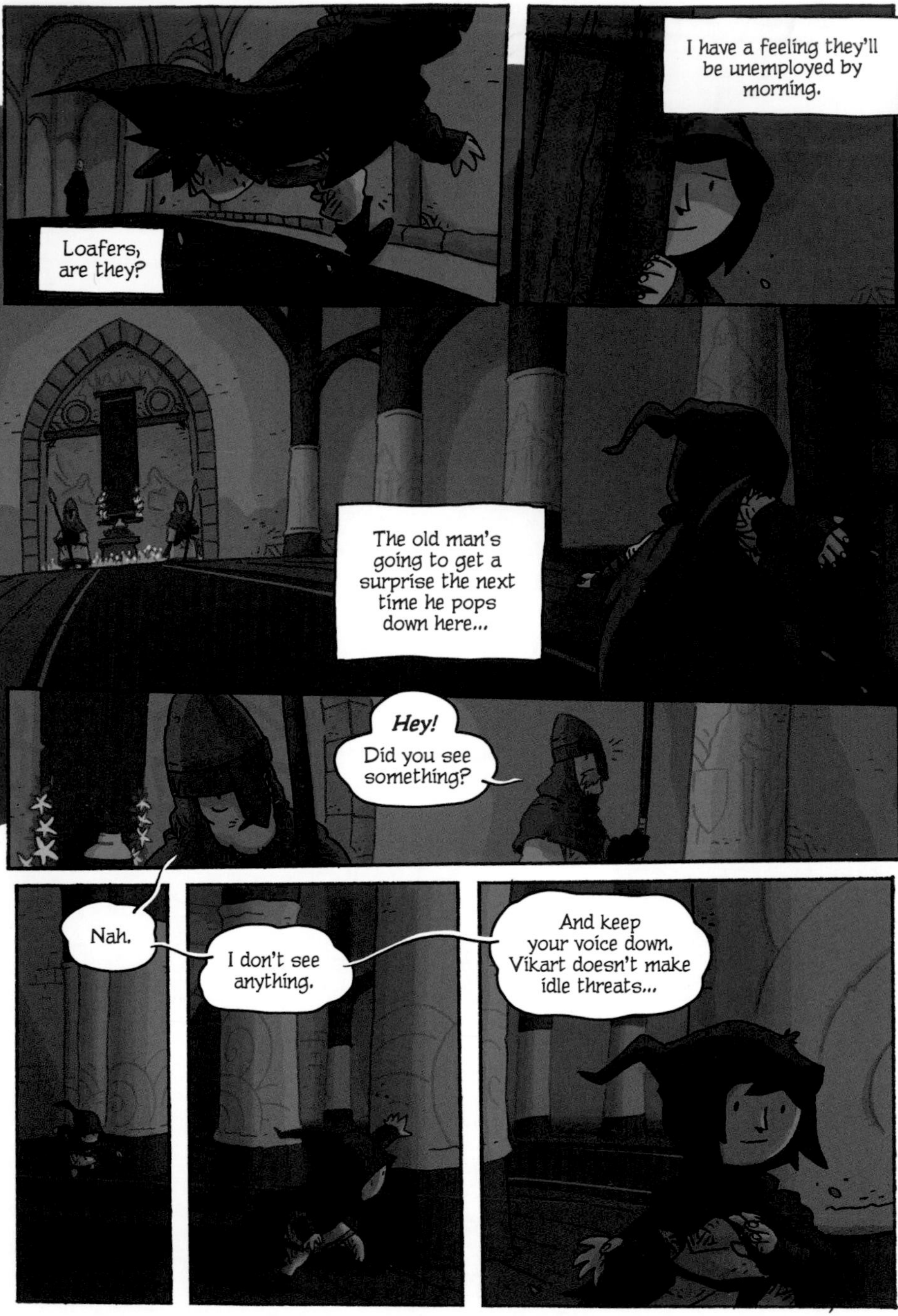
Loafers, are they?
I have a feeling they'll be unemployed by morning.
The old man's going to get a surprise the next time he pops down here...
Hey!
Did you see something?
Nah.
I don't see anything.
And keep your voice down. Vikart doesn't make idle threats...

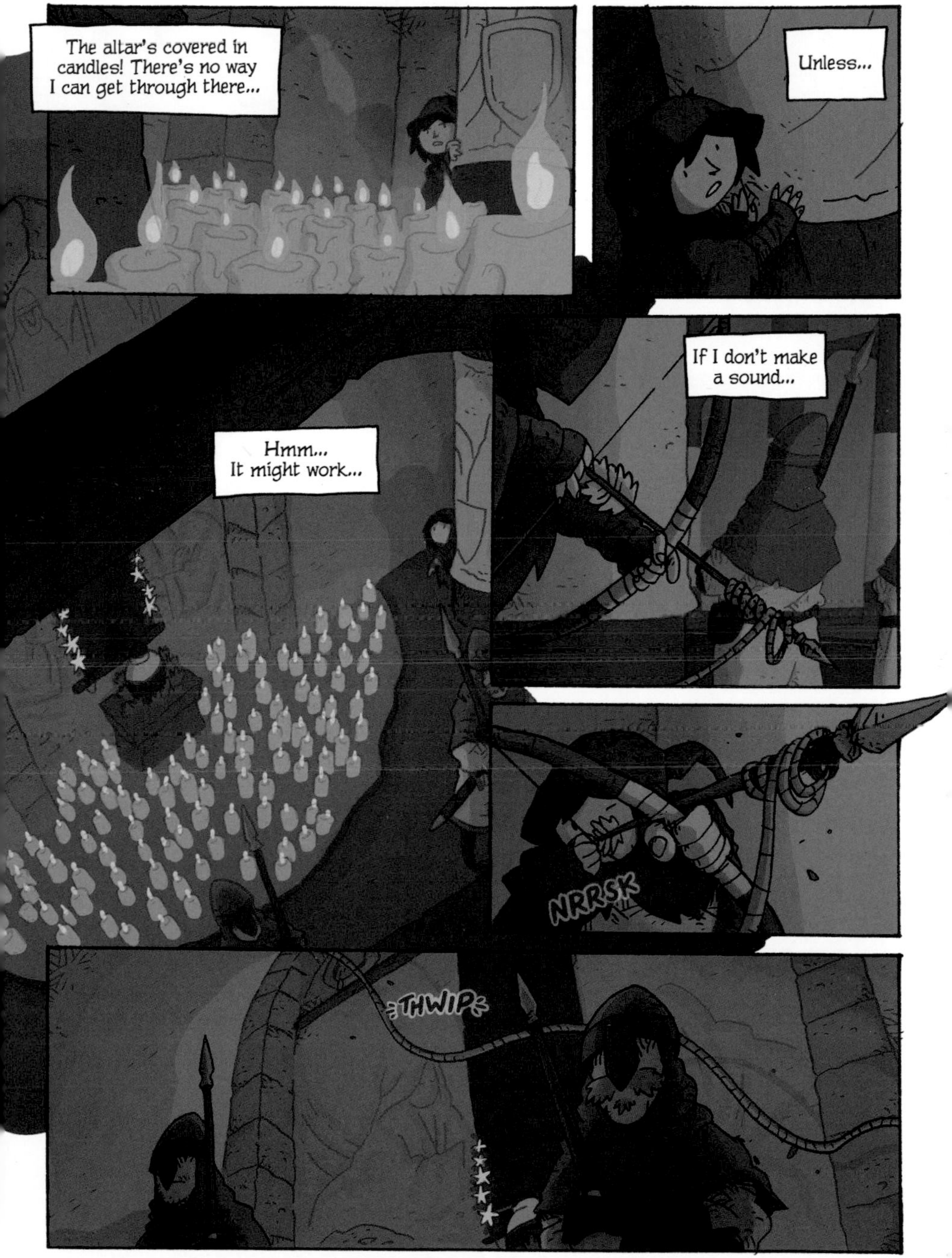
The altar's covered in candles! There's no way I can get through there...
Unless...
Hmm... It might work...
If I don't make a sound...
NRRSK
THWIP

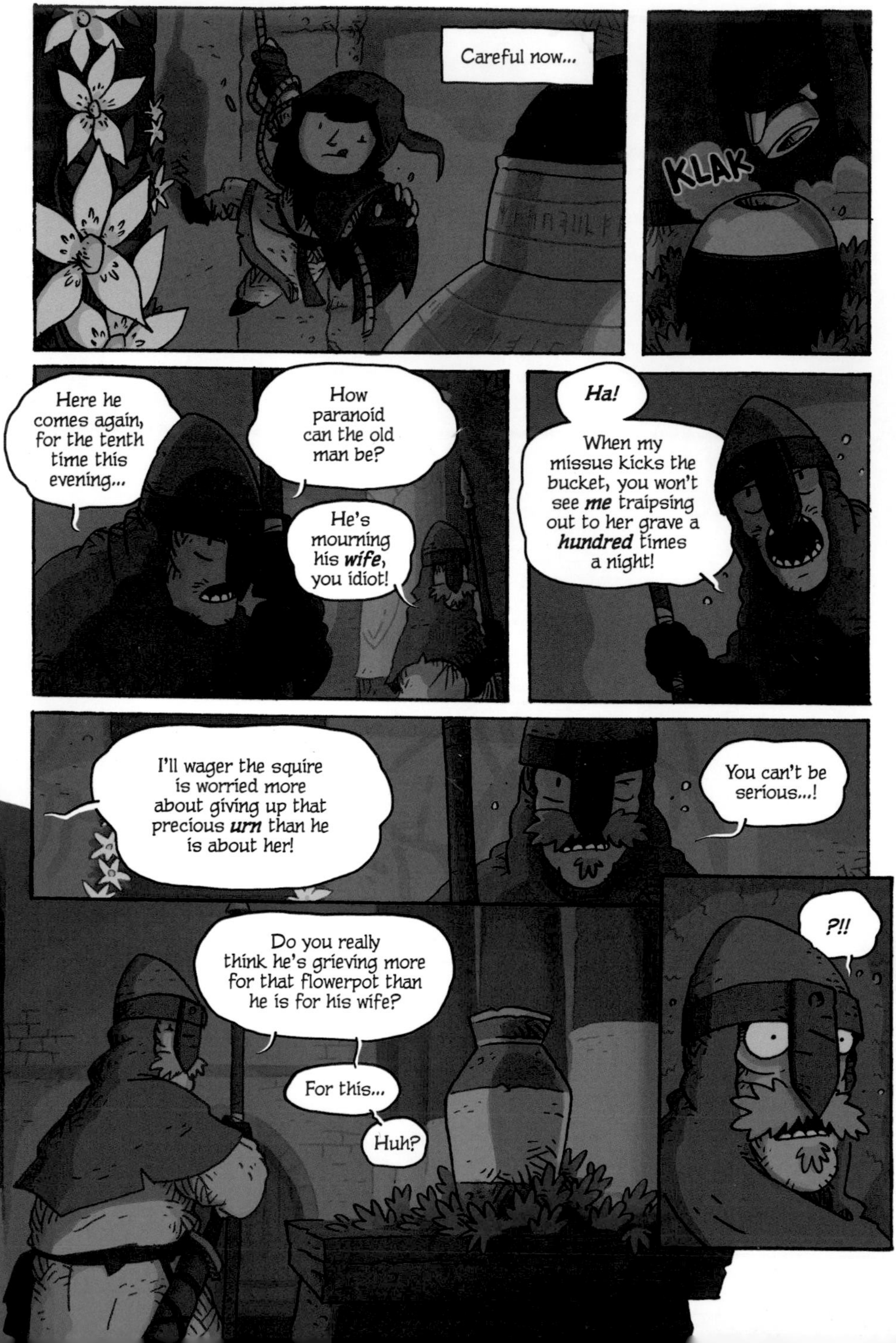
Careful now...
KLAK
Here he comes again, for the tenth time this evening...
How paranoid can the old man be?
He's mourning his wife, you idiot!
Ha!
When my missus kicks the bucket, you won't see me traipsing out to her grave a hundred times a night!
I'll wager the squire is worried more about giving up that precious urn than he is about her!
You can't be serious...!
Do you really think he's grieving more for that flowerpot than he is for his wife?
For this...
Huh?
?!!

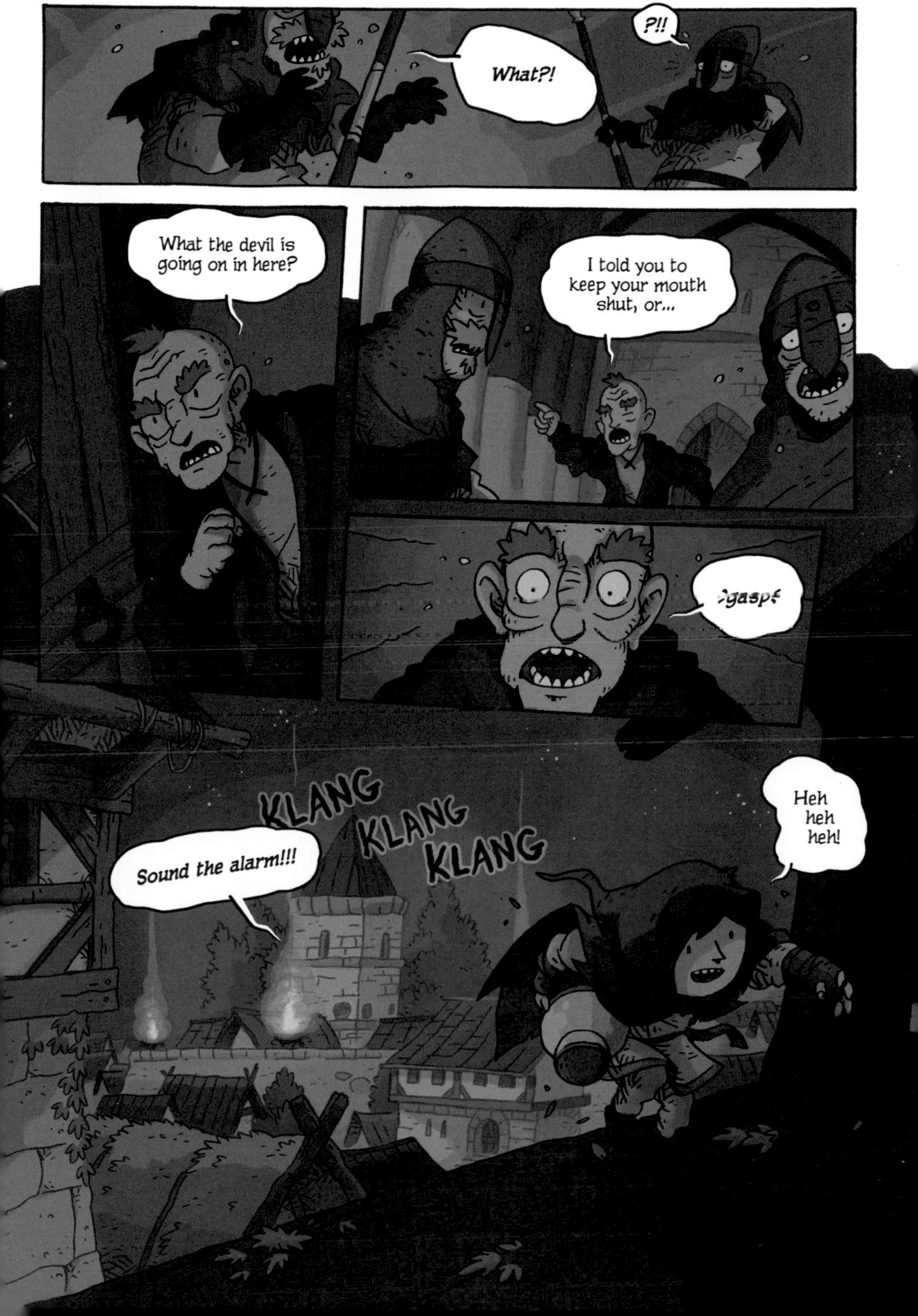
What?!
?!!
What the devil is going on in here?
I told you to keep your mouth shut, or...
gasp
KLANG KLANG KLANG
Sound the alarm!!!
Heh heh heh!

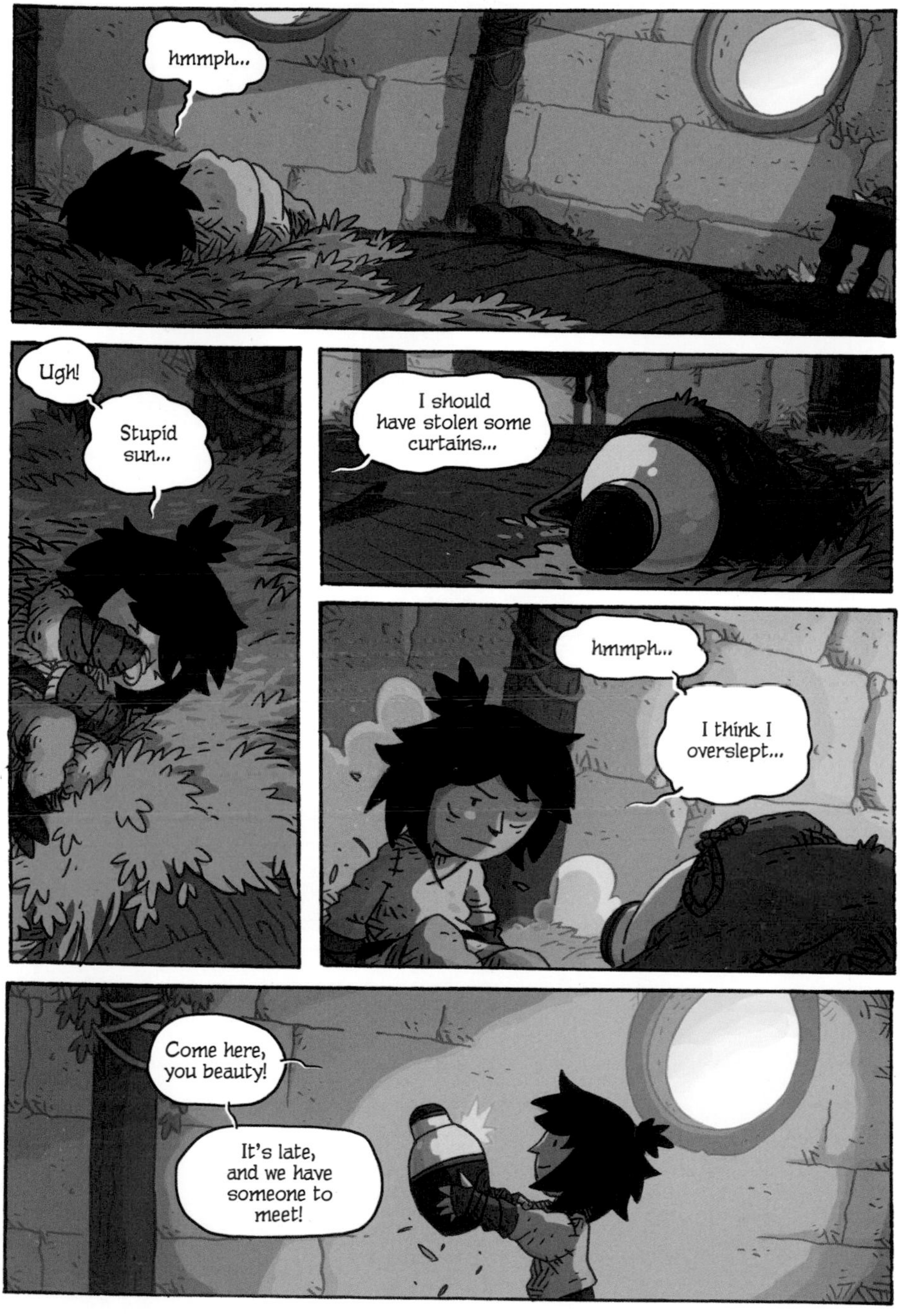
hmmph...
Ugh!
Stupid sun...
I should have stolen some curtains...
hmmph...
I think I overslept...
Come here, you beauty!
It's late, and we have someone to meet!

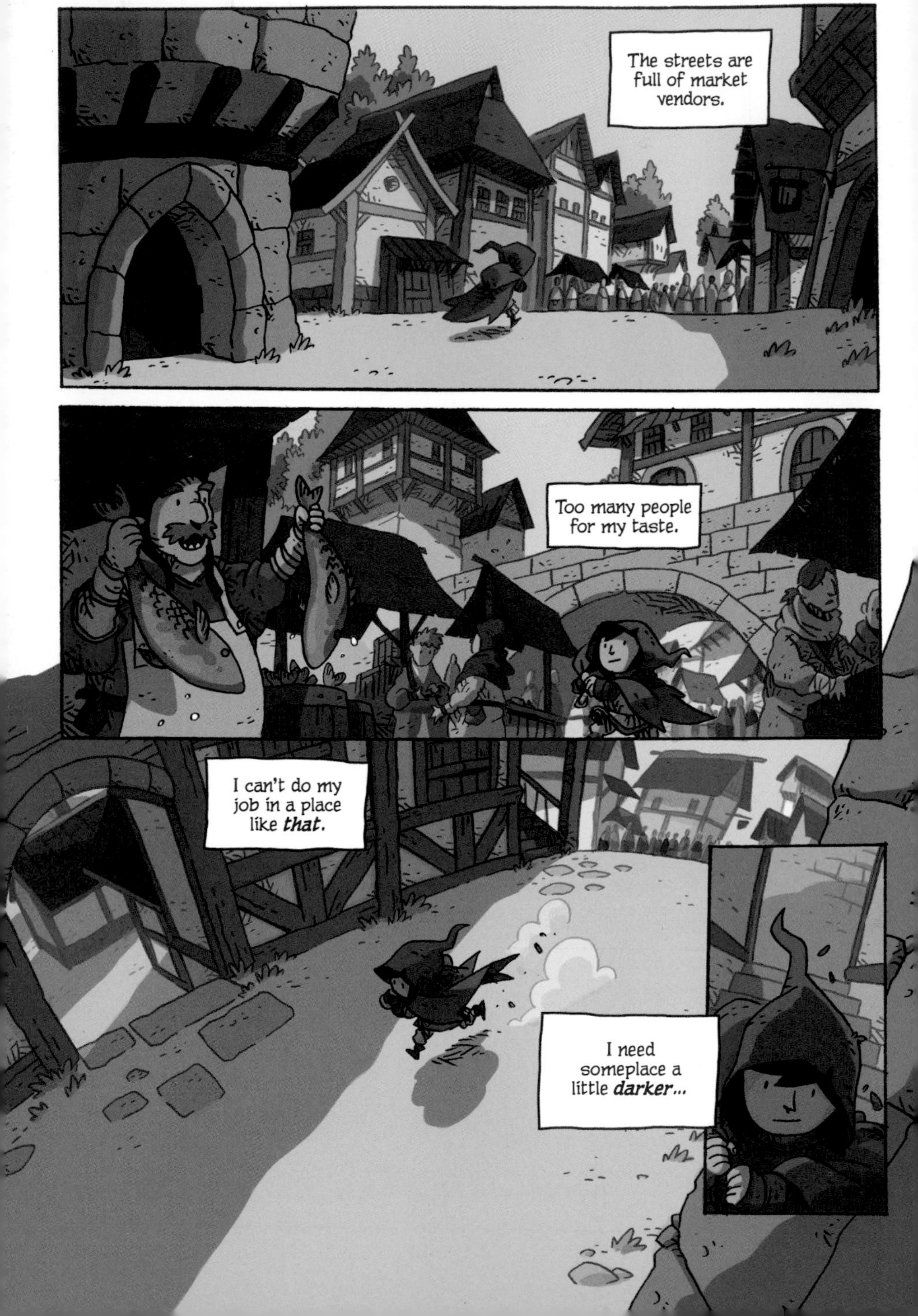
The streets are full of market vendors.
Too many people for my taste.
I can't do my job in a place like *that*.
I need someplace a little *darker*...

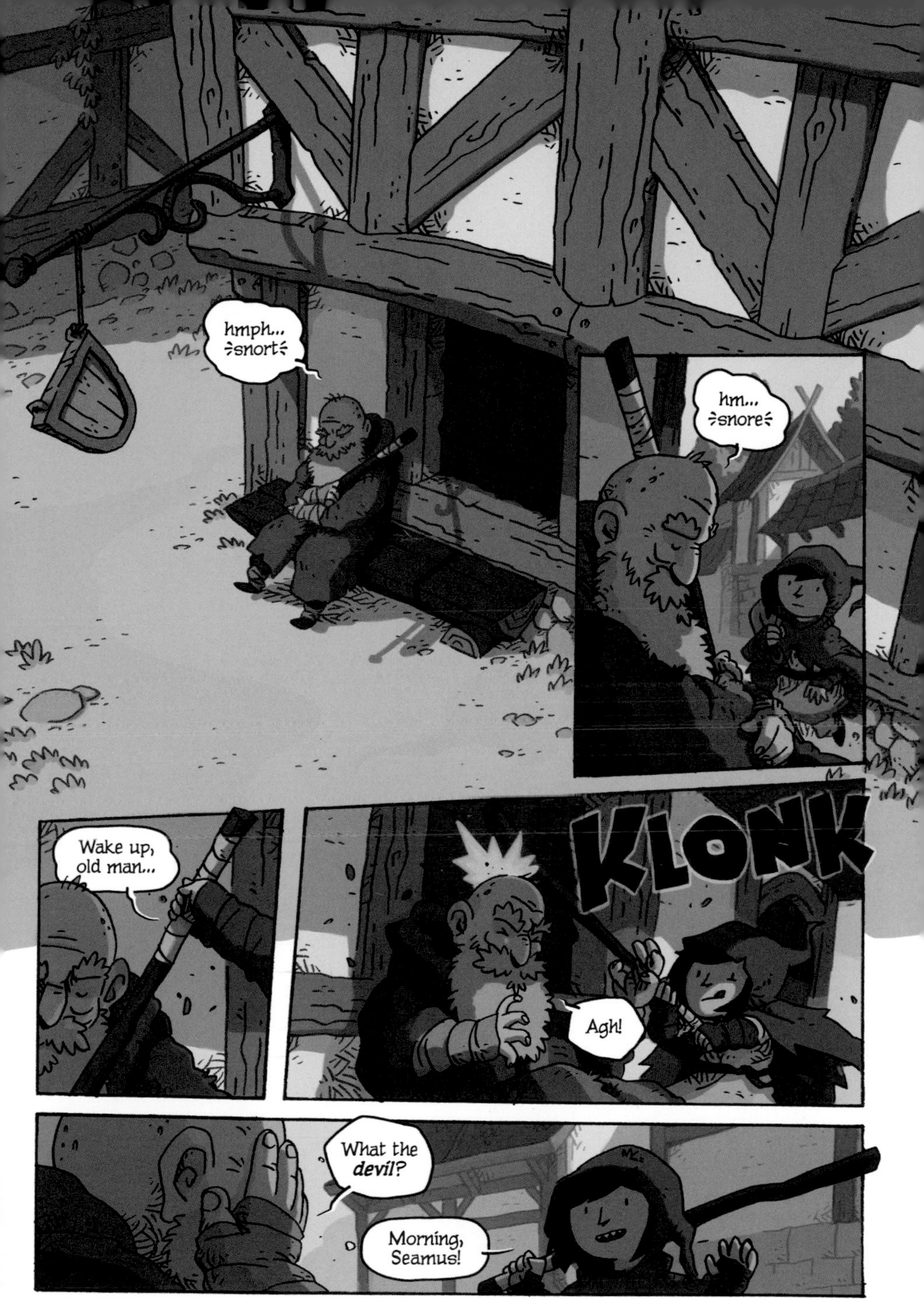
hmph...
≑snort≑
hm...
≑snore≑
Wake up, old man...
KLONK
Agh!
What the *devil*?
Morning, Seamus!

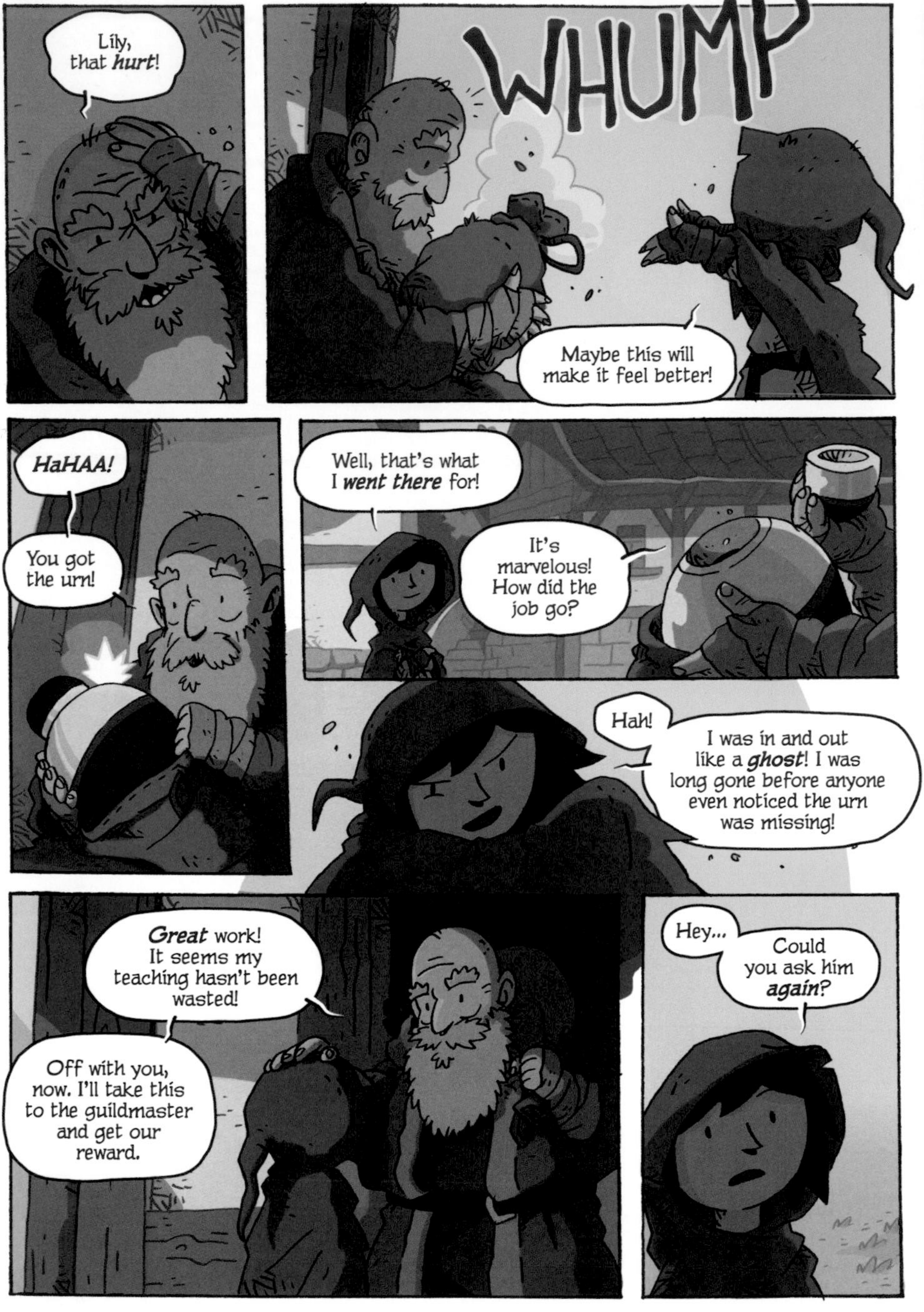

Lily, that *hurt*!
WHUMP
Maybe this will make it feel better!
HaHAA!
You got the urn!
Well, that's what I *went there* for!
It's marvelous! How did the job go?
Hah!
I was in and out like a *ghost*! I was long gone before anyone even noticed the urn was missing!
Great work! It seems my teaching hasn't been wasted!
Off with you, now. I'll take this to the guildmaster and get our reward.
Hey...
Could you ask him *again*?

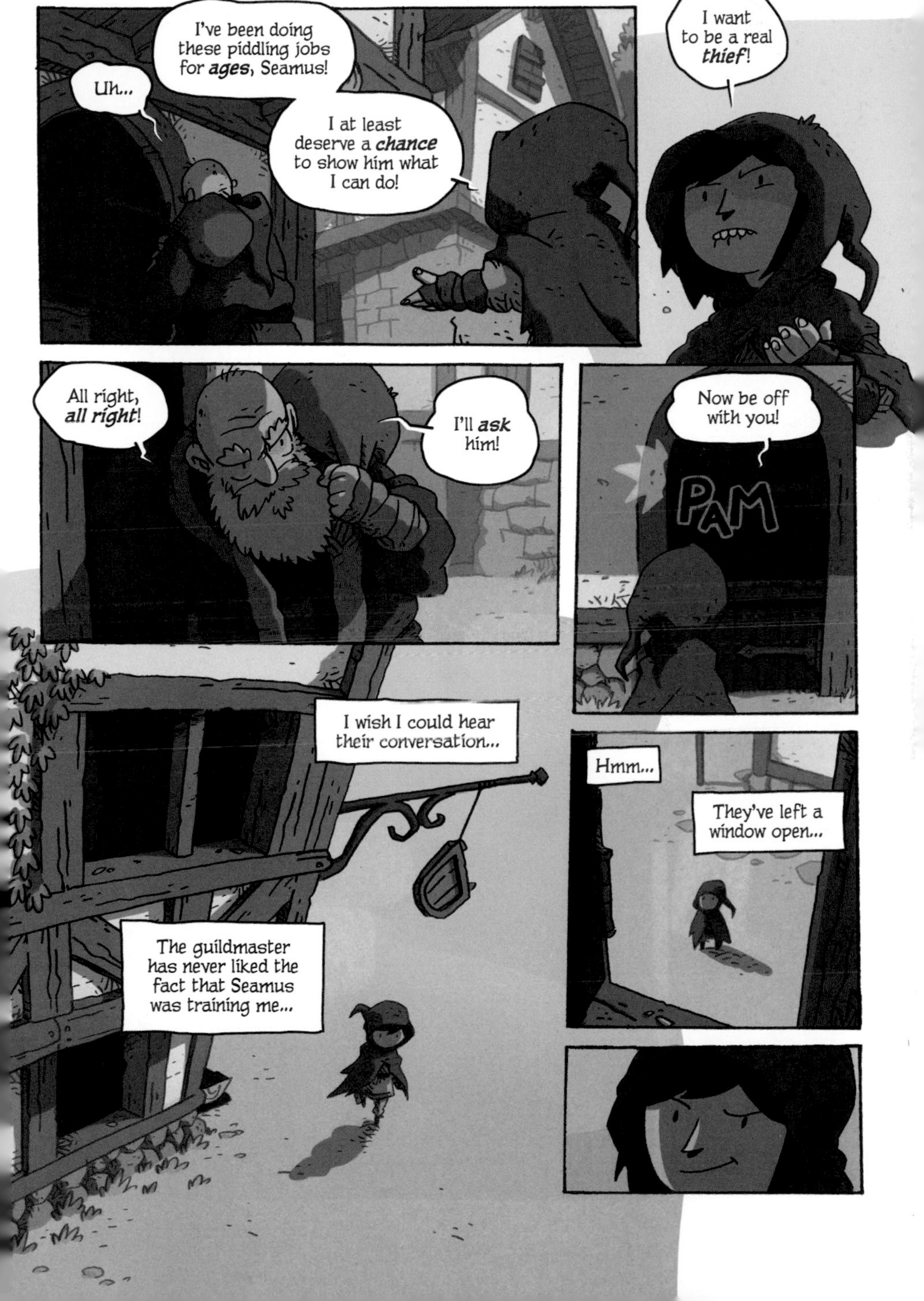
I've been doing these piddling jobs for ***ages***, Seamus!
Uh...
I at least deserve a ***chance*** to show him what I can do!
I want to be a real ***thief***!
All right, ***all right***!
I'll ***ask*** him!
Now be off with you!
PAM
I wish I could hear their conversation...
The guildmaster has never liked the fact that Seamus was training me...
Hmm...
They've left a window open...

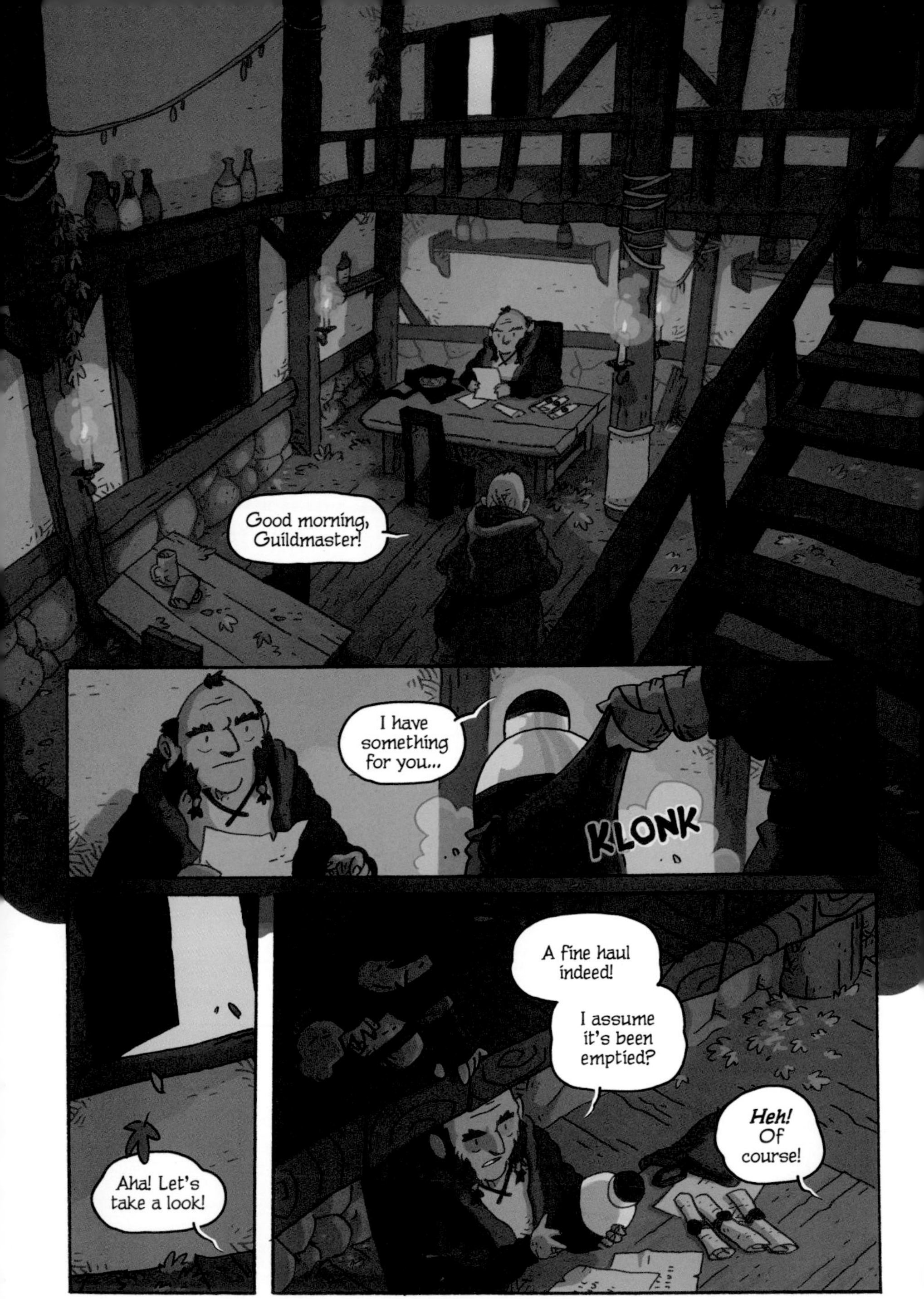
Good morning, Guildmaster!
I have something for you...
KLONK
Aha! Let's take a look!
A fine haul indeed!
I assume it's been emptied?
Heh! Of course!

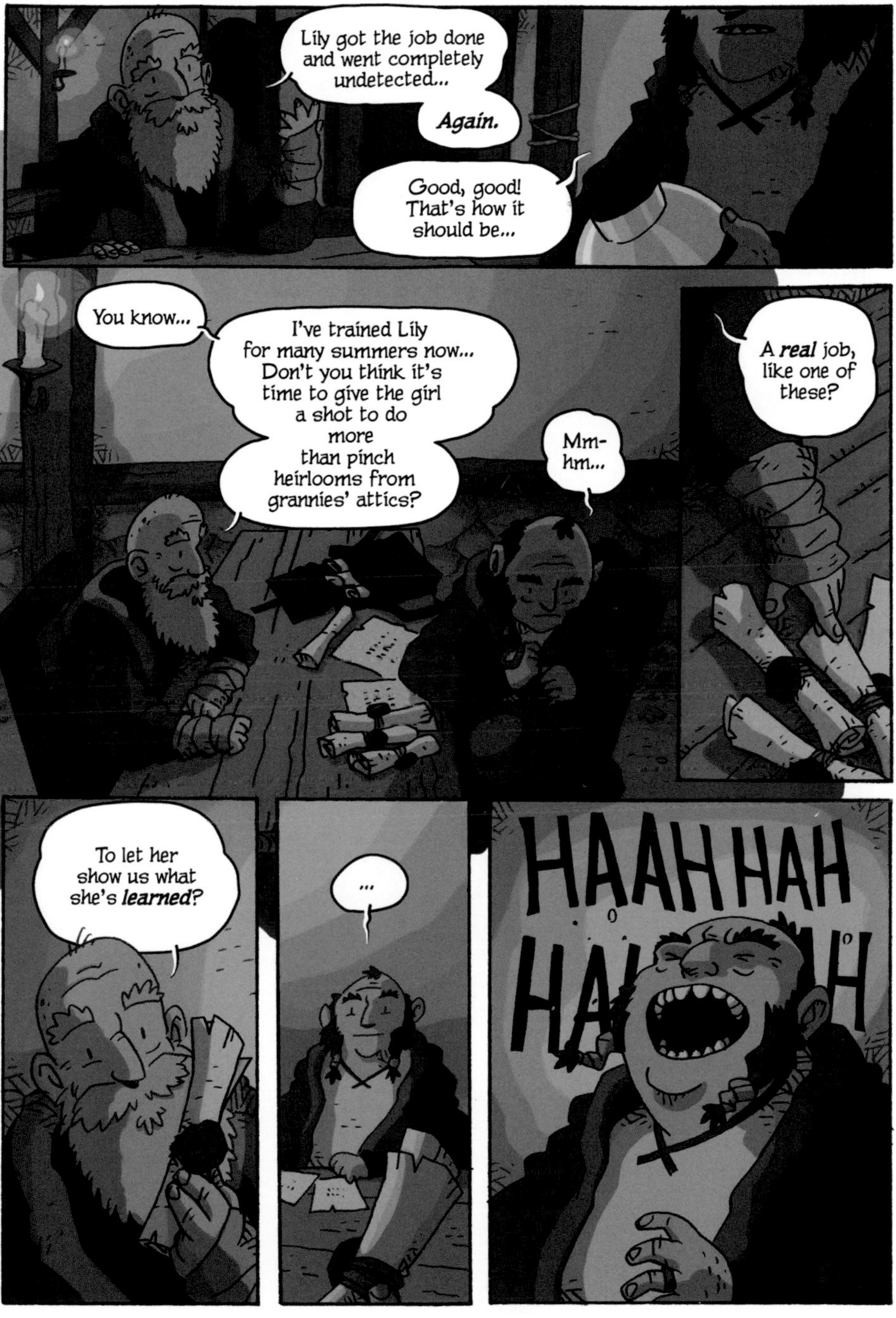
Lily got the job done and went completely undetected...
Again.
Good, good! That's how it should be...
You know...
I've trained Lily for many summers now... Don't you think it's time to give the girl a shot to do more than pinch heirlooms from grannies' attics?
Mm-hm...
A real job, like one of these?
To let her show us what she's learned?
...
HAAHHAH
HA

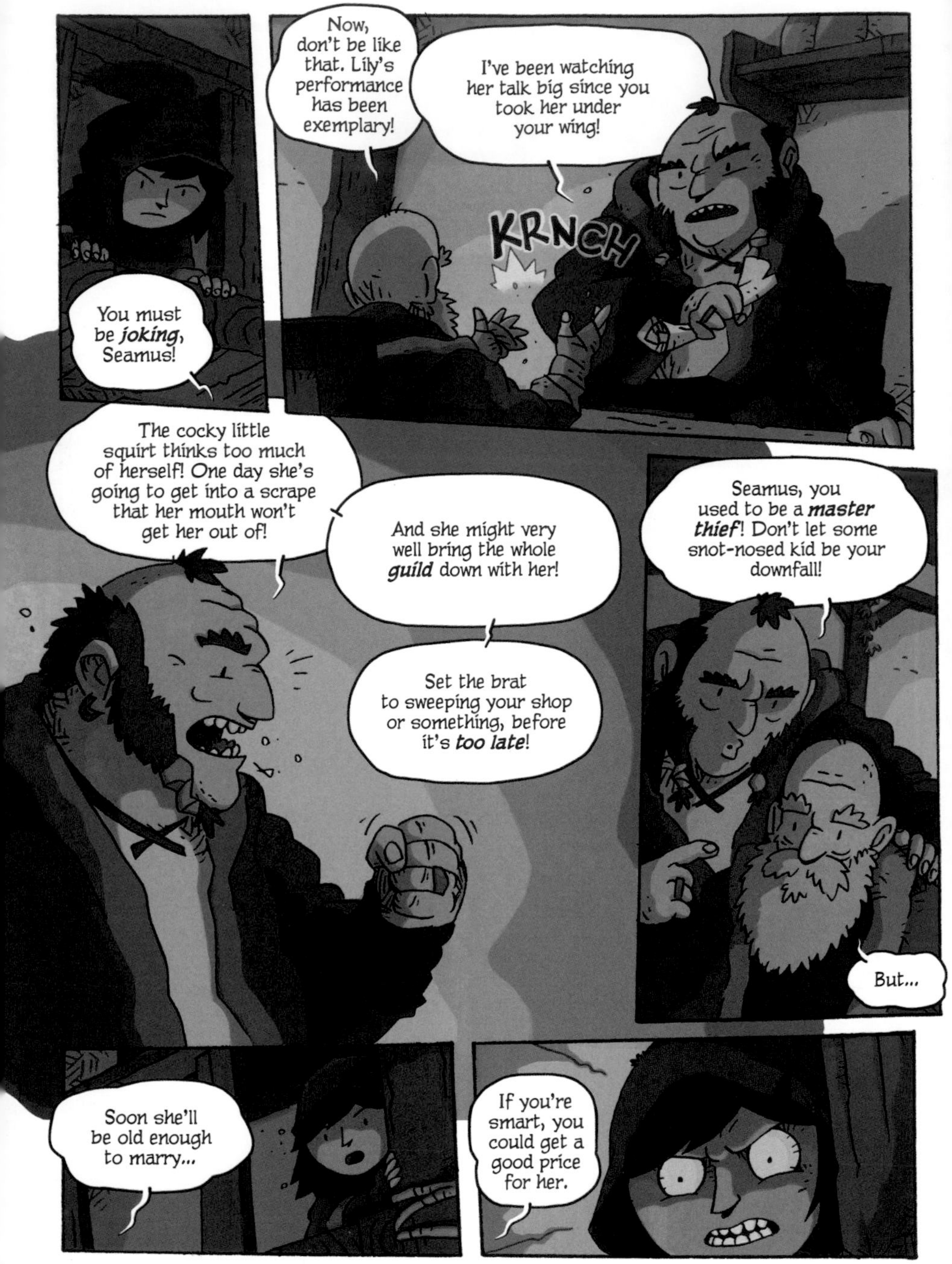
Now, don't be like that. Lily's performance has been exemplary!
I've been watching her talk big since you took her under your wing!
KRNCH
You must be *joking*, Seamus!
The cocky little squirt thinks too much of herself! One day she's going to get into a scrape that her mouth won't get her out of!
And she might very well bring the whole *guild* down with her!
Set the brat to sweeping your shop or something, before it's *too late*!
Seamus, you used to be a *master thief*! Don't let some snot-nosed kid be your downfall!
But...
Soon she'll be old enough to marry...
If you're smart, you could get a good price for her.

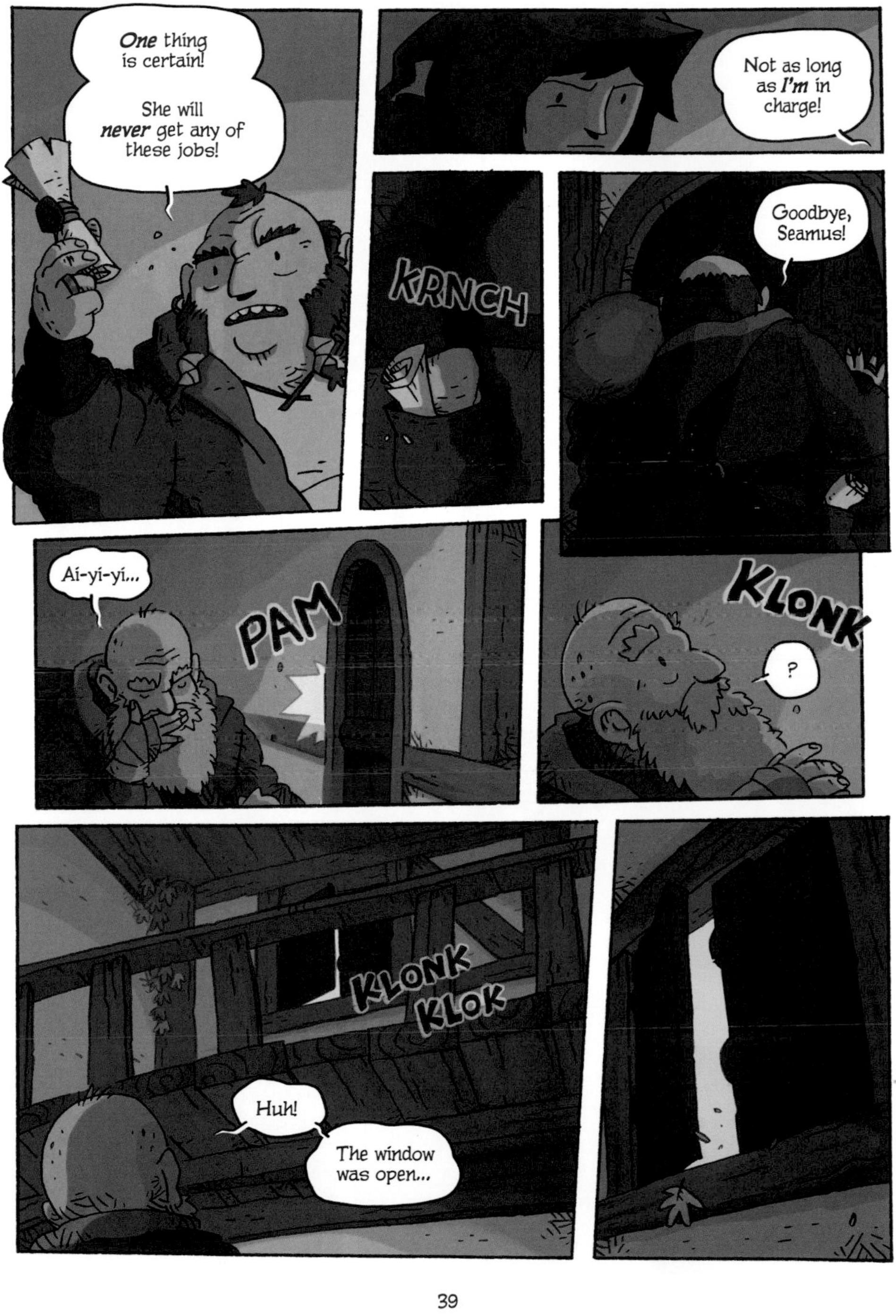

One thing is certain!
She will ***never*** get any of these jobs!
Not as long as ***I'm*** in charge!
KRNCH
Goodbye, Seamus!
Ai-yi-yi...
PAM
KLONK
?
KLONK KLOK
Huh!
The window was open...

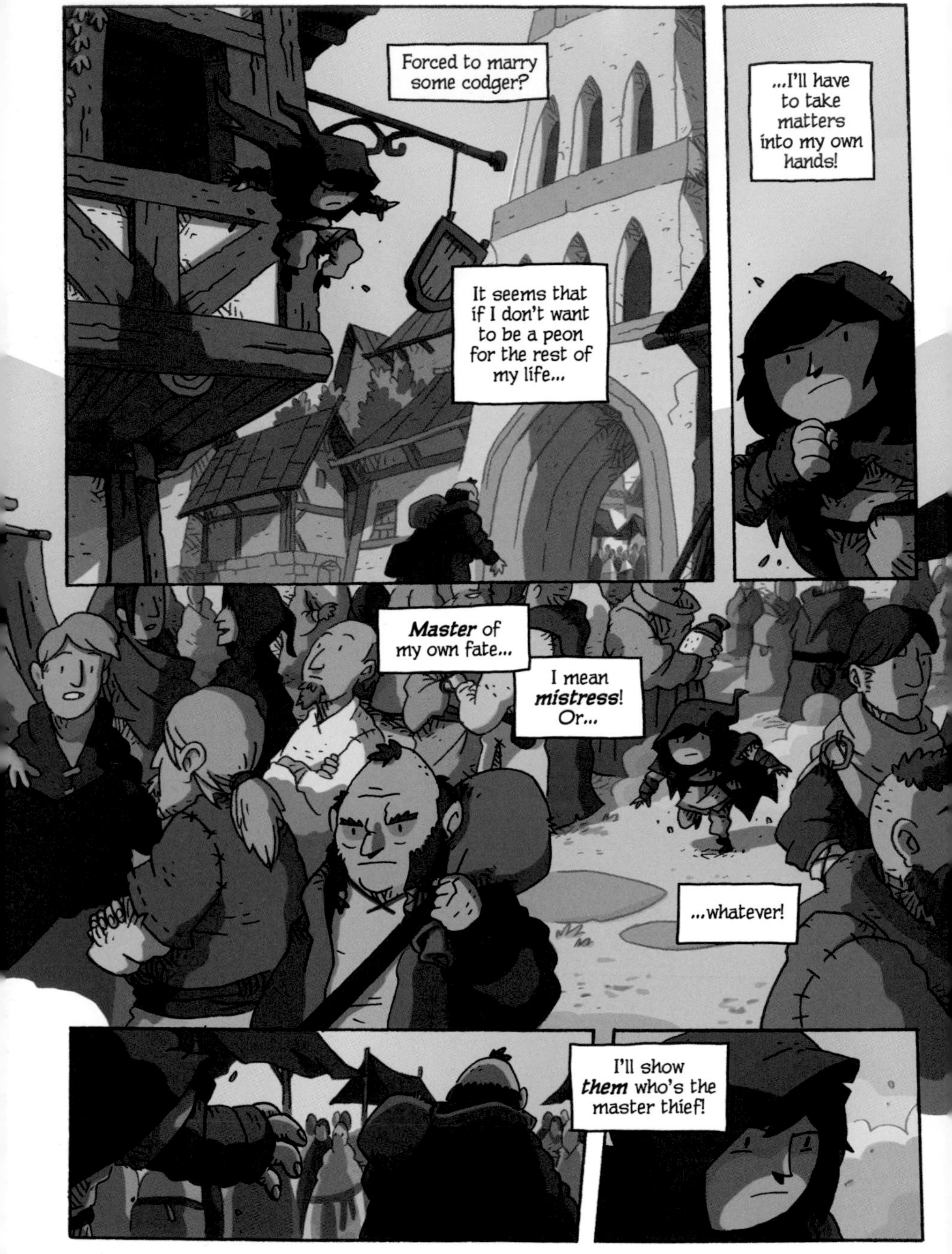
Forced to marry some codger?
It seems that if I don't want to be a peon for the rest of my life...
...I'll have to take matters into my own hands!
Master of my own fate...
I mean *mistress*! Or...
...whatever!
I'll show *them* who's the master thief!

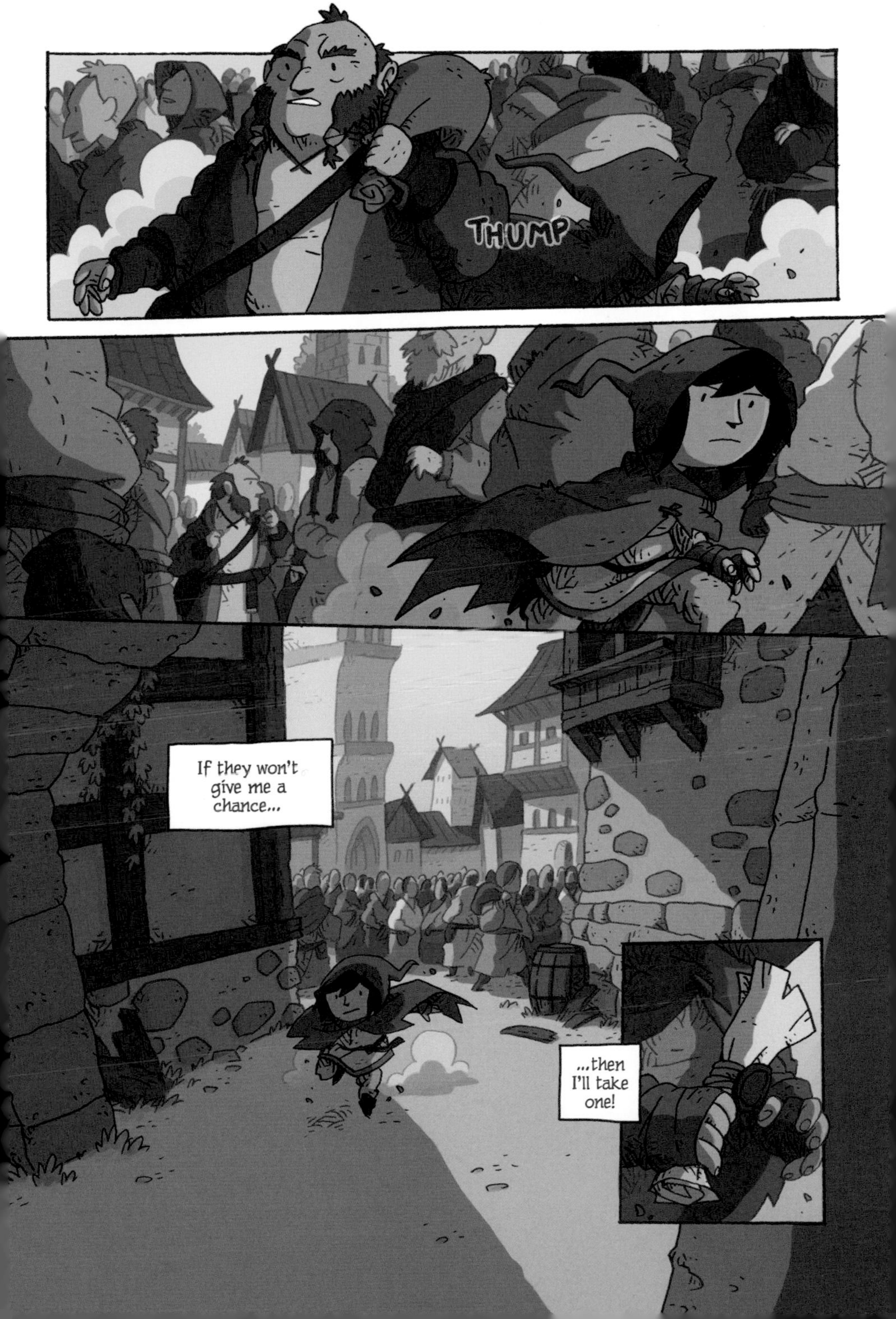
THUMP
If they won't give me a chance...
...then I'll take one!

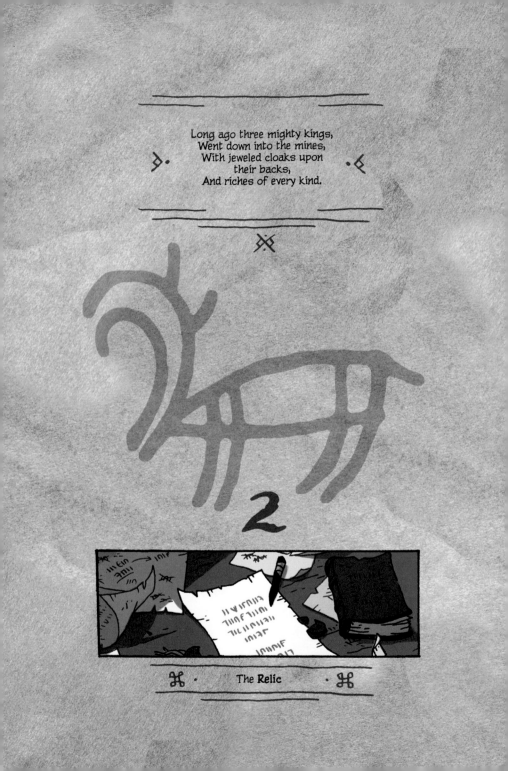

Long ago three mighty kings,
Went down into the mines,
With jeweled cloaks upon
their backs,
And riches of every kind.

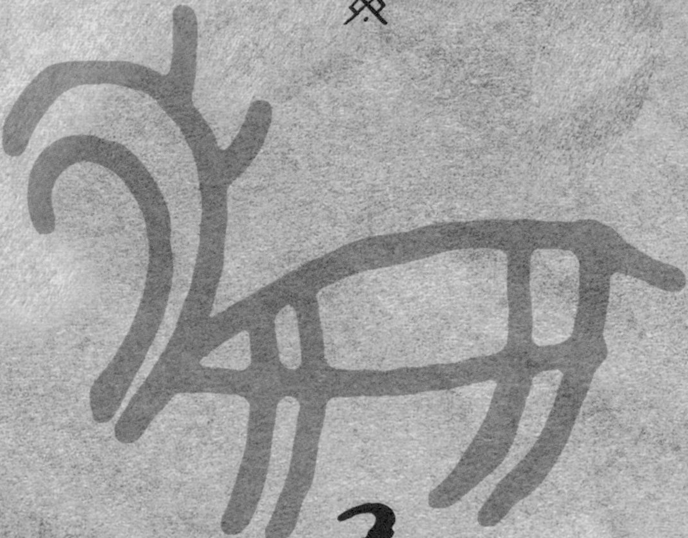

2

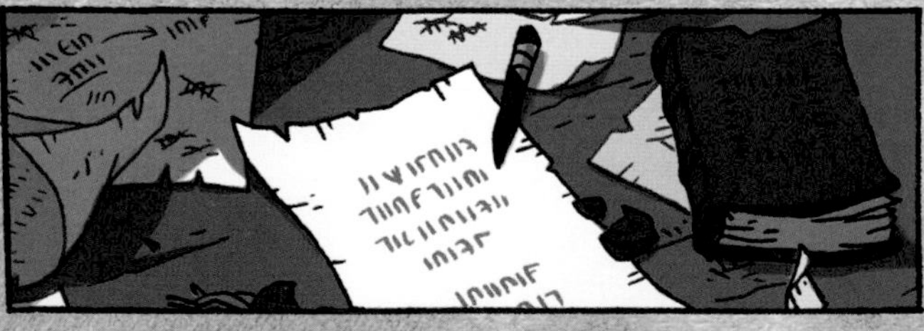

The Relic

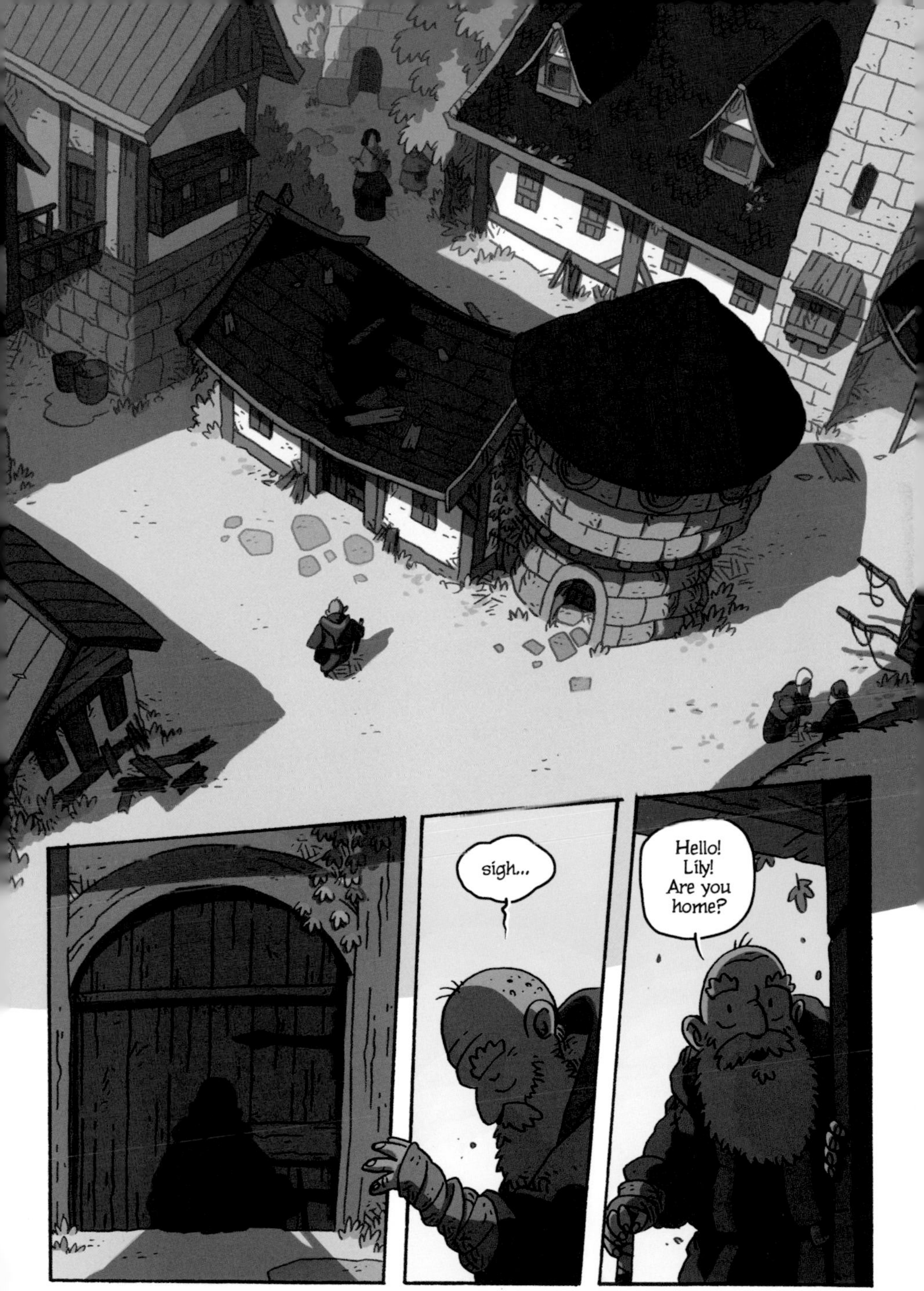
sigh...
Hello! Lily! Are you home?

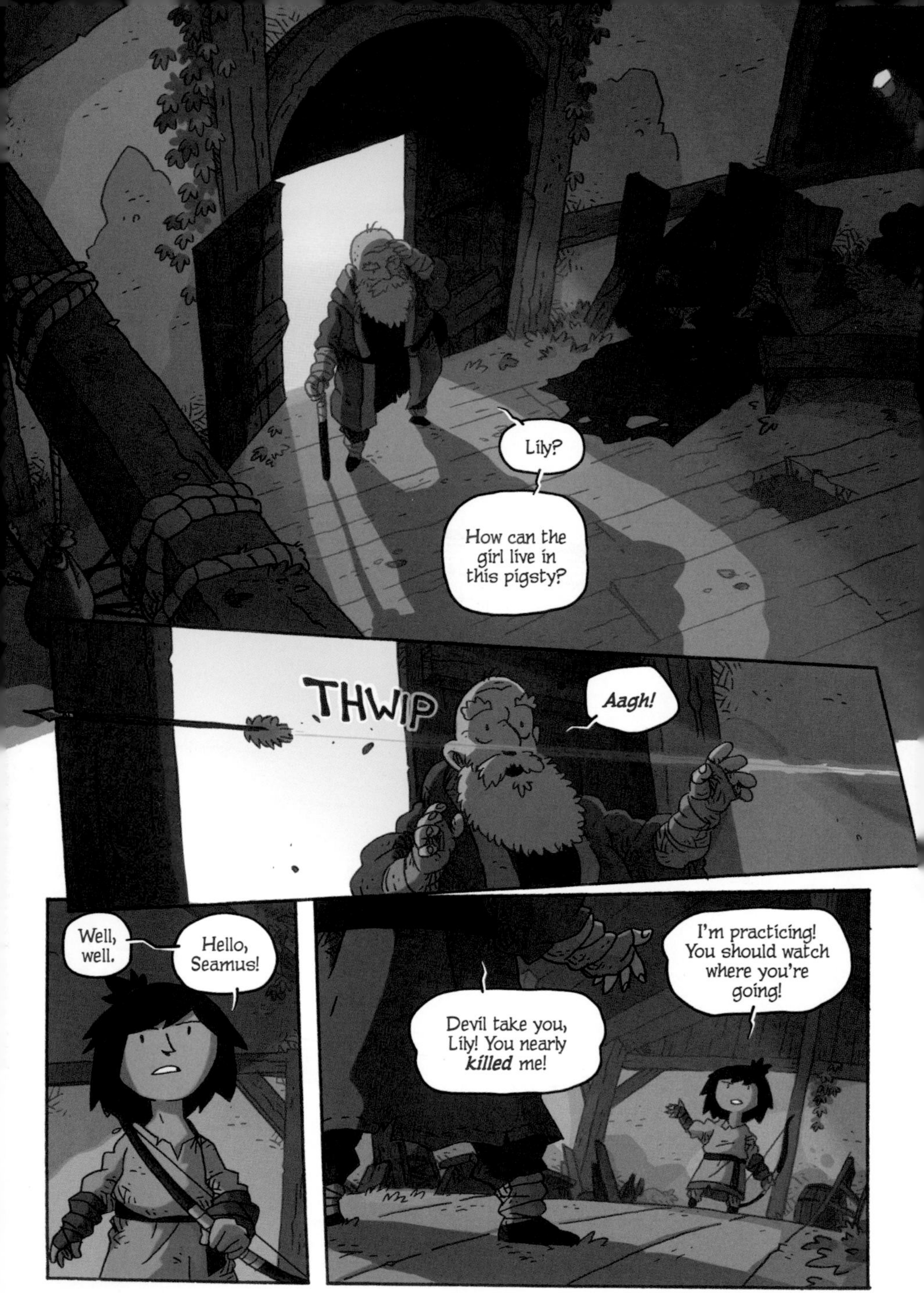
Lily?
How can the girl live in this pigsty?
THWIP
Aagh!
Well, well.
Hello, Seamus!
Devil take you, Lily! You nearly *killed* me!
I'm practicing! You should watch where you're going!

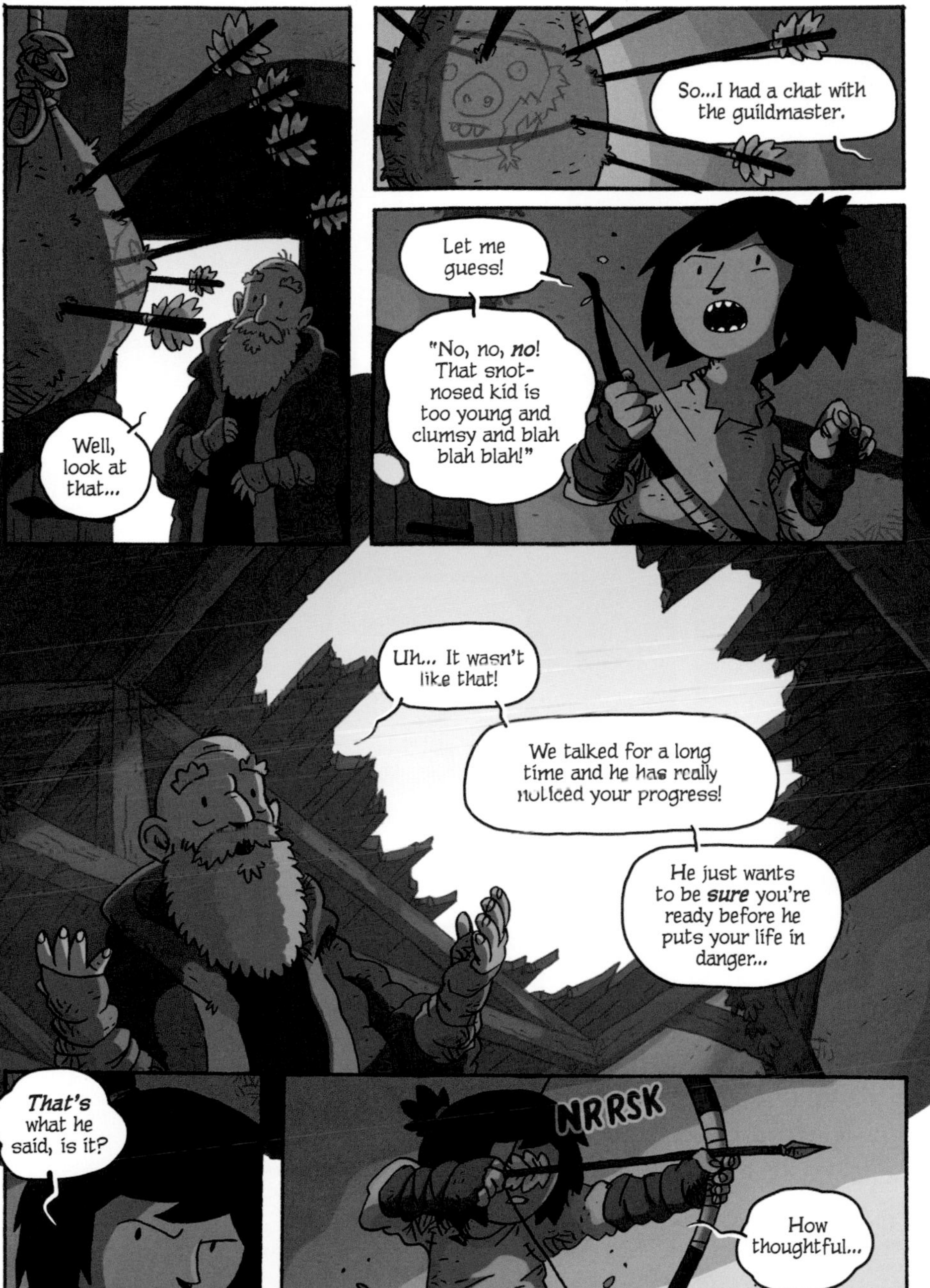
Well, look at that...
So...I had a chat with the guildmaster.
Let me guess!
"No, no, *no*! That snot-nosed kid is too young and clumsy and blah blah blah!"
Uh... It wasn't like that!
We talked for a long time and he has really noticed your progress!
He just wants to be *sure* you're ready before he puts your life in danger...
That's what he said, is it?
NRRSK
How thoughtful...

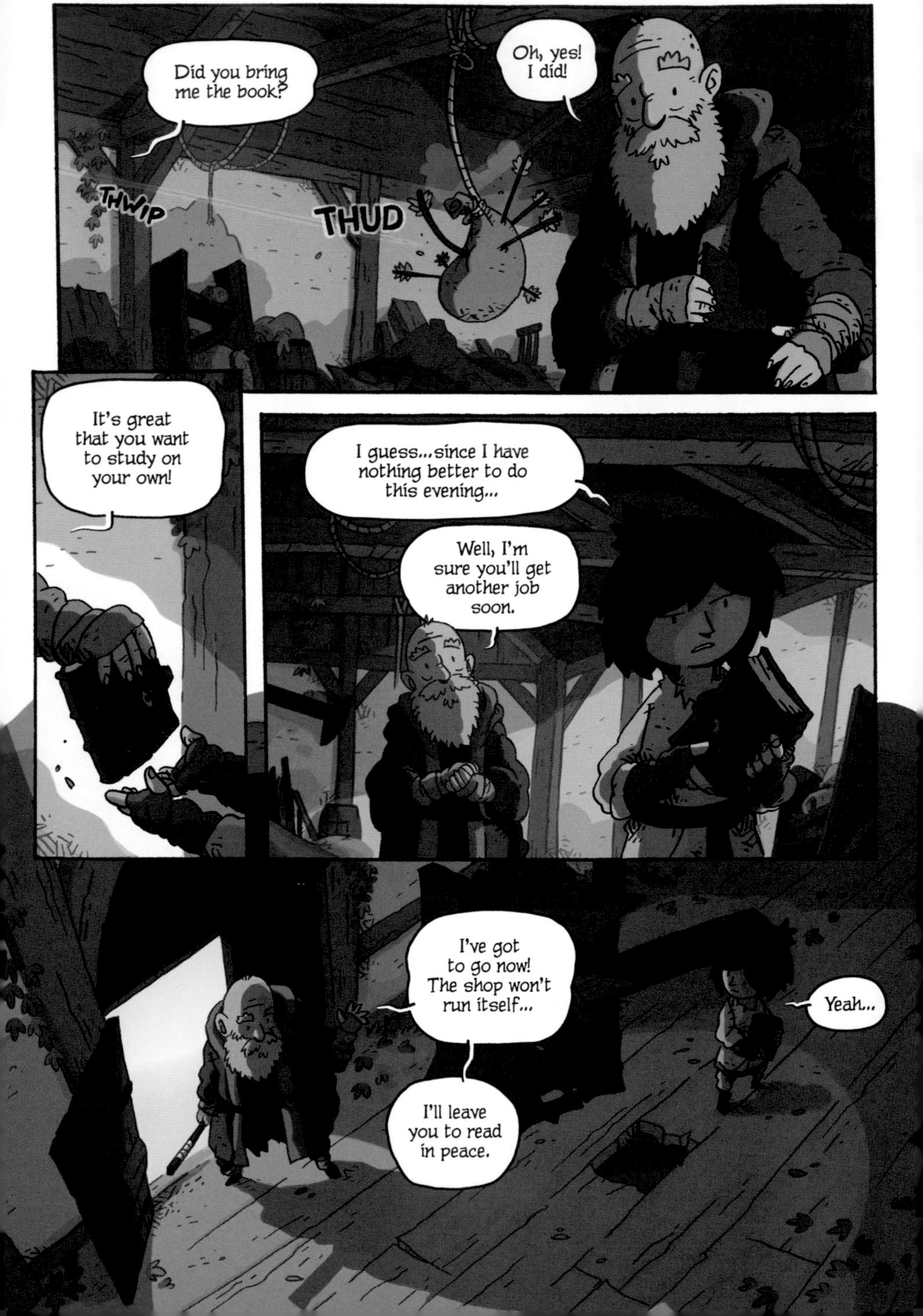
Did you bring me the book?
Oh, yes! I did!
THWIP
THUD
It's great that you want to study on your own!
I guess...since I have nothing better to do this evening...
Well, I'm sure you'll get another job soon.
I've got to go now! The shop won't run itself...
I'll leave you to read in peace.
Yeah...

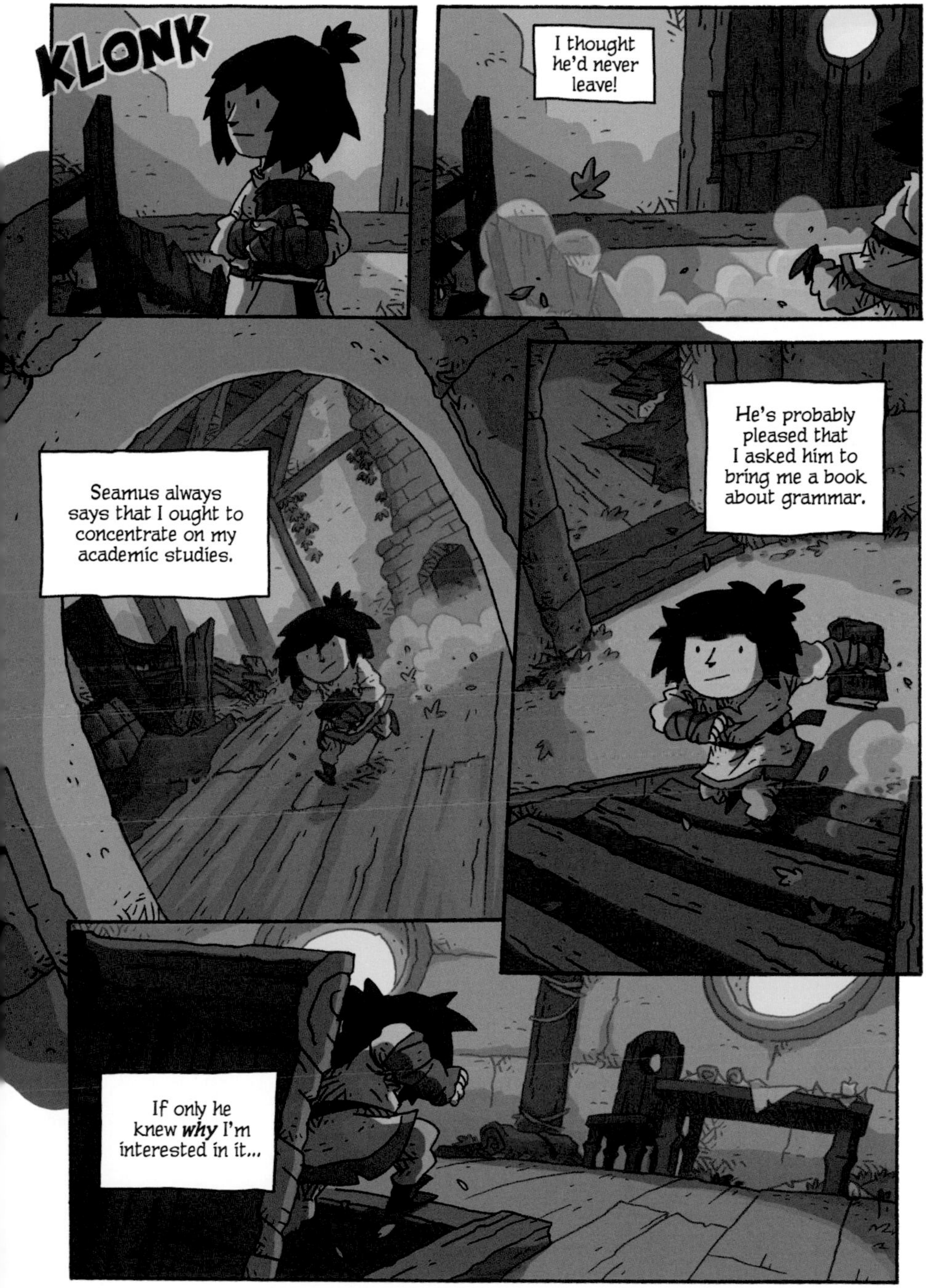
KLONK
I thought he'd never leave!
Seamus always says that I ought to concentrate on my academic studies.
He's probably pleased that I asked him to bring me a book about grammar.
If only he knew *why* I'm interested in it...

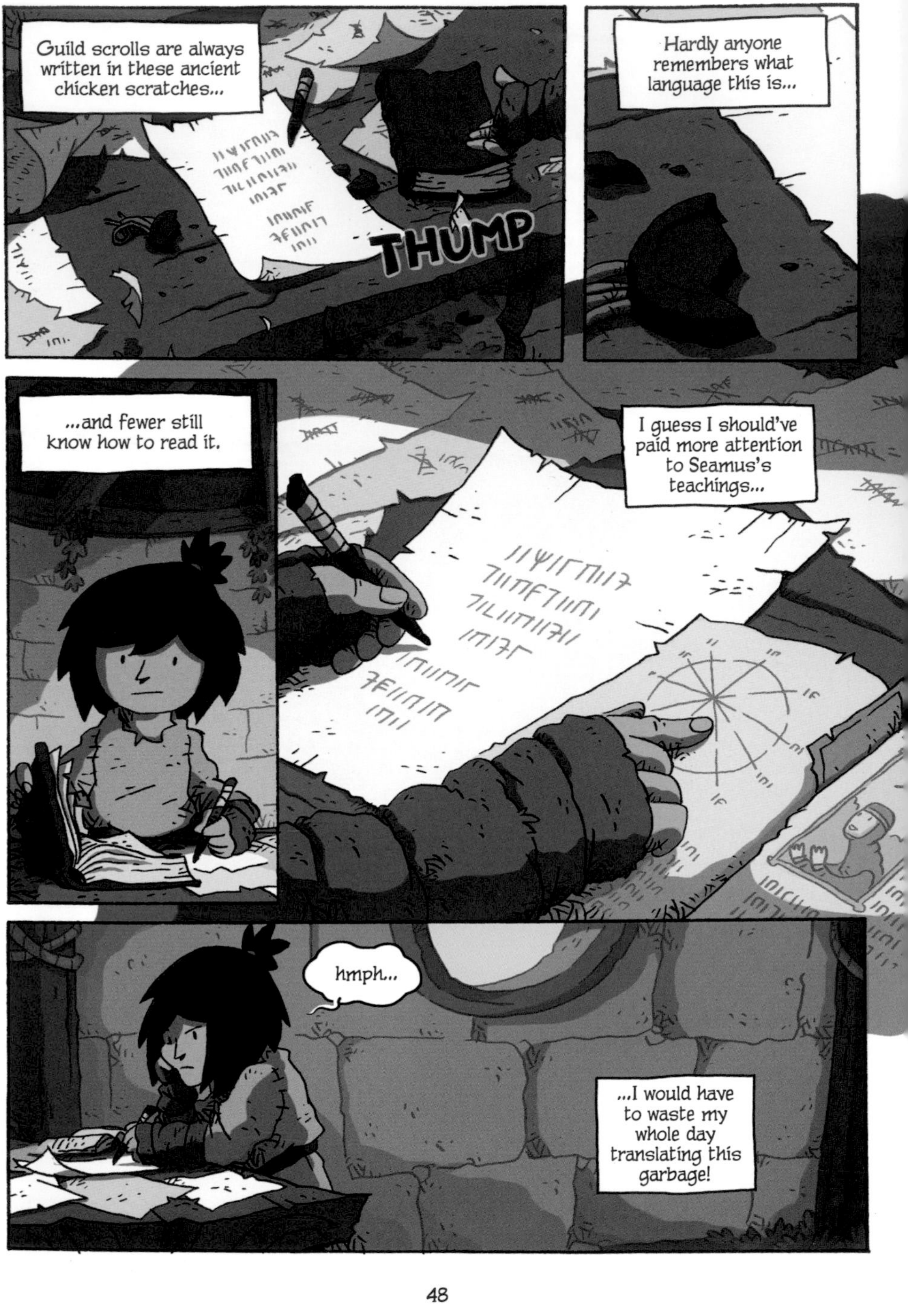
Guild scrolls are always written in these ancient chicken scratches...
THUMP
Hardly anyone remembers what language this is...
...and fewer still know how to read it.
I guess I should've paid more attention to Seamus's teachings...
hmph...
...I would have to waste my whole day translating this garbage!

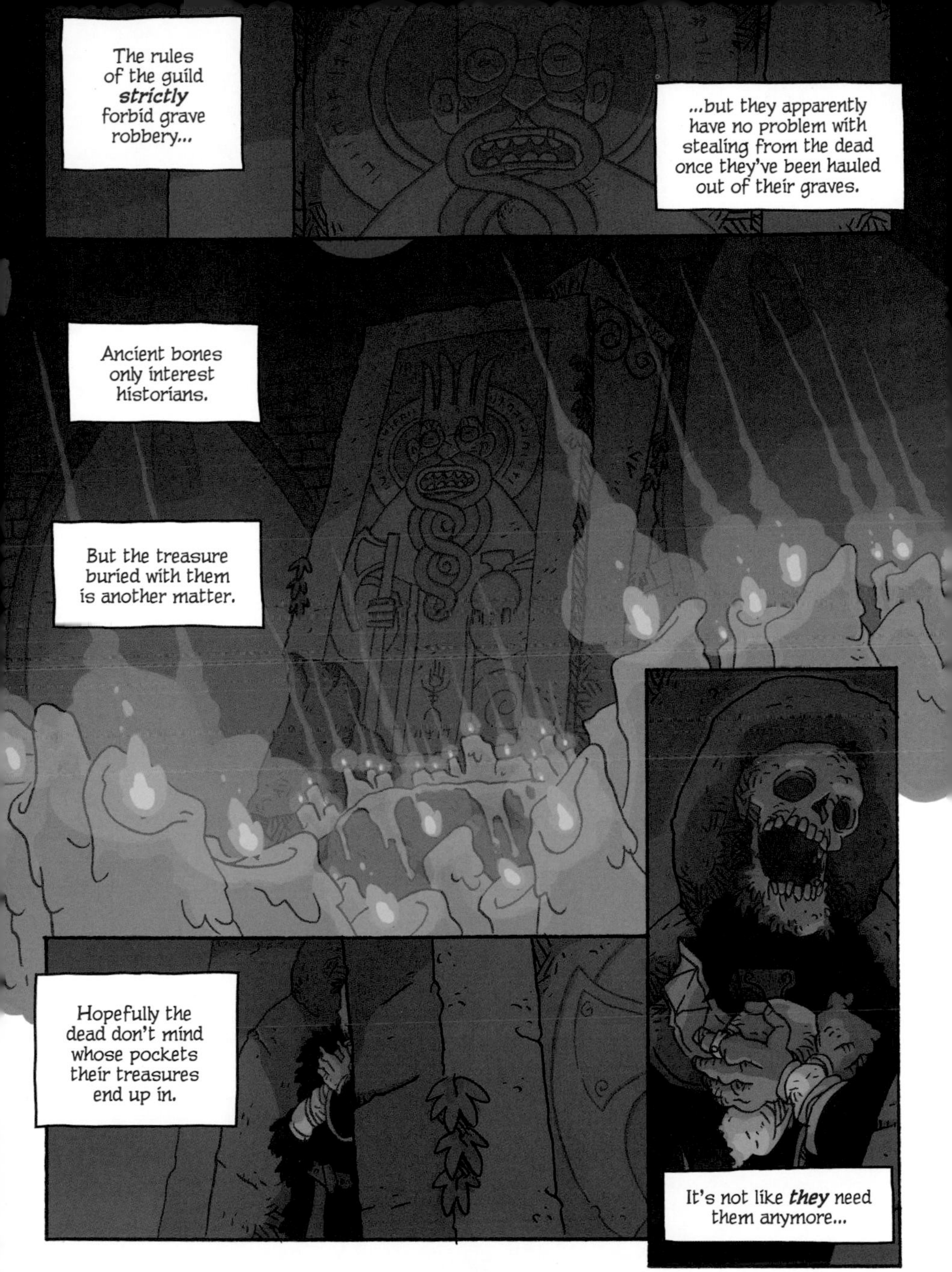
The rules of the guild *strictly* forbid grave robbery...
...but they apparently have no problem with stealing from the dead once they've been hauled out of their graves.
Ancient bones only interest historians.
But the treasure buried with them is another matter.
Hopefully the dead don't mind whose pockets their treasures end up in.
It's not like *they* need them anymore...

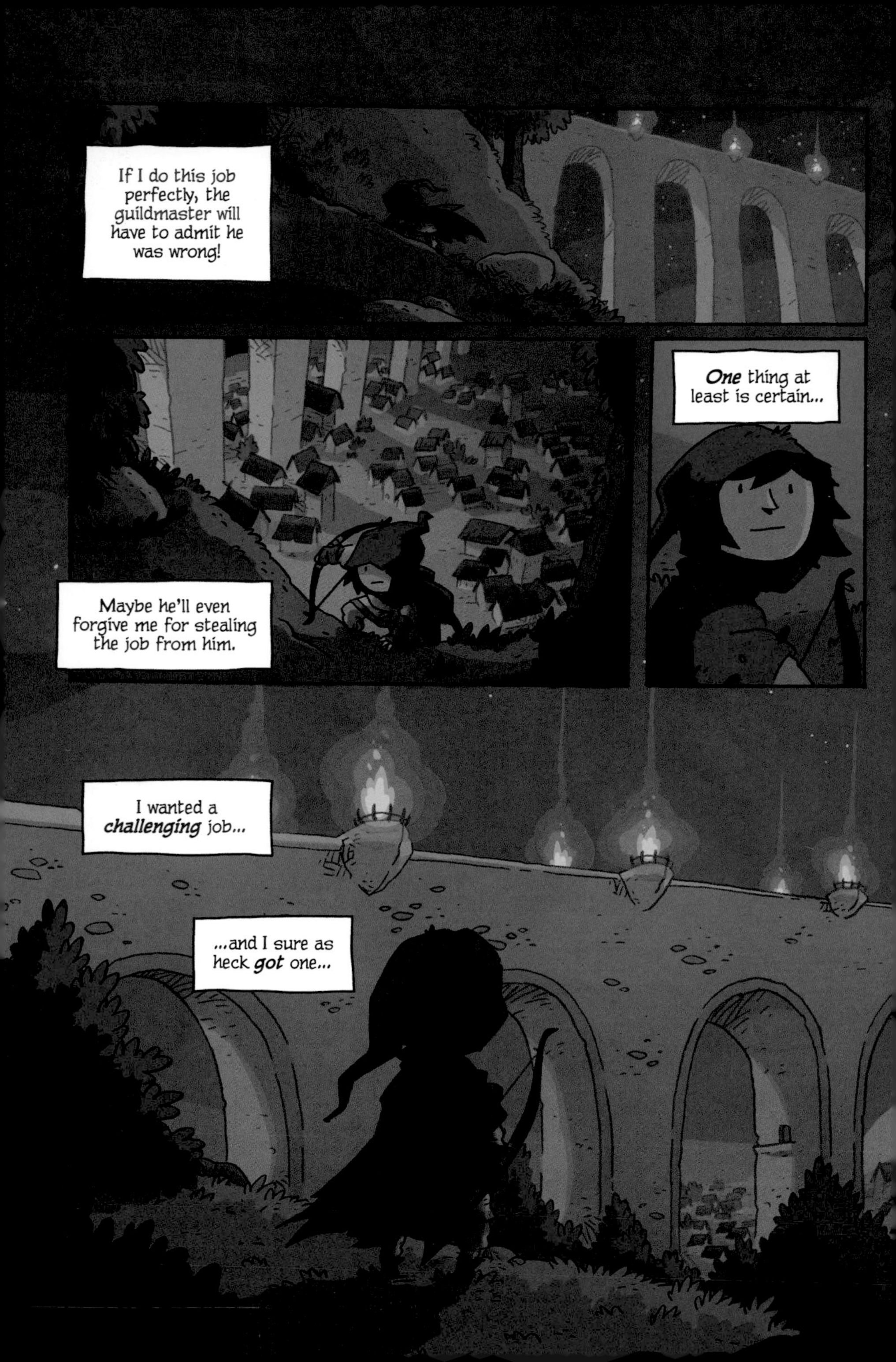

If I do this job perfectly, the guildmaster will have to admit he was wrong!
Maybe he'll even forgive me for stealing the job from him.
One thing at least is certain...
I wanted a *challenging* job...
...and I sure as heck *got* one...

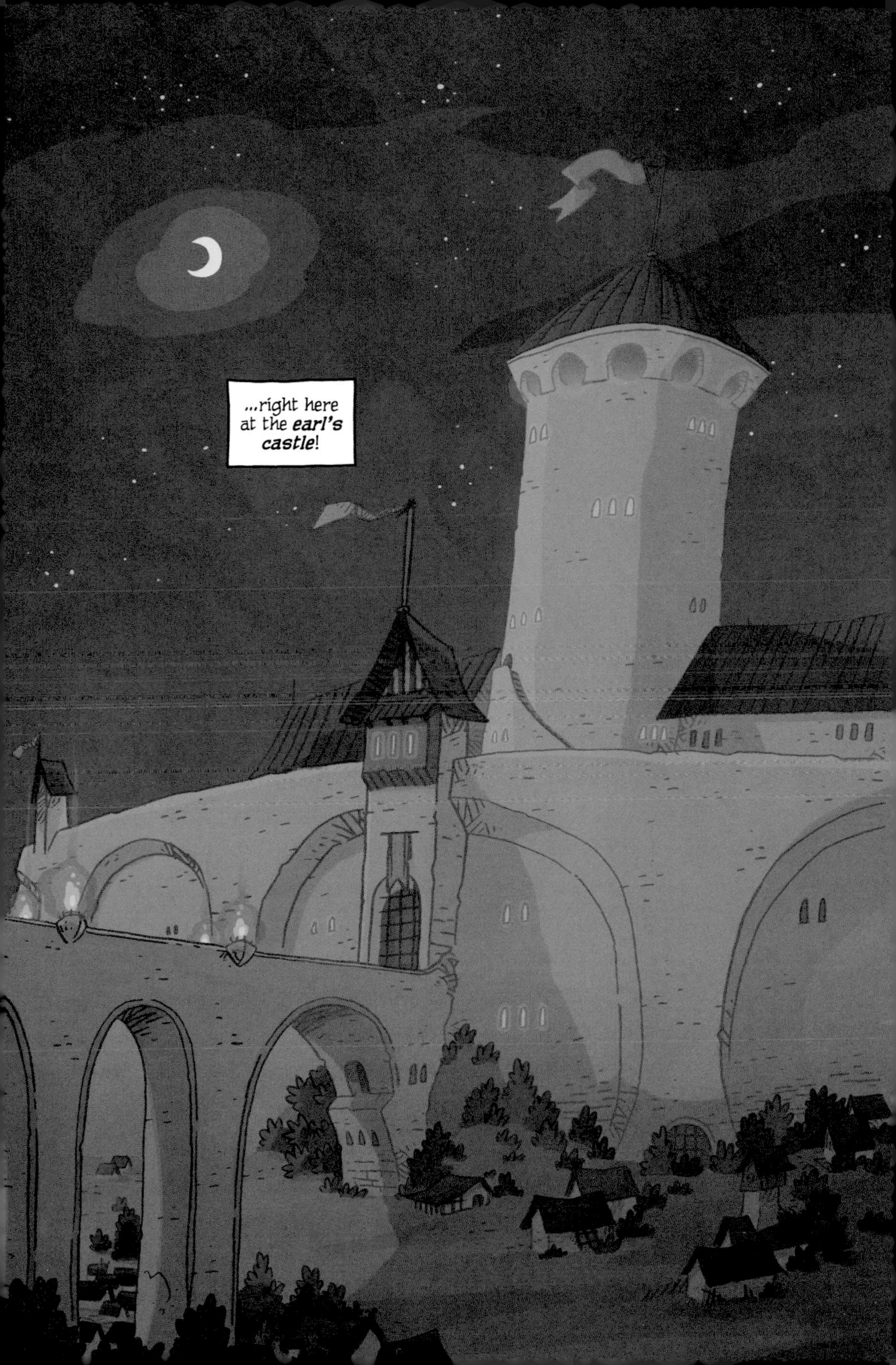
...right here at the ***earl's castle***!

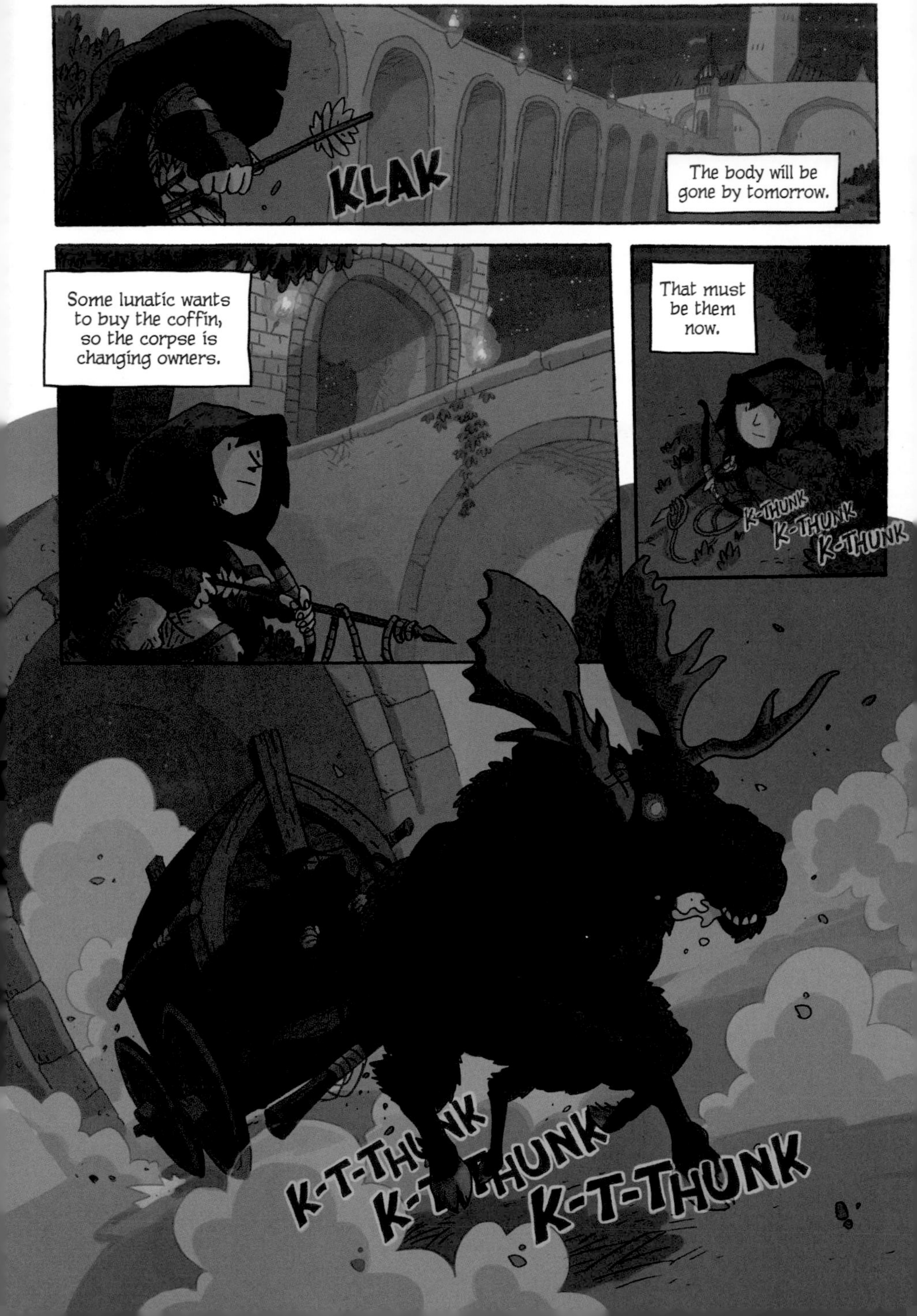
KLAK
The body will be gone by tomorrow.
Some lunatic wants to buy the coffin, so the corpse is changing owners.
That must be them now.
K-THUNK
K-THUNK
K-THUNK
K-T-THUNK
K-T-THUNK
K-T-THUNK

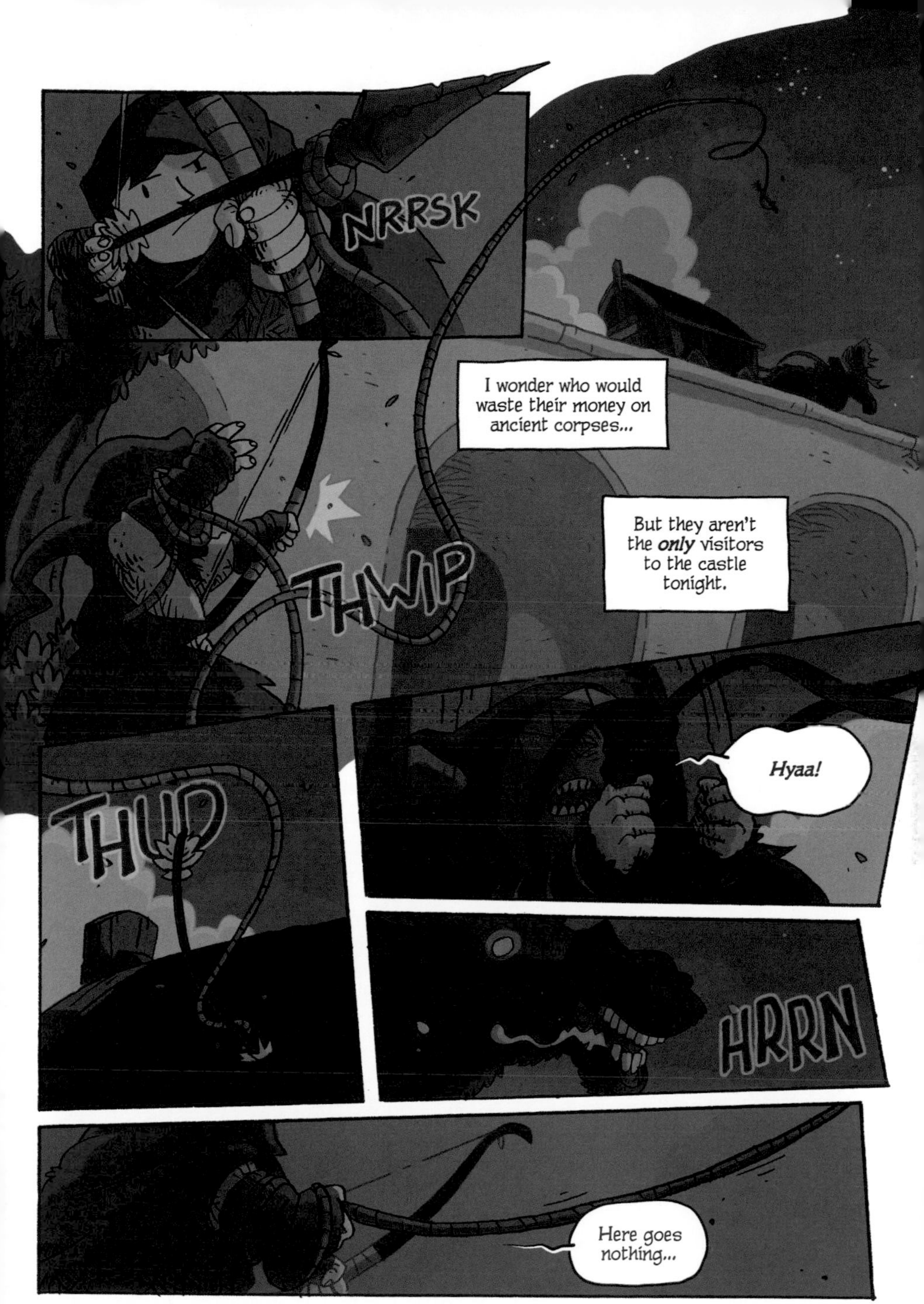
NRRSK
I wonder who would waste their money on ancient corpses...
THWIP
But they aren't the *only* visitors to the castle tonight.
THUD
Hyaa!
HRRN
Here goes nothing...

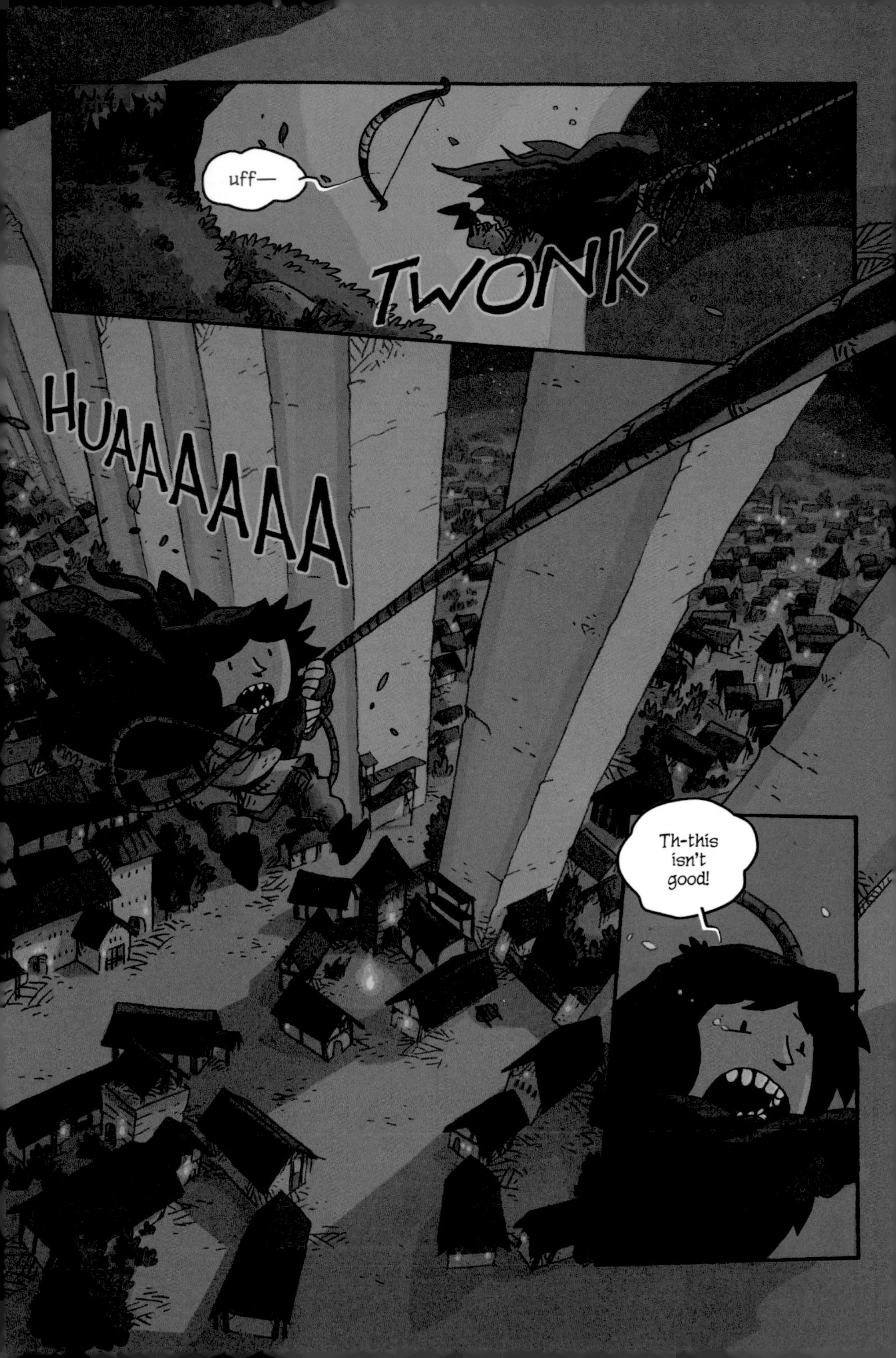
uff—
TWONK
HUAAAAAAA
Th-this isn't good!

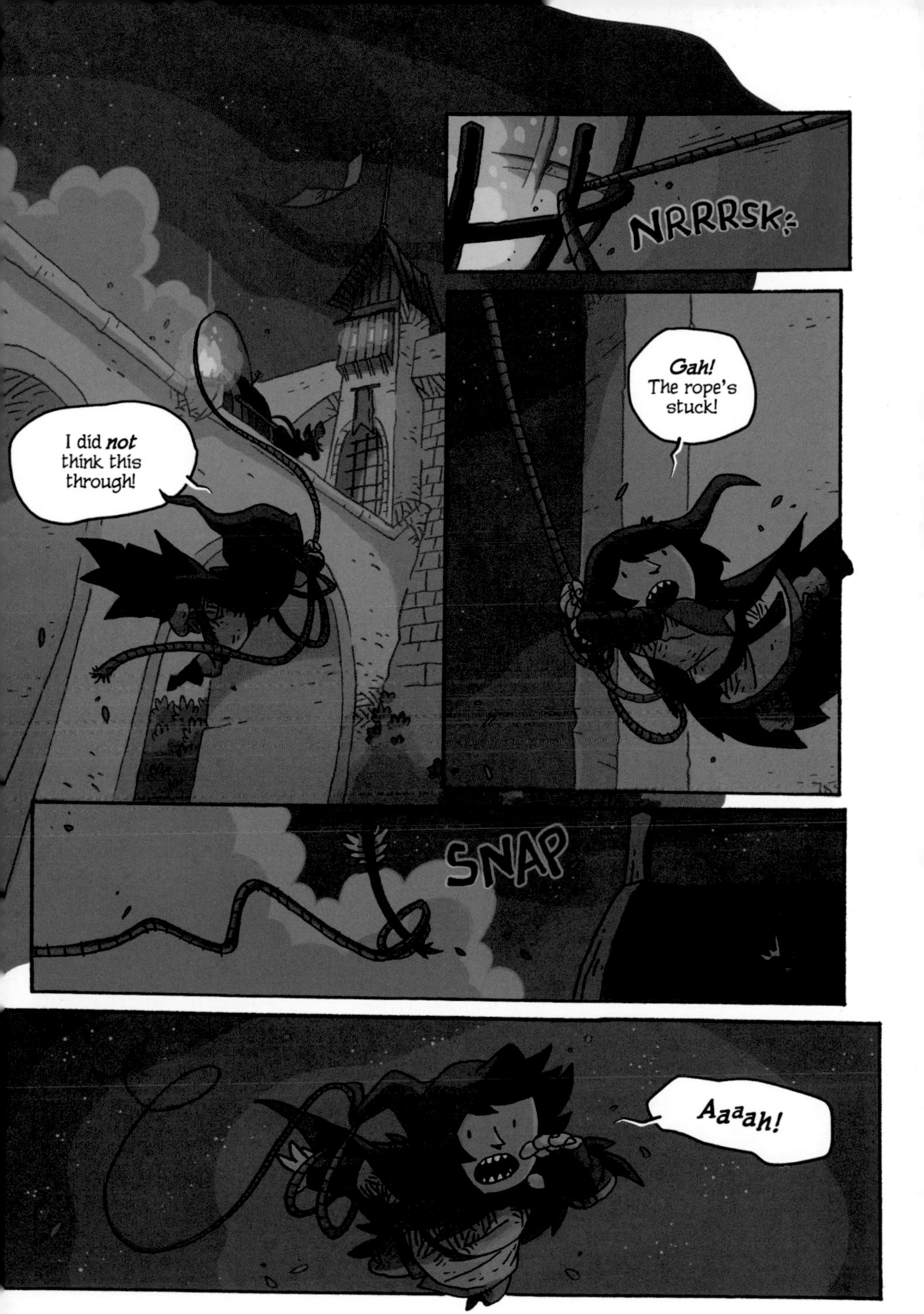
NRRRSK
I did *not* think this through!
Gah! The rope's stuck!
SNAP
Aaaah!

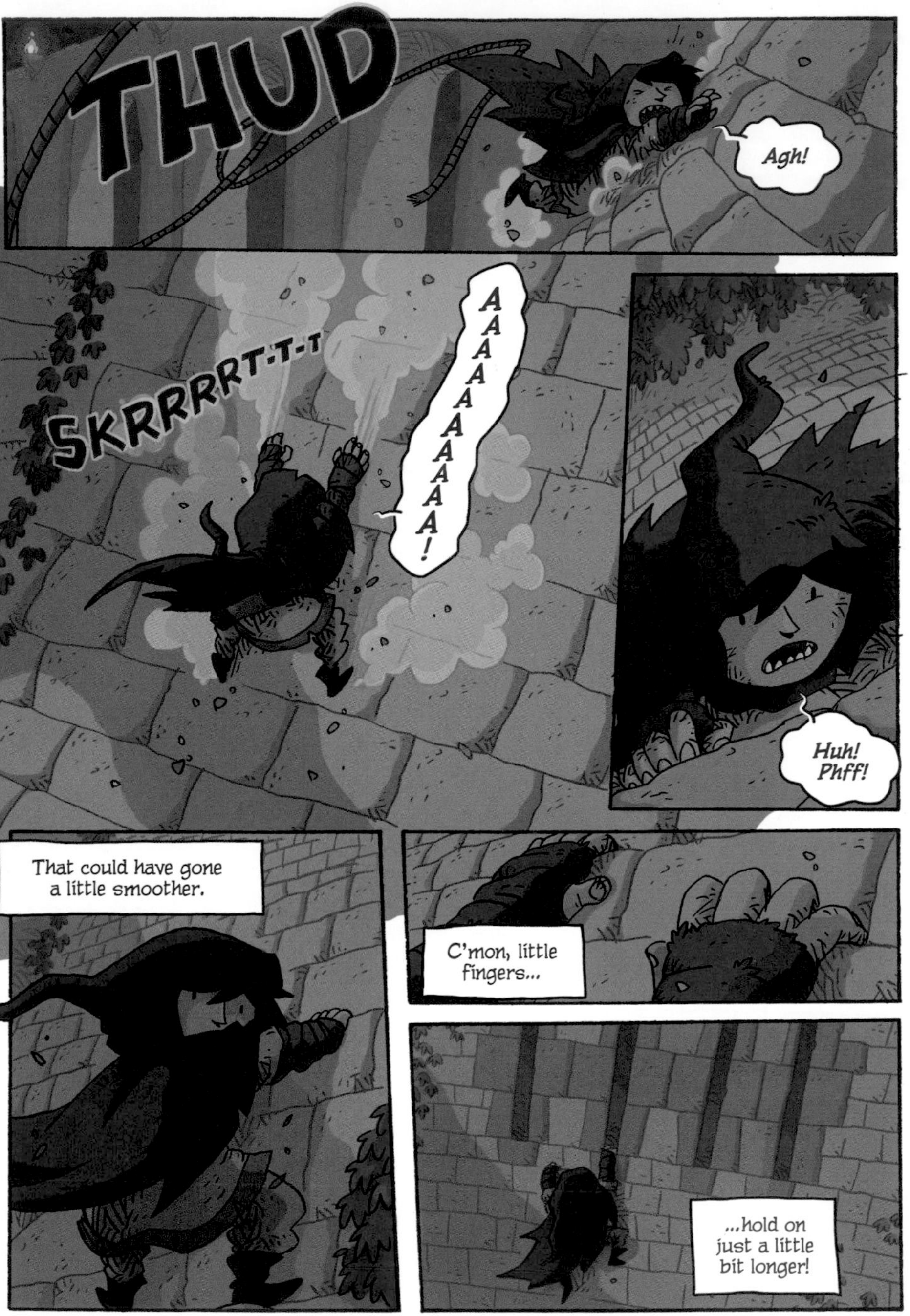
THUD
Agh!
SKRRRRT-T-T
AAAAAAAAAAAA!
Huh! Phff!
That could have gone a little smoother.
C'mon, little fingers...
...hold on just a little bit longer!

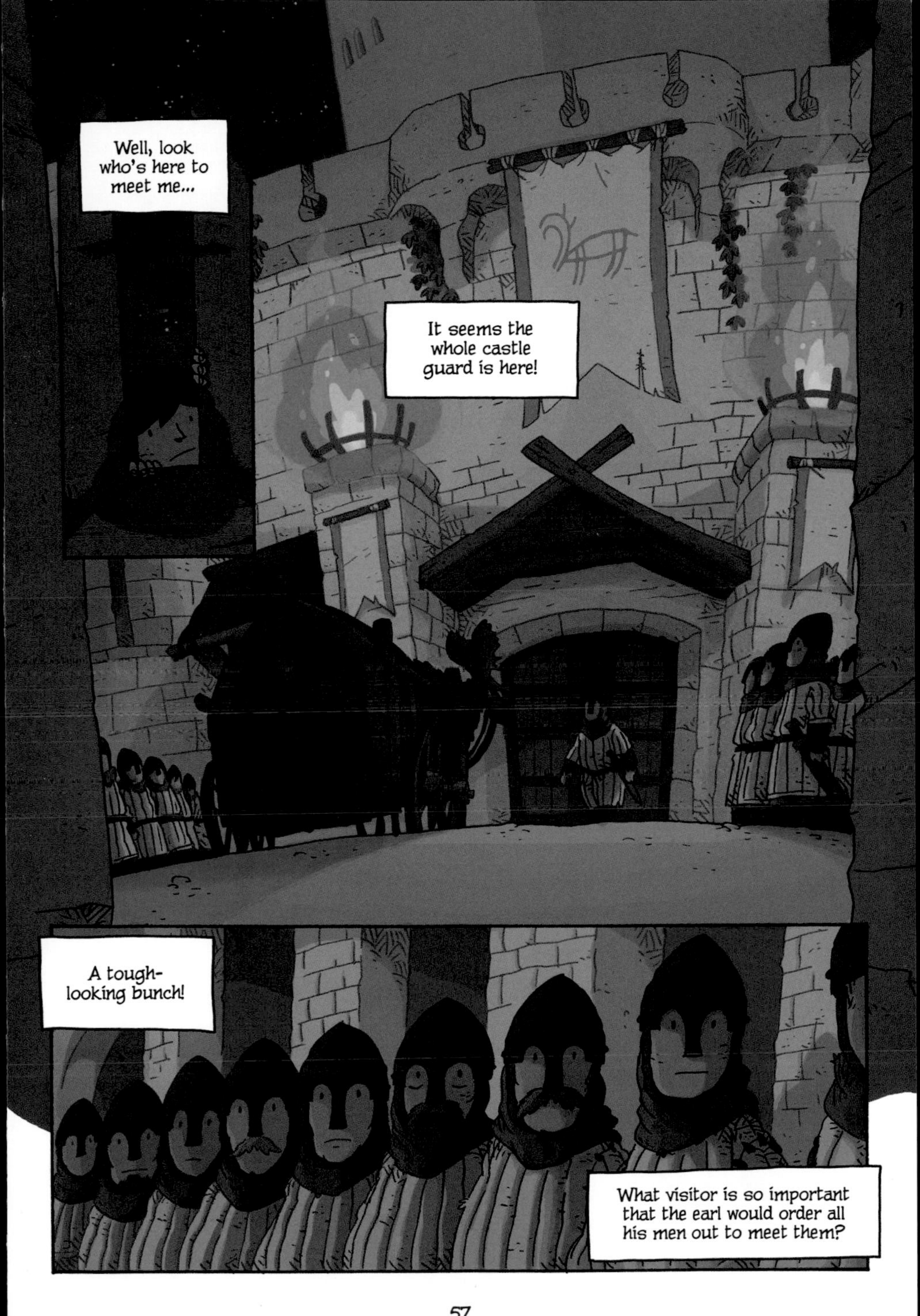
Well, look who's here to meet me...
It seems the whole castle guard is here!
A tough-looking bunch!
What visitor is so important that the earl would order all his men out to meet them?

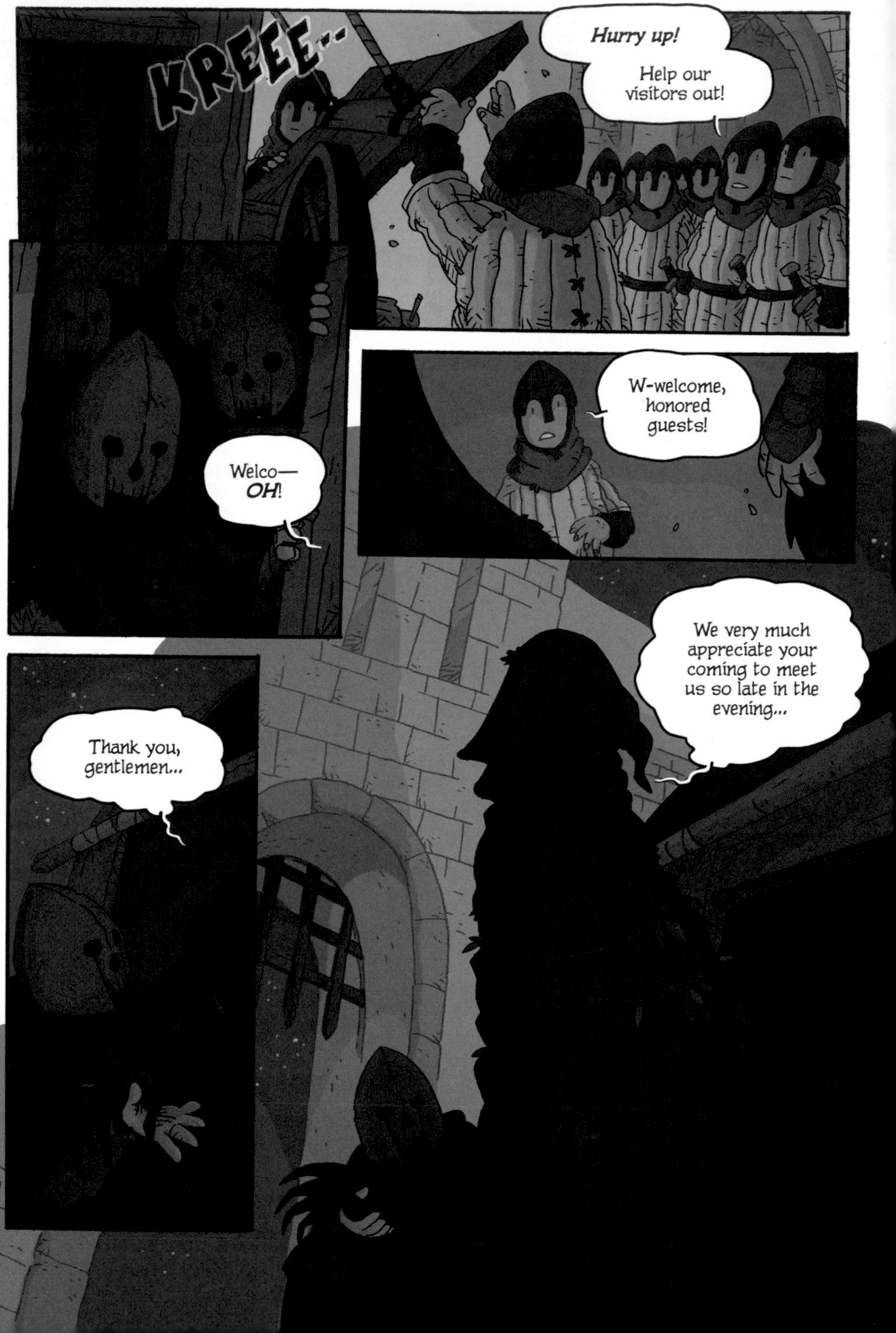
KREEE..
Hurry up!
Help our visitors out!
Welco— OH!
W-welcome, honored guests!
We very much appreciate your coming to meet us so late in the evening...
Thank you, gentlemen...

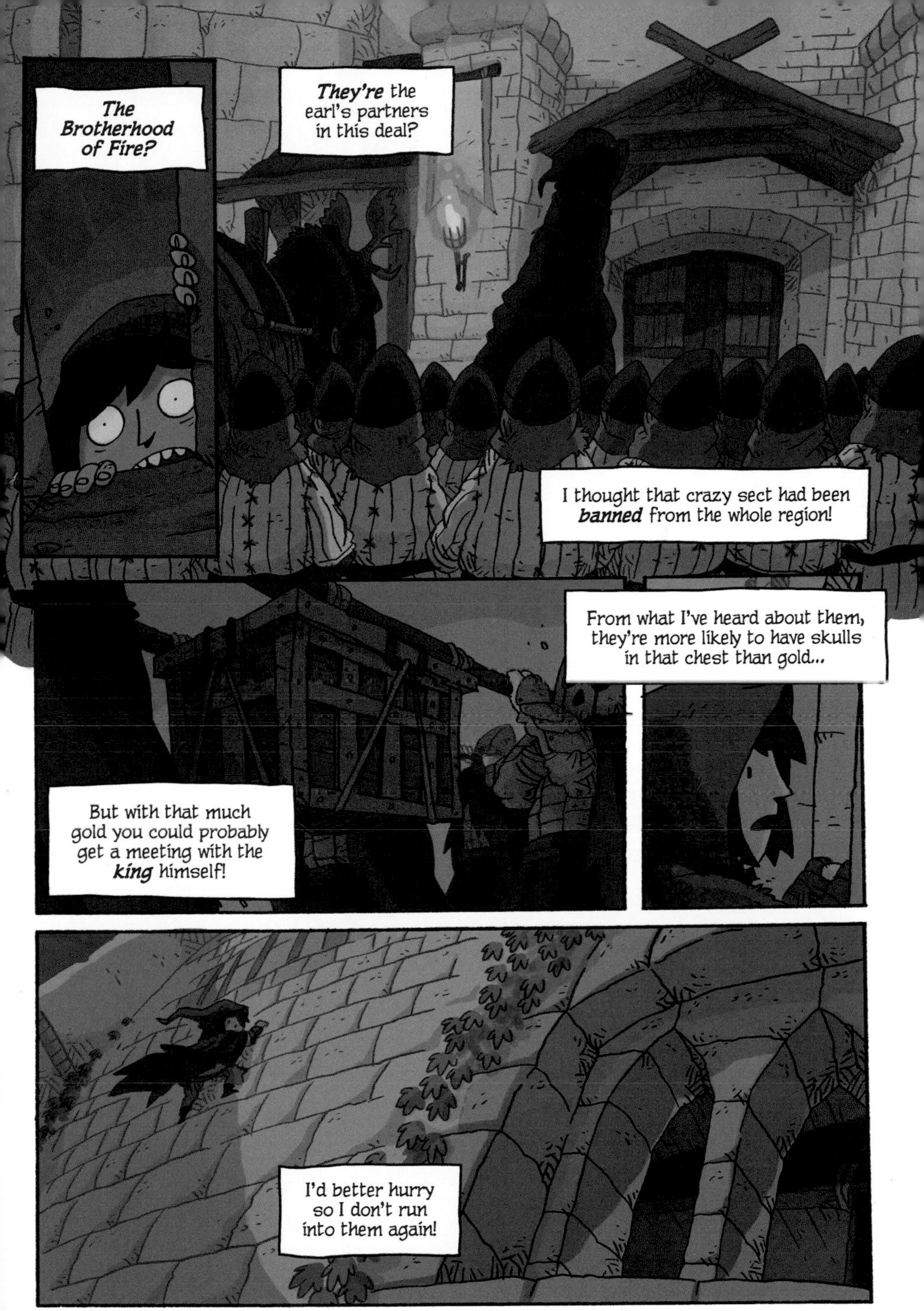
The Brotherhood of Fire?
They're the earl's partners in this deal?
I thought that crazy sect had been banned from the whole region!
But with that much gold you could probably get a meeting with the king himself!
From what I've heard about them, they're more likely to have skulls in that chest than gold...
I'd better hurry so I don't run into them again!

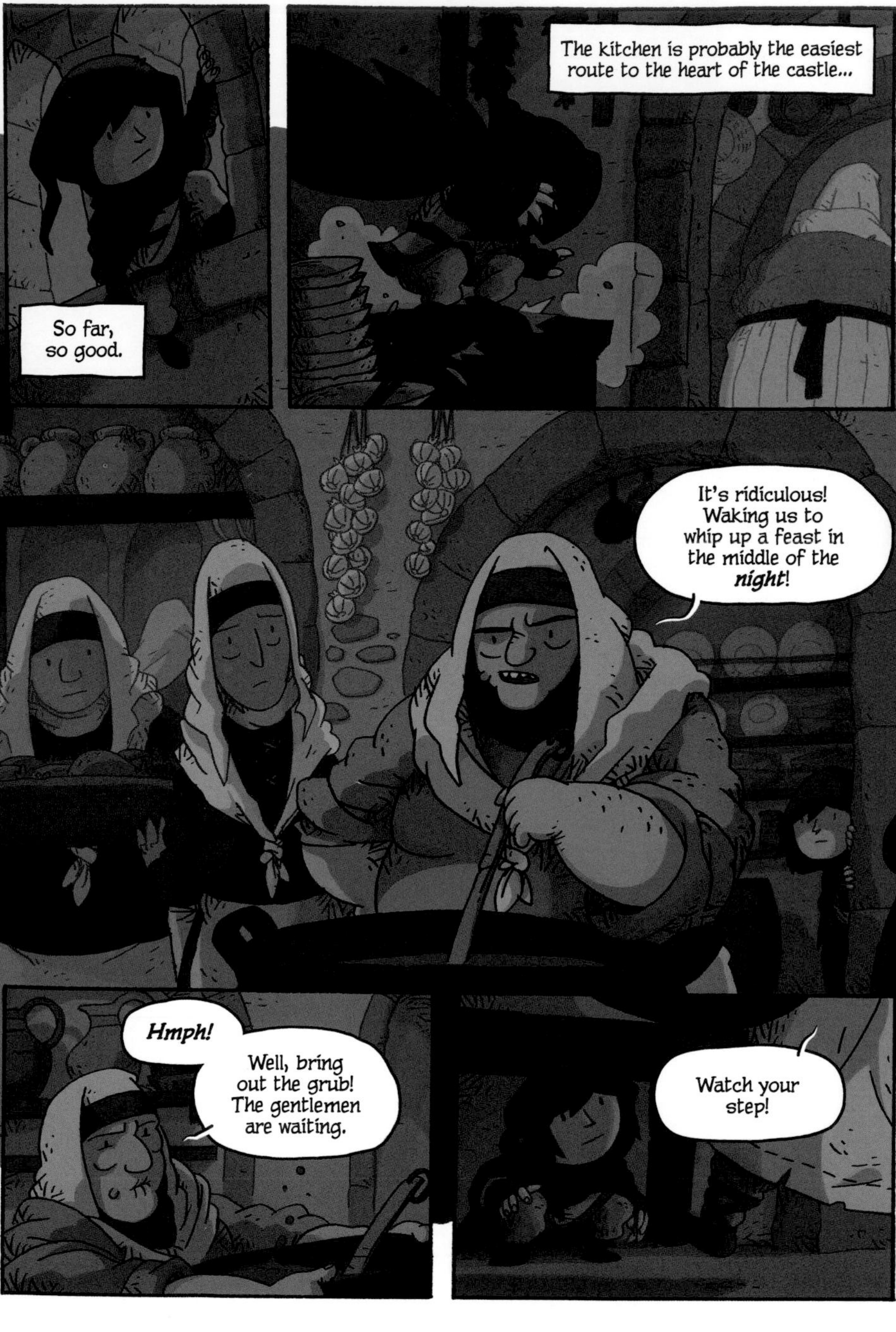
So far, so good.
The kitchen is probably the easiest route to the heart of the castle...
It's ridiculous! Waking us to whip up a feast in the middle of the *night*!
Hmph!
Well, bring out the grub! The gentlemen are waiting.
Watch your step!

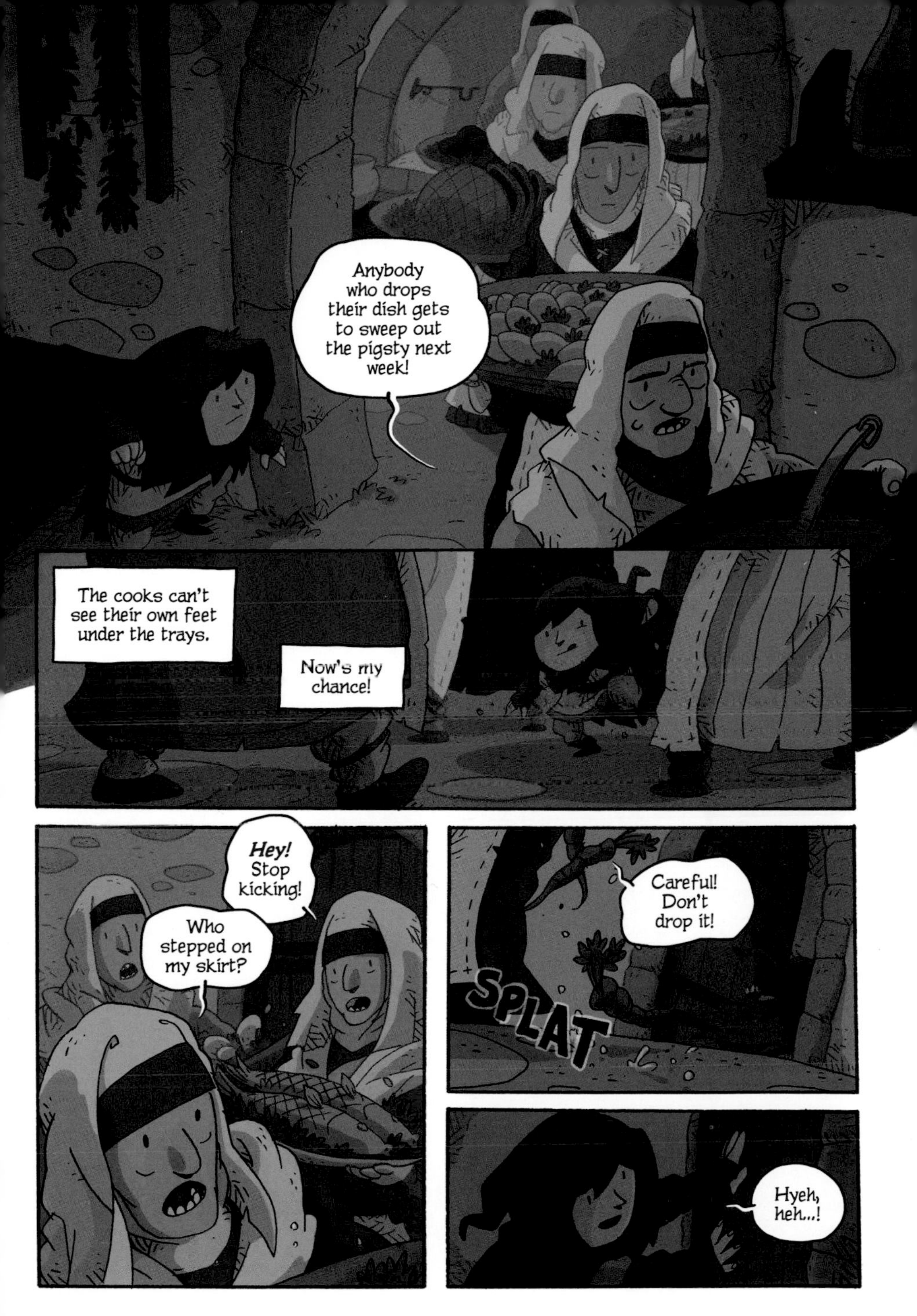
Anybody who drops their dish gets to sweep out the pigsty next week!
The cooks can't see their own feet under the trays.
Now's my chance!
Hey! Stop kicking!
Who stepped on my skirt?
Careful! Don't drop it!
SPLAT
Hyeh, heh...!

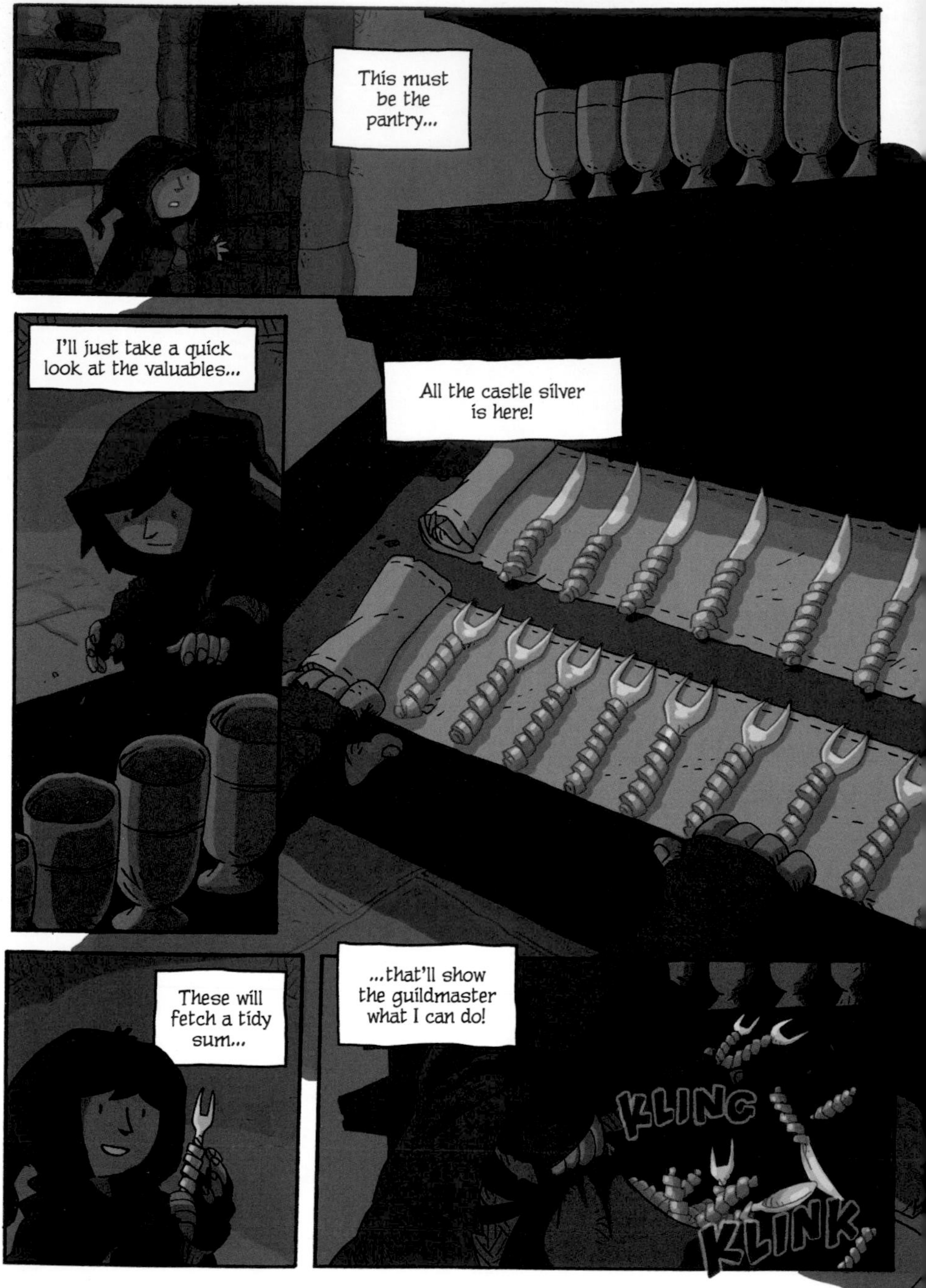
This must be the pantry...
I'll just take a quick look at the valuables...
All the castle silver is here!
These will fetch a tidy sum...
...that'll show the guildmaster what I can do!
KLING
KLINK

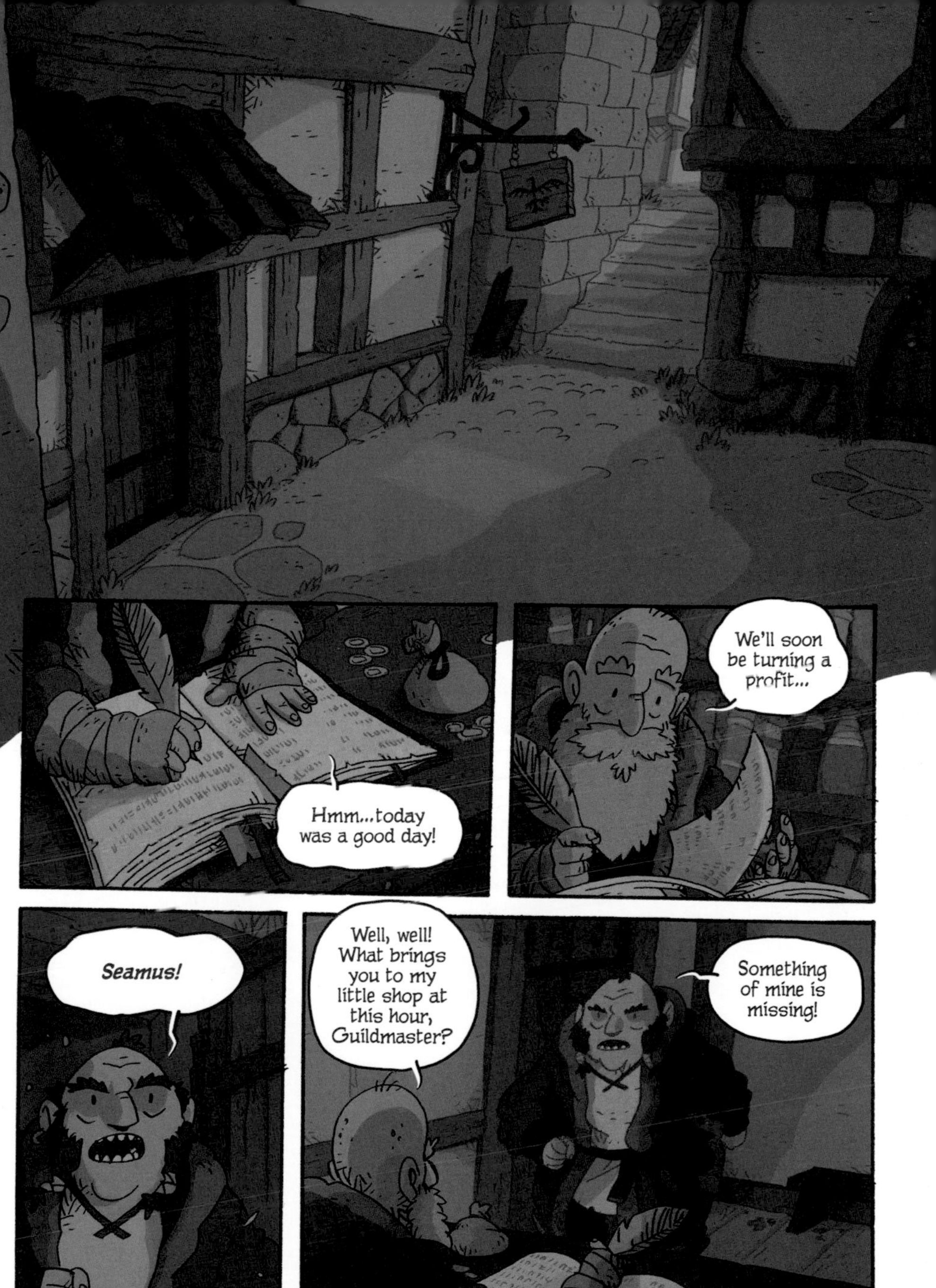
Hmm...today was a good day!
We'll soon be turning a profit...
Seamus!
Well, well! What brings you to my little shop at this hour, Guildmaster?
Something of mine is missing!

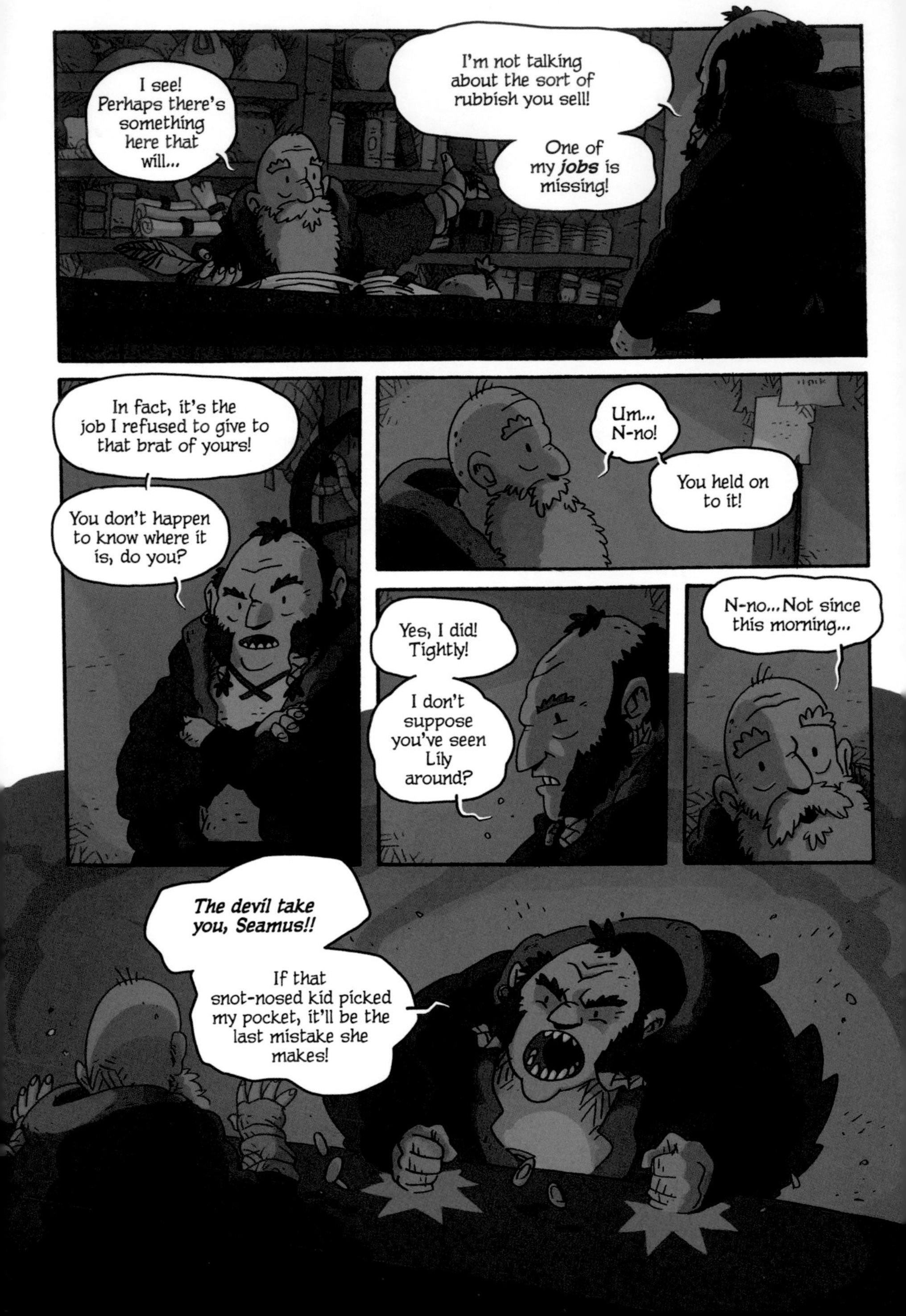
I see! Perhaps there's something here that will...
I'm not talking about the sort of rubbish you sell!
One of my ***jobs*** is missing!
In fact, it's the job I refused to give to that brat of yours!
You don't happen to know where it is, do you?
Um... N-no!
You held on to it!
Yes, I did! Tightly!
I don't suppose you've seen Lily around?
N-no... Not since this morning...
The devil take you, Seamus!!
If that snot-nosed kid picked my pocket, it'll be the last mistake she makes!

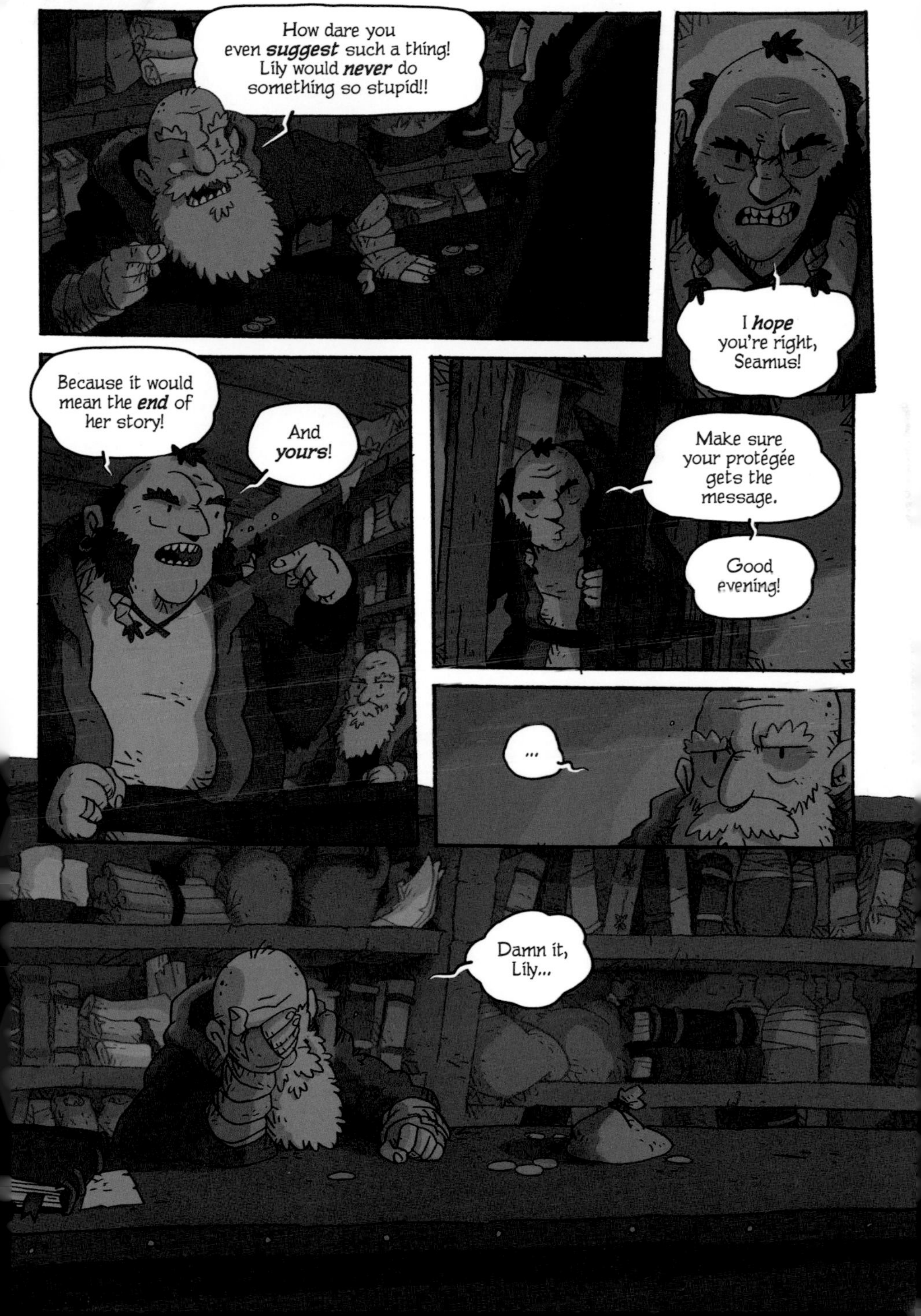
How dare you even *suggest* such a thing! Lily would *never* do something so stupid!!
I *hope* you're right, Seamus!
Because it would mean the *end* of her story!
And *yours*!
Make sure your protégée gets the message.
Good evening!
...
Damn it, Lily...

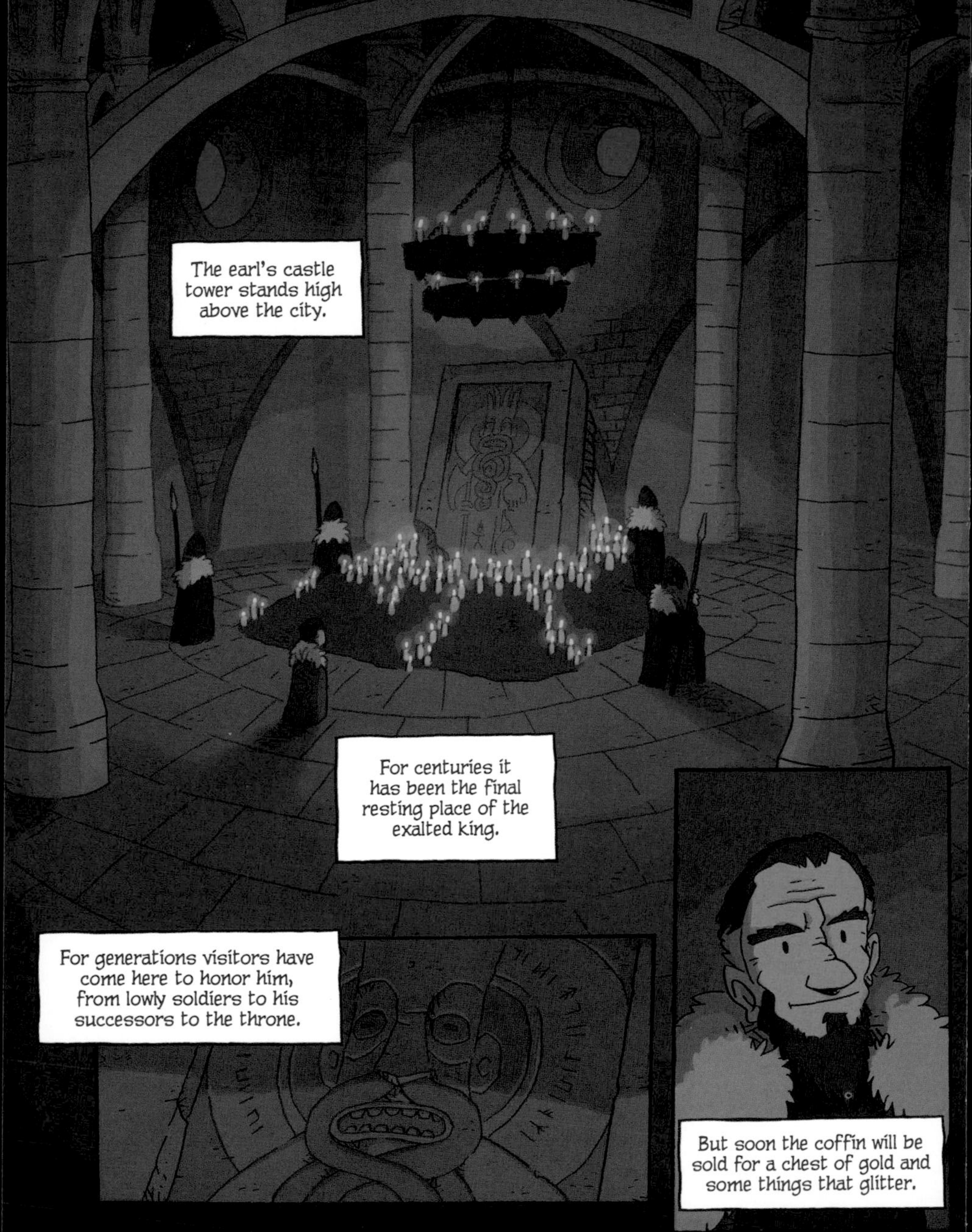

The earl's castle tower stands high above the city.
For centuries it has been the final resting place of the exalted king.
For generations visitors have come here to honor him, from lowly soldiers to his successors to the throne.
But soon the coffin will be sold for a chest of gold and some things that glitter.

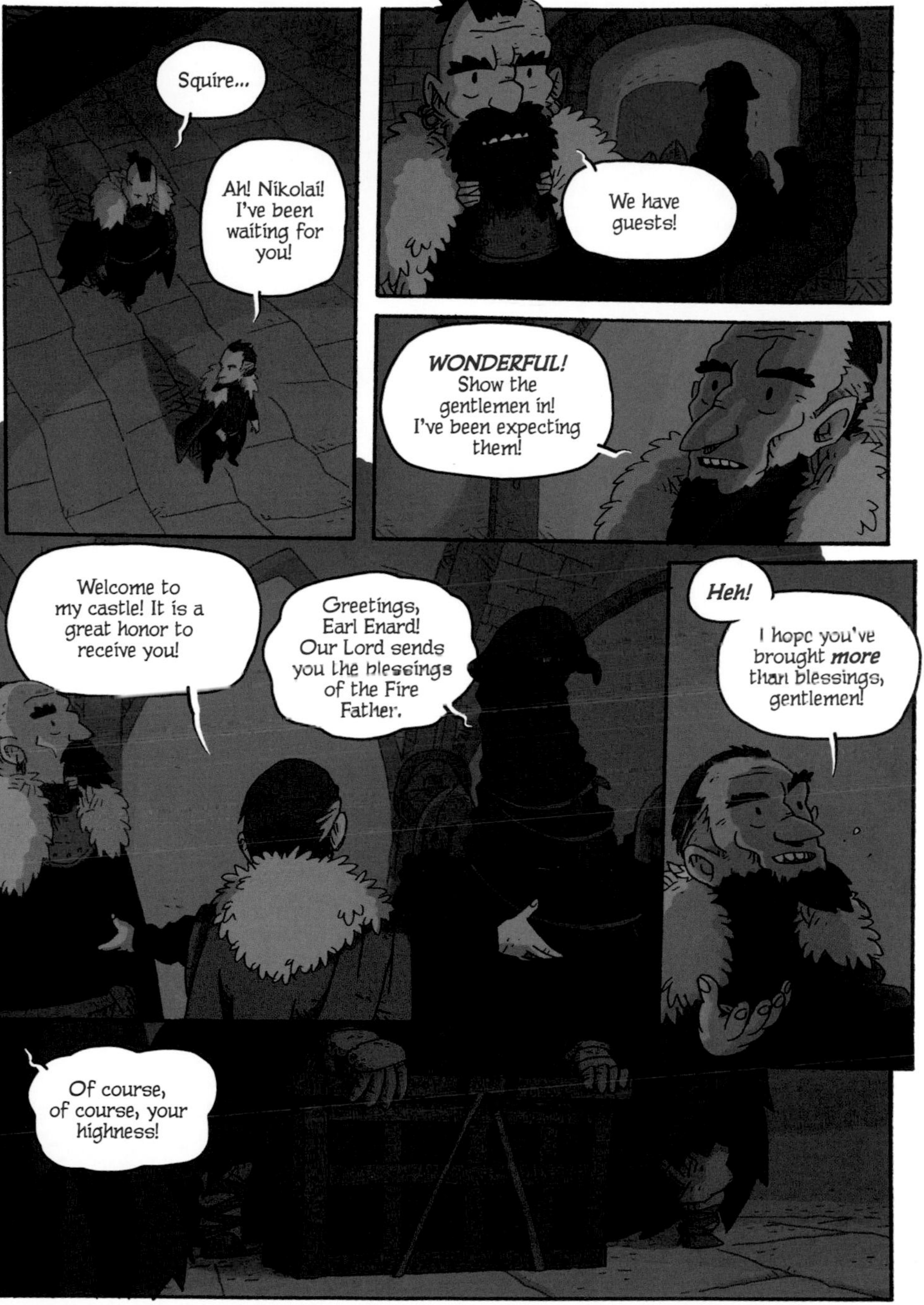
Squire...
Ah! Nikolai! I've been waiting for you!
We have guests!
WONDERFUL! Show the gentlemen in! I've been expecting them!
Welcome to my castle! It is a great honor to receive you!
Greetings, Earl Enard! Our Lord sends you the blessings of the Fire Father.
Heh!
I hope you've brought *more* than blessings, gentlemen!
Of course, of course, your highness!

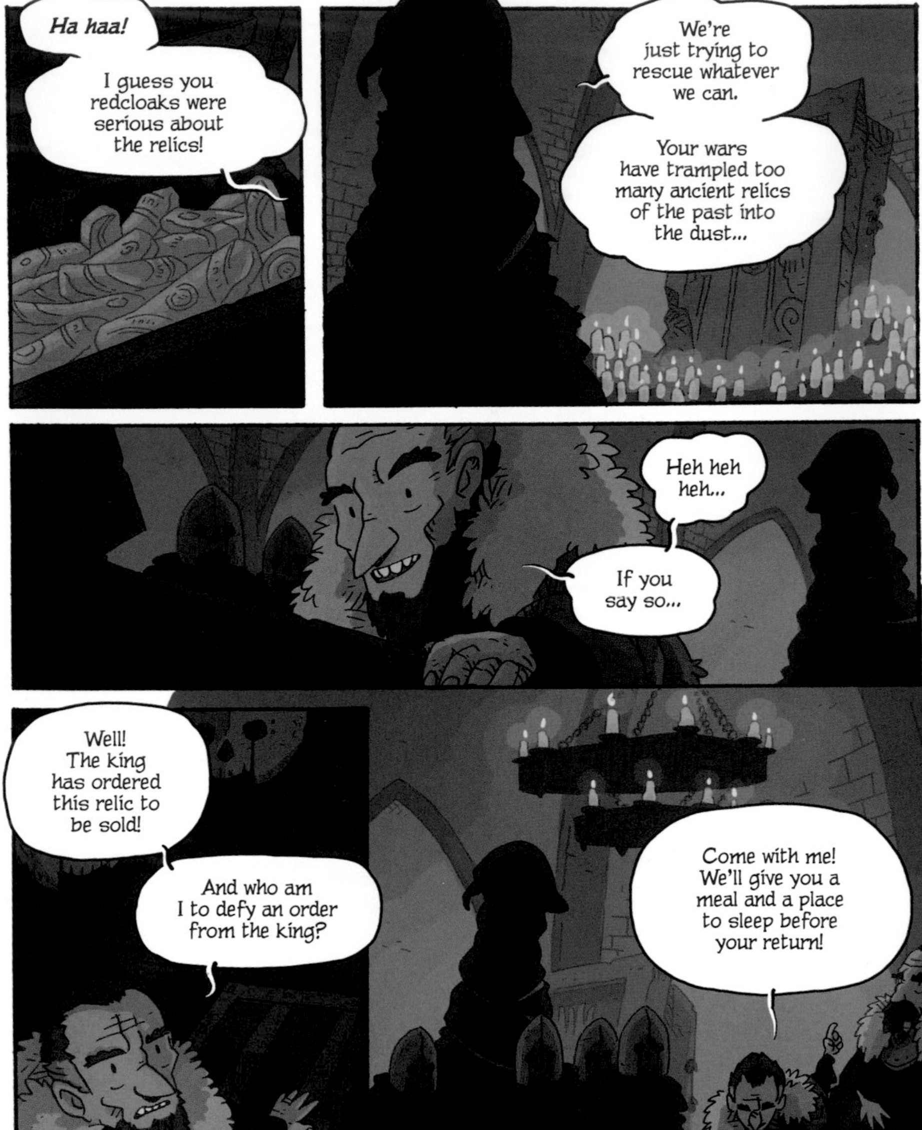

Ha haa!
I guess you redcloaks were serious about the relics!
We're just trying to rescue whatever we can.
Your wars have trampled too many ancient relics of the past into the dust...
Heh heh heh...
If you say so...
Well! The king has ordered this relic to be sold!
And who am I to defy an order from the king?
Come with me! We'll give you a meal and a place to sleep before your return!

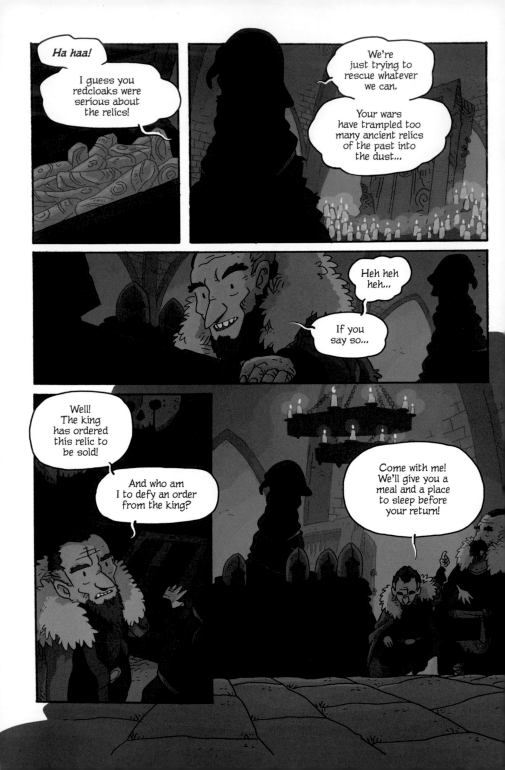

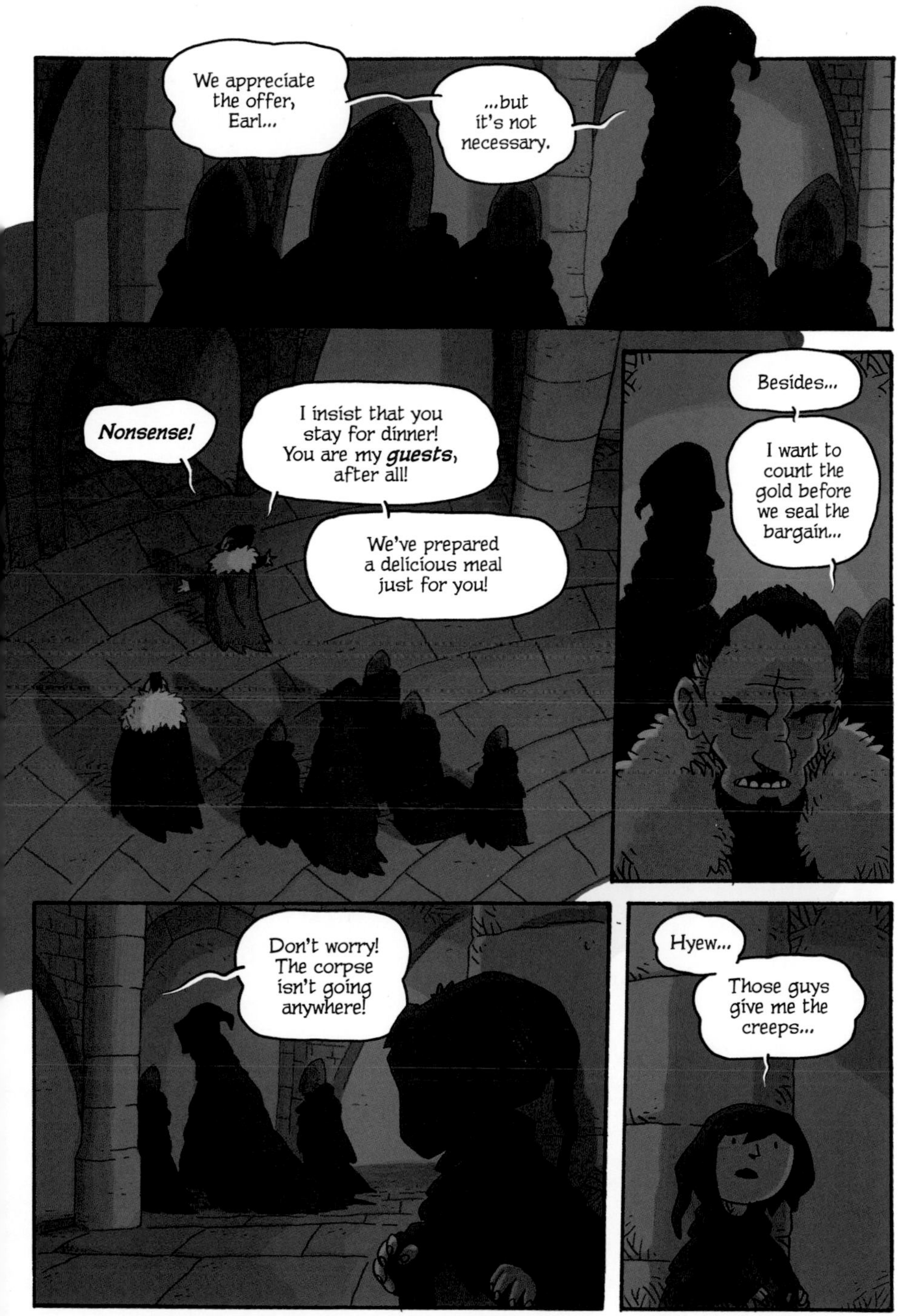

We appreciate the offer, Earl...
...but it's not necessary.
Nonsense!
I insist that you stay for dinner! You are my **guests**, after all!
We've prepared a delicious meal just for you!
Besides...
I want to count the gold before we seal the bargain...
Don't worry! The corpse isn't going anywhere!
Hyew...
Those guys give me the creeps...

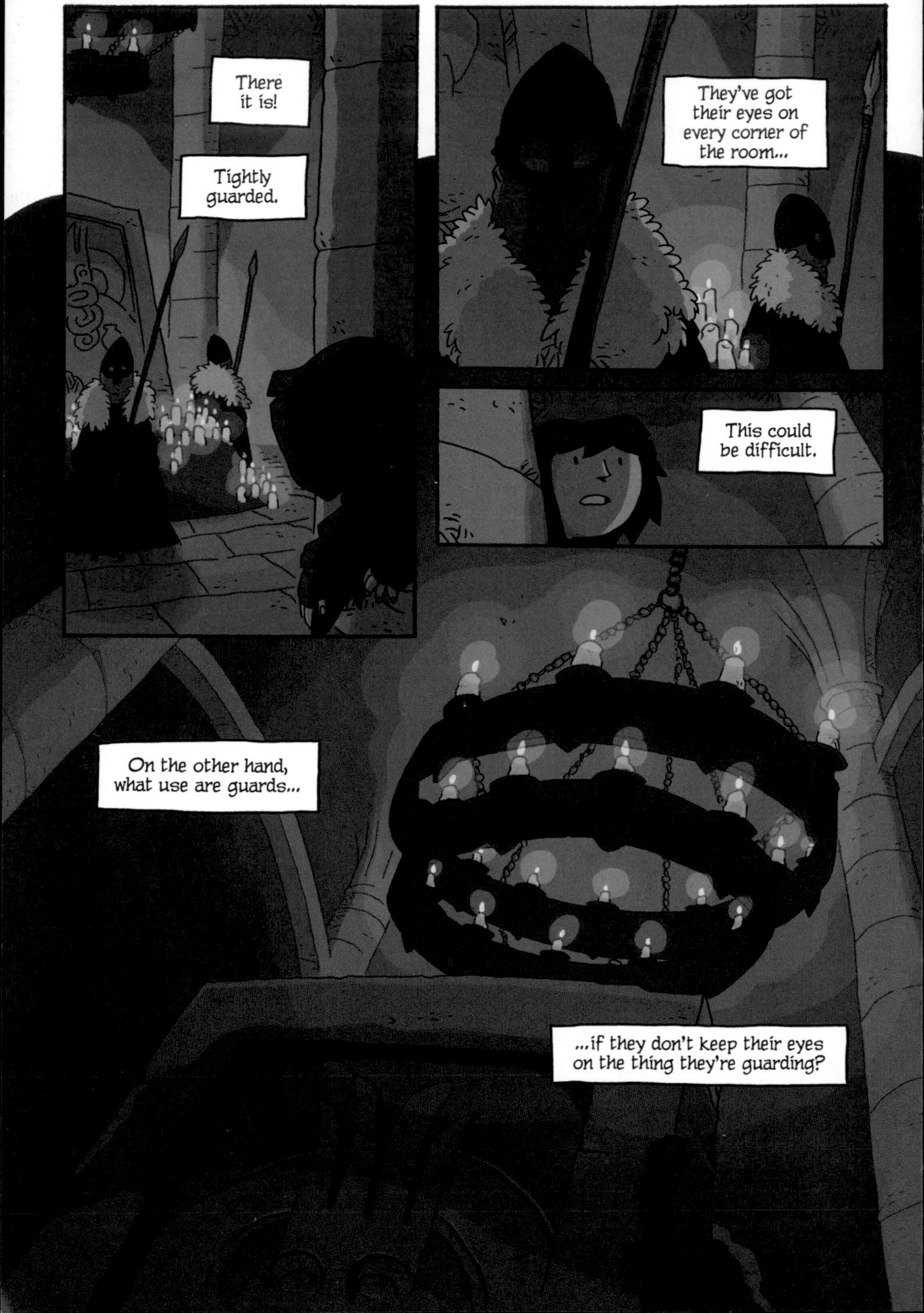
There it is!
Tightly guarded.
They've got their eyes on every corner of the room...
This could be difficult.
On the other hand, what use are guards...
...if they don't keep their eyes on the thing they're guarding?

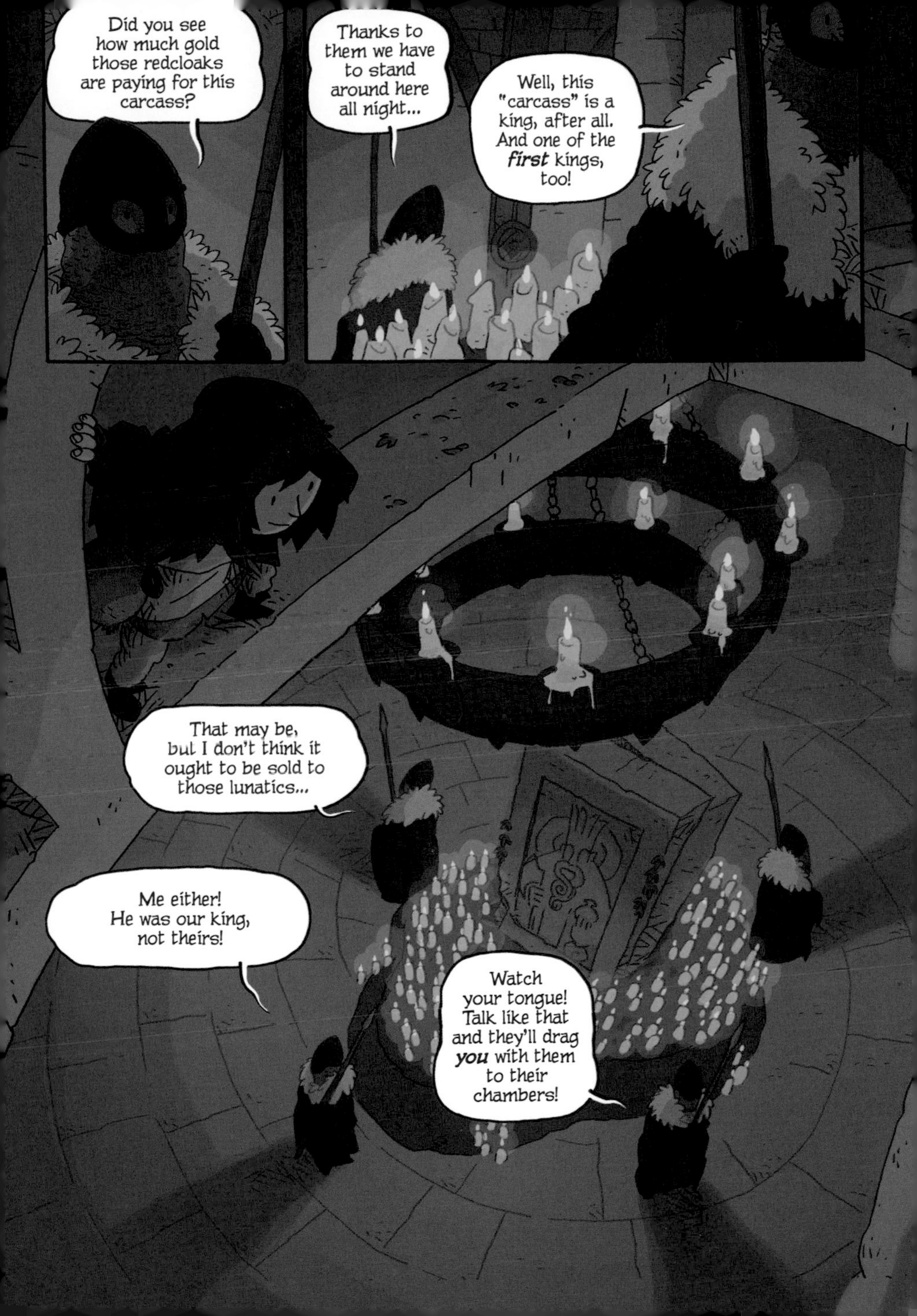
Did you see how much gold those redcloaks are paying for this carcass?
Thanks to them we have to stand around here all night...
Well, this "carcass" is a king, after all. And one of the *first* kings, too!
That may be, but I don't think it ought to be sold to those lunatics...
Me either! He was our king, not theirs!
Watch your tongue! Talk like that and they'll drag *you* with them to their chambers!

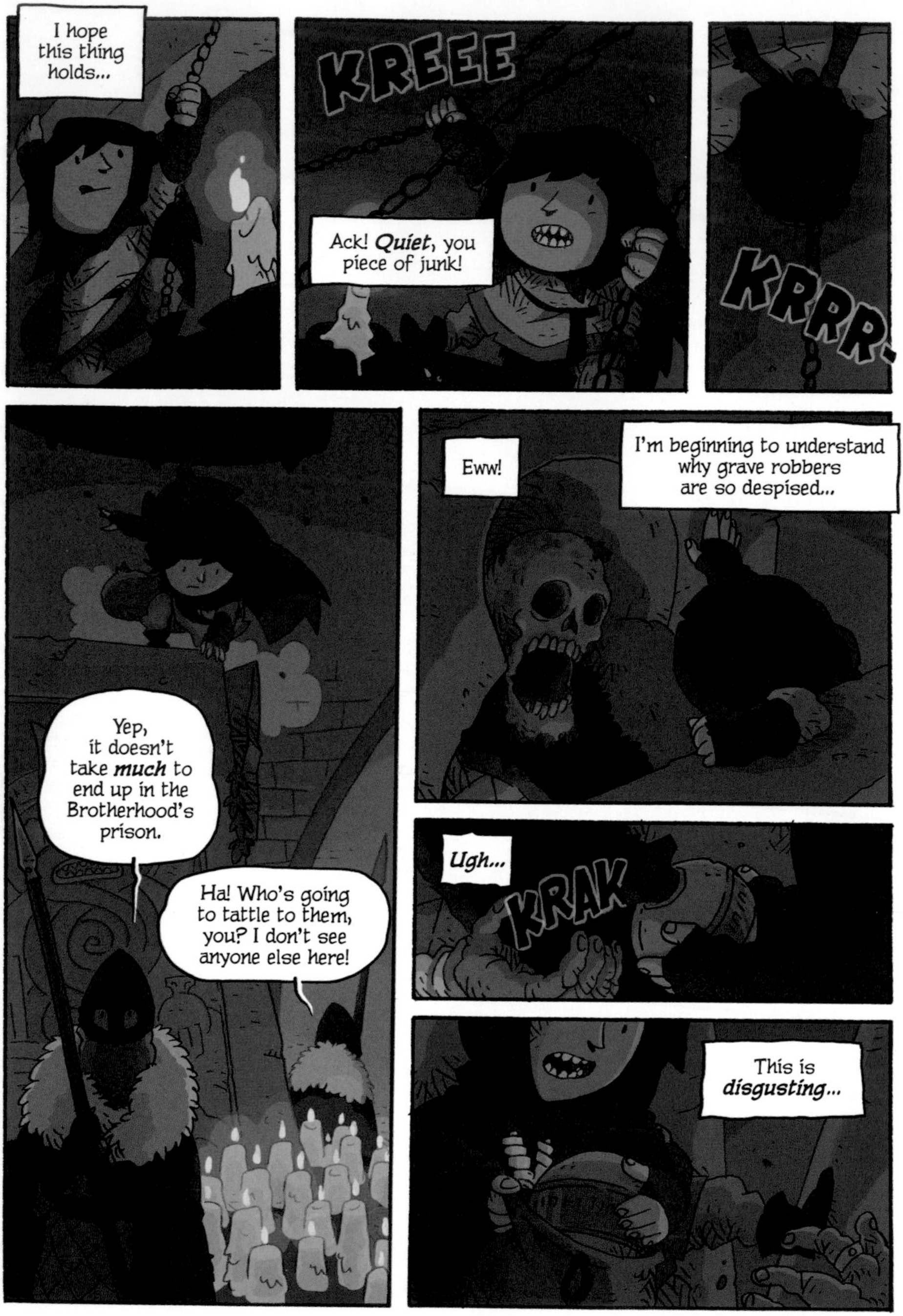
I hope this thing holds...
KREEE
Ack! *Quiet*, you piece of junk!
KRRR-
Yep, it doesn't take *much* to end up in the Brotherhood's prison.
Ha! Who's going to tattle to them, you? I don't see anyone else here!
Eww!
I'm beginning to understand why grave robbers are so despised...
Ugh...
KRAK
This is *disgusting*...

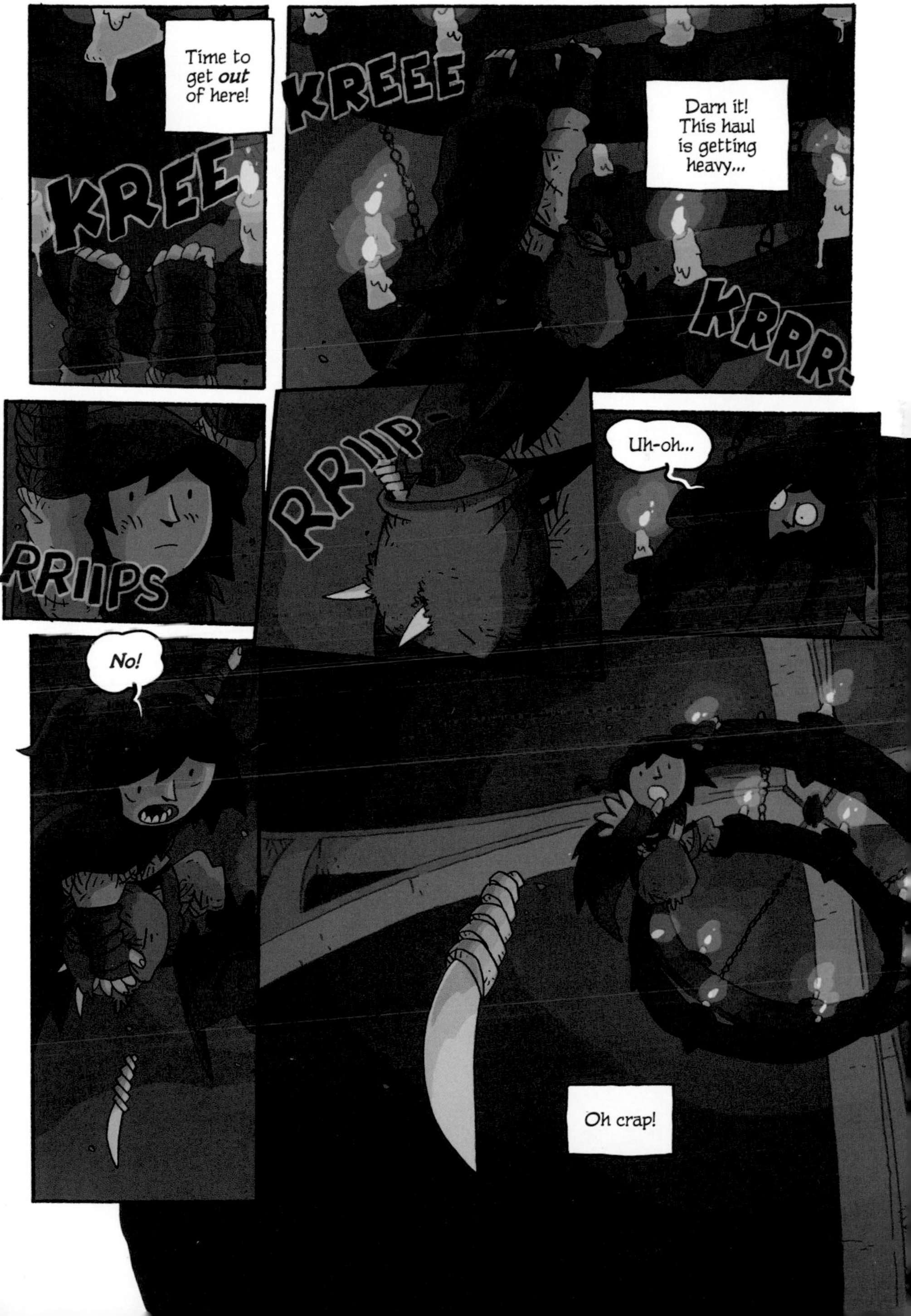
Time to get *out* of here!
KREE
KREEE
Darn it! This haul is getting heavy...
KRRR-
RRIIPS
RRIIP
Uh-oh...
No!
Oh crap!

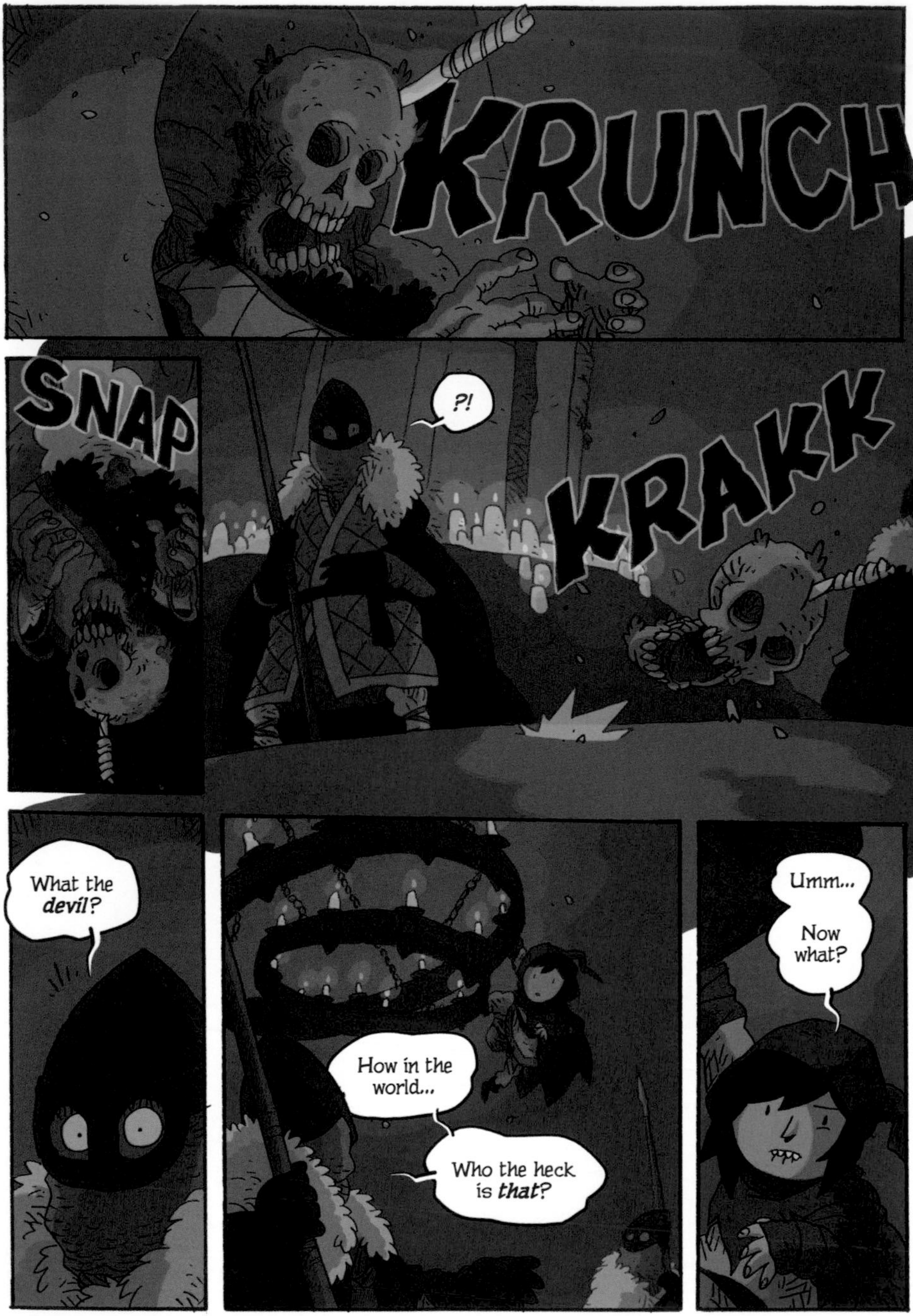
KRUNCH
SNAP
?!
KRAKK
What the *devil*?
How in the world...
Who the heck is *that*?
Umm...
Now what?

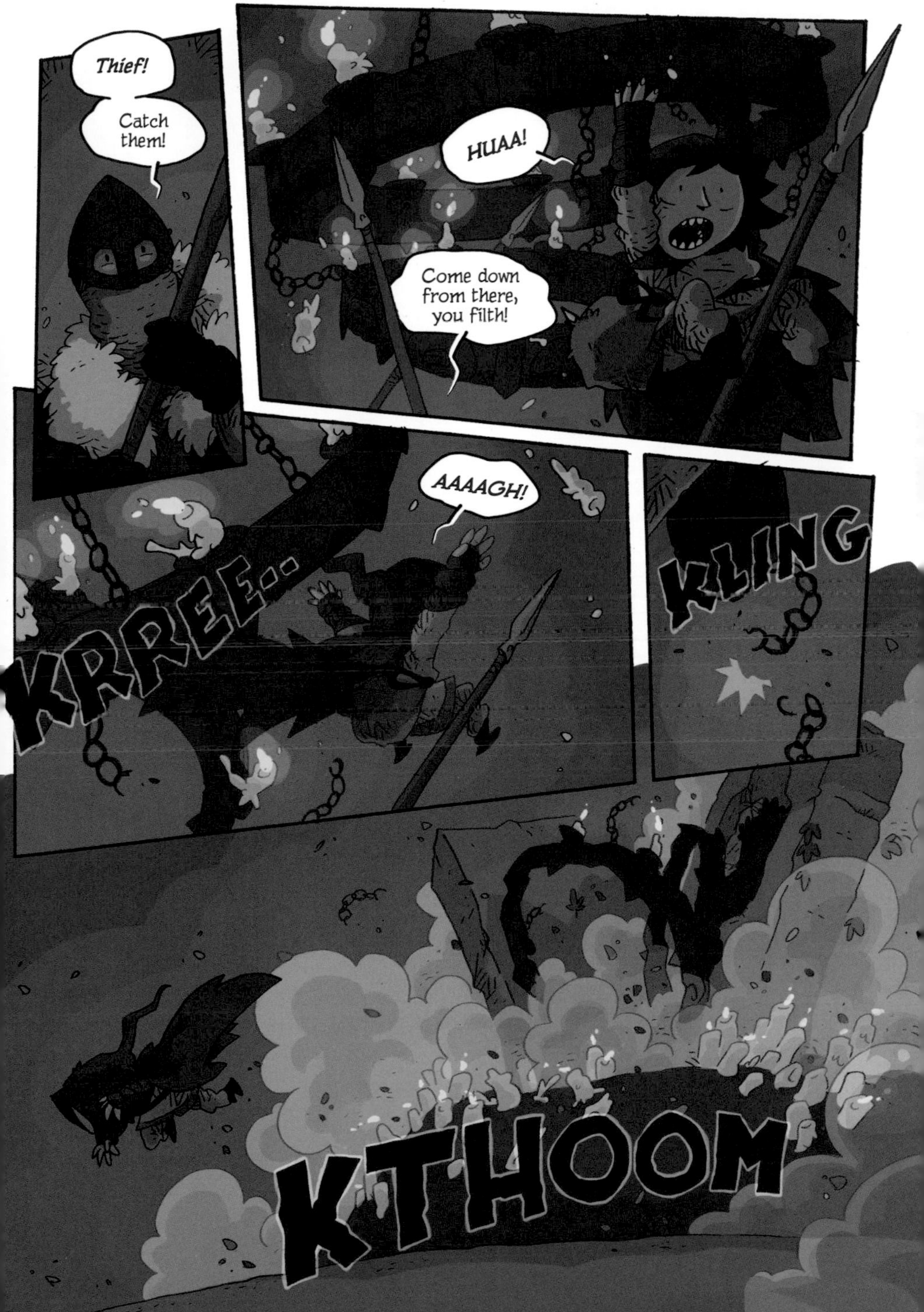
Thief!
Catch them!
HUAA!
Come down from there, you filth!
AAAAGH!
KRREE..
KLING
KTHOOM

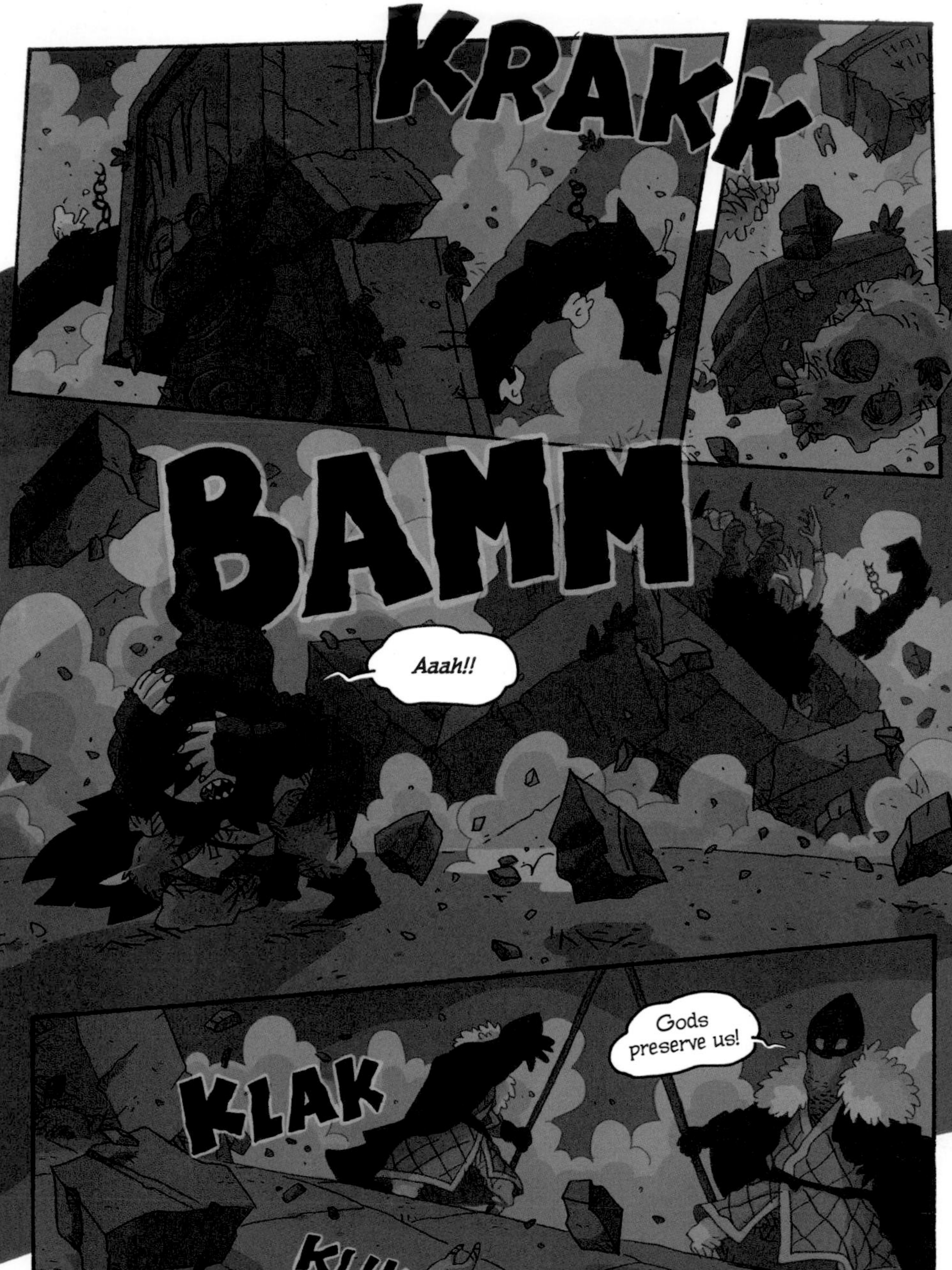
KRAKK
BAMM
Aaah!!
Gods preserve us!
KLAK
KLIK

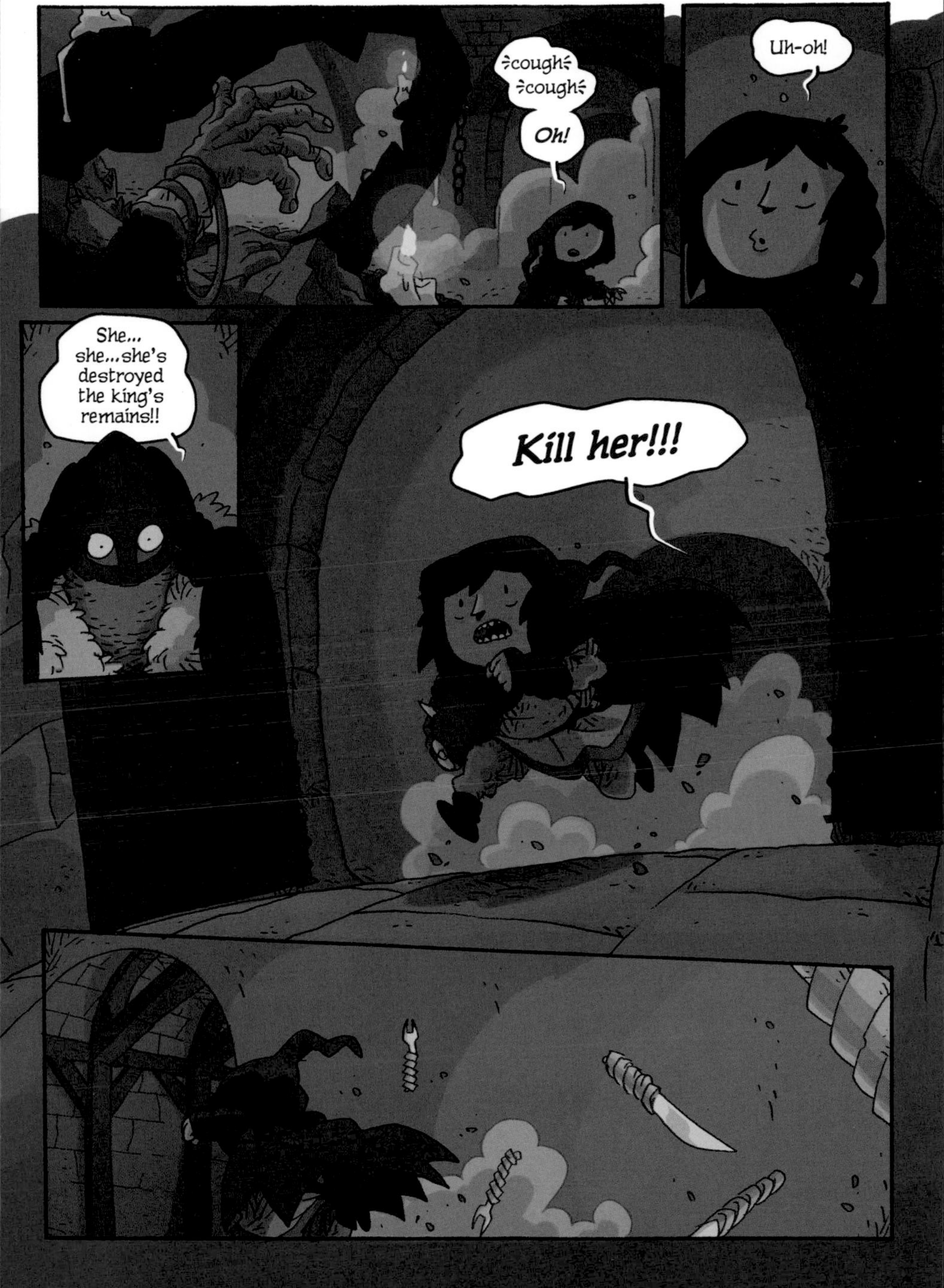

cough cough
Oh!
Uh-oh!
She... she...she's destroyed the king's remains!!
Kill her!!!

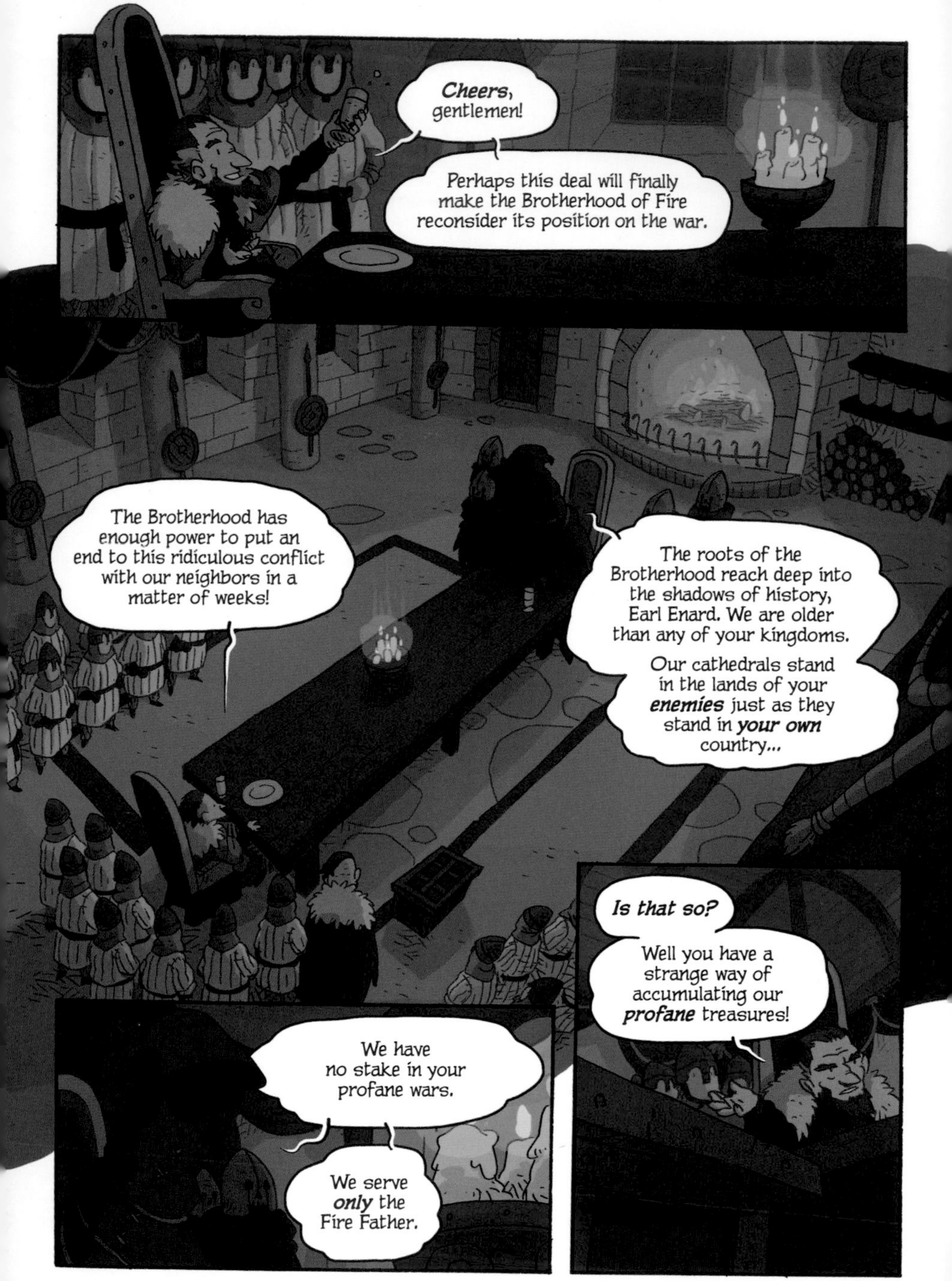
Cheers, gentlemen!
Perhaps this deal will finally make the Brotherhood of Fire reconsider its position on the war.
The Brotherhood has enough power to put an end to this ridiculous conflict with our neighbors in a matter of weeks!
The roots of the Brotherhood reach deep into the shadows of history, Earl Enard. We are older than any of your kingdoms.
Our cathedrals stand in the lands of your *enemies* just as they stand in *your own* country...
We have no stake in your profane wars.
We serve *only* the Fire Father.
Is that so?
Well you have a strange way of accumulating our *profane* treasures!

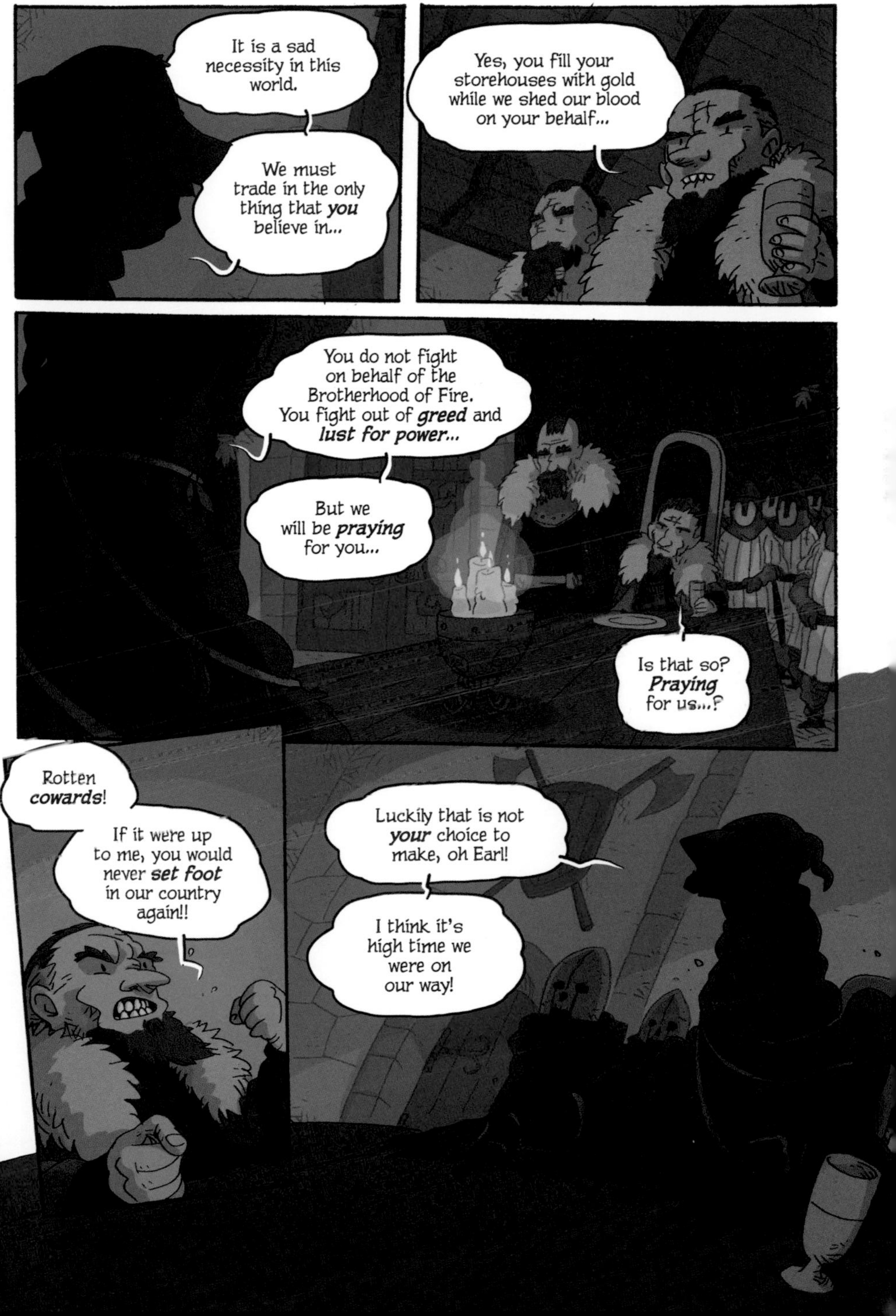

It is a sad necessity in this world.
We must trade in the only thing that *you* believe in...
Yes, you fill your storehouses with gold while we shed our blood on your behalf...
You do not fight on behalf of the Brotherhood of Fire. You fight out of ***greed*** and ***lust for power...***
But we will be ***praying*** for you...
Is that so? ***Praying*** for us...?
Rotten ***cowards***!
If it were up to me, you would never ***set foot*** in our country again!!
Luckily that is not ***your*** choice to make, oh Earl!
I think it's high time we were on our way!

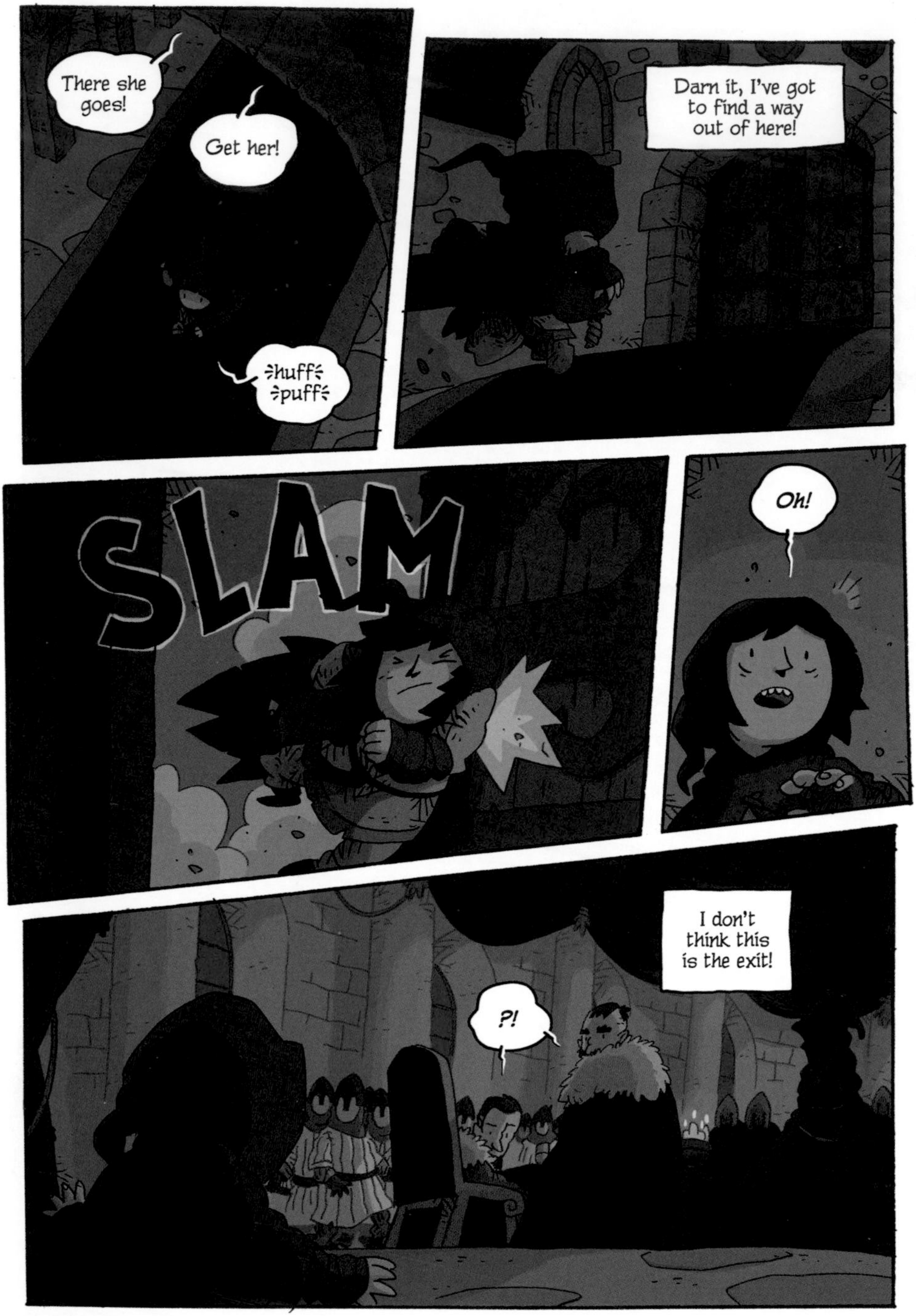
There she goes!
Get her!
huff puff
Darn it, I've got to find a way out of here!
SLAM
Oh!
I don't think this is the exit!
?!

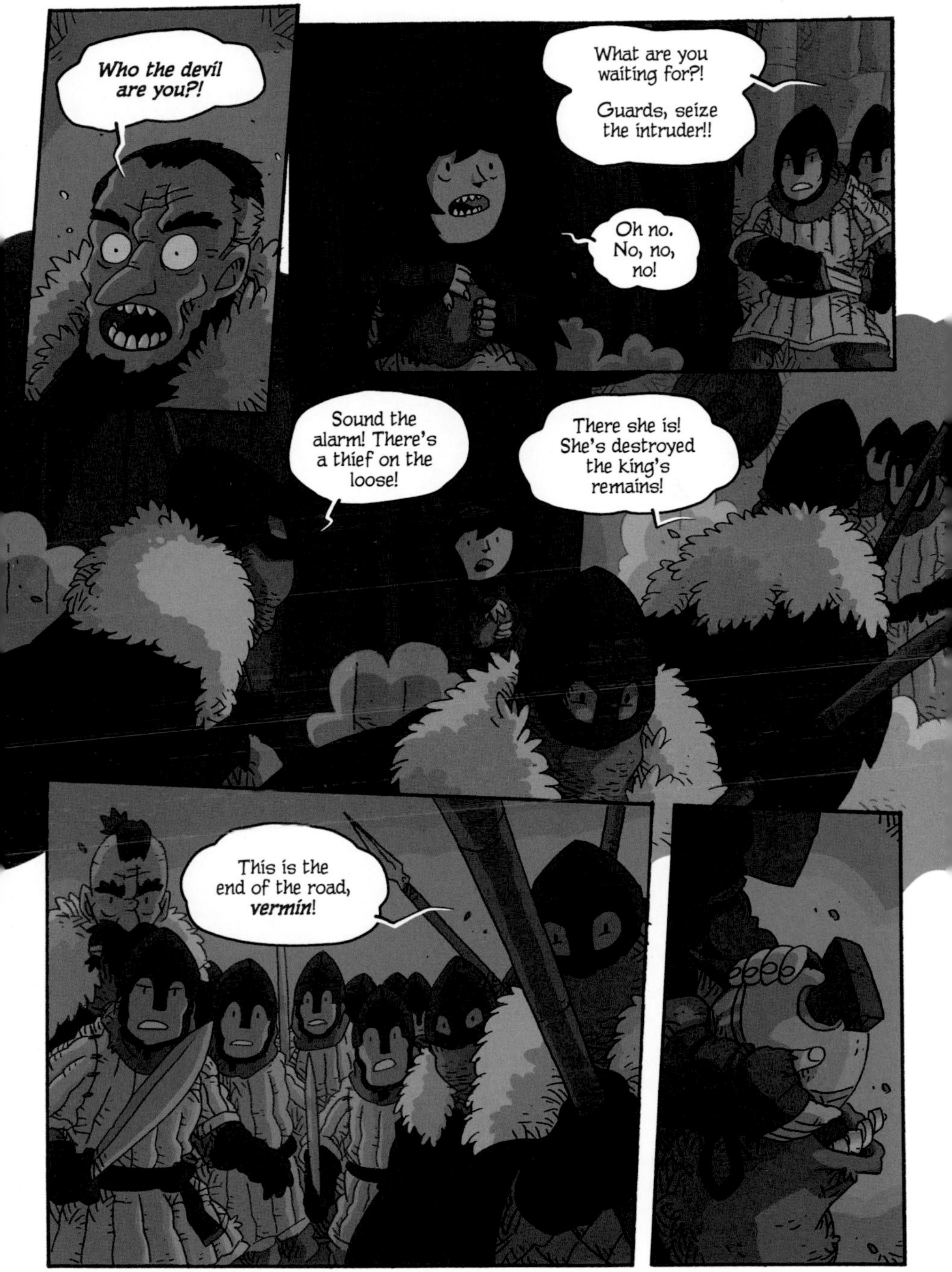
Who the devil are you?!
What are you waiting for?!
Guards, seize the intruder!!
Oh no. No, no, no!
Sound the alarm! There's a thief on the loose!
There she is! She's destroyed the king's remains!
This is the end of the road, ***vermin***!

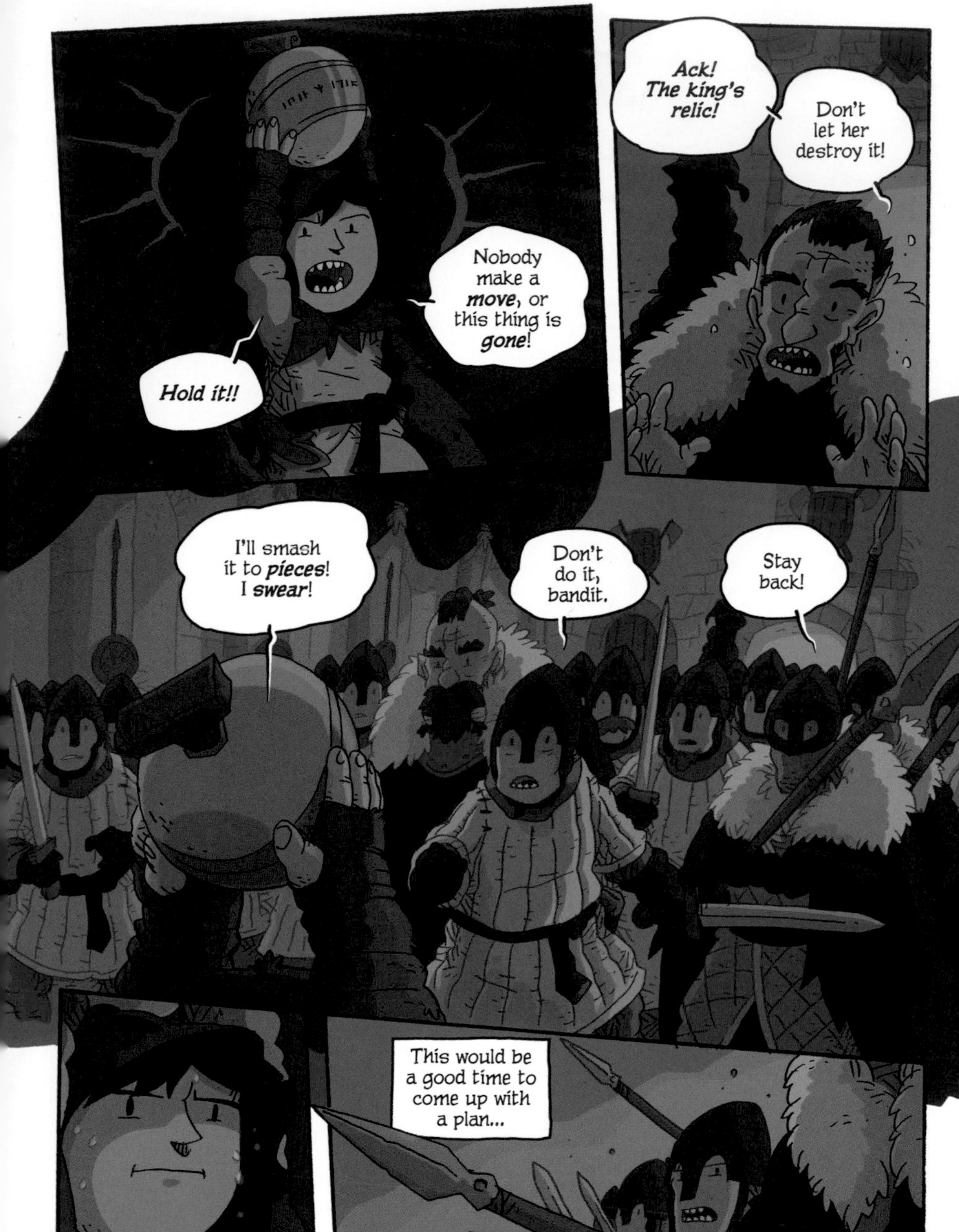
Nobody make a *move*, or this thing is *gone*!
Hold it!!
Ack! The king's relic!
Don't let her destroy it!
I'll smash it to *pieces*! I *swear*!
Don't do it, bandit.
Stay back!
This would be a good time to come up with a plan...

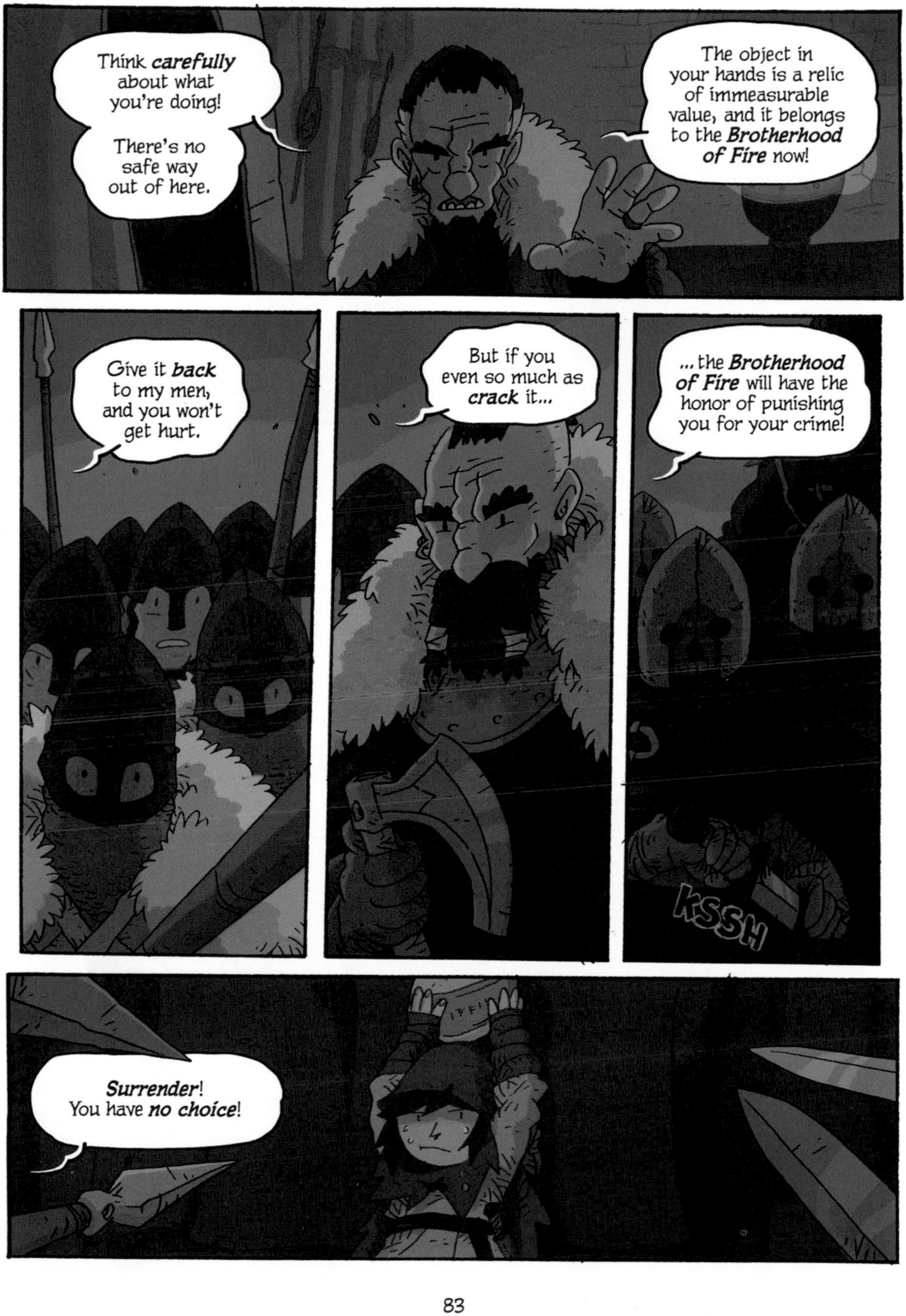
Think **carefully** about what you're doing!
There's no safe way out of here.
The object in your hands is a relic of immeasurable value, and it belongs to the **Brotherhood of Fire** now!
Give it **back** to my men, and you won't get hurt.
But if you even so much as **crack** it...
...the **Brotherhood of Fire** will have the honor of punishing you for your crime!
KSSH
Surrender! You have **no choice**!

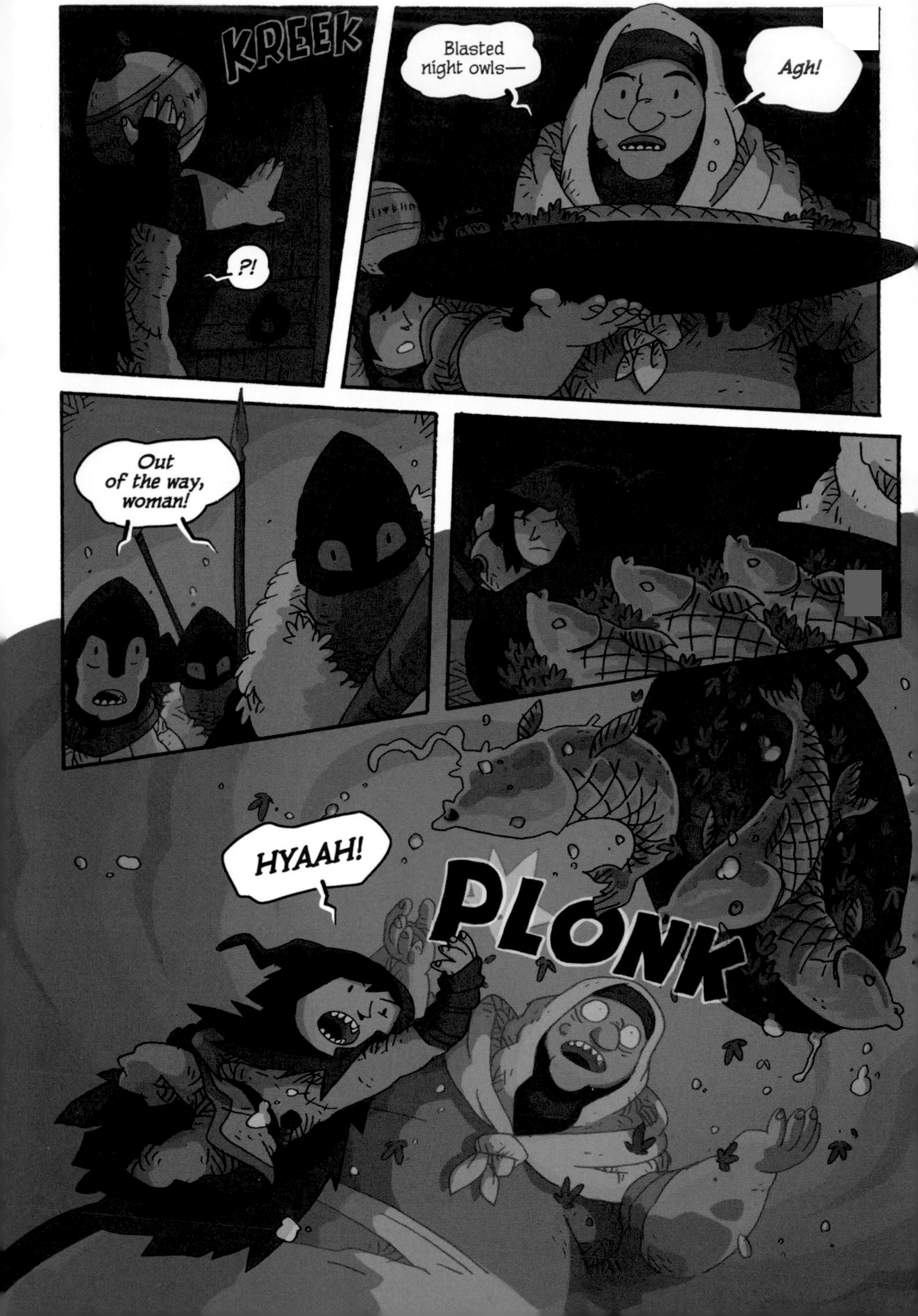
KREEK
?!
Blasted night owls—
Agh!
Out of the way, woman!
HYAAH!
PLONK

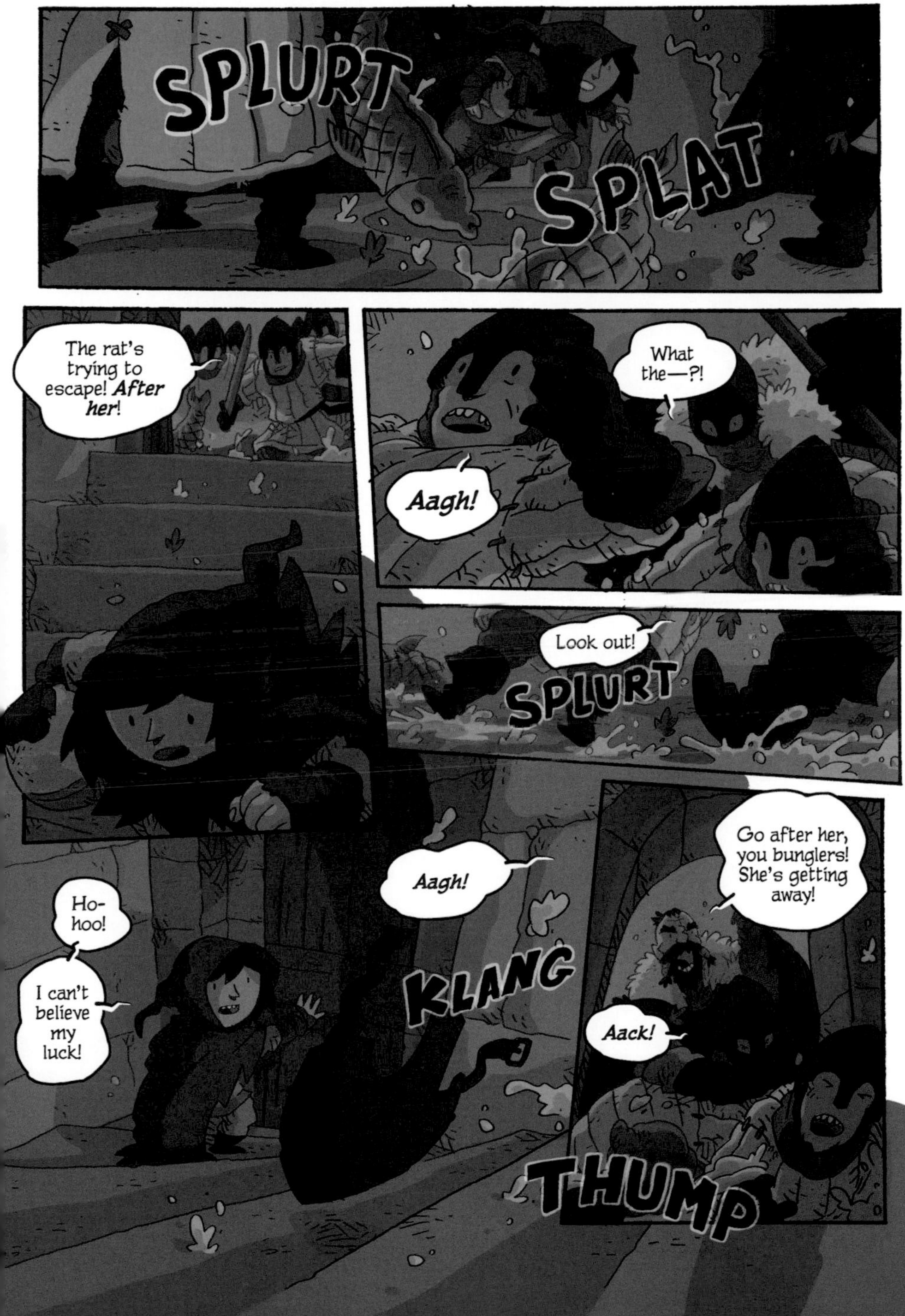
SPLURT
SPLAT
The rat's trying to escape! After her!
What the—?!
Aagh!
Look out!
SPLURT
Ho-hoo!
I can't believe my luck!
Aagh!
KLANG
Go after her, you bunglers! She's getting away!
Aack!
THUMP

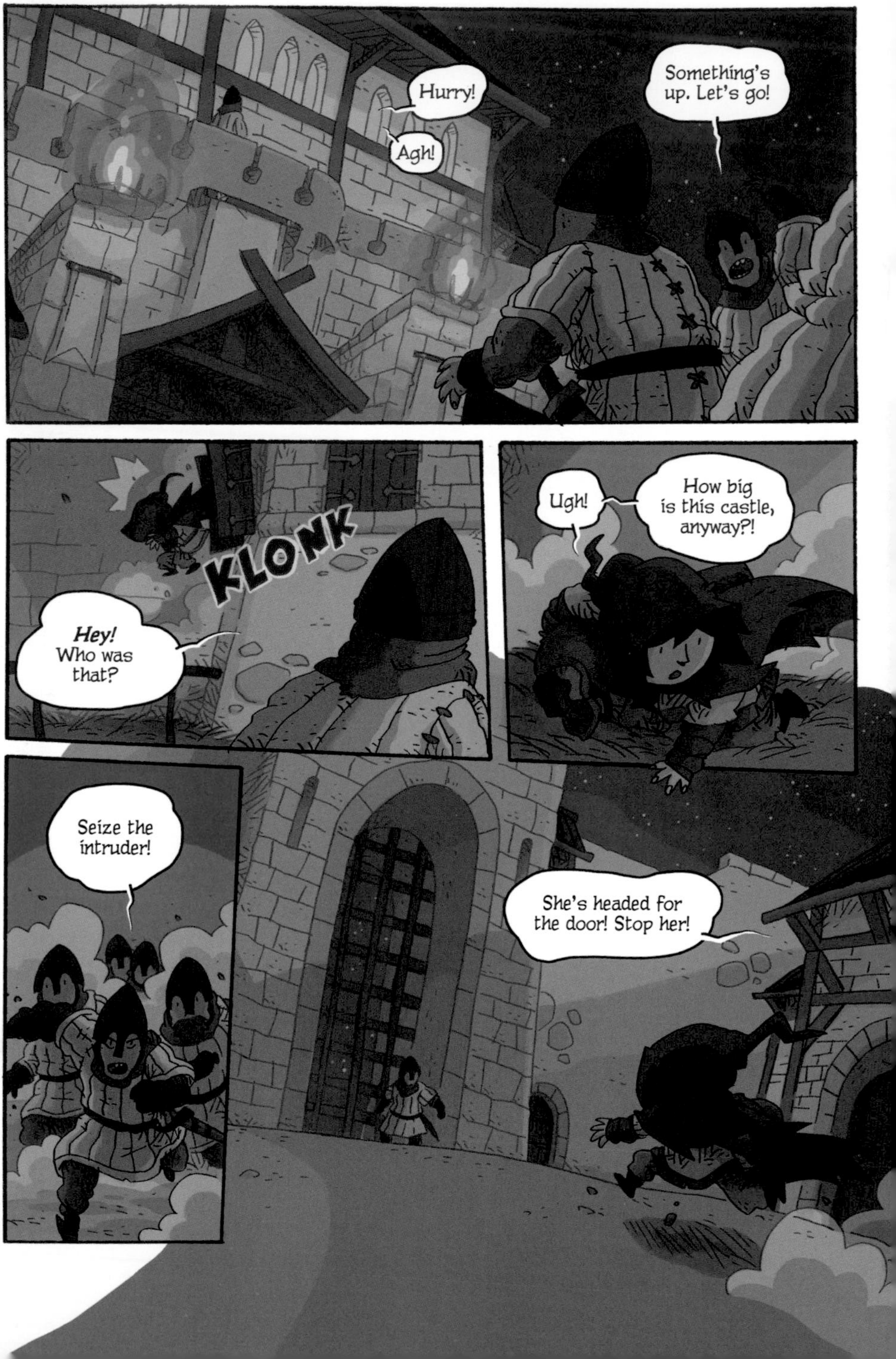
Hurry!
Agh!
Something's up. Let's go!
KLONK
Hey! Who was that?
Ugh!
How big is this castle, anyway?!
Seize the intruder!
She's headed for the door! Stop her!

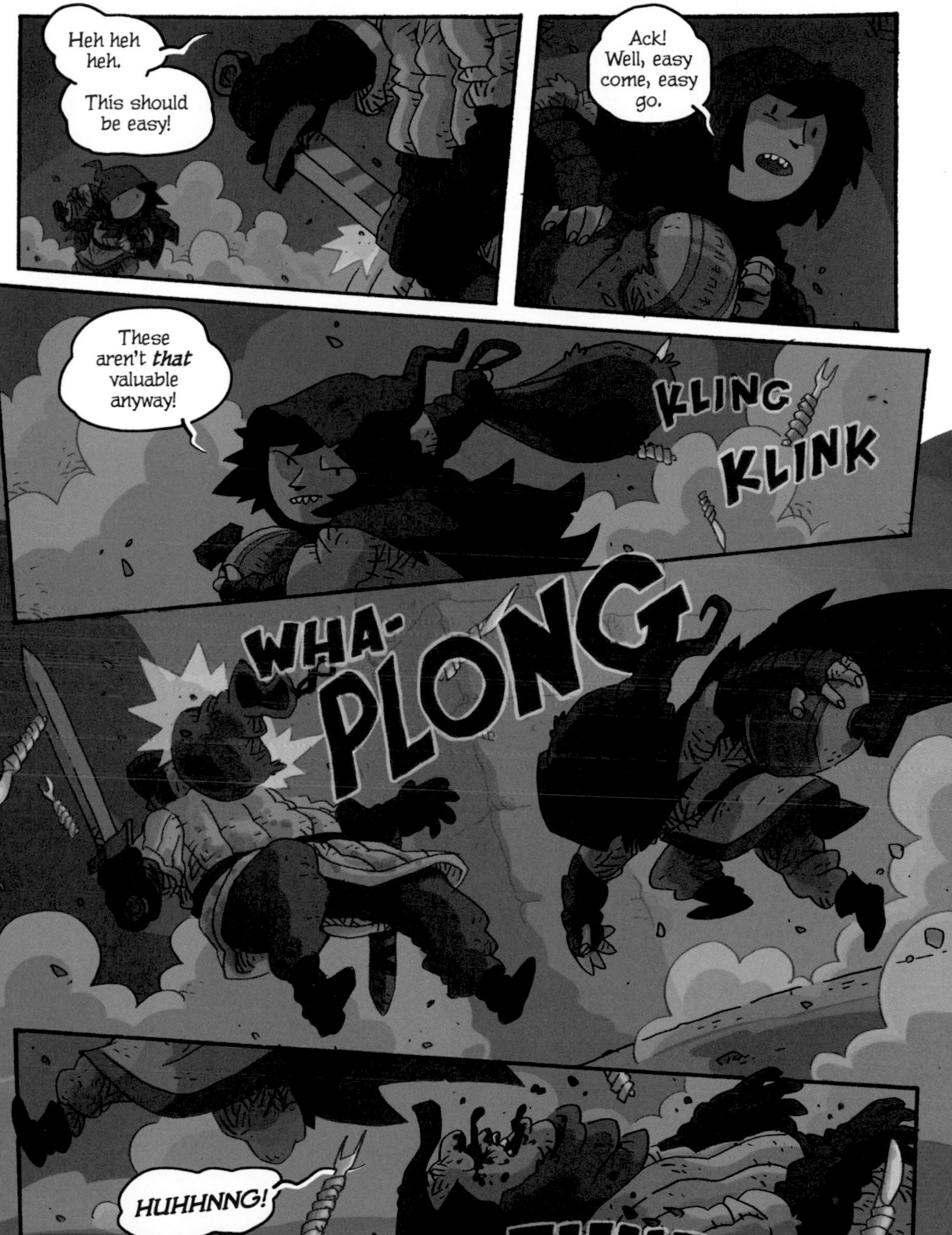
Heh heh heh.
This should be easy!
Ack! Well, easy come, easy go.
These aren't ***that*** valuable anyway!
KLING
KLINK
WHA-PLONG
HUHHNNG!
THUD

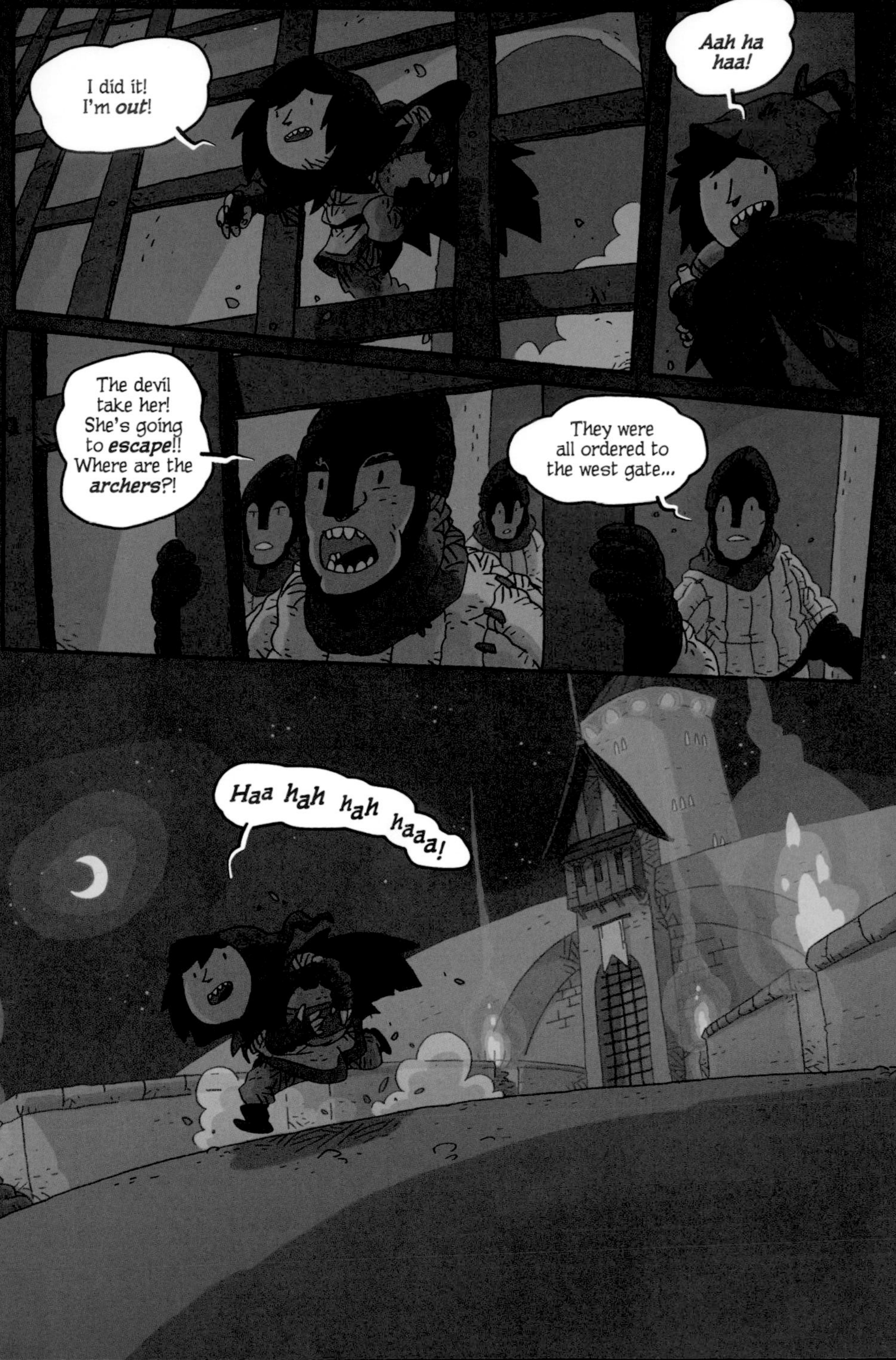
I did it! I'm *out*!
Aah ha haa!
The devil take her! She's going to ***escape***!! Where are the ***archers***?!
They were all ordered to the west gate...
Haa hah hah haaa!

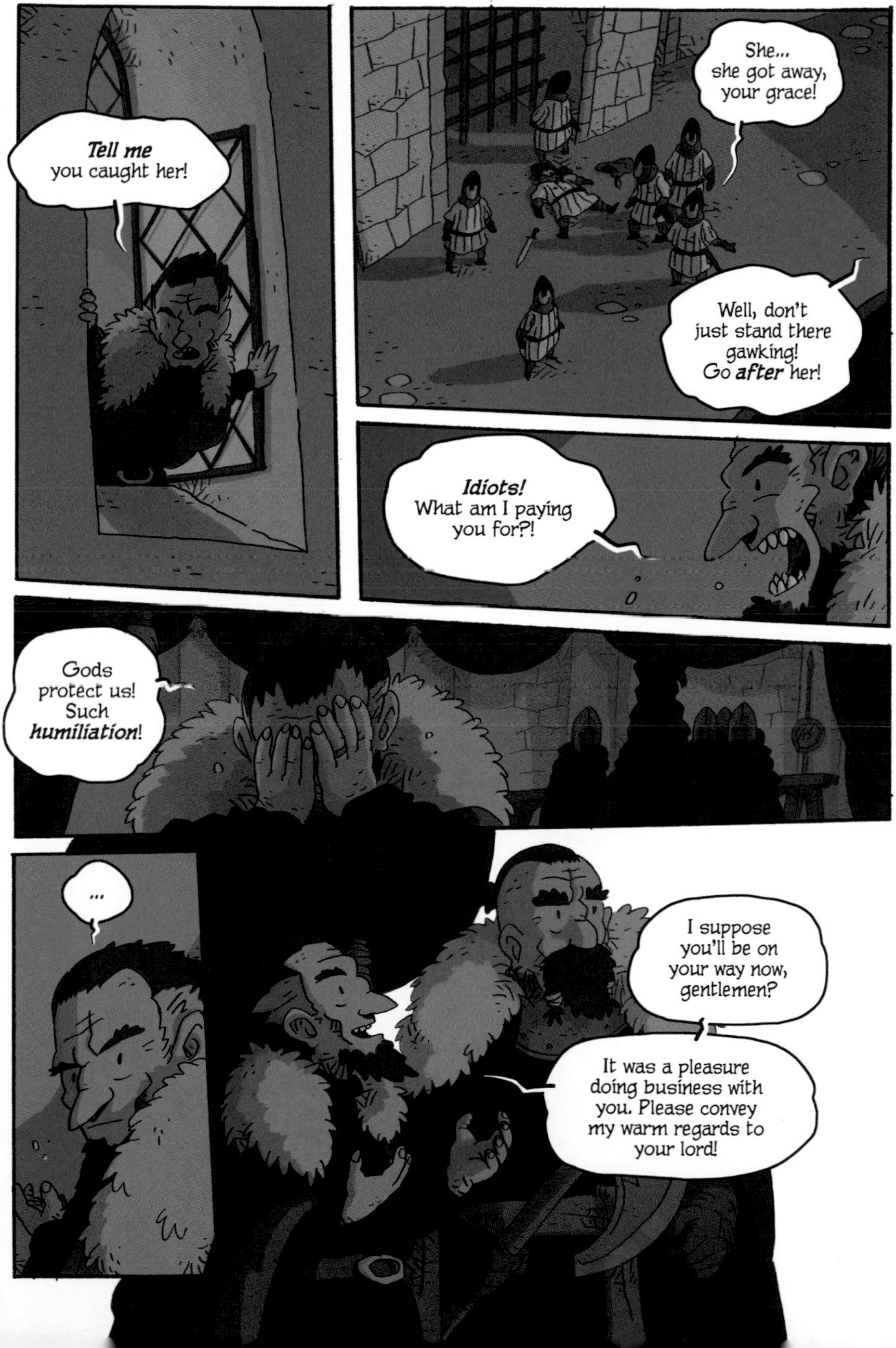

Tell me you caught her!
She... she got away, your grace!
Well, don't just stand there gawking! Go *after* her!
Idiots! What am I paying you for?!
Gods protect us! Such *humiliation*!
...
I suppose you'll be on your way now, gentlemen?
It was a pleasure doing business with you. Please convey my warm regards to your lord!

Secrets deep are whispered,
Of where a faint light flickers,
Upon a gleaming treasure,
Riches beyond measure,
Golden, upon gold.

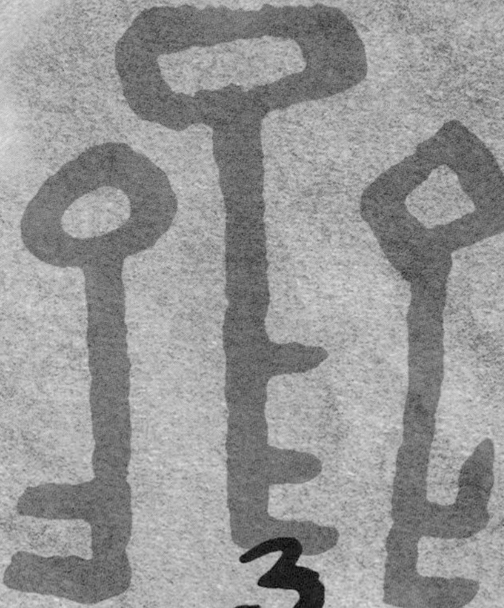

3

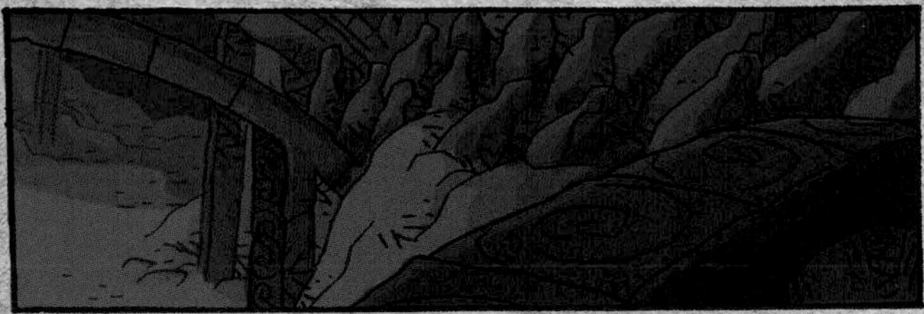

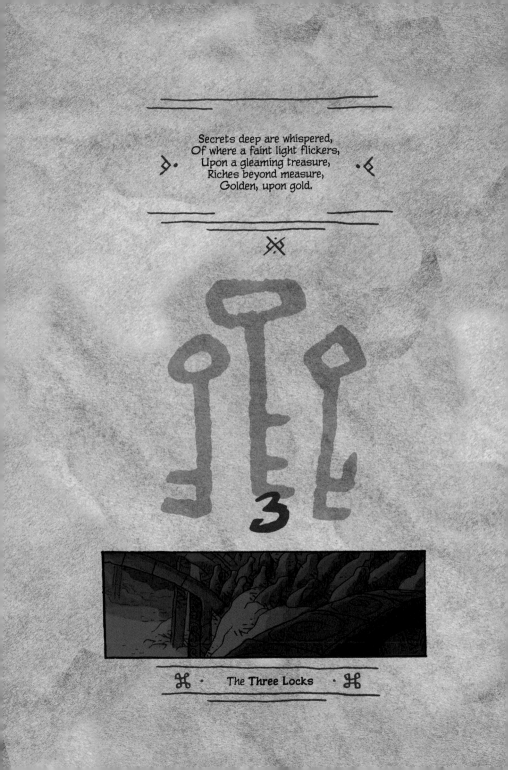

The Three Locks

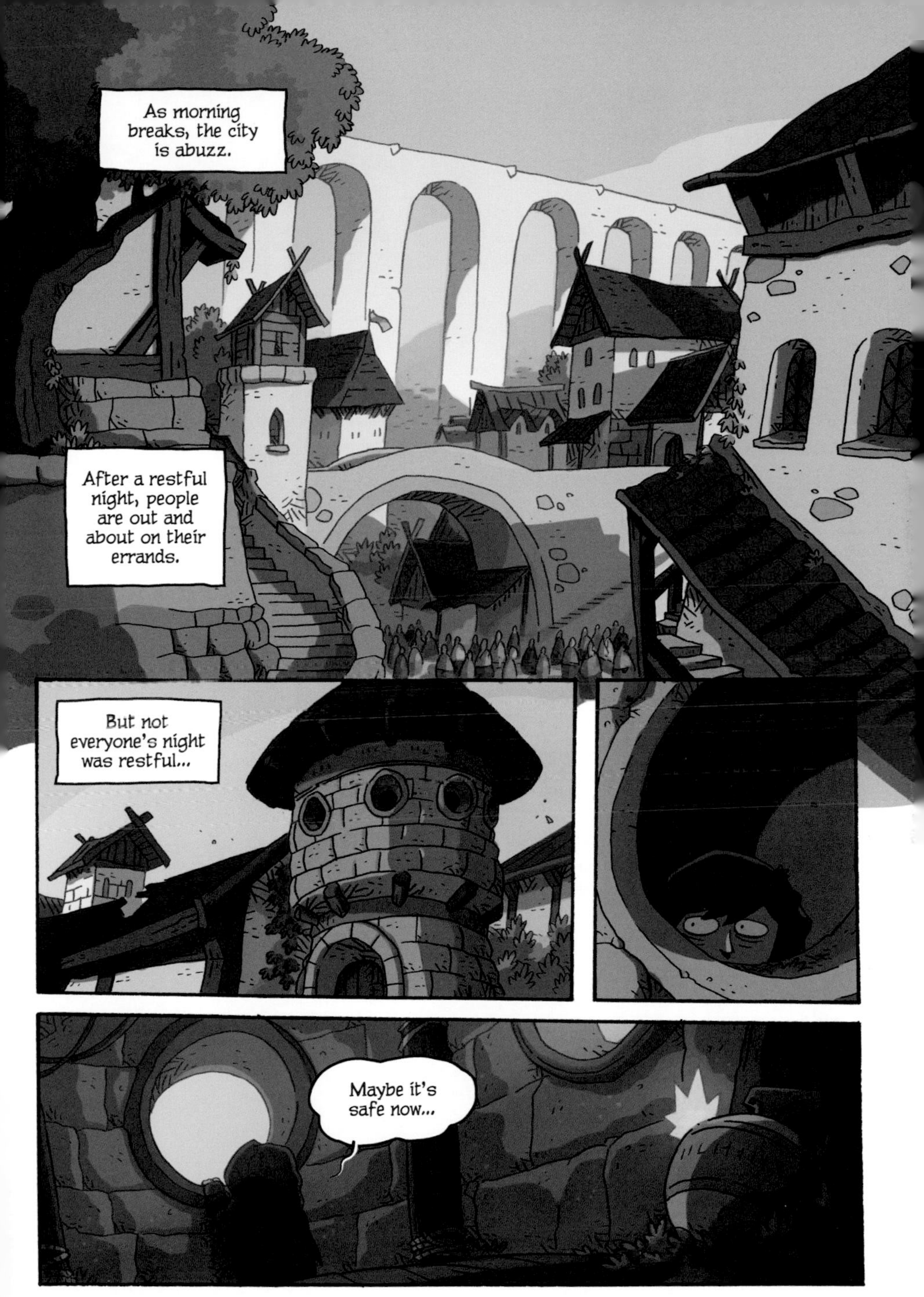
As morning breaks, the city is abuzz.
After a restful night, people are out and about on their errands.
But not everyone's night was restful...
Maybe it's safe now...

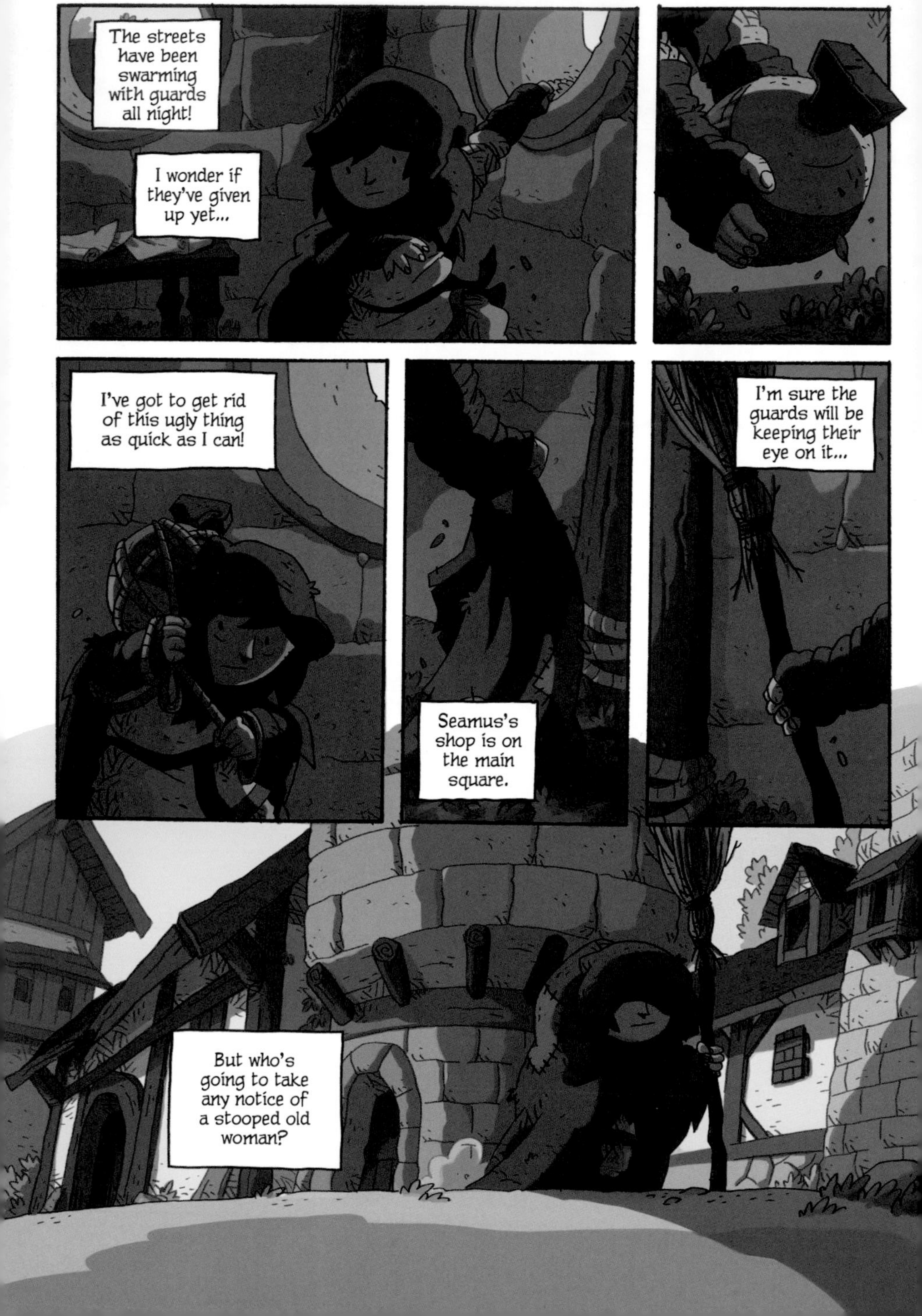
The streets have been swarming with guards all night!
I wonder if they've given up yet...
I've got to get rid of this ugly thing as quick as I can!
Seamus's shop is on the main square.
I'm sure the guards will be keeping their eye on it...
But who's going to take any notice of a stooped old woman?

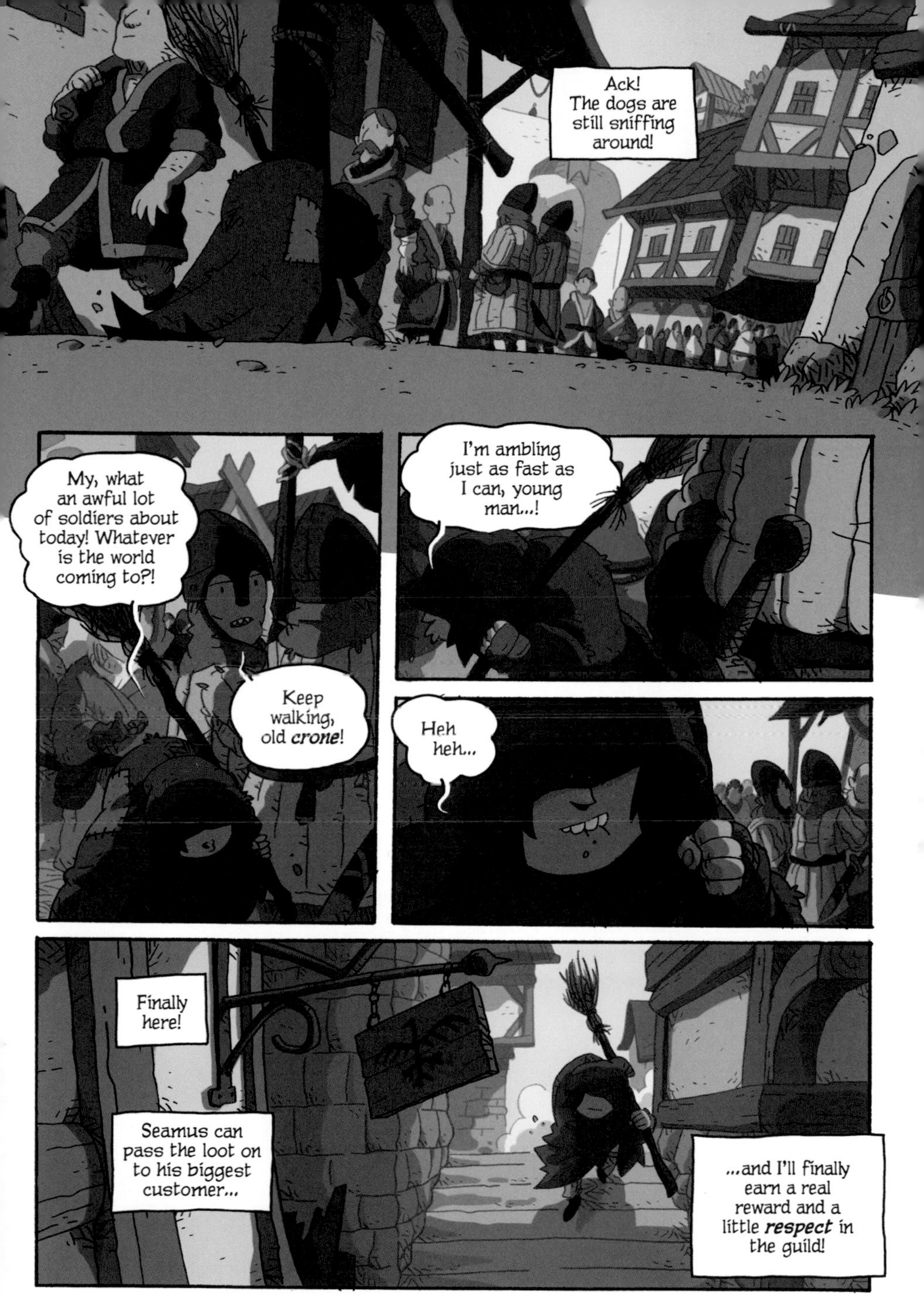

Ack! The dogs are still sniffing around!
My, what an awful lot of soldiers about today! Whatever is the world coming to?!
Keep walking, old *crone*!
I'm ambling just as fast as I can, young man...!
Heh heh...
Finally here!
Seamus can pass the loot on to his biggest customer...
...and I'll finally earn a real reward and a little ***respect*** in the guild!

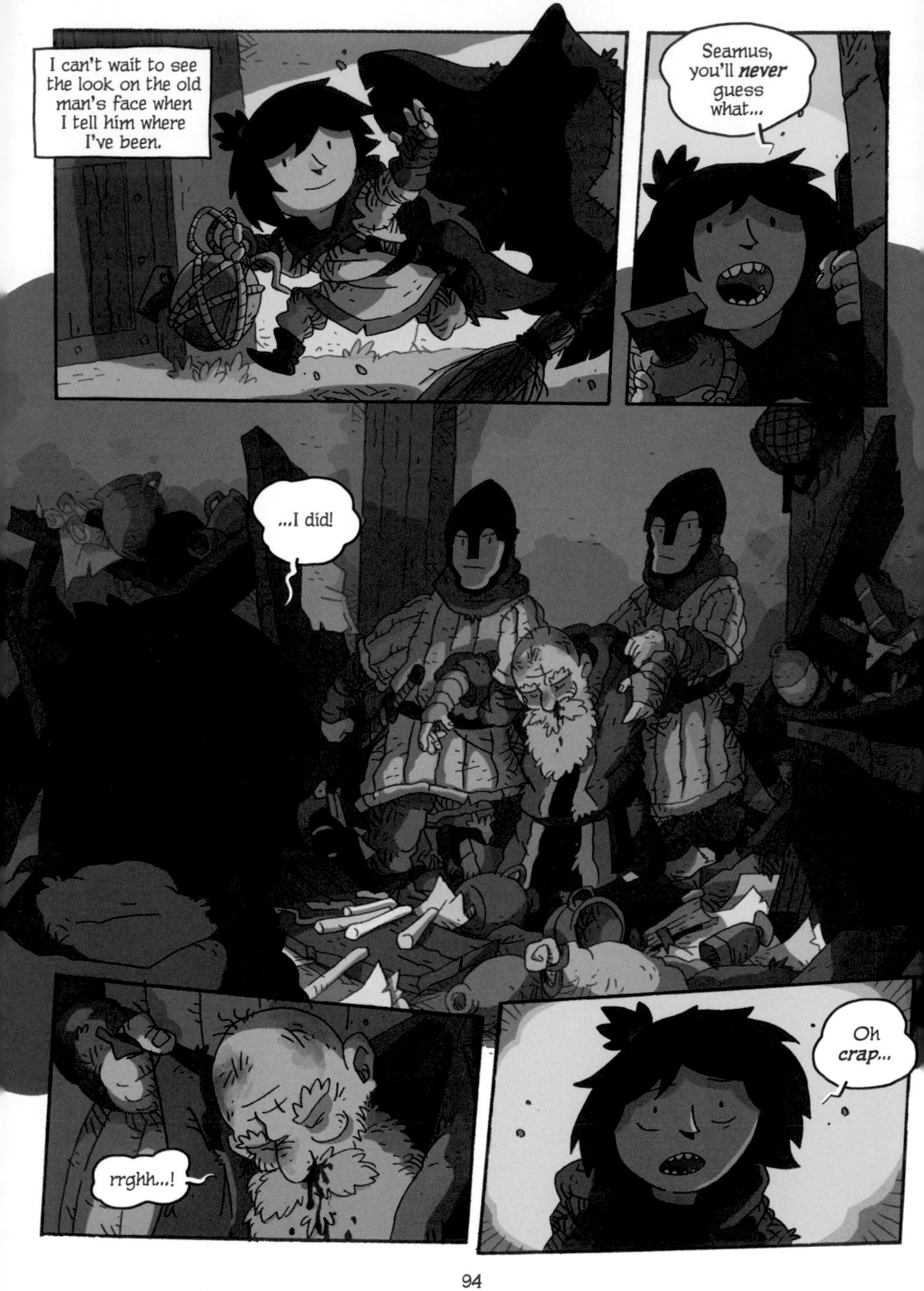
I can't wait to see the look on the old man's face when I tell him where I've been.
Seamus, you'll ***never*** guess what...
...I did!
rrghh...!
Oh *crap*...

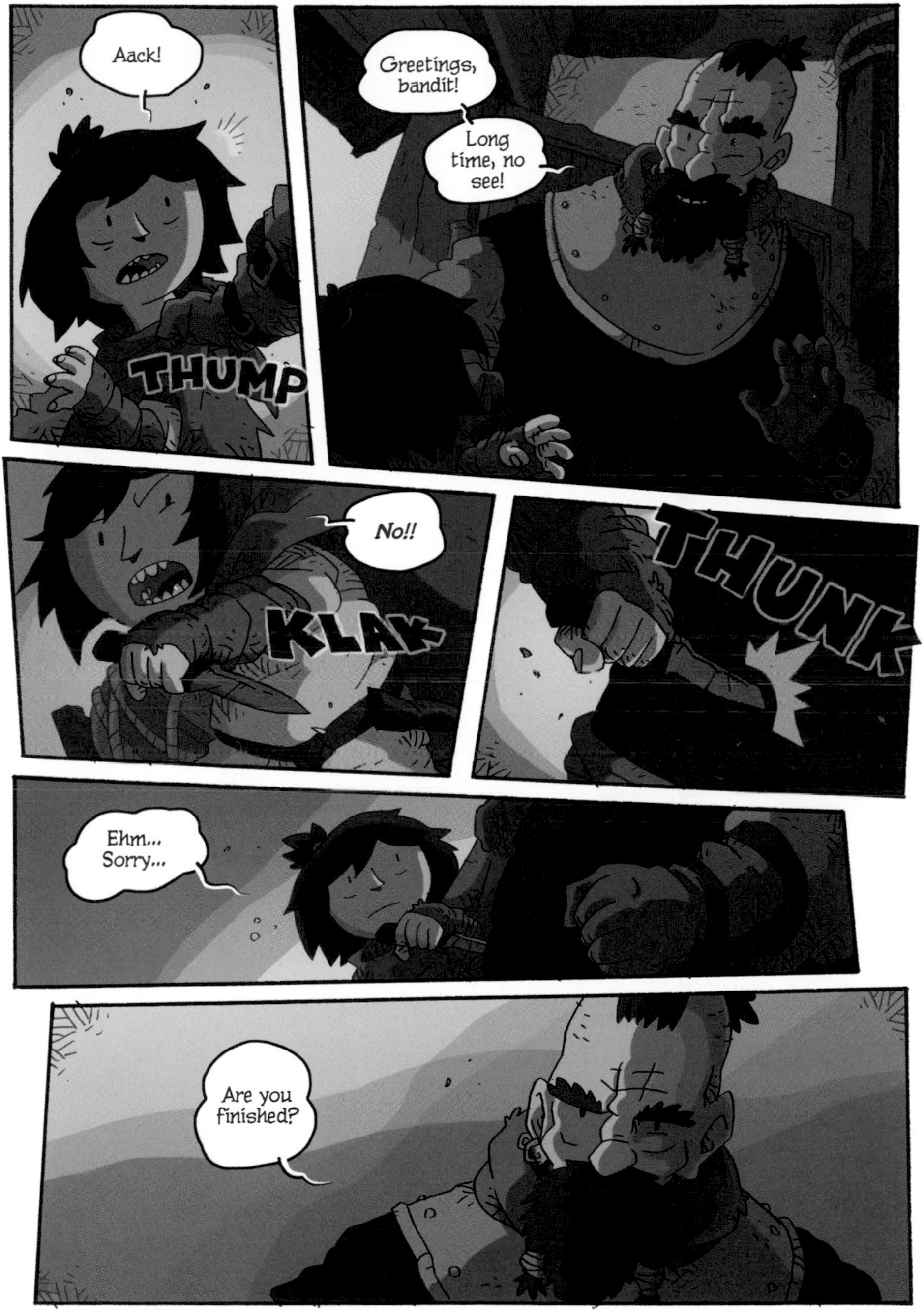
Aack!
THUMP
Greetings, bandit!
Long time, no see!
No!!
KLAK
THUNK
Ehm... Sorry...
Are you finished?

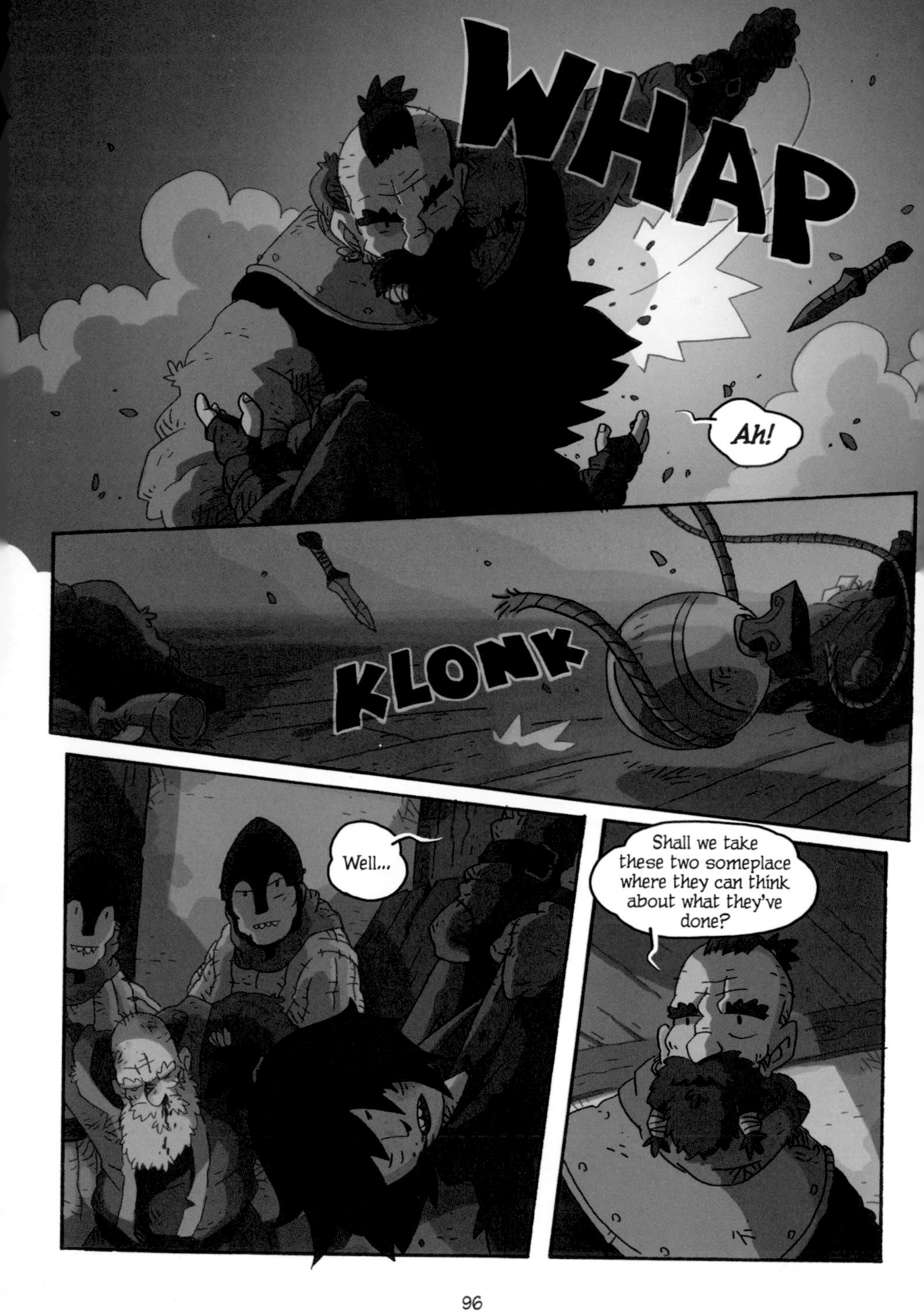
WHAP
Ah!
KLONK
Well...
Shall we take these two someplace where they can think about what they've done?

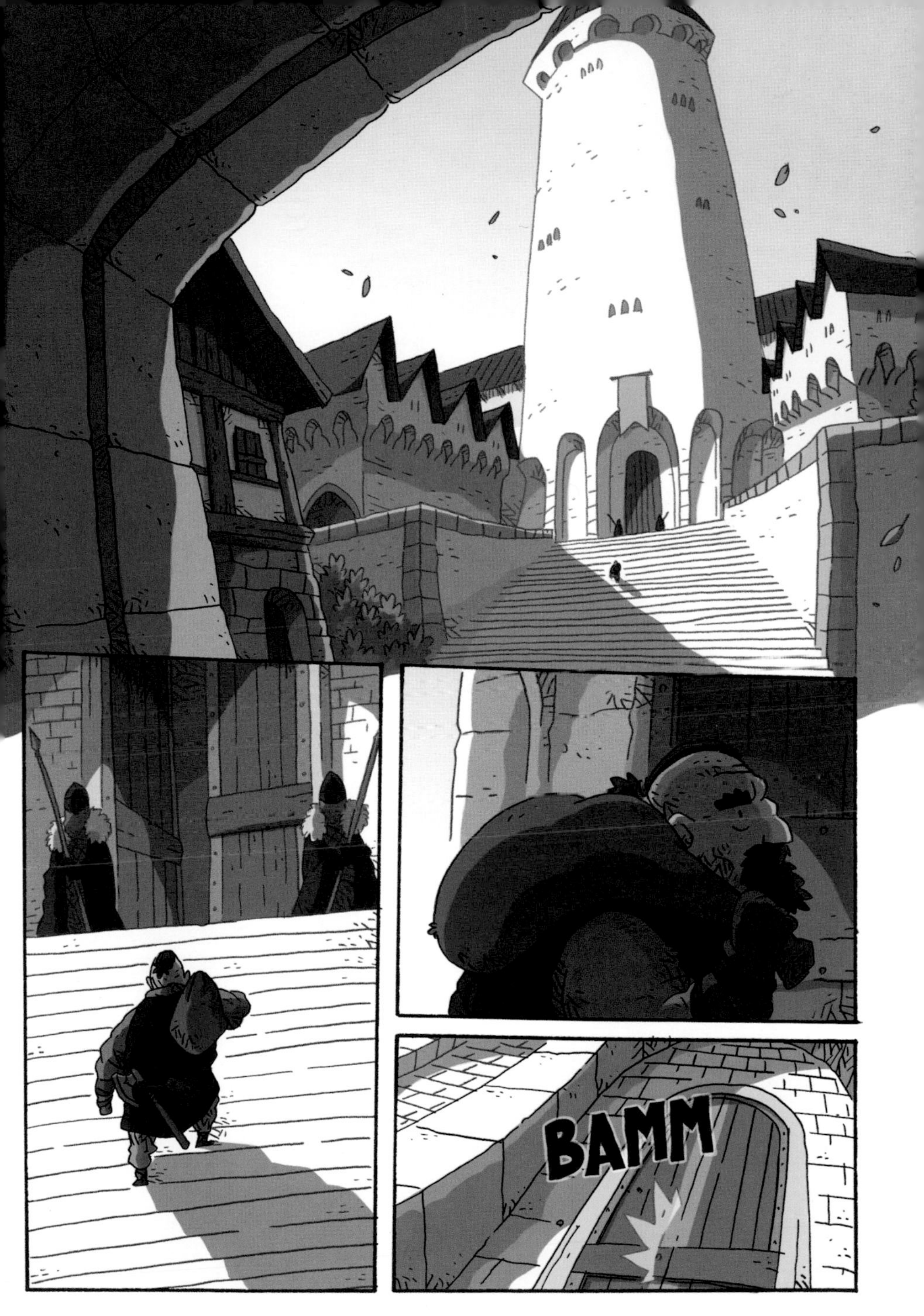
BAMM

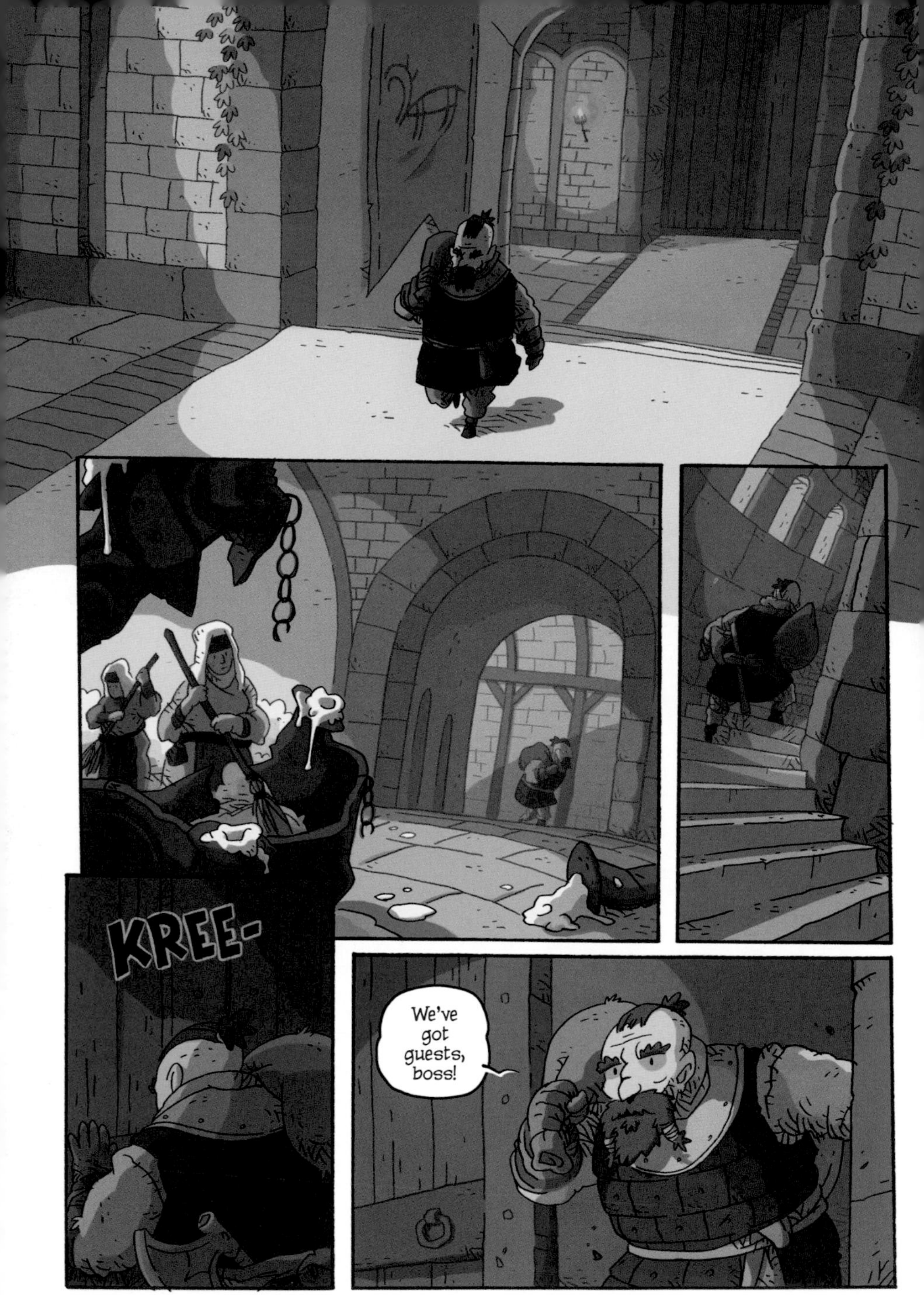
KREE-
We've got guests, boss!

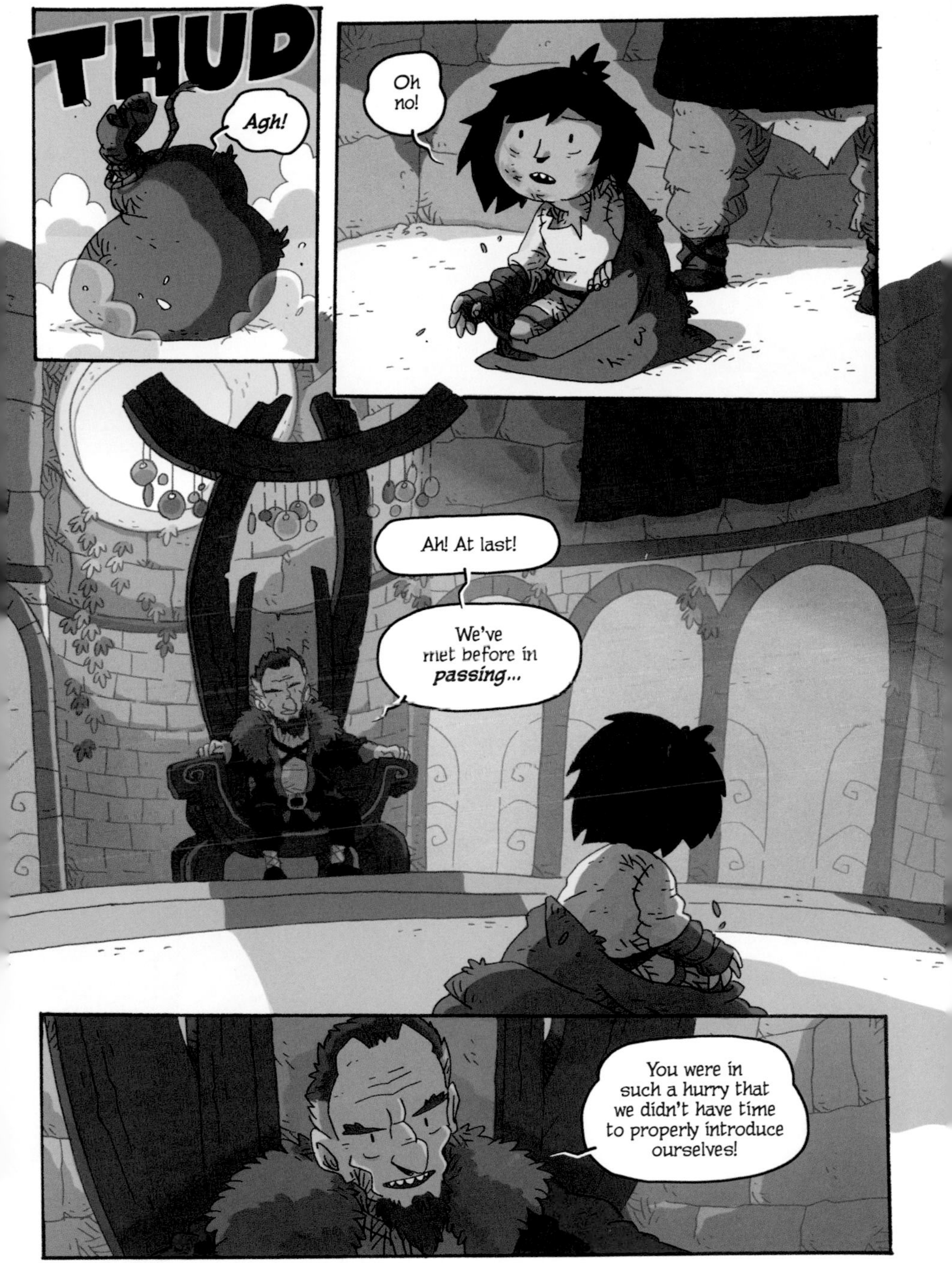
THUD
Agh!
Oh no!
Ah! At last!
We've met before in *passing*...
You were in such a hurry that we didn't have time to properly introduce ourselves!

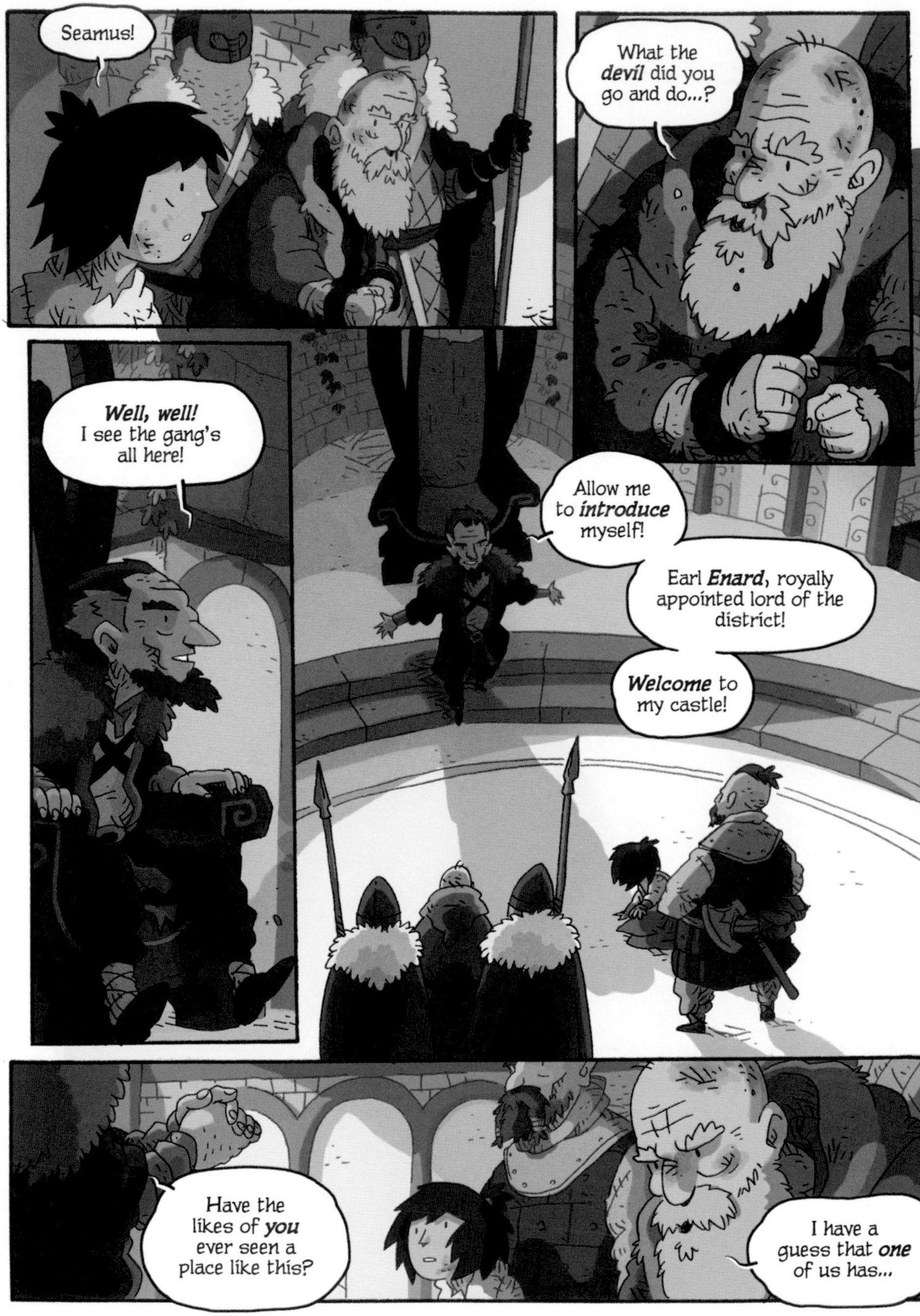
Seamus!
What the *devil* did you go and do...?
Well, well! I see the gang's all here!
Allow me to *introduce* myself!
Earl *Enard*, royally appointed lord of the district!
Welcome to my castle!
Have the likes of *you* ever seen a place like this?
I have a guess that *one* of us has...

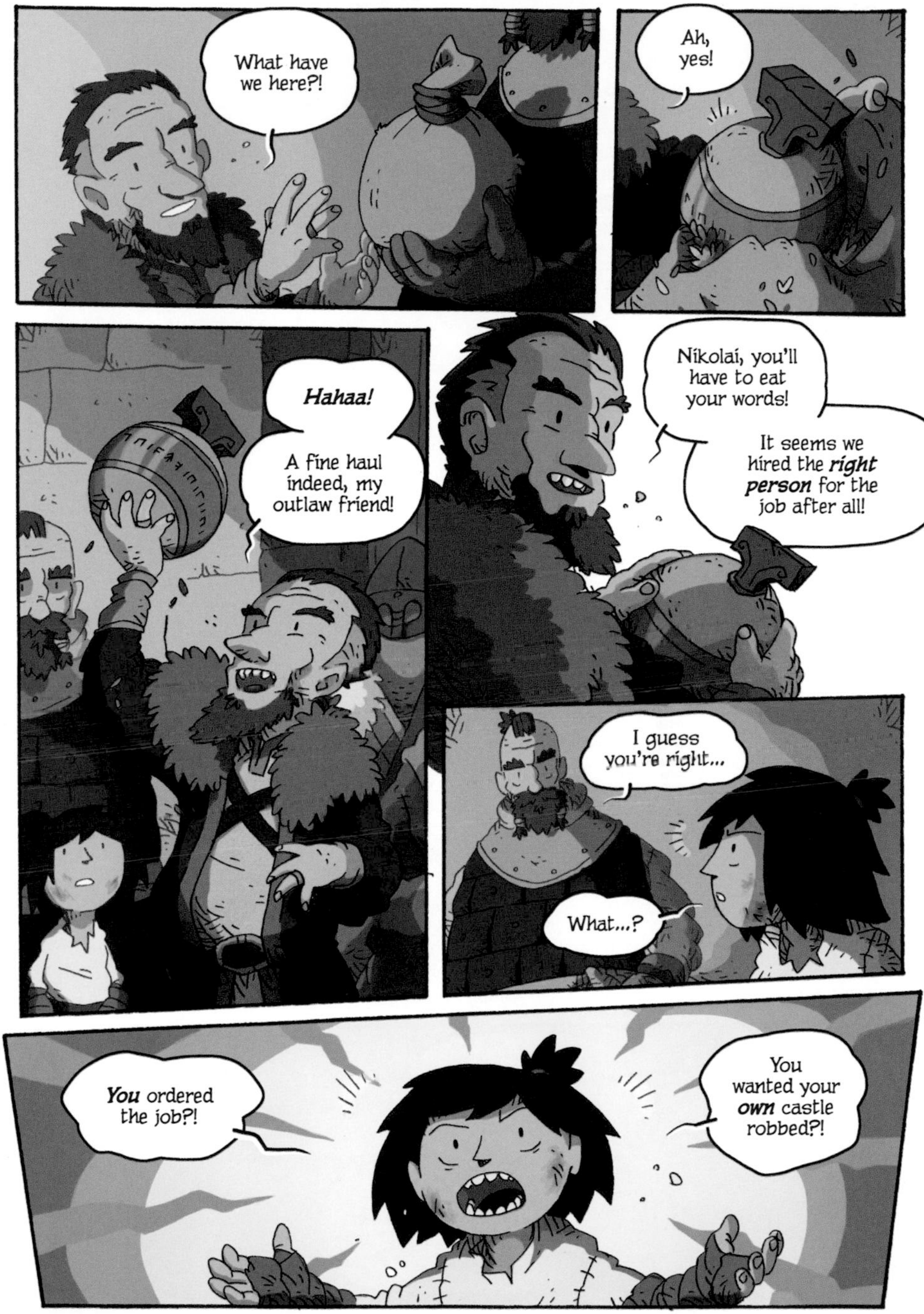
What have we here?!
Ah, yes!
Hahaa!
A fine haul indeed, my outlaw friend!
Nikolai, you'll have to eat your words!
It seems we hired the ***right person*** for the job after all!
I guess you're right...
What...?
You ordered the job?!
You wanted your ***own*** castle robbed?!

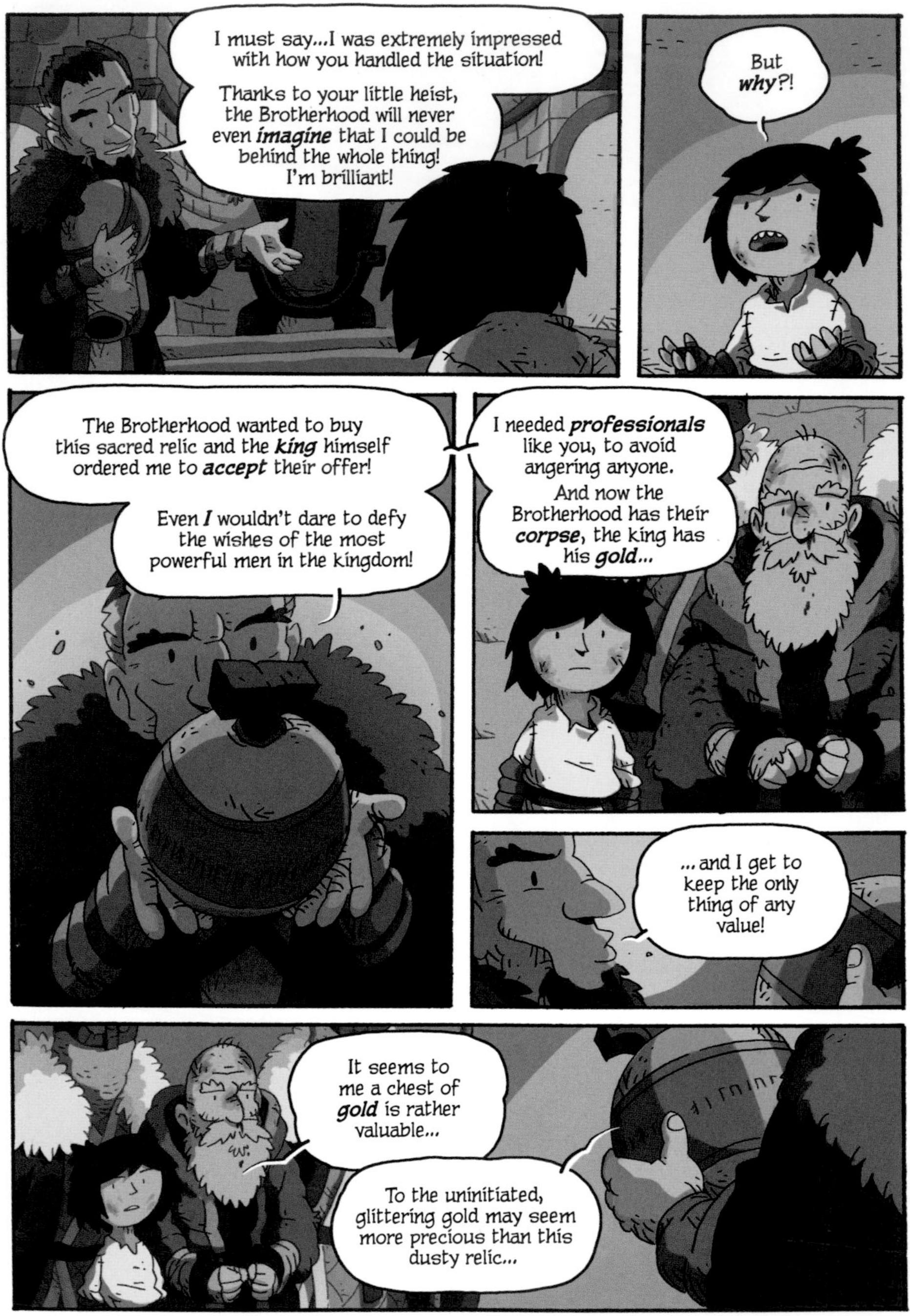
I must say...I was extremely impressed with how you handled the situation!
Thanks to your little heist, the Brotherhood will never even *imagine* that I could be behind the whole thing! I'm brilliant!
But *why*?!
The Brotherhood wanted to buy this sacred relic and the *king* himself ordered me to *accept* their offer!
Even *I* wouldn't dare to defy the wishes of the most powerful men in the kingdom!
I needed *professionals* like you, to avoid angering anyone.
And now the Brotherhood has their *corpse*, the king has his *gold*...
...and I get to keep the only thing of any value!
It seems to me a chest of *gold* is rather valuable...
To the uninitiated, glittering gold may seem more precious than this dusty relic...

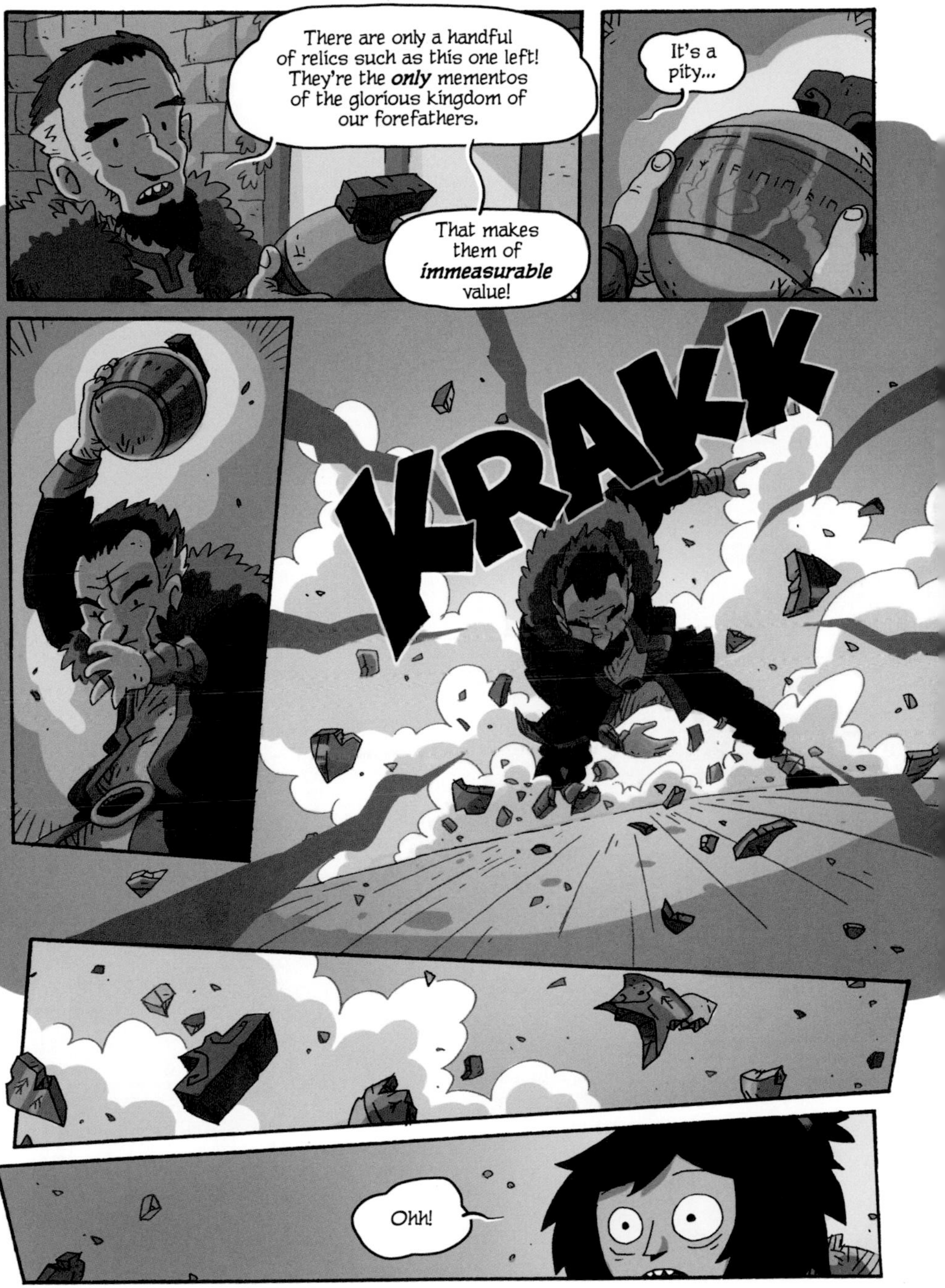
There are only a handful of relics such as this one left! They're the **only** mementos of the glorious kingdom of our forefathers.
That makes them of **immeasurable** value!
It's a pity...
KRAKK
Ohh!

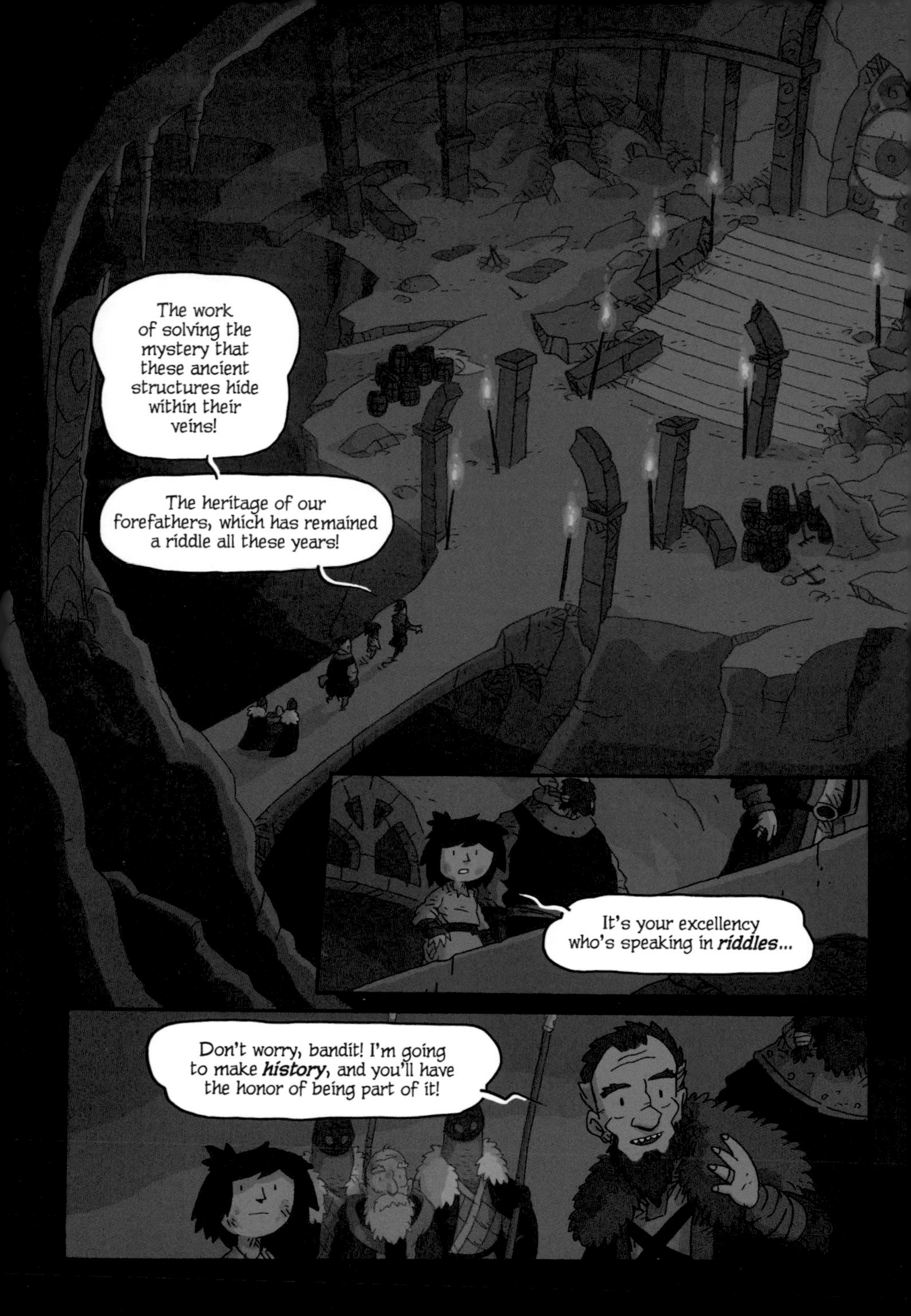
The work of solving the mystery that these ancient structures hide within their veins!
The heritage of our forefathers, which has remained a riddle all these years!
It's your excellency who's speaking in ***riddles***...
Don't worry, bandit! I'm going to make ***history***, and you'll have the honor of being part of it!

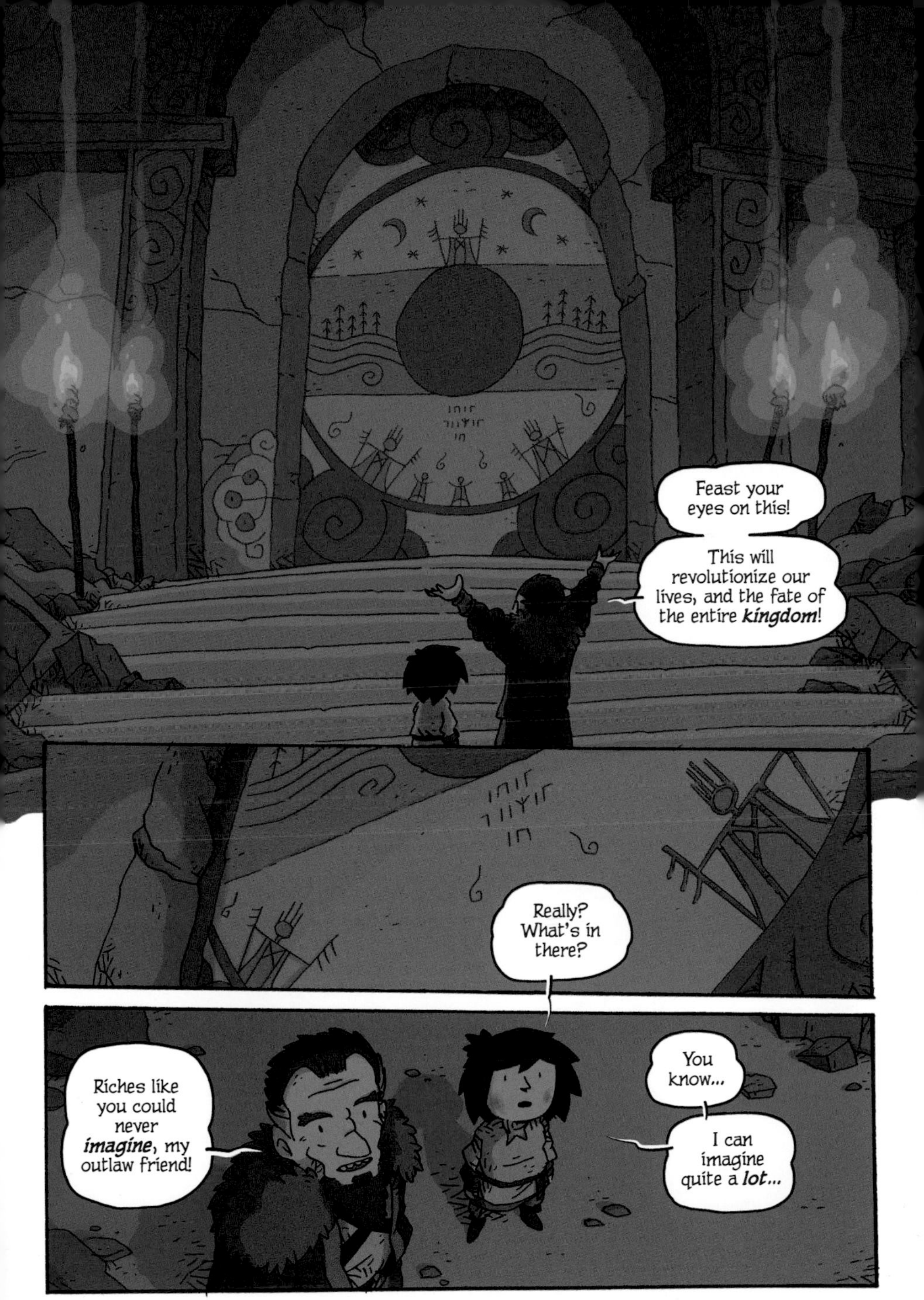
Feast your eyes on this!
This will revolutionize our lives, and the fate of the entire ***kingdom***!
Really? What's in there?
Riches like you could never ***imagine***, my outlaw friend!
You know...
I can imagine quite a ***lot***...

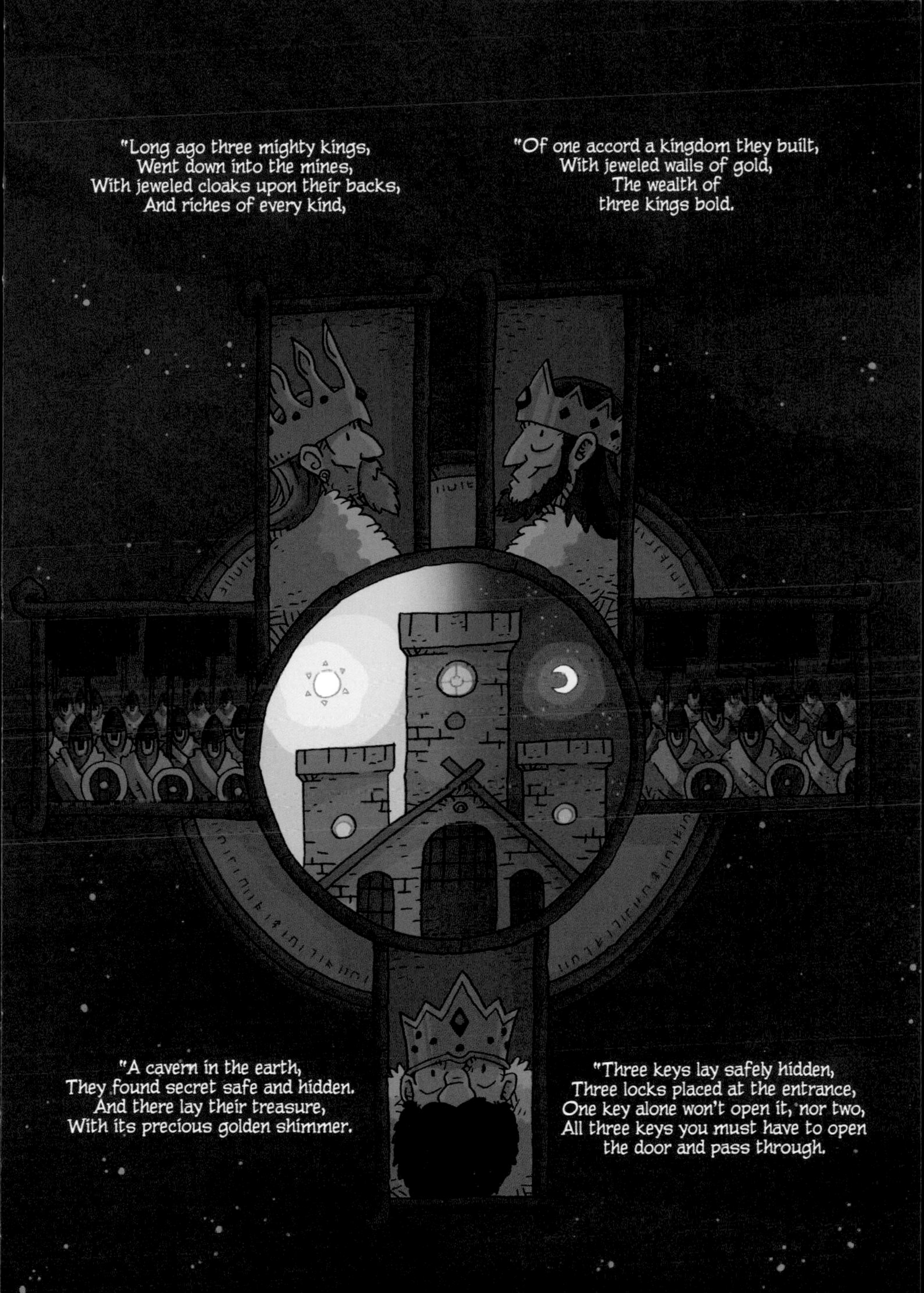
"Long ago three mighty kings,
Went down into the mines,
With jeweled cloaks upon their backs,
And riches of every kind,
"Of one accord a kingdom they built,
With jeweled walls of gold,
The wealth of
three kings bold.
"A cavern in the earth,
They found secret safe and hidden.
And there lay their treasure,
With its precious golden shimmer.
"Three keys lay safely hidden,
Three locks placed at the entrance,
One key alone won't open it, nor two,
All three keys you must have to open
the door and pass through.

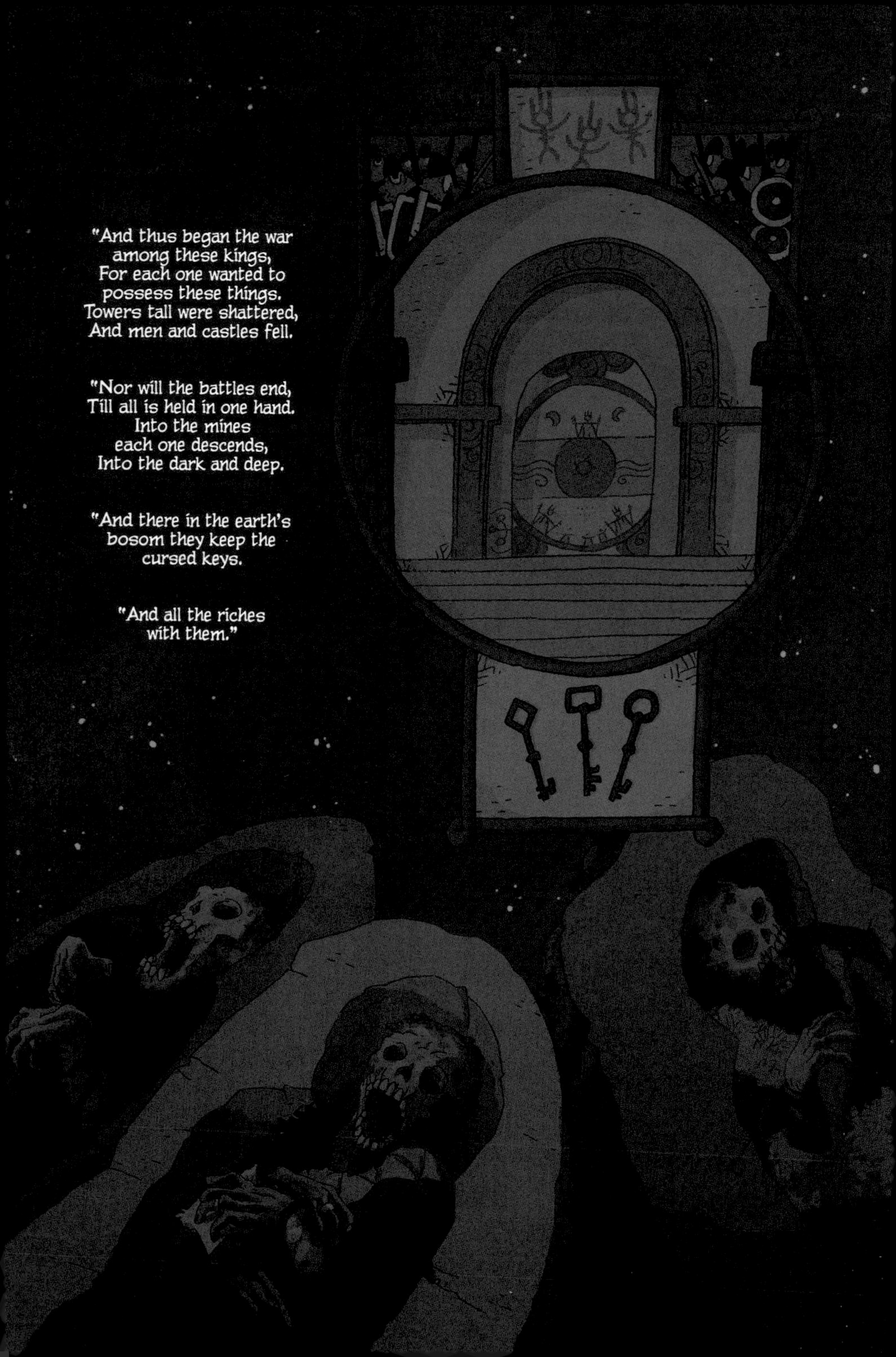
"And thus began the war
among these kings,
For each one wanted to
possess these things.
Towers tall were shattered,
And men and castles fell.
"Nor will the battles end,
Till all is held in one hand.
Into the mines
each one descends,
Into the dark and deep.
"And there in the earth's
bosom they keep the
cursed keys.
"And all the riches
with them."

116

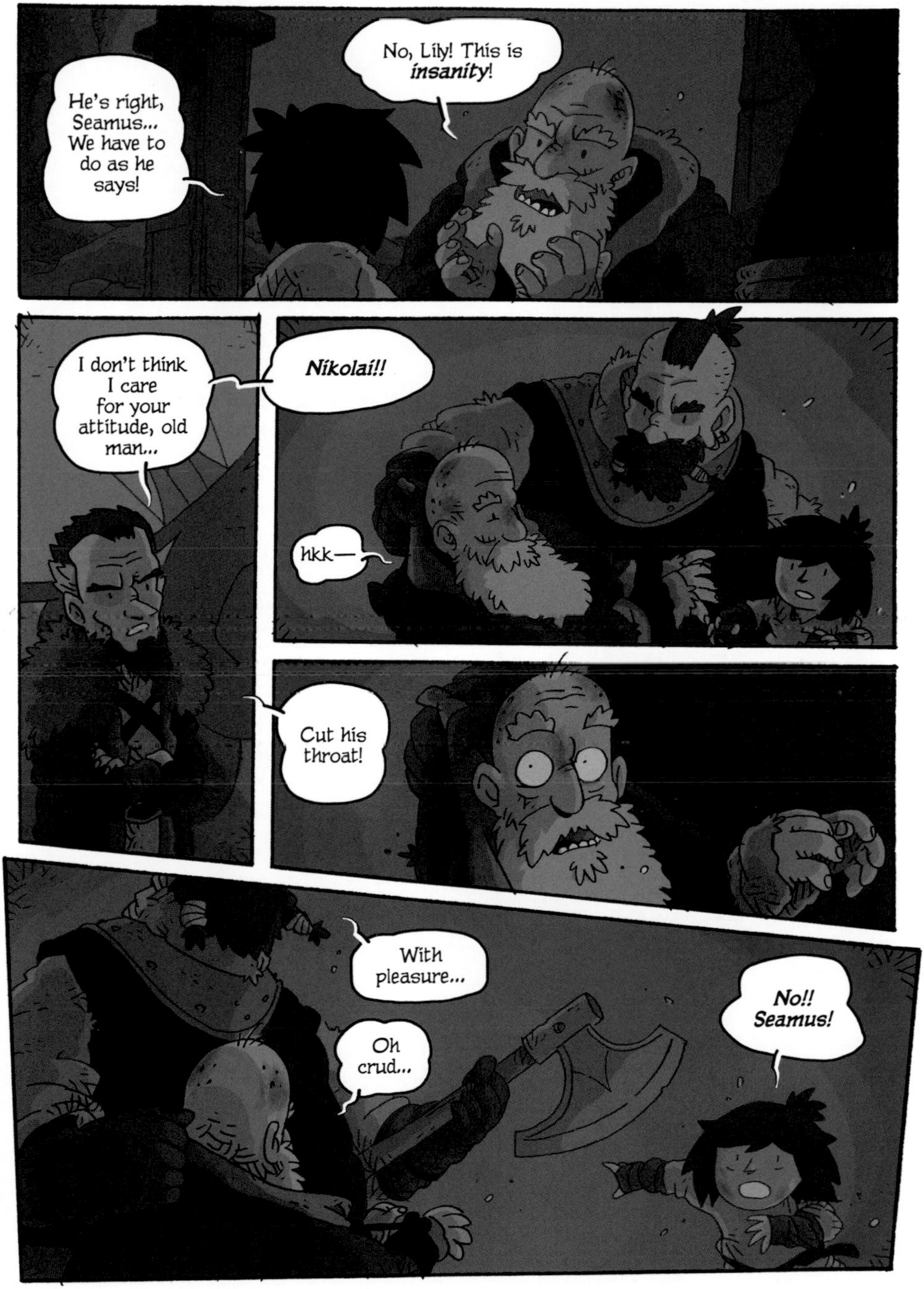
No, Lily! This is *insanity*!
He's right, Seamus... We have to do as he says!
I don't think I care for your attitude, old man...
Nikolai!!
hkk—
Cut his throat!
With pleasure...
Oh crud...
No!! Seamus!

118

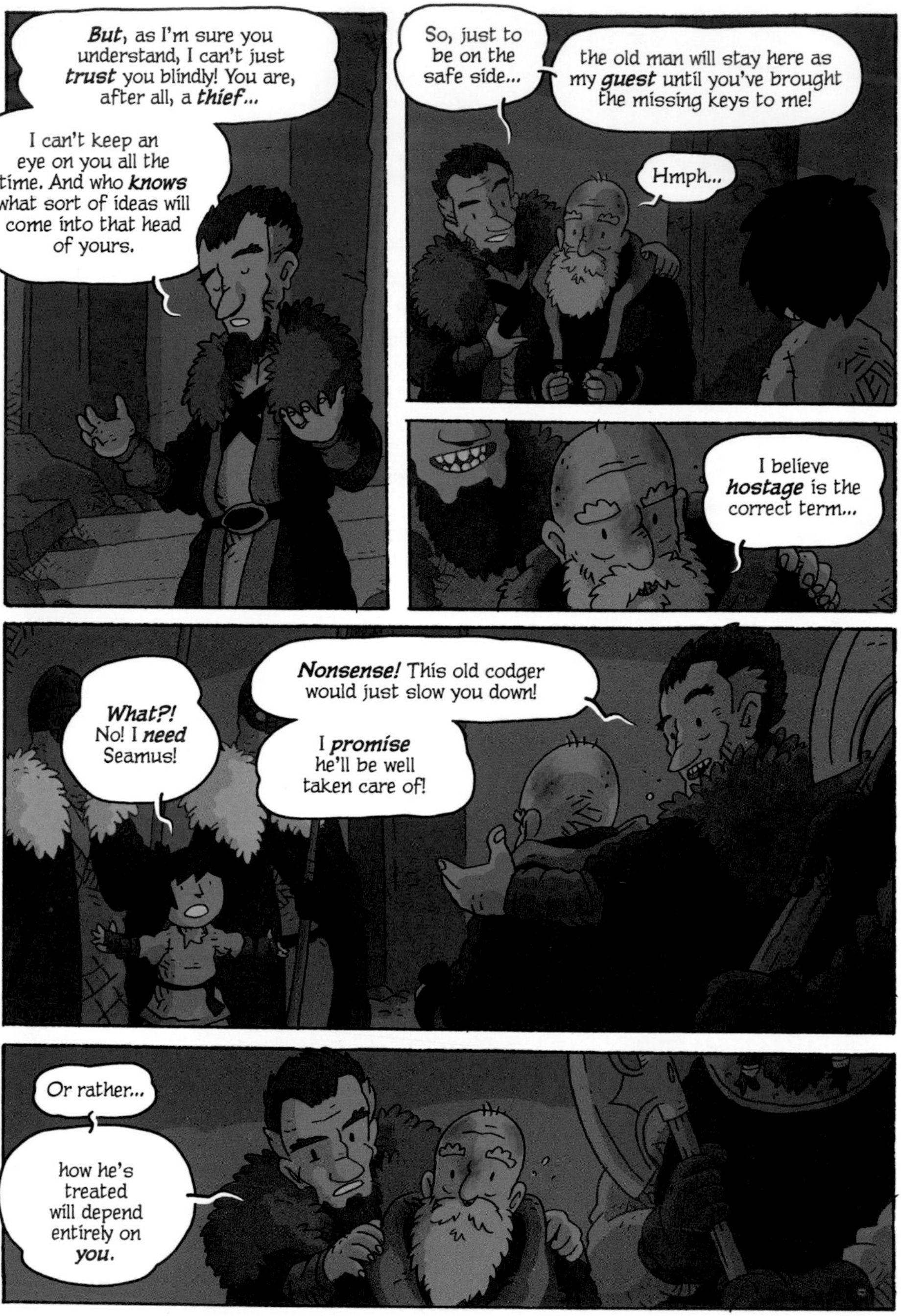
But, as I'm sure you understand, I can't just *trust* you blindly! You are, after all, a *thief*...
I can't keep an eye on you all the time. And who *knows* what sort of ideas will come into that head of yours.
So, just to be on the safe side...
the old man will stay here as my *guest* until you've brought the missing keys to me!
Hmph...
I believe *hostage* is the correct term...
What?! No! I *need* Seamus!
Nonsense! This old codger would just slow you down!
I *promise* he'll be well taken care of!
Or rather...
how he's treated will depend entirely on *you*.

Gleam of steel,
Glow of coals,
Chase wickedness away,
Out the evil goes.
The breath of the Brotherhood,
Blows life upon the embers.

4

H · The Dungeon · H

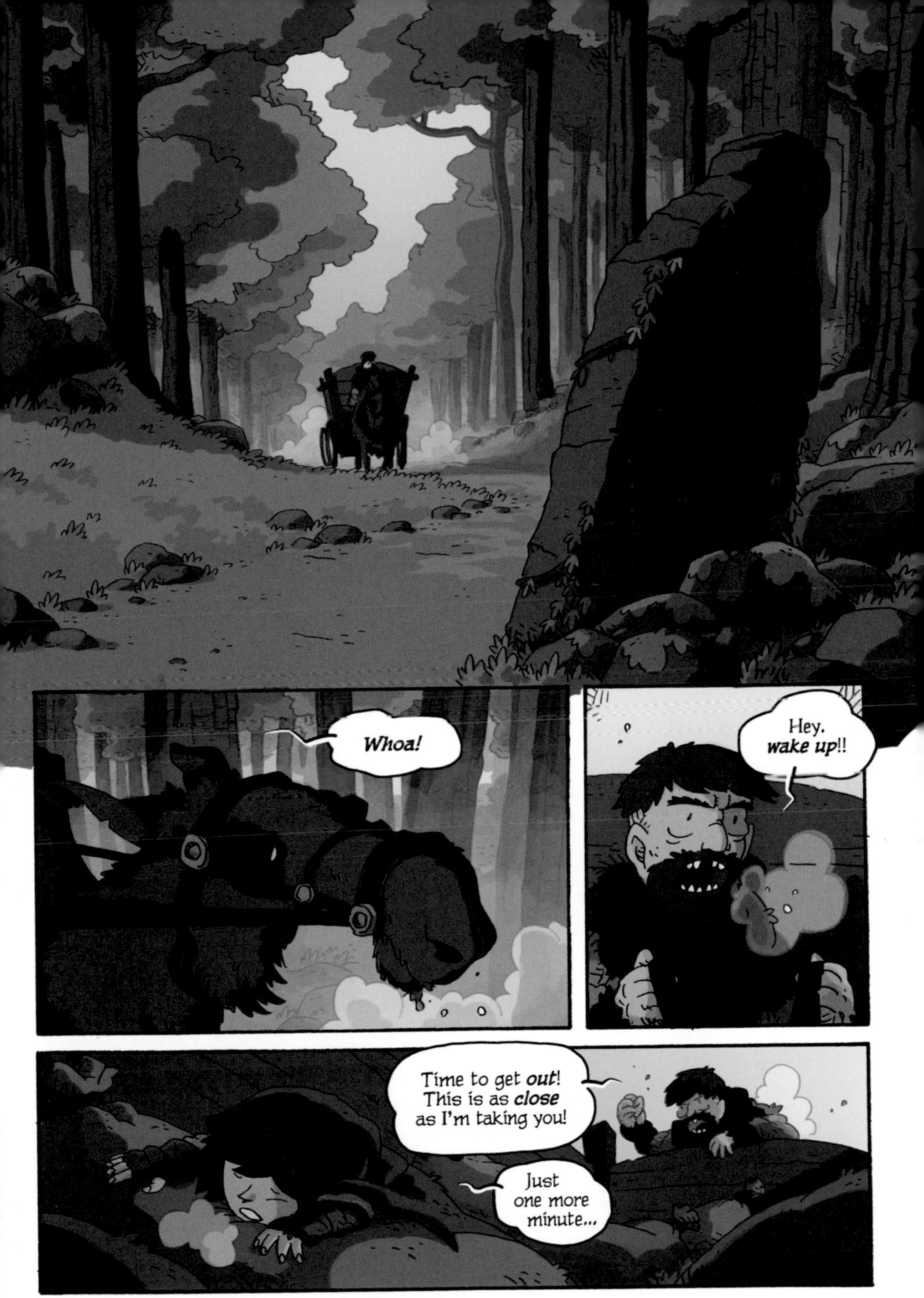
Whoa!
Hey. wake up!!
Time to get out! This is as close as I'm taking you!
Just one more minute...

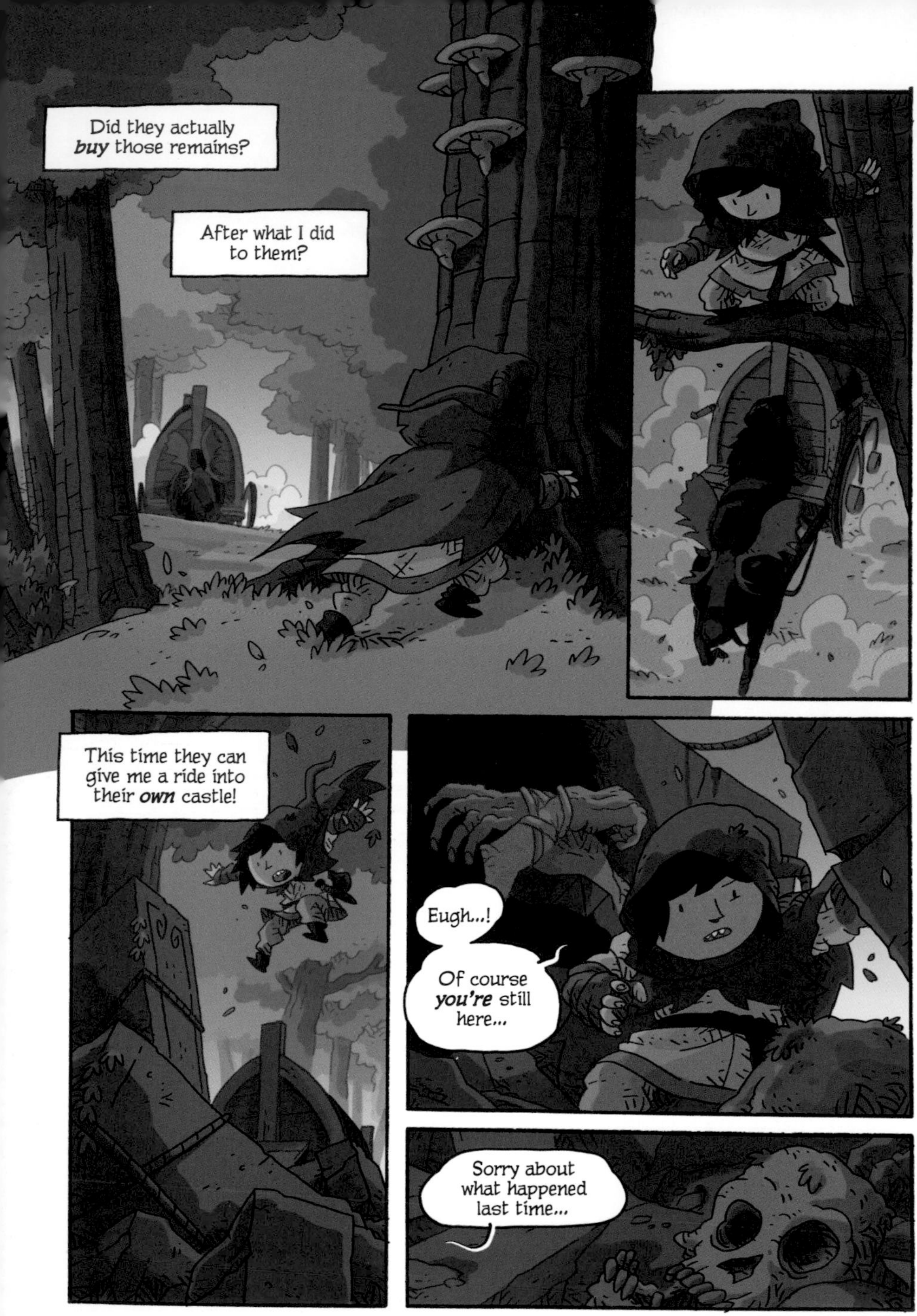

Did they actually *buy* those remains?
After what I did to them?
This time they can give me a ride into their *own* castle!
Eugh...!
Of course *you're* still here...
Sorry about what happened last time...

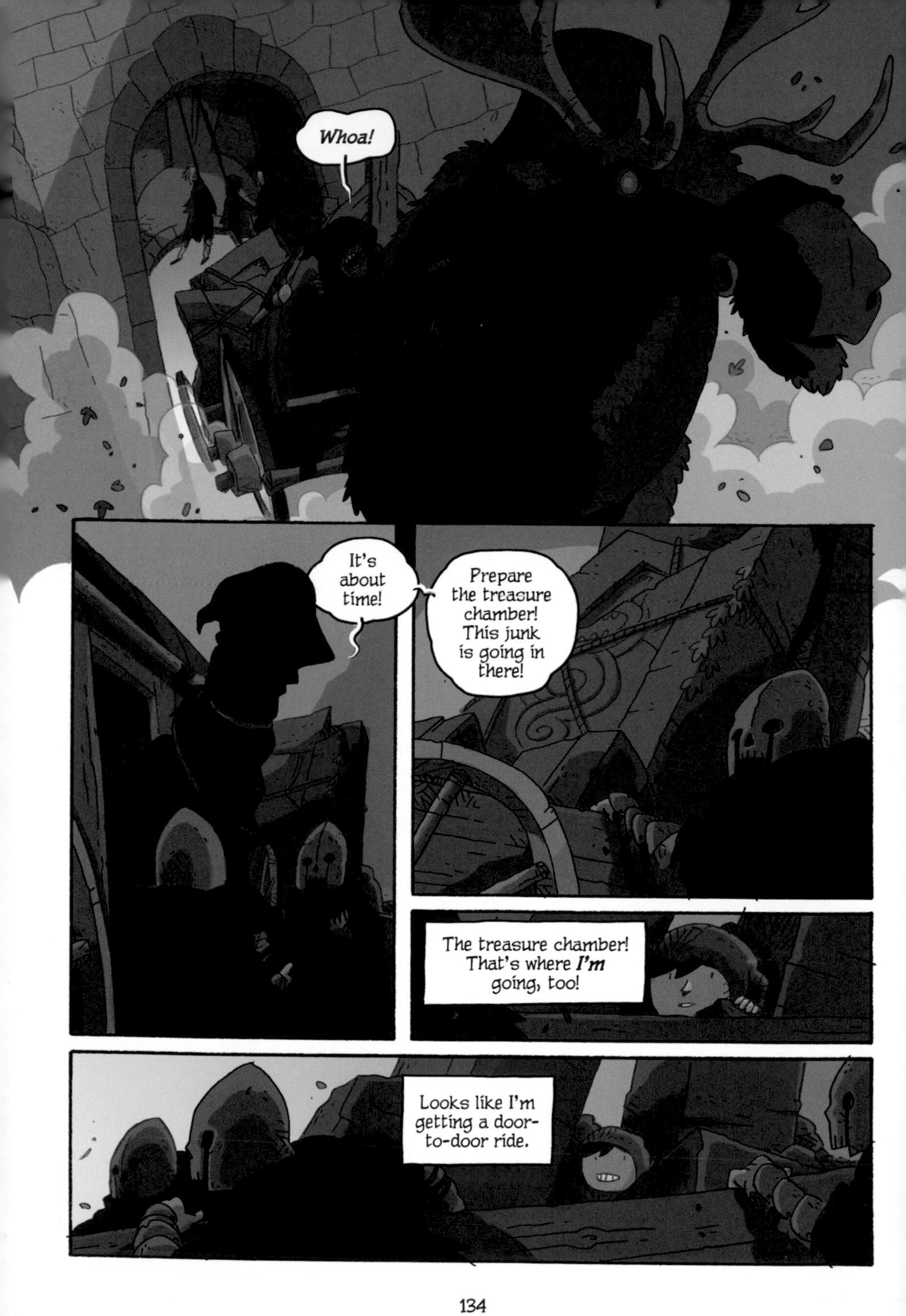

Whoa!
It's about time!
Prepare the treasure chamber! This junk is going in there!
The treasure chamber! That's where ***I'm*** going, too!
Looks like I'm getting a door-to-door ride.

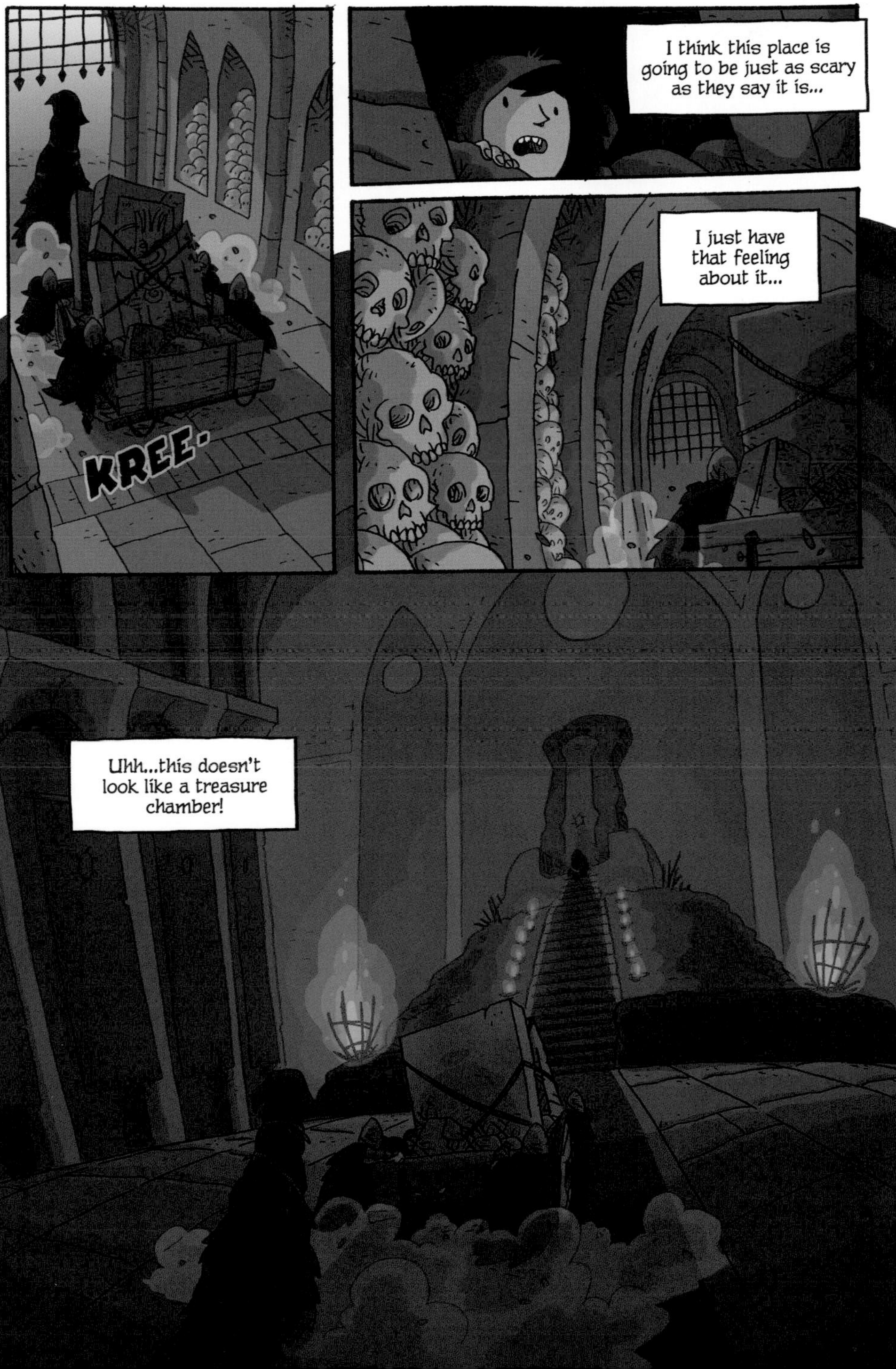
KREE-
I think this place is going to be just as scary as they say it is...
I just have that feeling about it...
Uhh...this doesn't look like a treasure chamber!

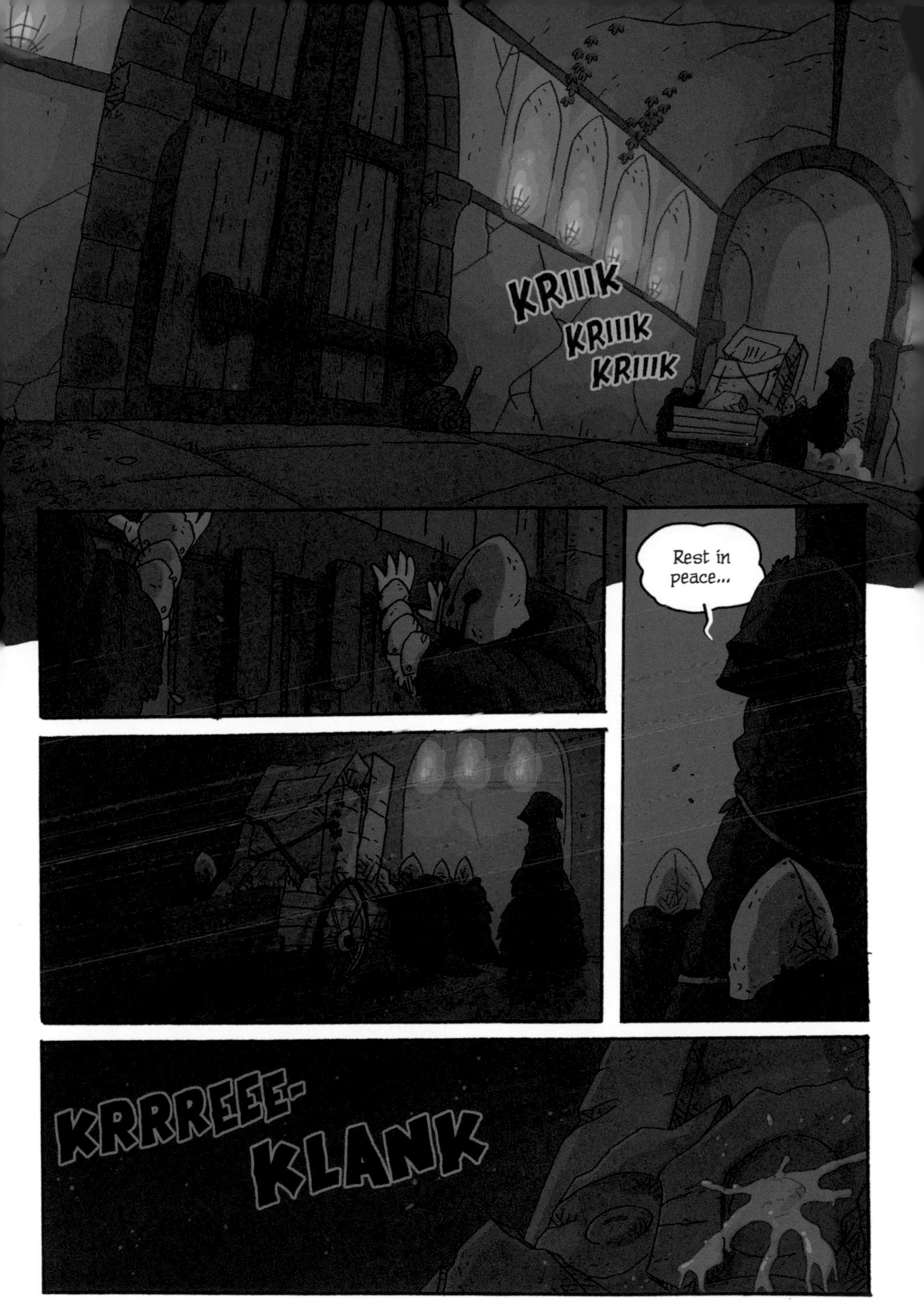
KRIIIK
KRIIIK
KRIIIK
Rest in peace...
KRRREEE-
KLANK

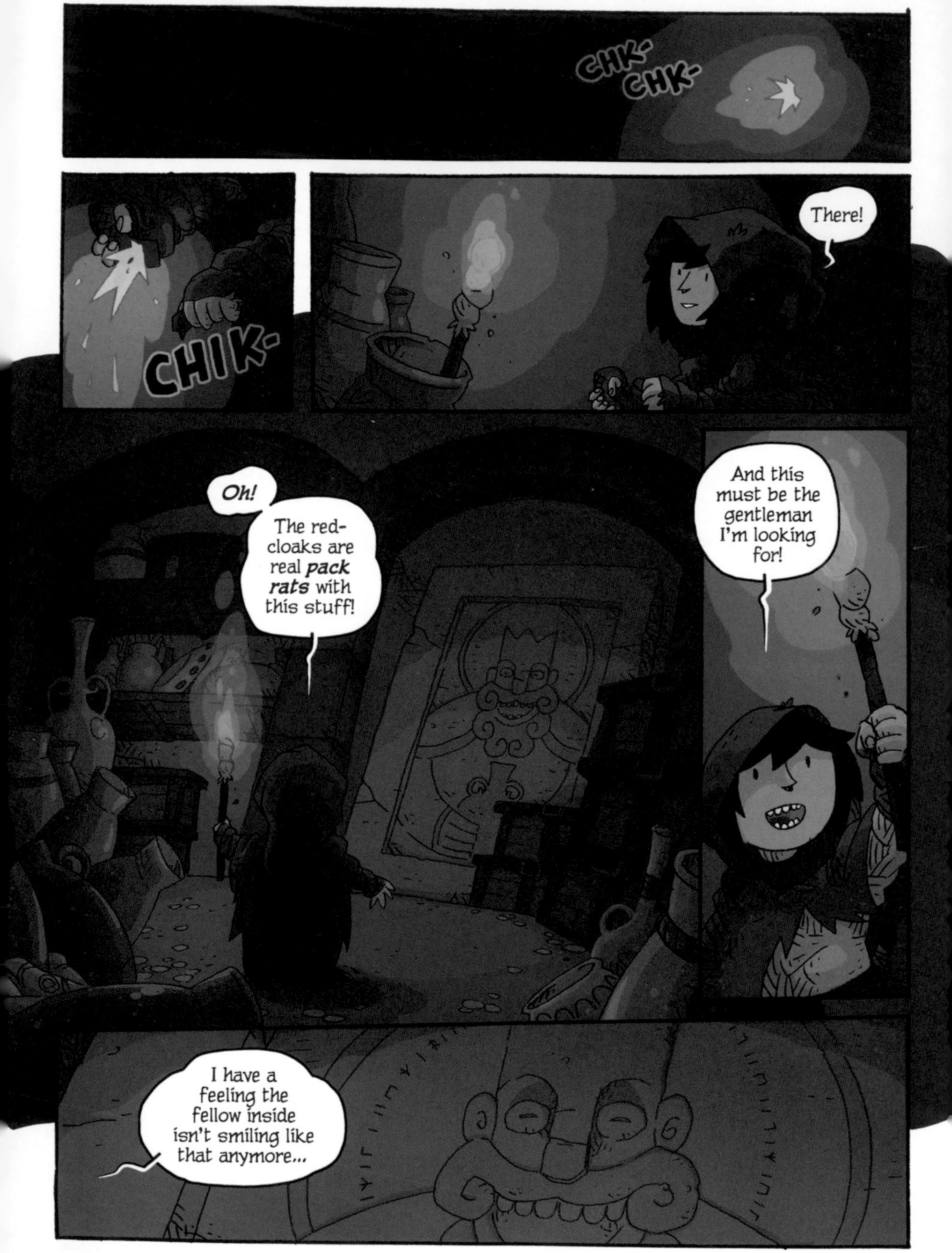
CHK-
CHK-
CHIK-
There!
Oh!
The red-cloaks are real *pack rats* with this stuff!
And this must be the gentleman I'm looking for!
I have a feeling the fellow inside isn't smiling like that anymore...

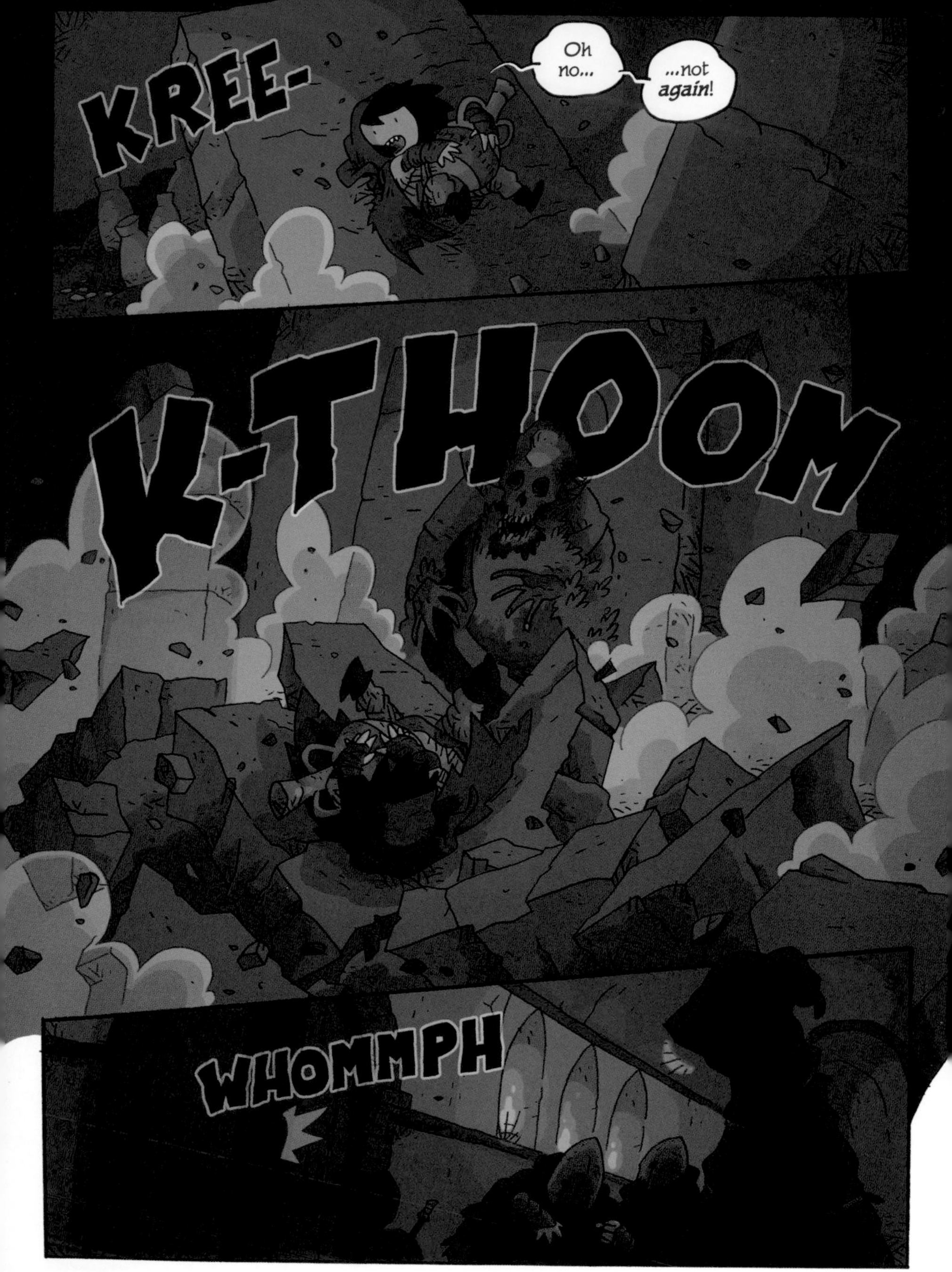
KREE-
Oh no...
...not again!
K-THOOM
WHOMMPH

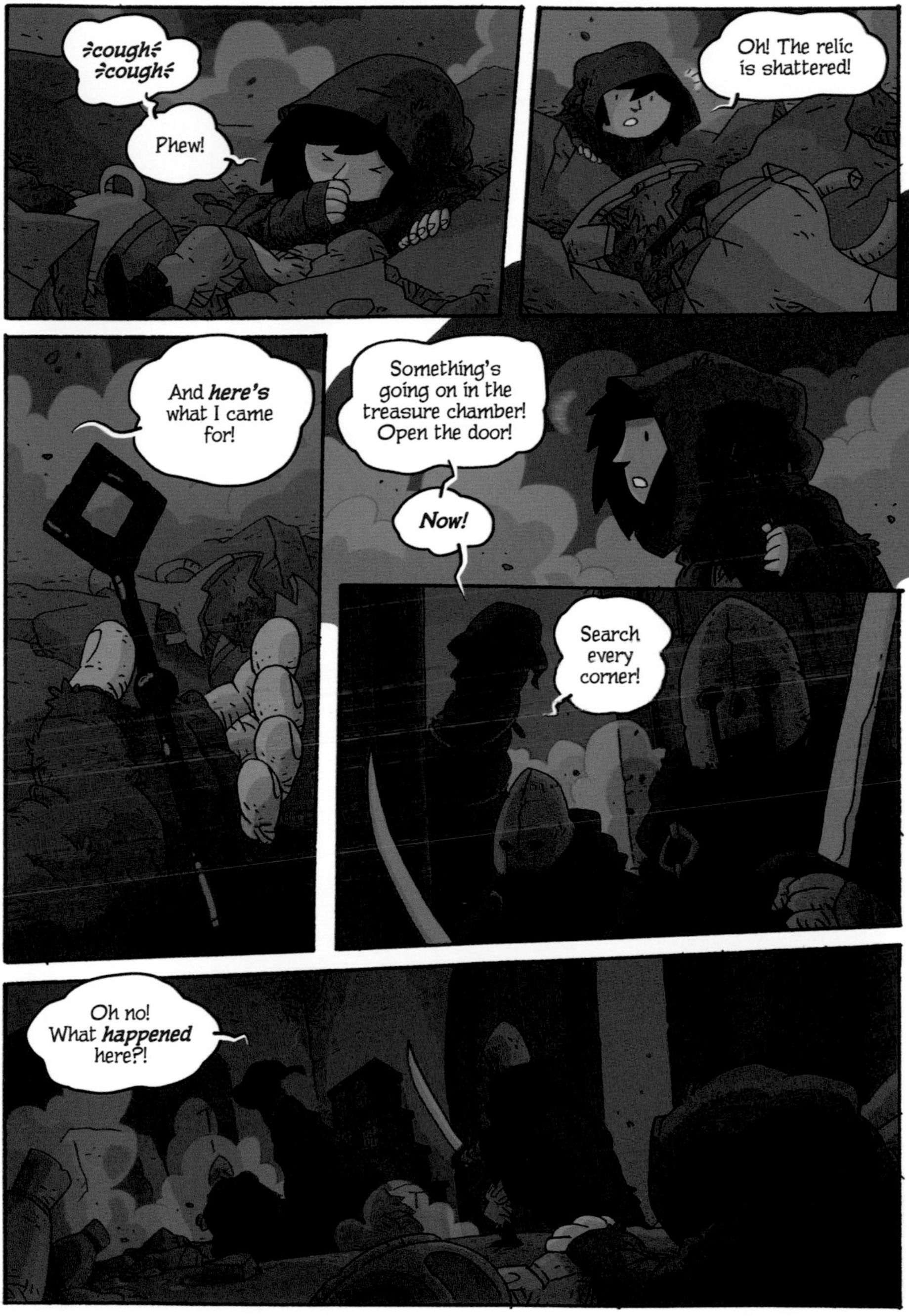
cough *cough*
Phew!
Oh! The relic is shattered!
And **here's** what I came for!
Something's going on in the treasure chamber! Open the door!
Now!
Search every corner!
Oh no! What **happened** here?!

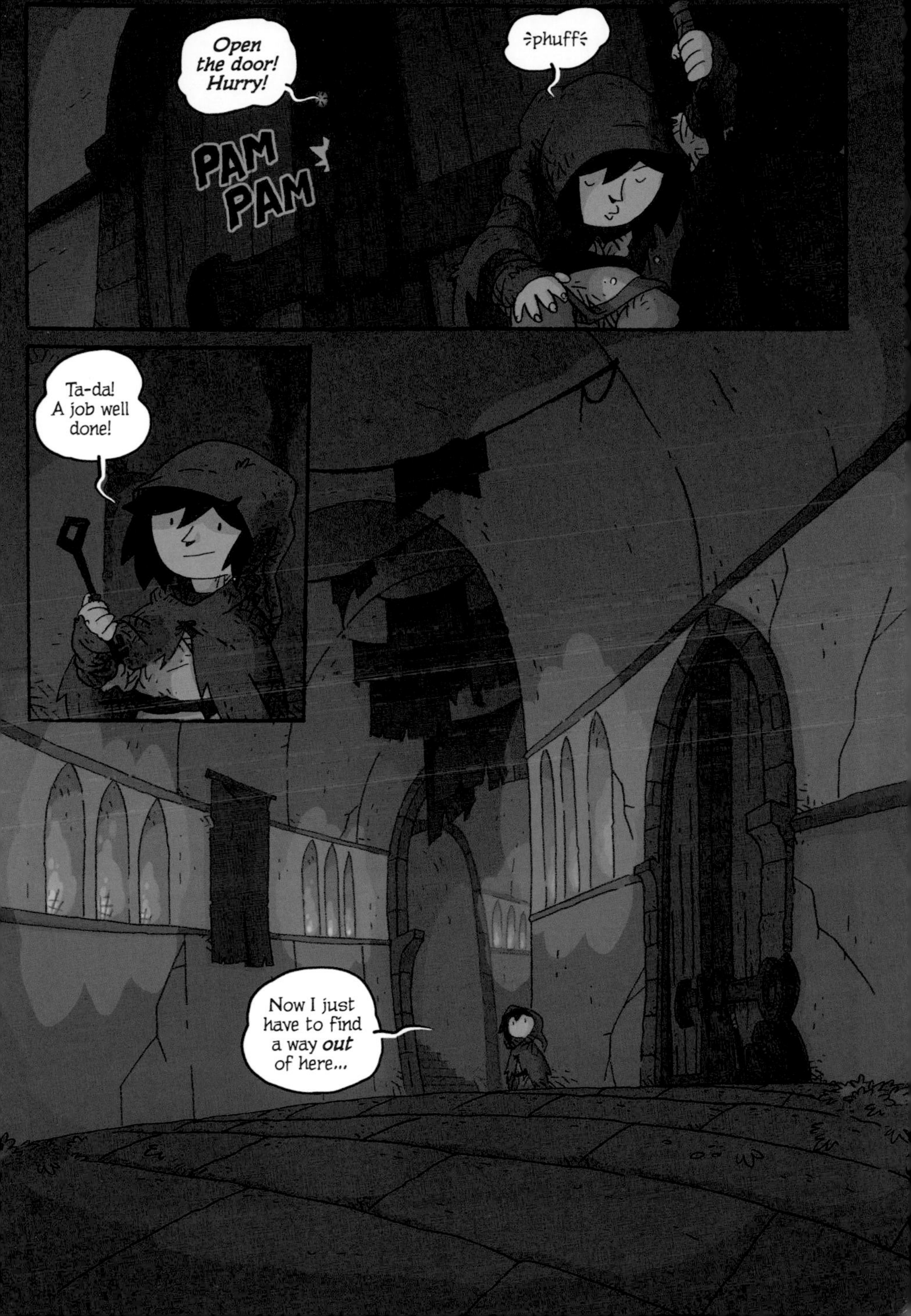
Open the door! Hurry!
PAM PAM
phuff
Ta-da! A job well done!
Now I just have to find a way *out* of here...

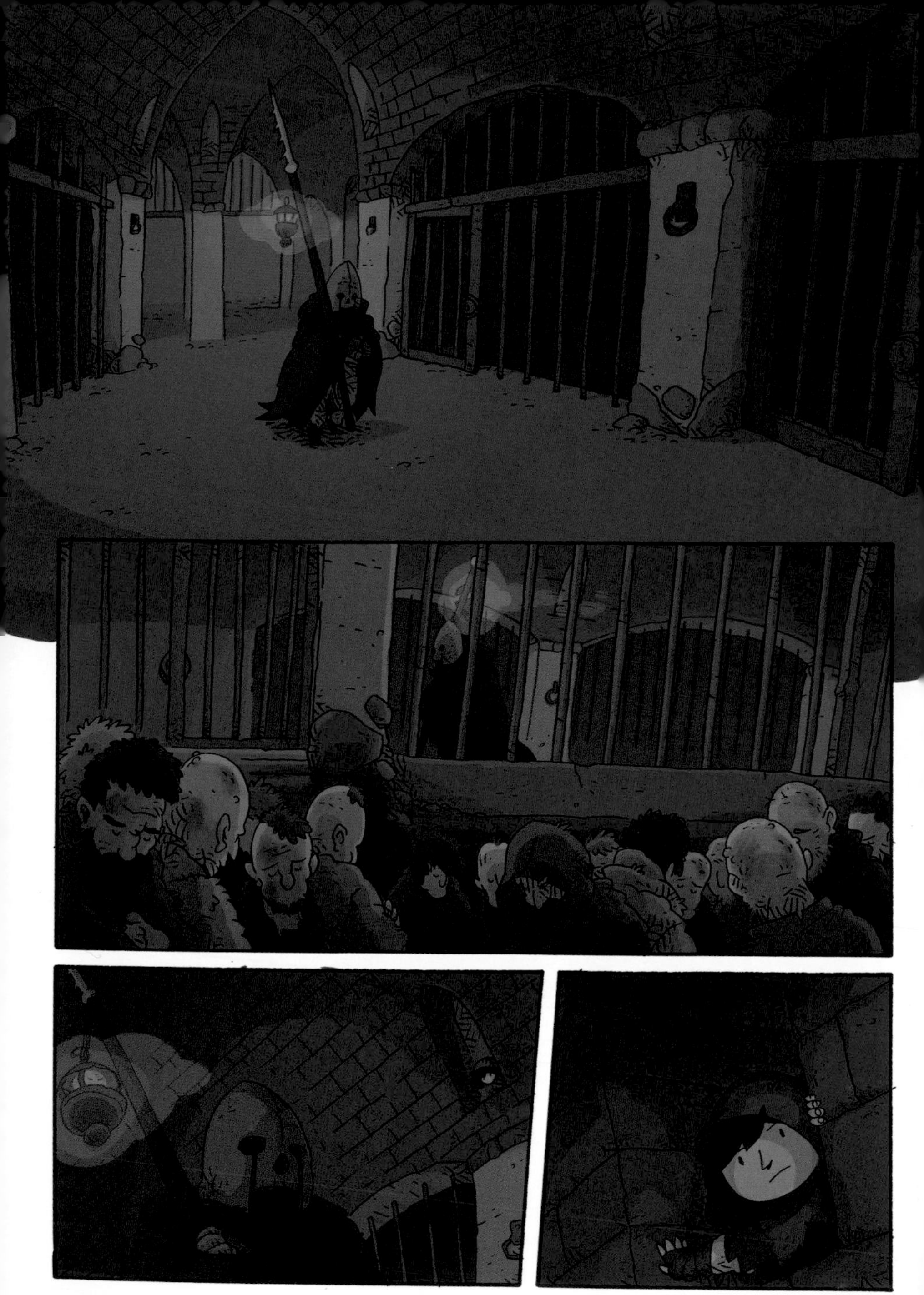

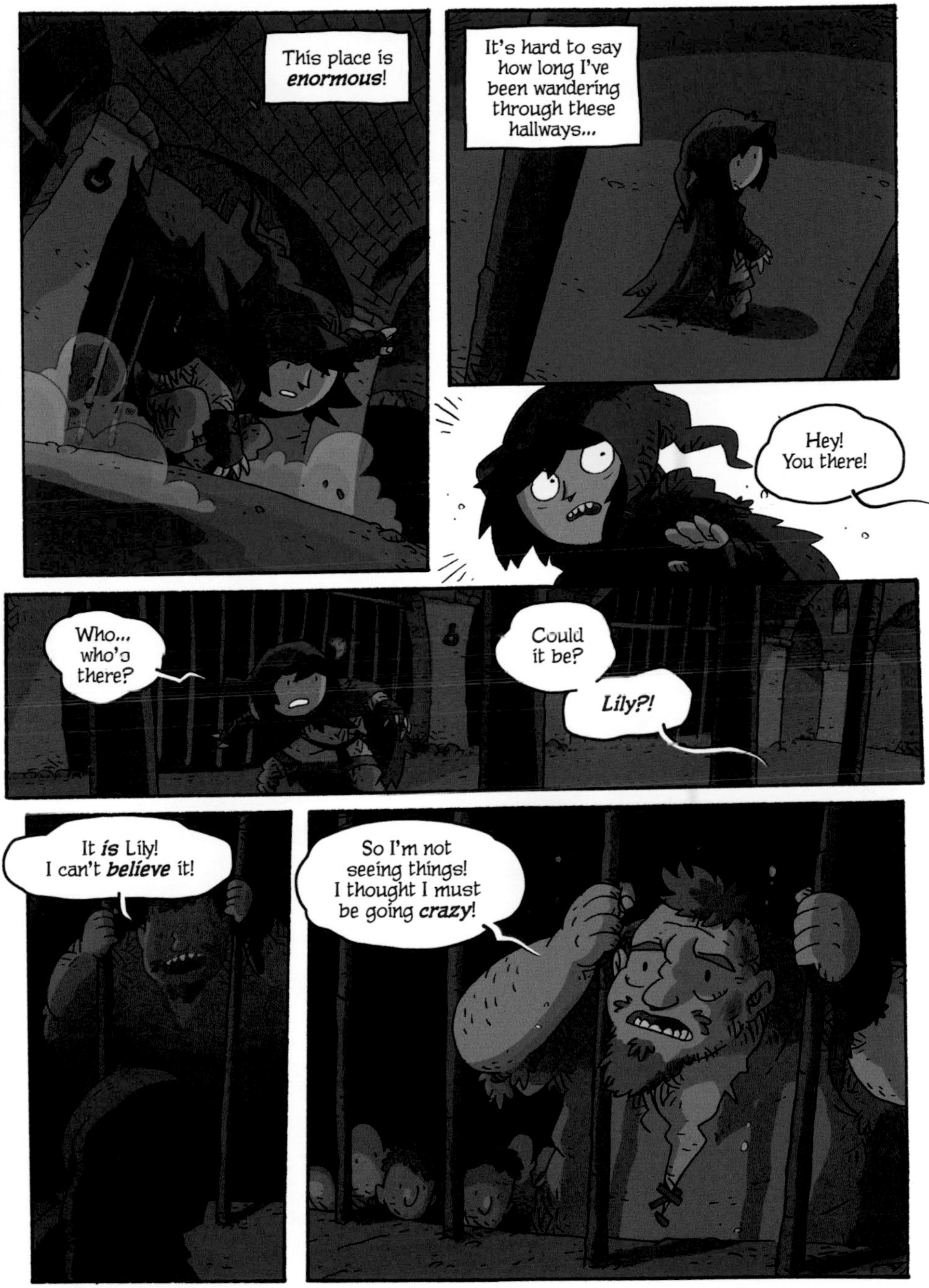
This place is *enormous*!
It's hard to say how long I've been wandering through these hallways...
Hey! You there!
Who... who's there?
Could it be?
Lily?!
It *is* Lily! I can't *believe* it!
So I'm not seeing things! I thought I must be going *crazy*!

148

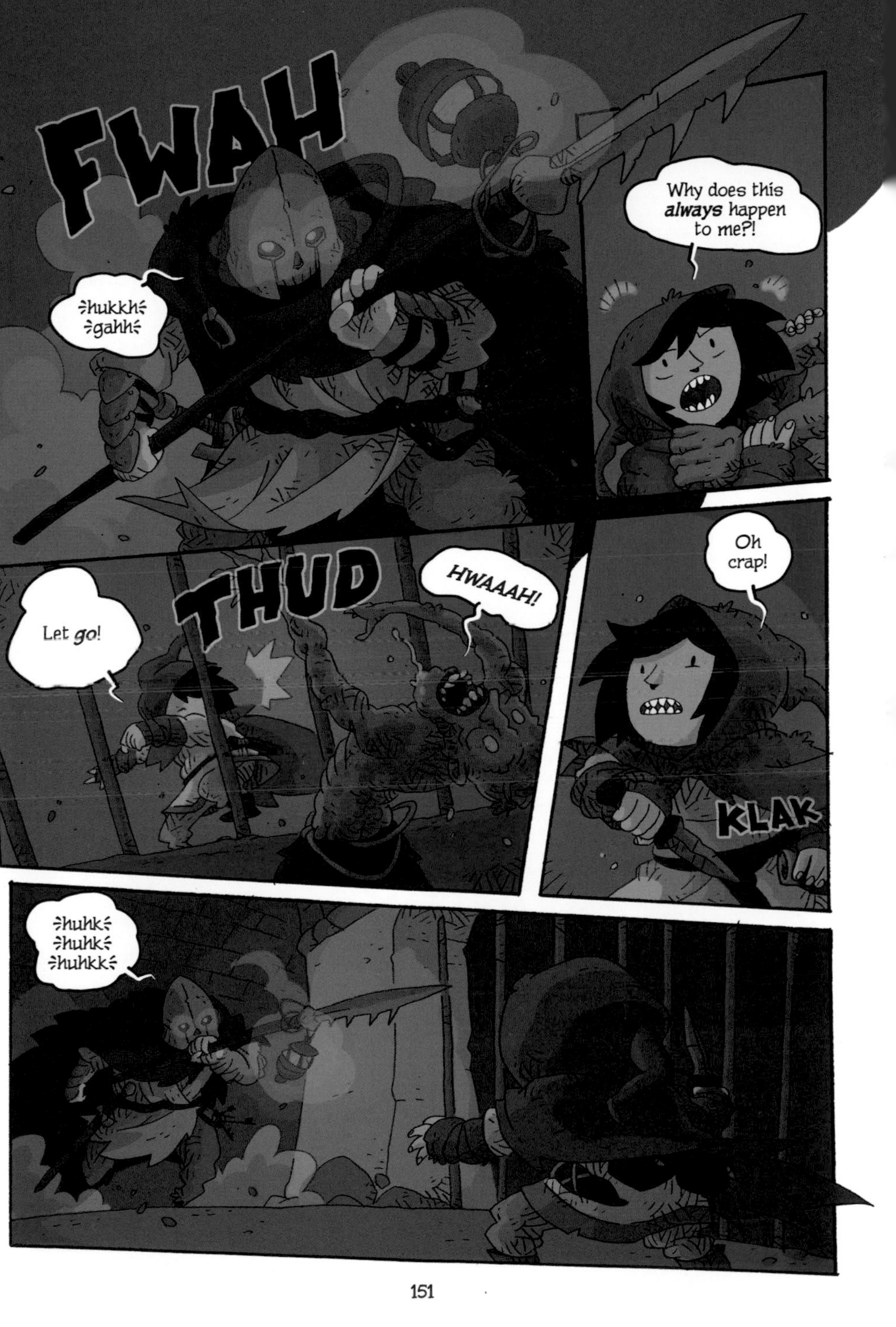
FWAH
⇛hukkh⇚ ⇛gahh⇚
Why does this always happen to me?!
THUD
HWAAAH!
Let go!
Oh crap!
KLAK
⇛huhk⇚ ⇛huhk⇚ ⇛huhkk⇚

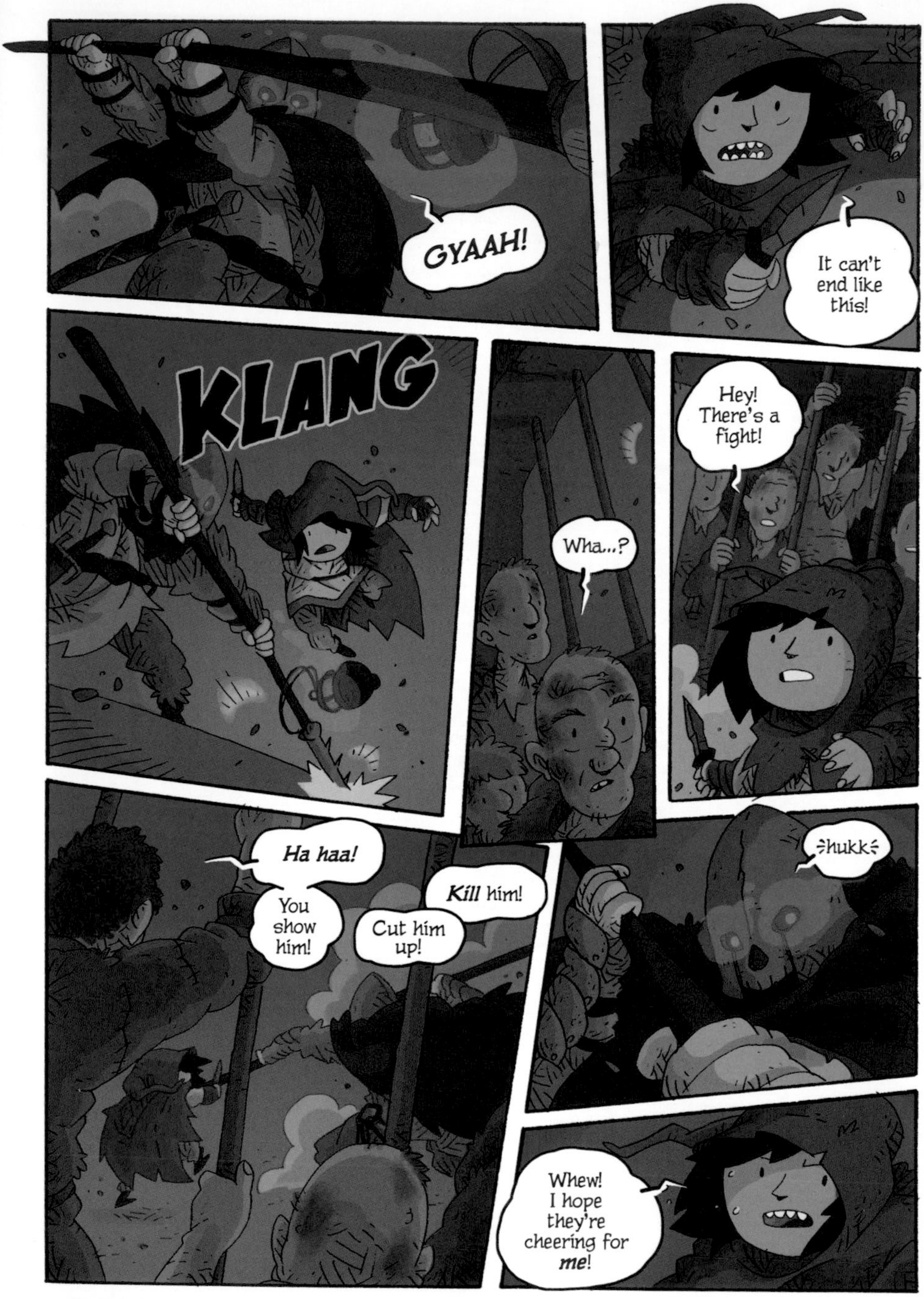
GYAAH!
It can't end like this!
KLANG
Wha...?
Hey! There's a fight!
Ha haa!
You show him!
Cut him up!
Kill him!
hukk
Whew! I hope they're cheering for me!

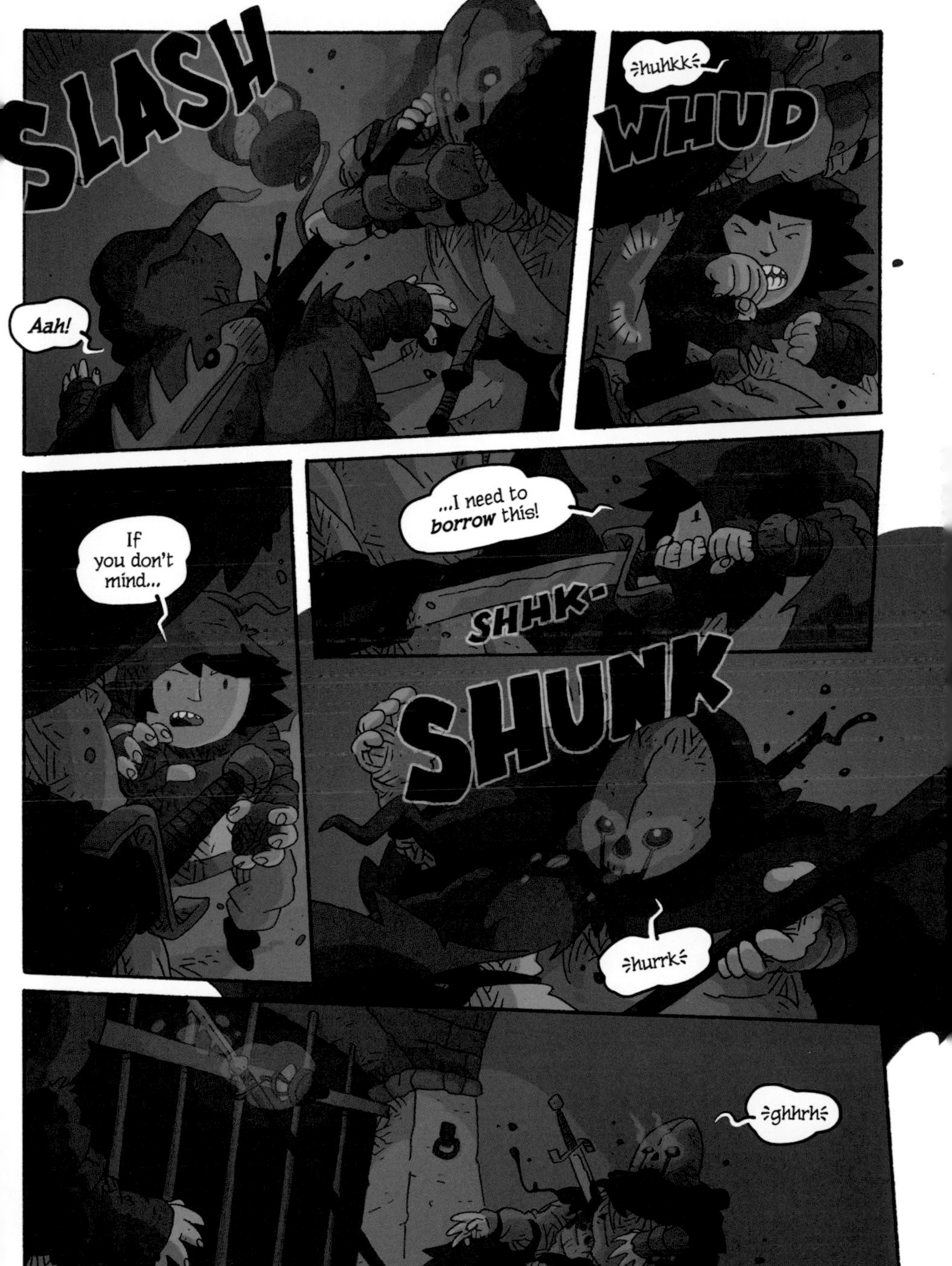
SLASH
Aah!
huhkk
WHUD
If you don't mind...
...I need to *borrow* this!
SHHK-
SHUNK
hurrk
ghhrh

154

155

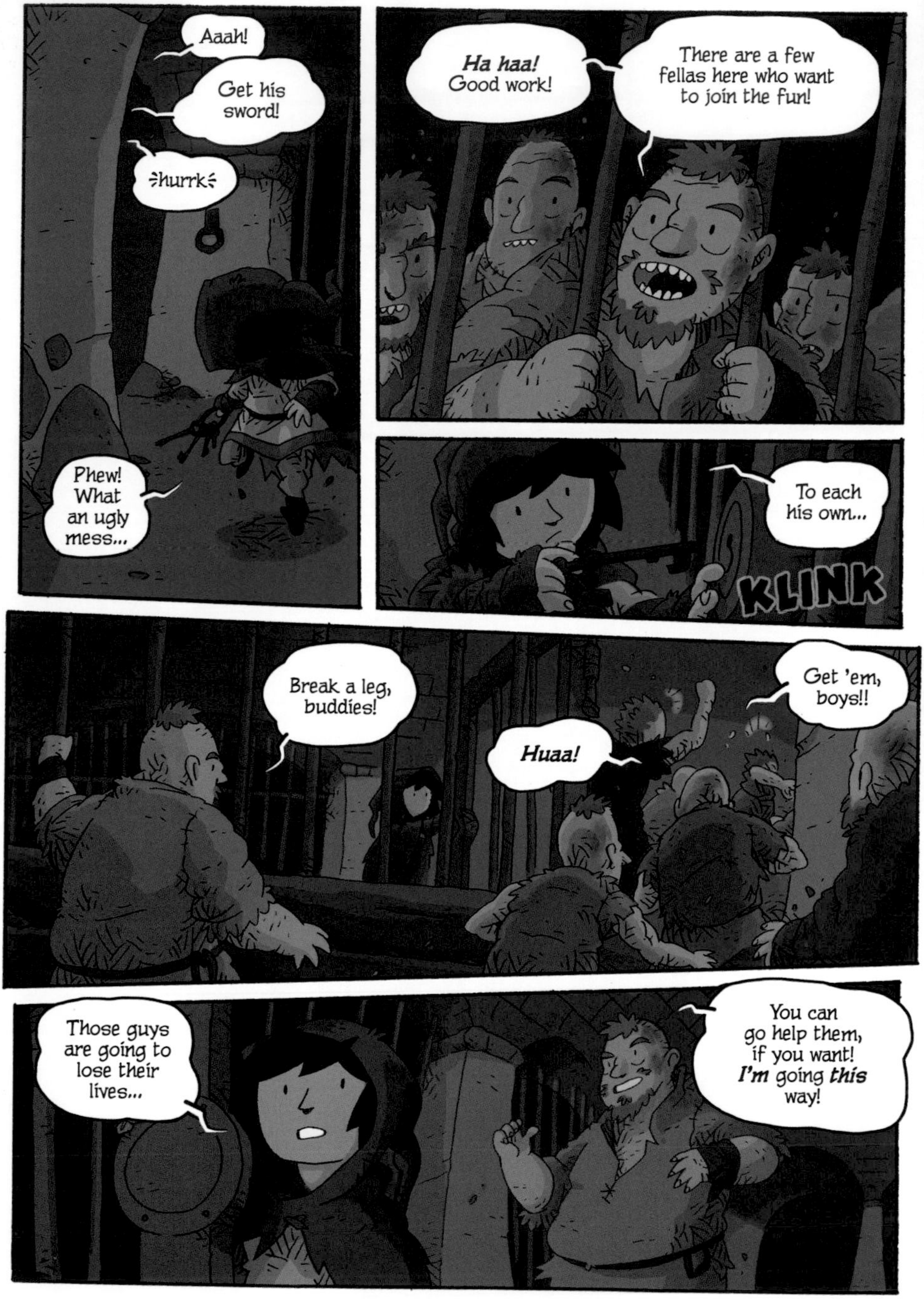
Aaah!
Get his sword!
hurrk
Phew! What an ugly mess...
Ha haa! Good work!
There are a few fellas here who want to join the fun!
To each his own...
KLINK
Break a leg, buddies!
Get 'em, boys!!
Huaa!
Those guys are going to lose their lives...
You can go help them, if you want! ***I'm*** going ***this*** way!

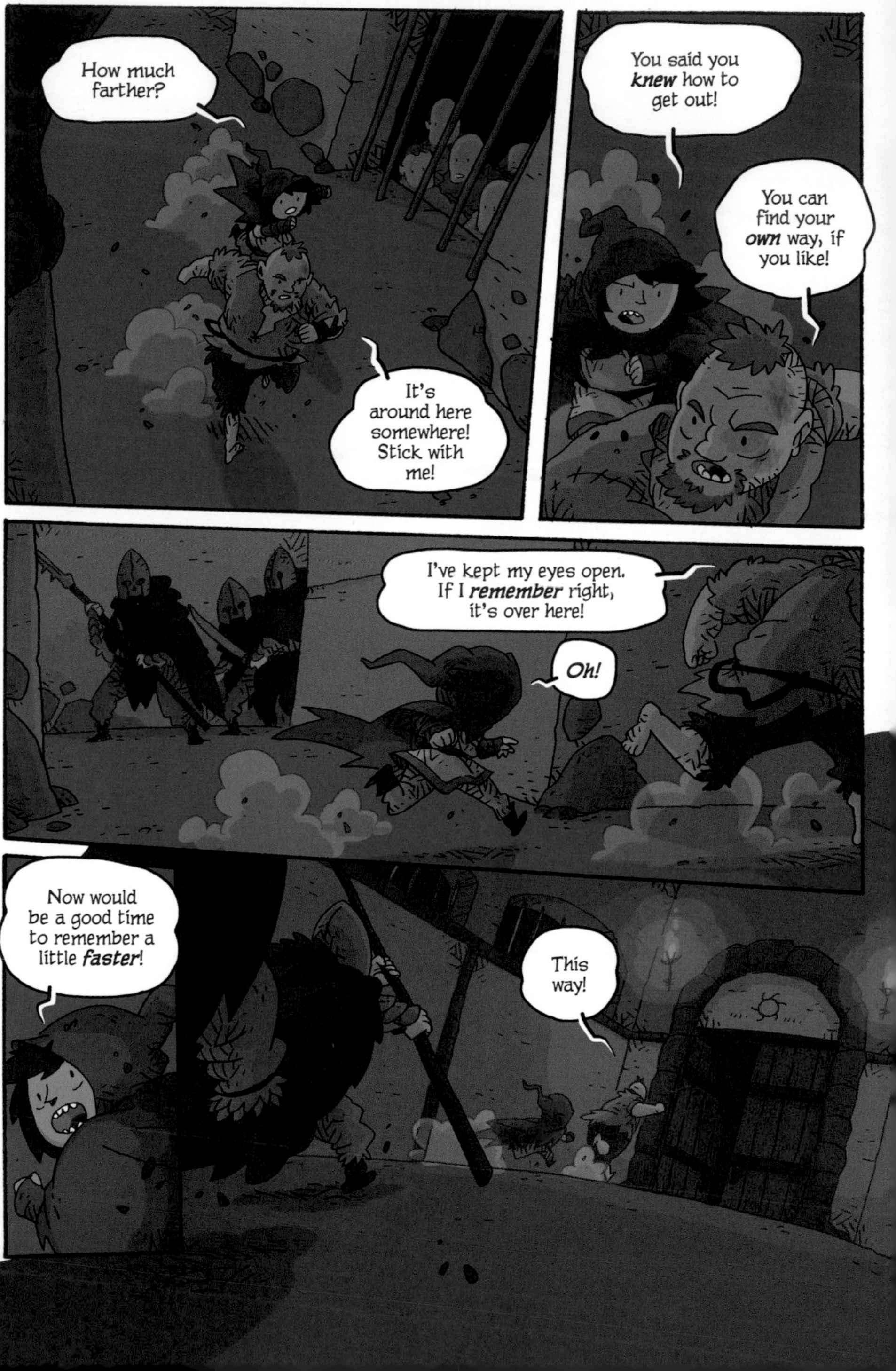
How much farther?
It's around here somewhere! Stick with me!
You said you *knew* how to get out!
You can find your *own* way, if you like!
I've kept my eyes open. If I *remember* right, it's over here!
Oh!
Now would be a good time to remember a little *faster*!
This way!

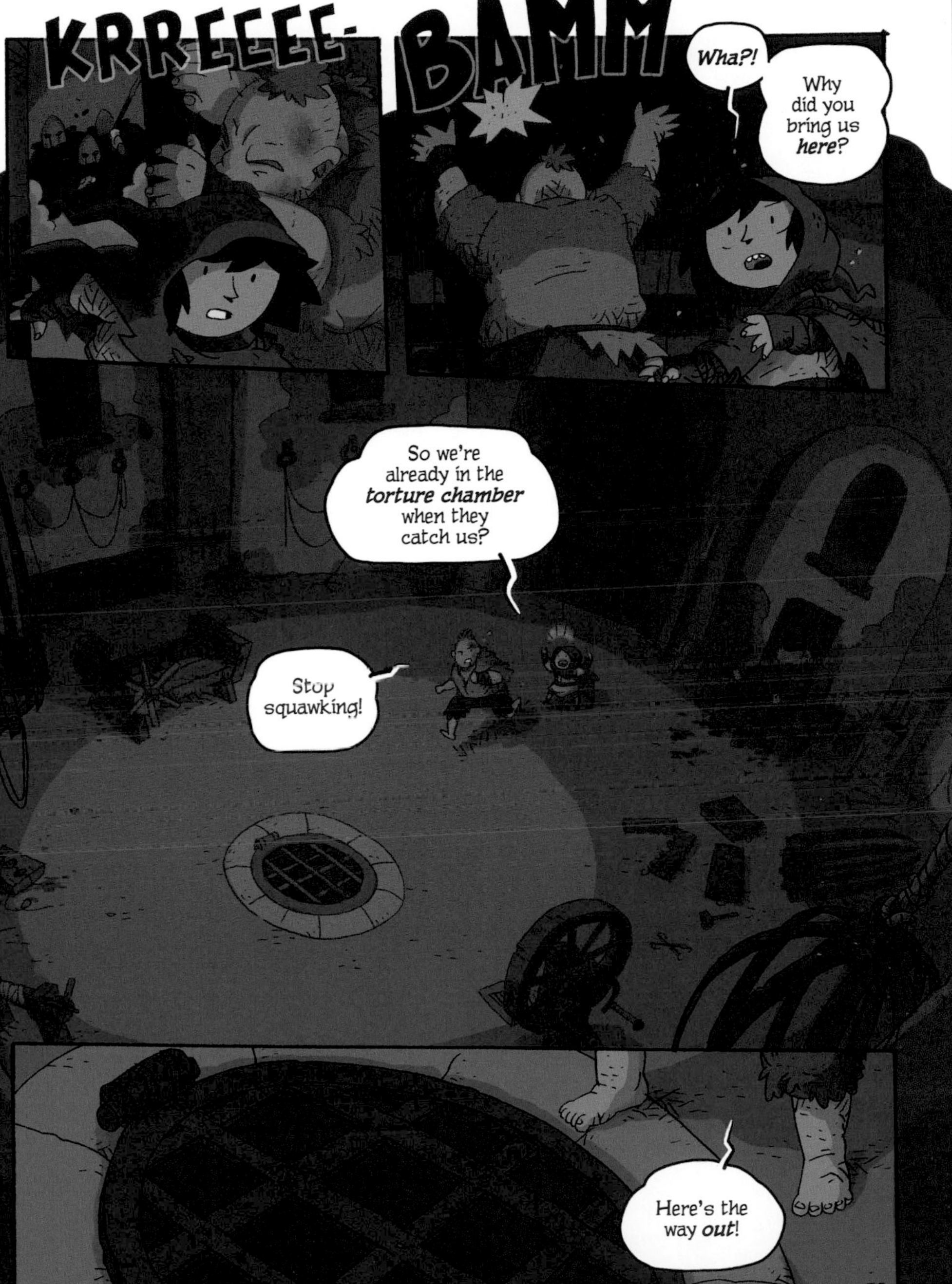
KRREEEE-
BAMM
Wha?!
Why did you bring us *here*?
So we're already in the *torture chamber* when they catch us?
Stop squawking!
Here's the way *out*!

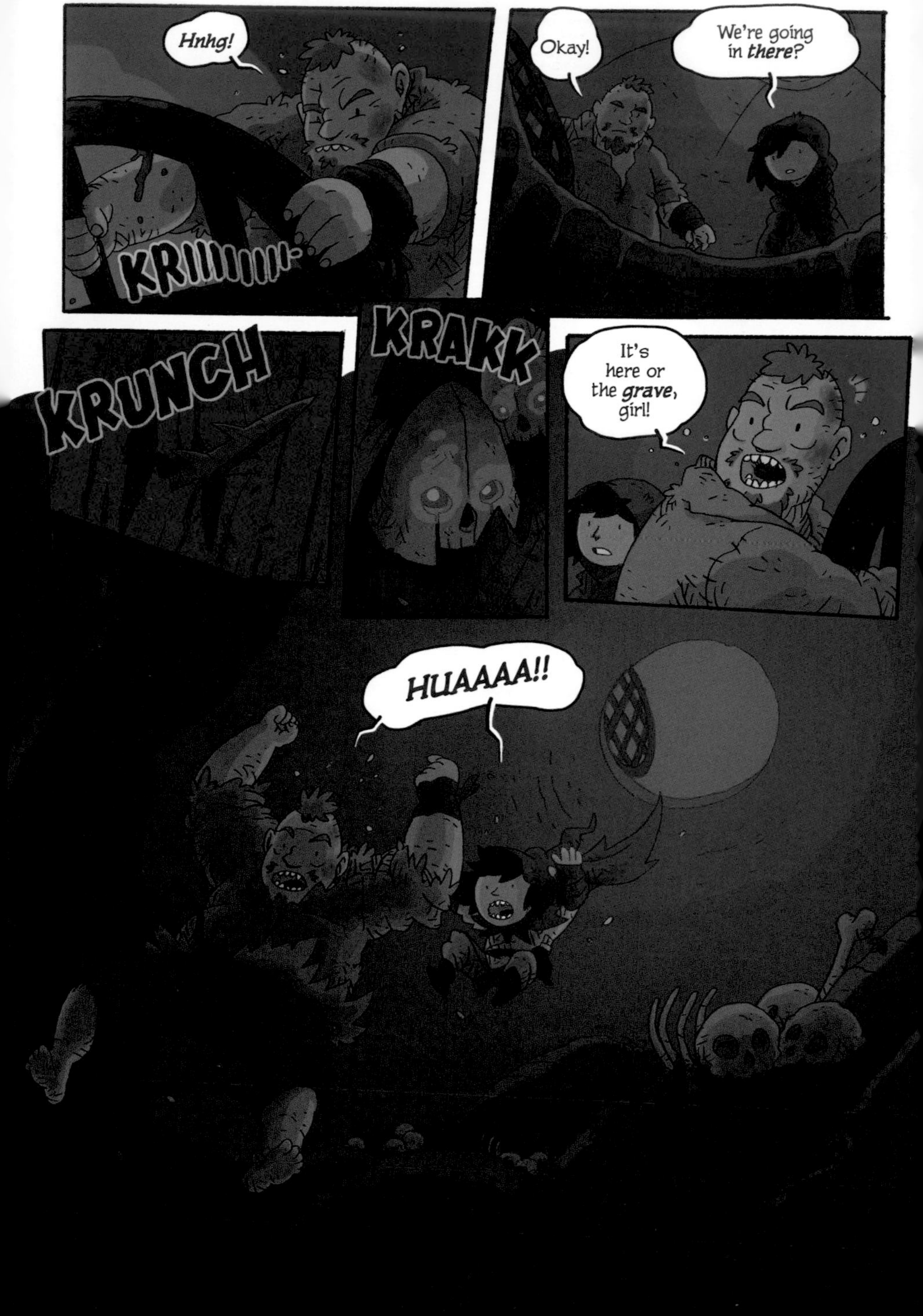
Hnhg!
KRIIIIIIII-
Okay!
We're going in *there*?
KRUNCH
KRAKK
It's here or the *grave*, girl!
HUAAAA!!

161

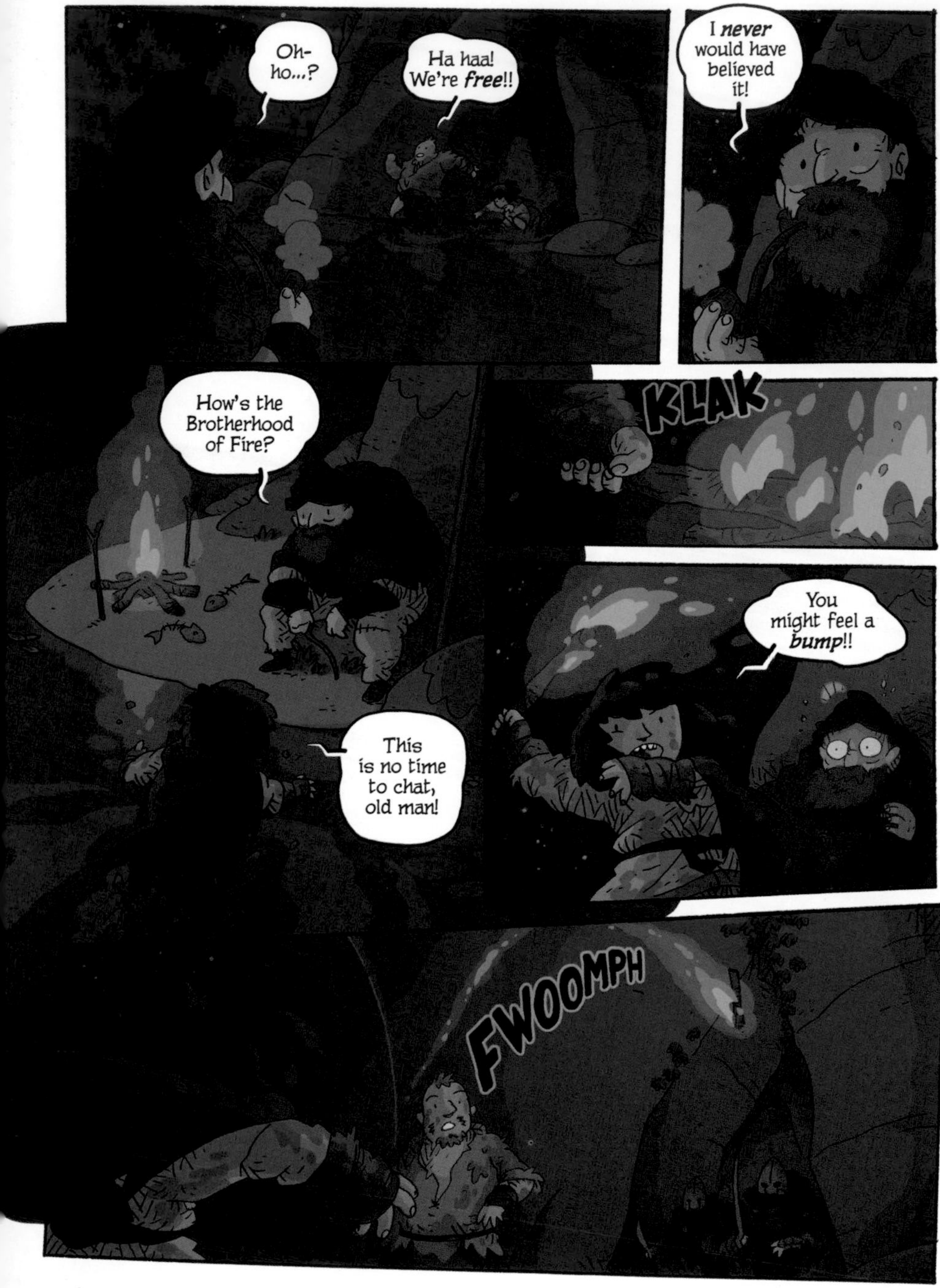
Oh-
ho...?
Ha haa! We're *free*!!
I *never* would have believed it!
How's the Brotherhood of Fire?
This is no time to chat, old man!
KLAK
You might feel a *bump*!!
FWOOMPH

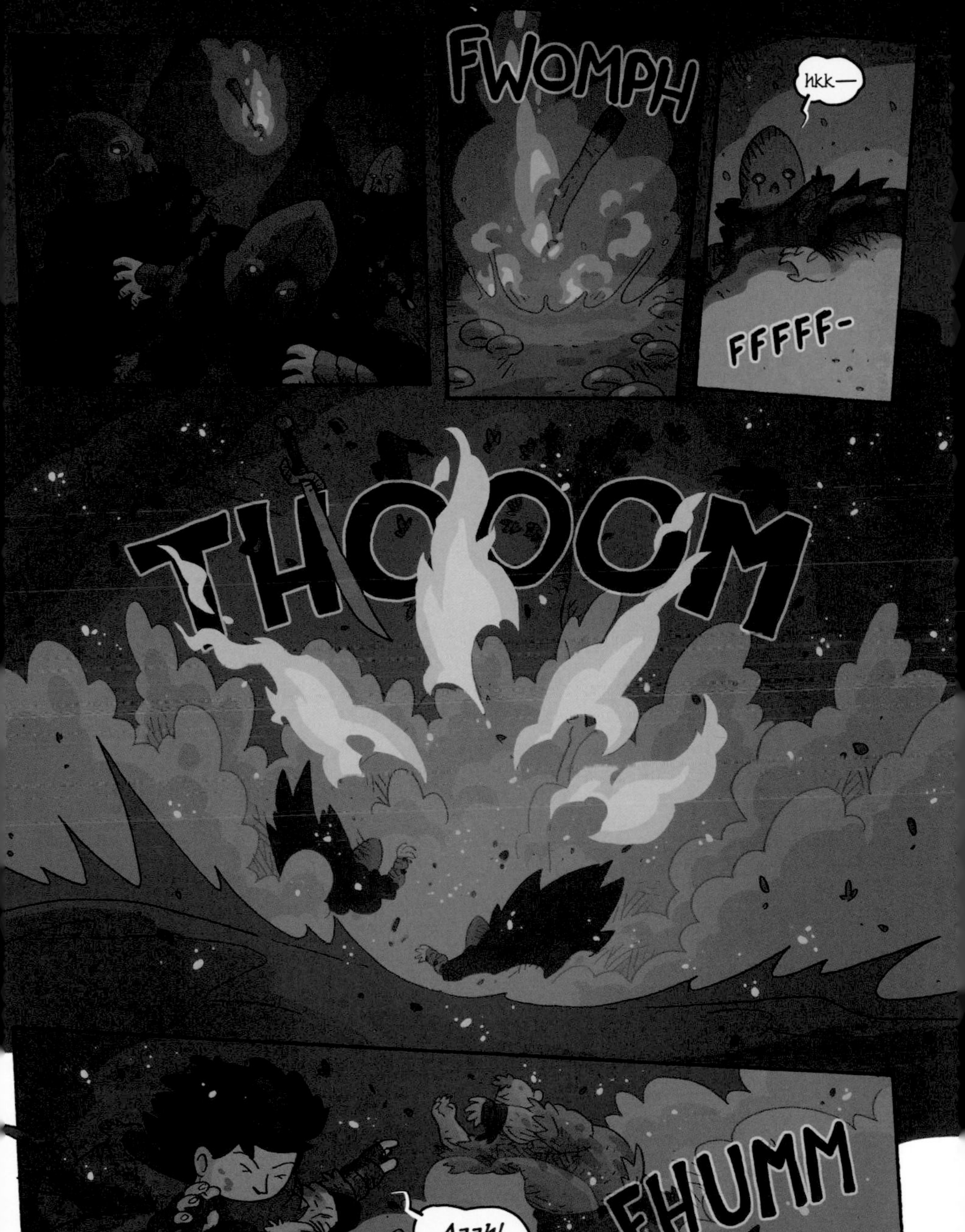
FWOMPH
hkk—
FFFFF-
THOOOM
Aaah!
FHUMM

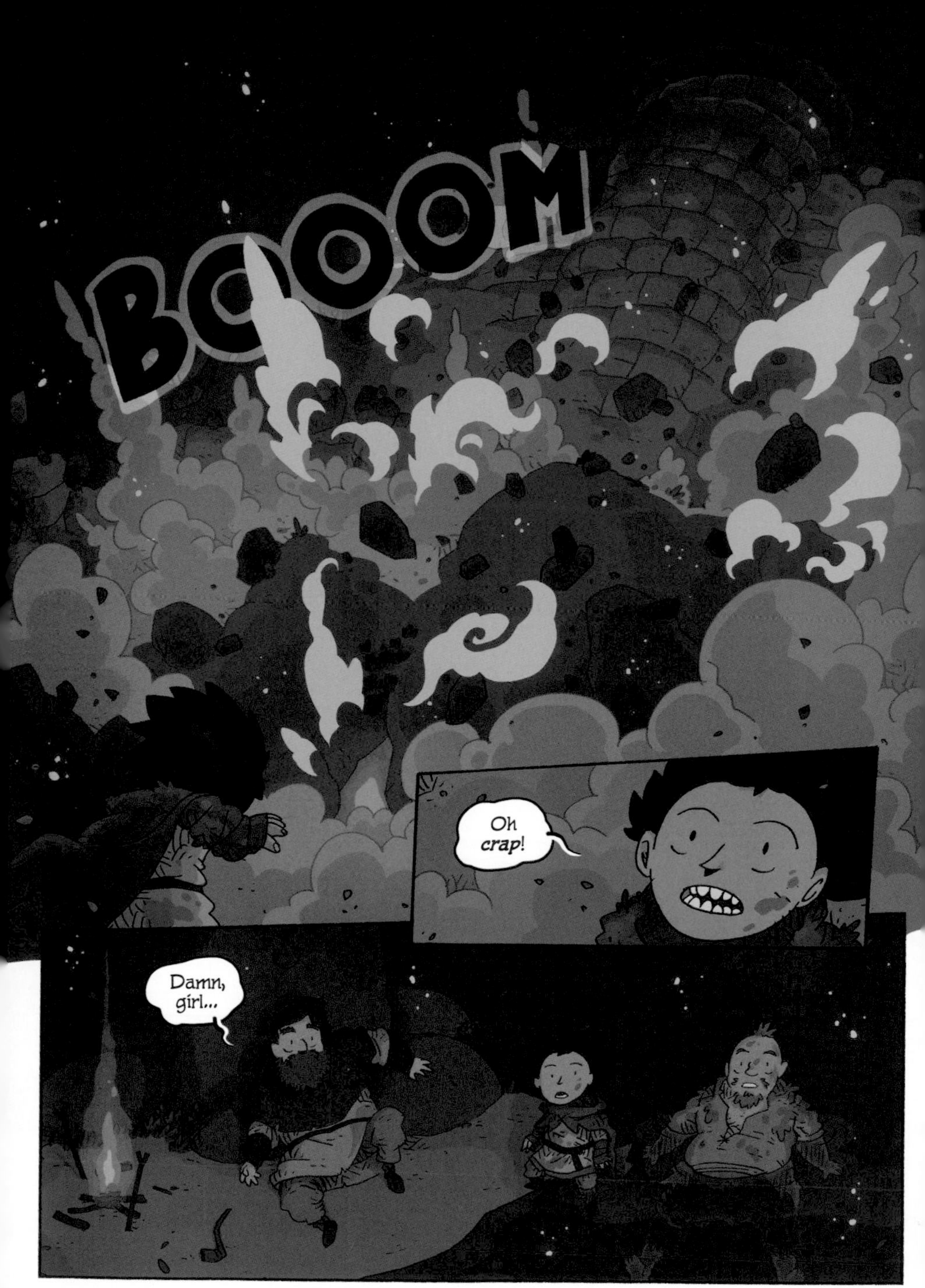
BOOOM
Oh crap!
Damn, girl...

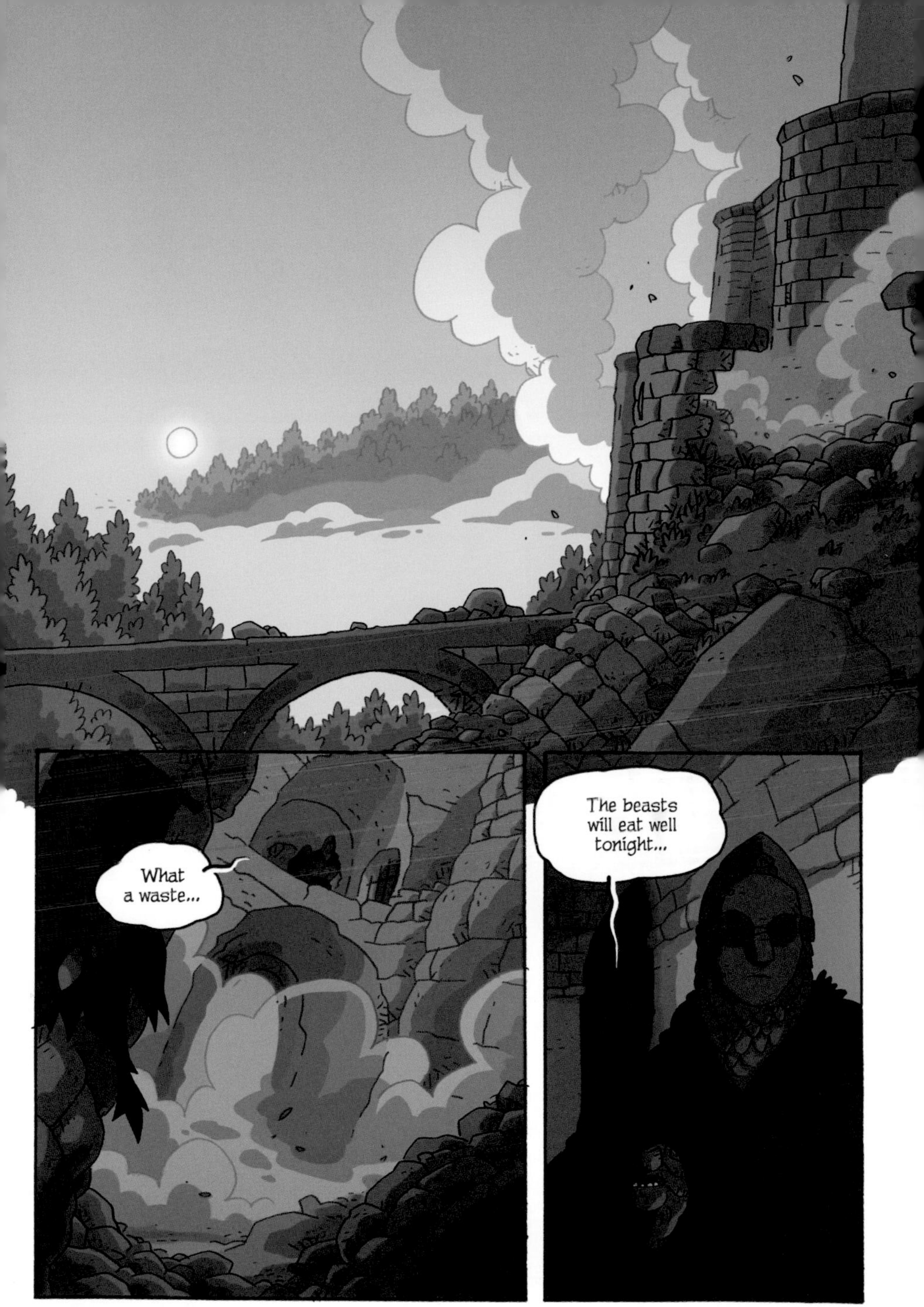
What a waste...
The beasts will eat well tonight...

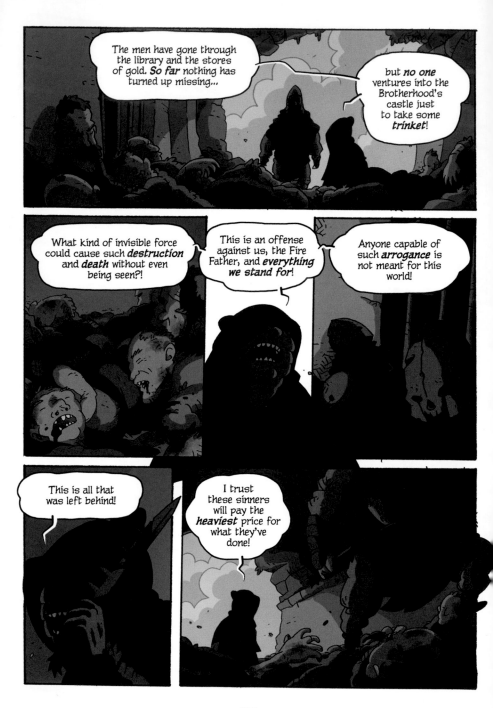

166

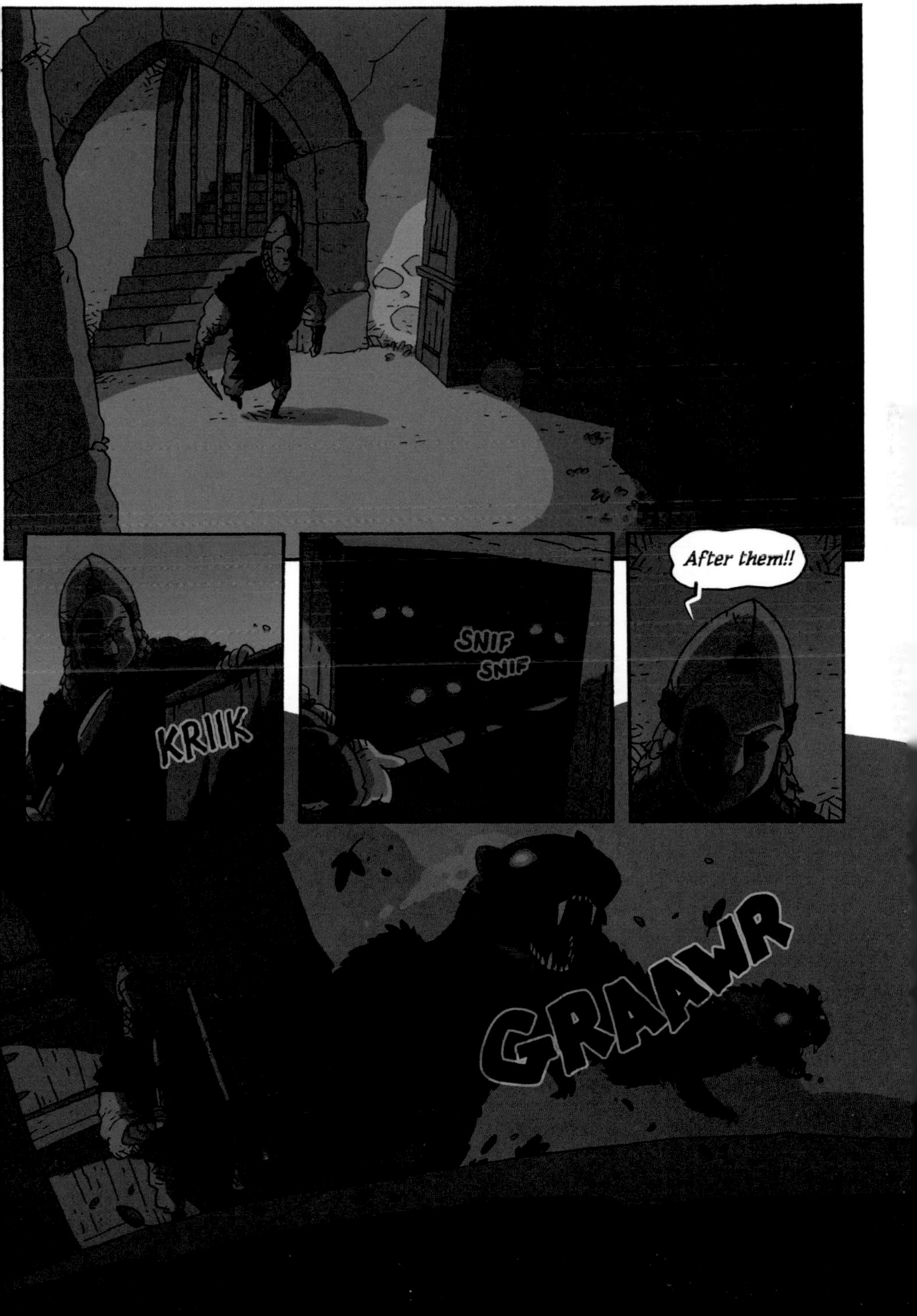
KRIIK
SNIF
SNIF
After them!!
GRAAWR

Each man against the march of days,
The old marching to the grave,
Legends and spells forgotten,
Never chanted or remembered,
The stories lost like dying embers,
Till all belongs to one.

5

The Trail

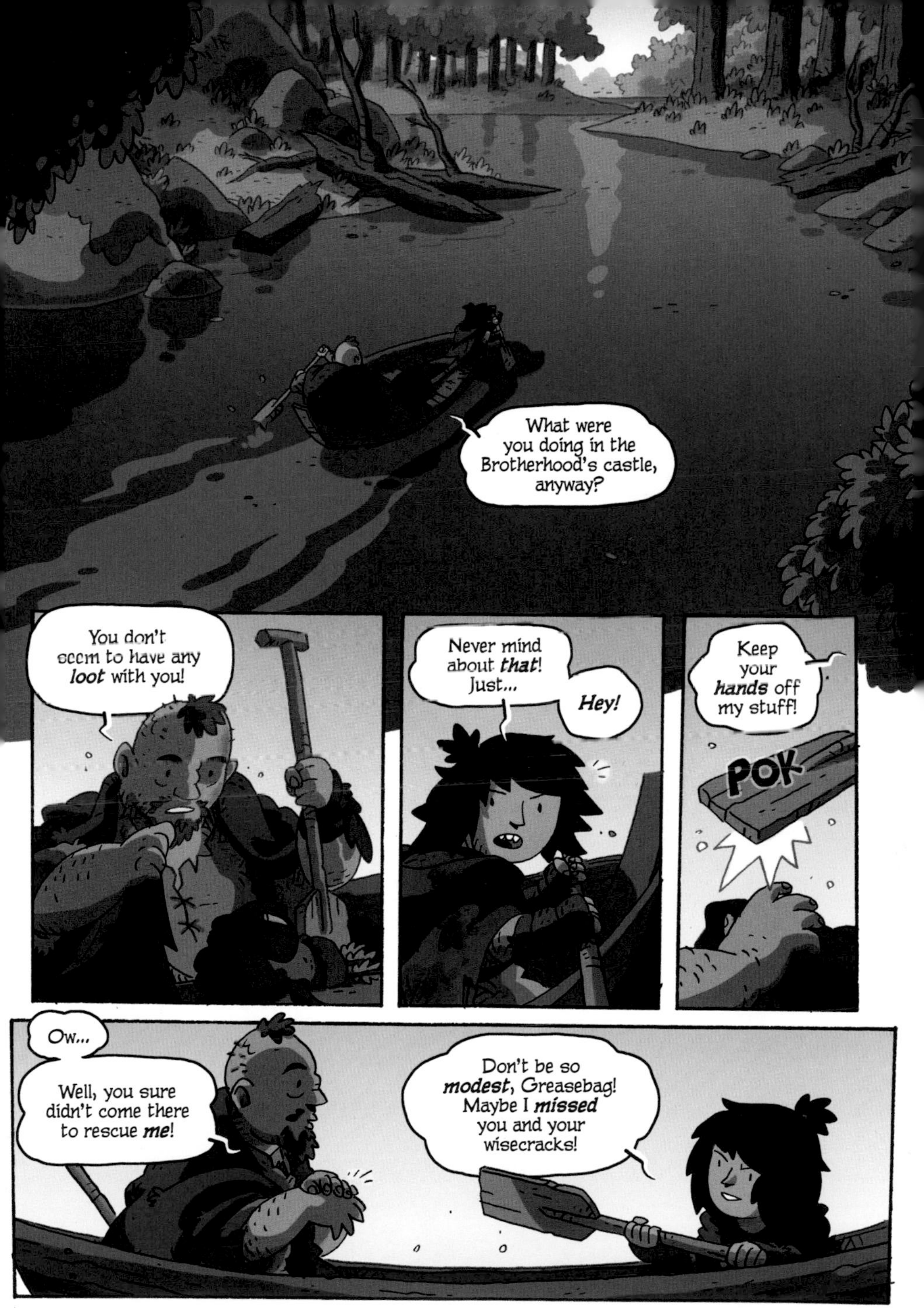
What were you doing in the Brotherhood's castle, anyway?
You don't seem to have any *loot* with you!
Never mind about *that*! Just...
Hey!
Keep your *hands* off my stuff!
POK
Ow...
Well, you sure didn't come there to rescue *me*!
Don't be so *modest*, Greasebag! Maybe I *missed* you and your wisecracks!

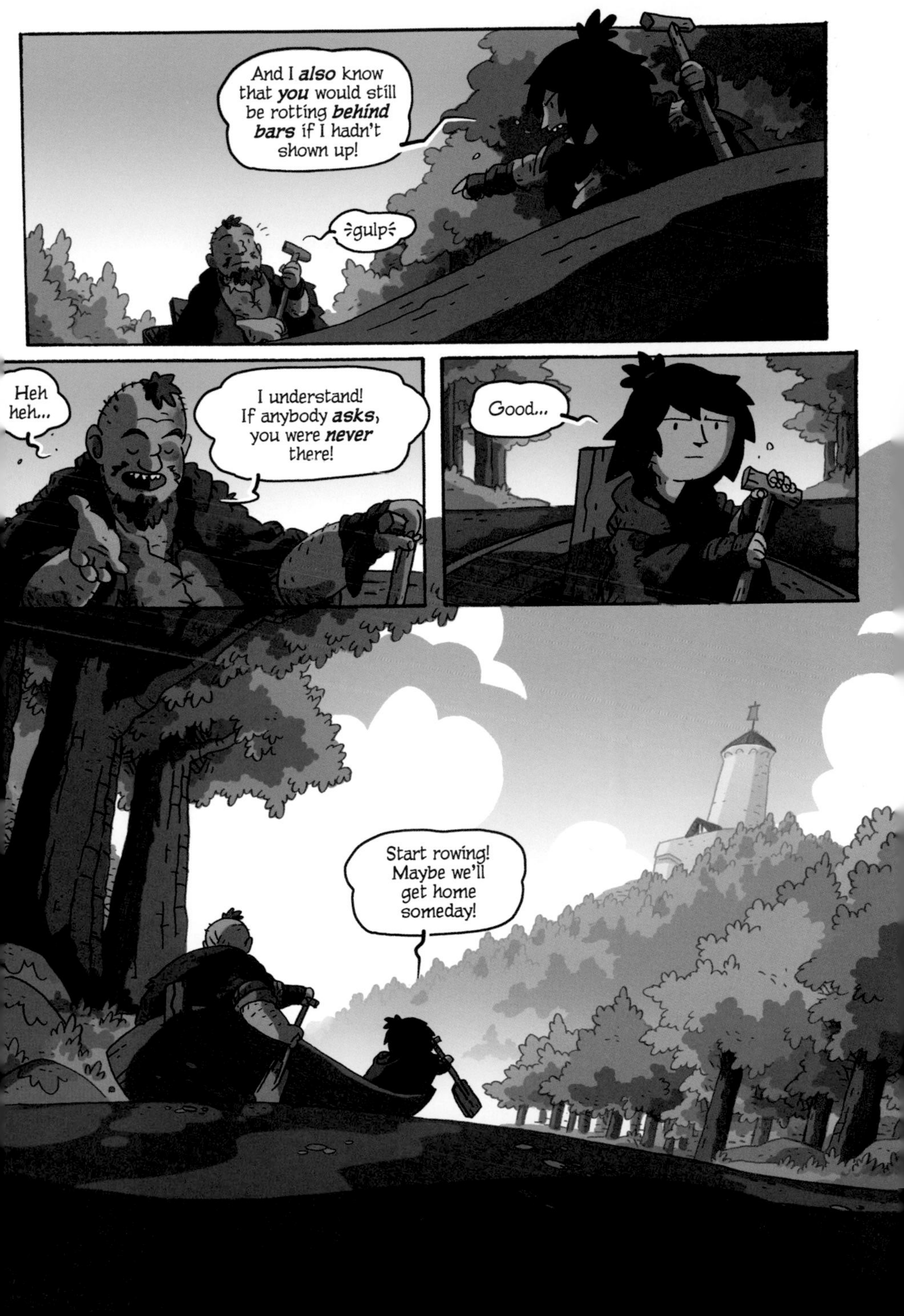
And I **also** know that **you** would still be rotting **behind bars** if I hadn't shown up!
gulp
Heh heh...
I understand! If anybody **asks**, you were **never** there!
Good...
Start rowing! Maybe we'll get home someday!

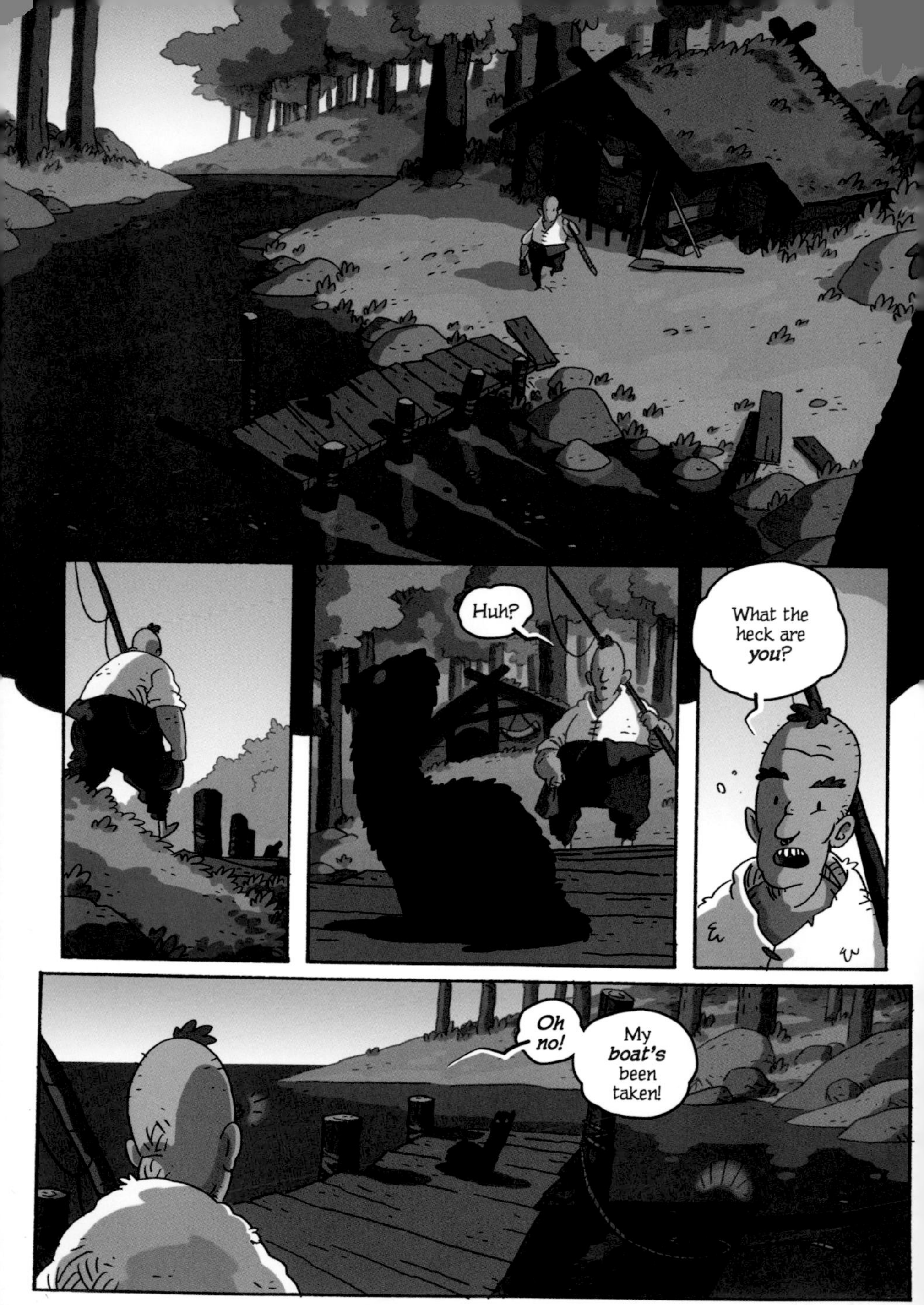
Huh?
What the heck are *you*?
Oh no!
My *boat's* been taken!

175

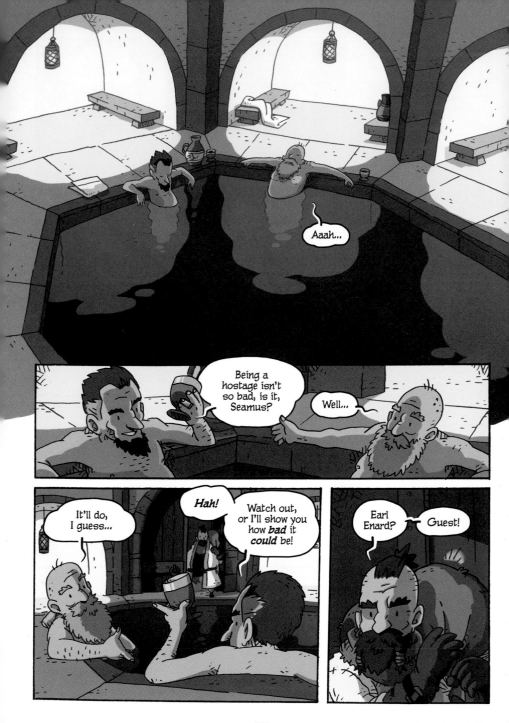

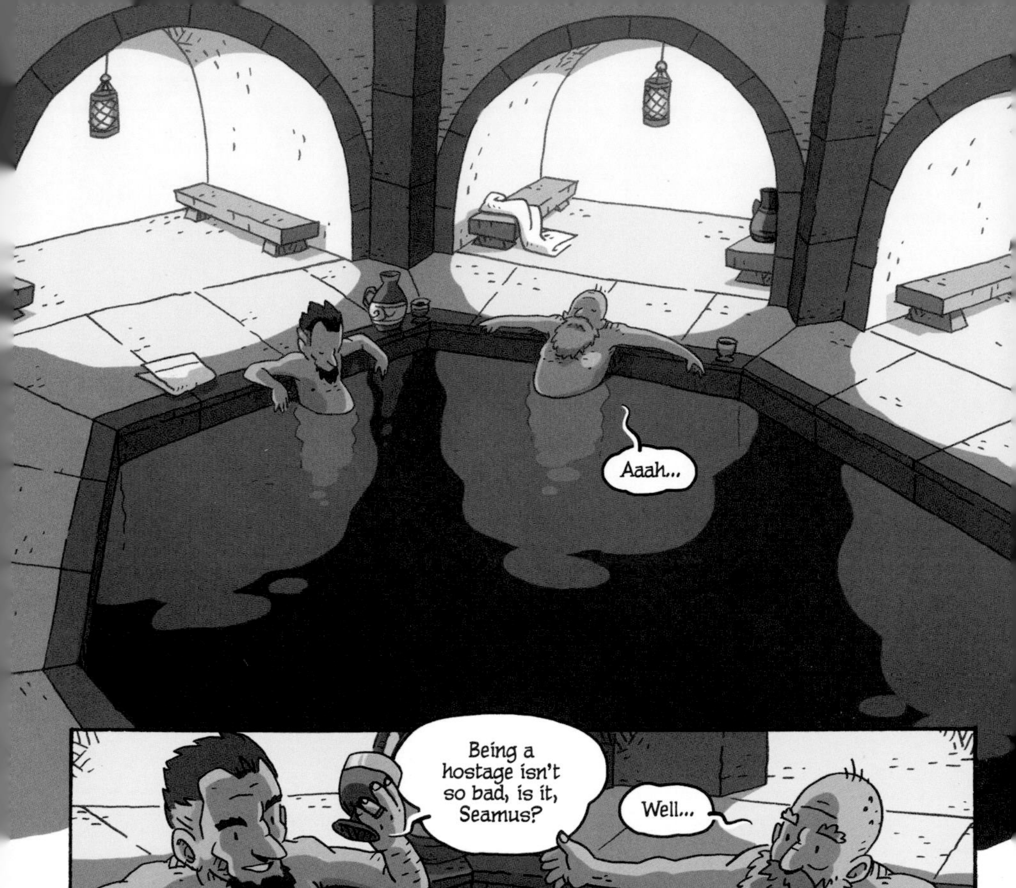
Aaah...
Being a hostage isn't so bad, is it, Seamus?
Well...
It'll do, I guess...
Hah!
Watch out, or I'll show you how ***bad*** it ***could*** be!
Earl Enard?
Guest!

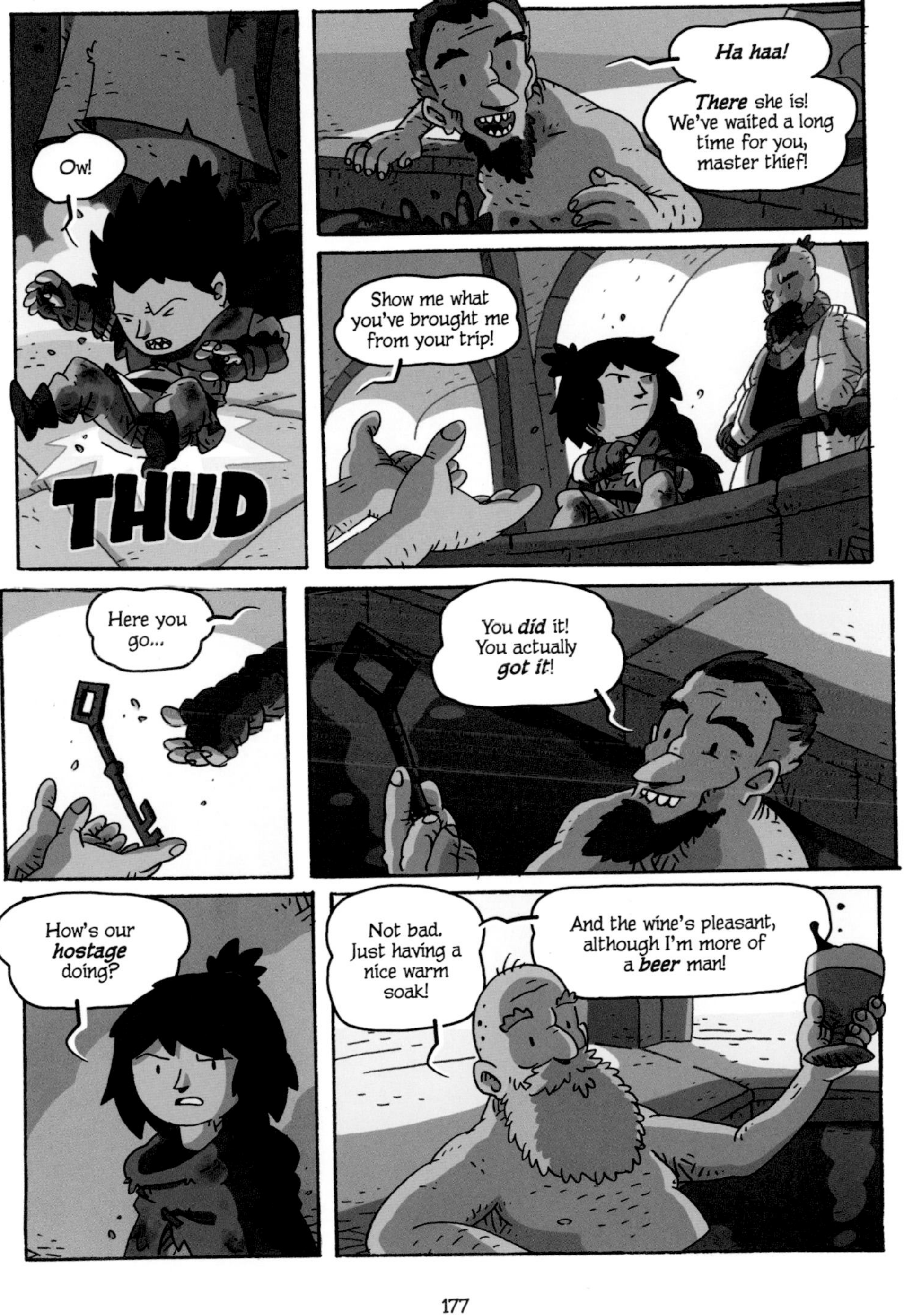
Ow!
THUD
Ha haa!
There she is! We've waited a long time for you, master thief!
Show me what you've brought me from your trip!
Here you go...
You ***did*** it! You actually ***got it***!
How's our ***hostage*** doing?
Not bad. Just having a nice warm soak!
And the wine's pleasant, although I'm more of a ***beer*** man!

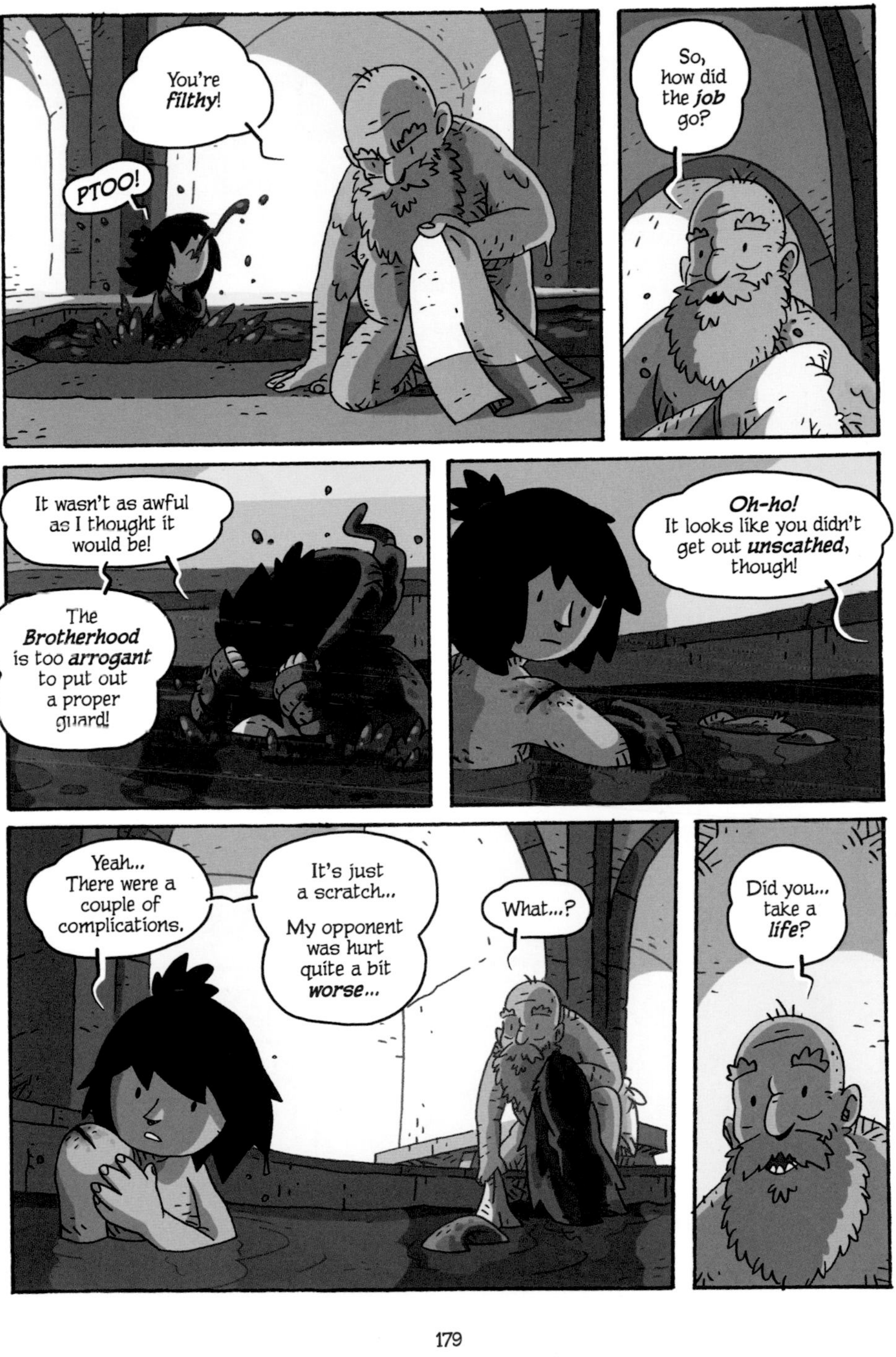

You're *filthy*!
PTOO!
So, how did the *job* go?
It wasn't as awful as I thought it would be!
The *Brotherhood* is too *arrogant* to put out a proper guard!
Oh-ho! It looks like you didn't get out *unscathed*, though!
Yeah... There were a couple of complications.
It's just a scratch...
My opponent was hurt quite a bit *worse*...
What...?
Did you... take a *life*?

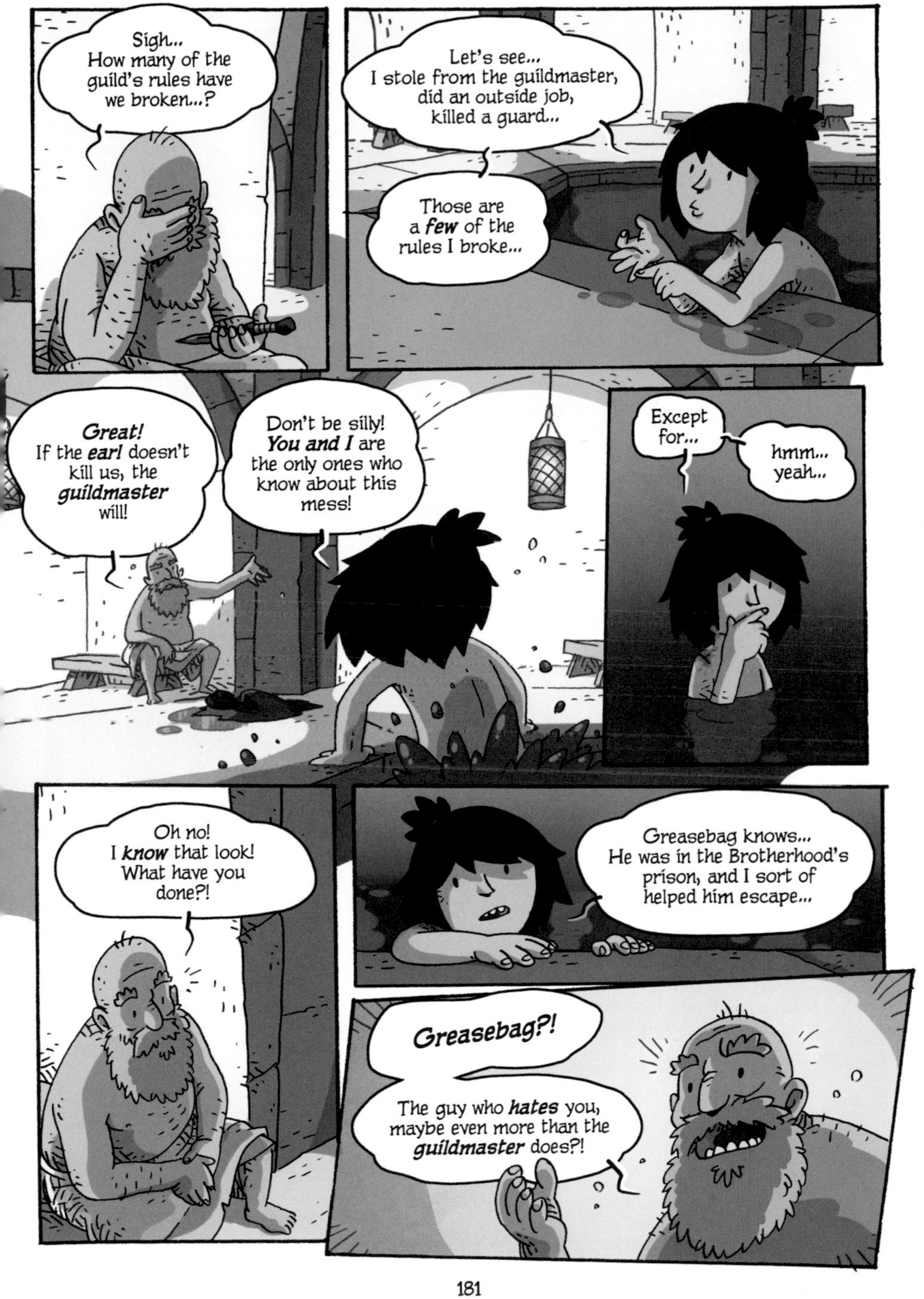
Sigh...
How many of the guild's rules have we broken...?
Let's see...
I stole from the guildmaster, did an outside job, killed a guard...
Those are a *few* of the rules I broke...
Great!
If the *earl* doesn't kill us, the *guildmaster* will!
Don't be silly! *You and I* are the only ones who know about this mess!
Except for...
hmm... yeah...
Oh no!
I *know* that look! What have you done?!
Greasebag knows...
He was in the Brotherhood's prison, and I sort of helped him escape...
Greasebag?!
The guy who *hates* you, maybe even more than the *guildmaster* does?!

183

188

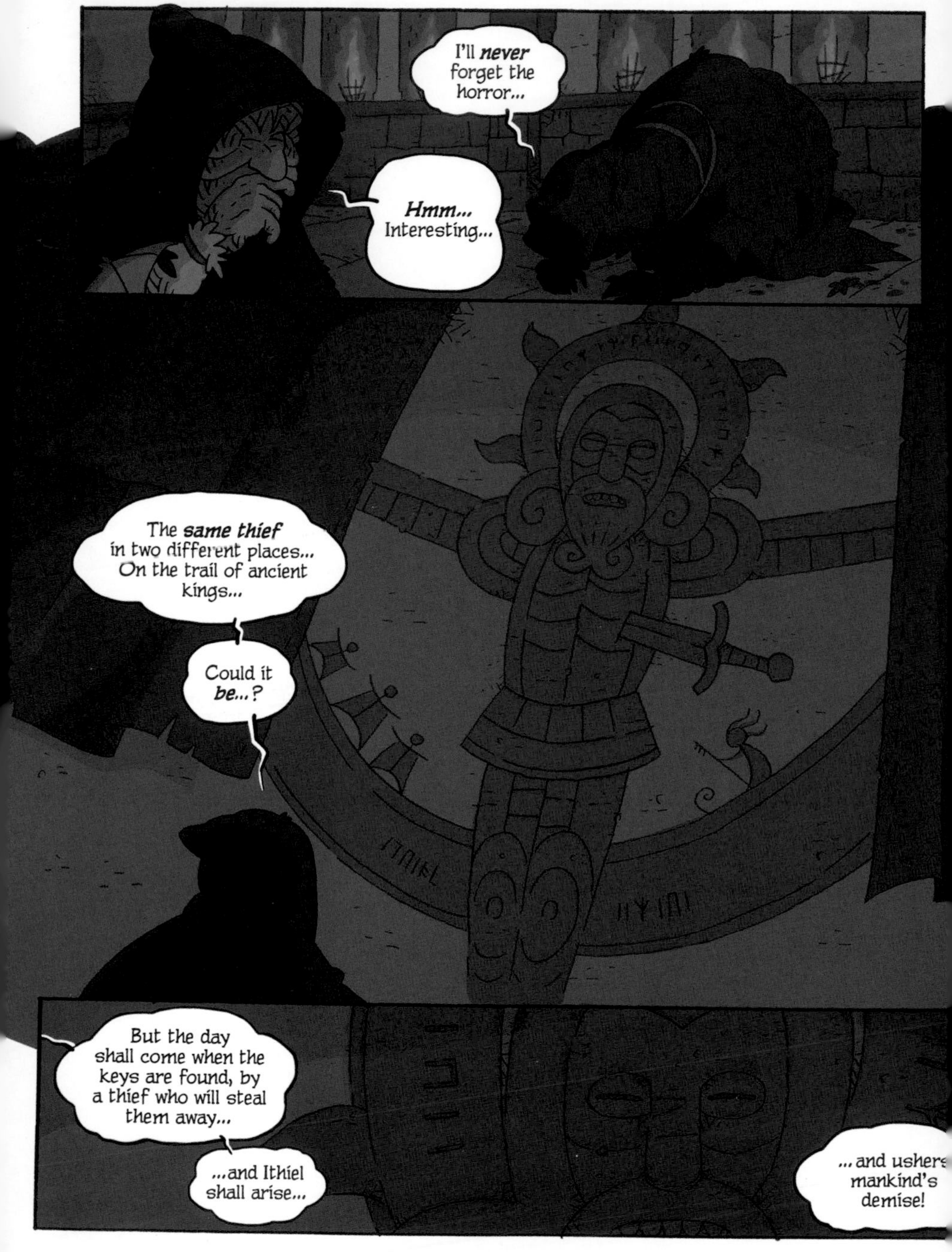
I'll *never* forget the horror...
Hmm... Interesting...
The *same thief* in two different places... On the trail of ancient kings...
Could it *be...?*
But the day shall come when the keys are found, by a thief who will steal them away...
...and Ithiel shall arise...
...and ushers mankind's demise!

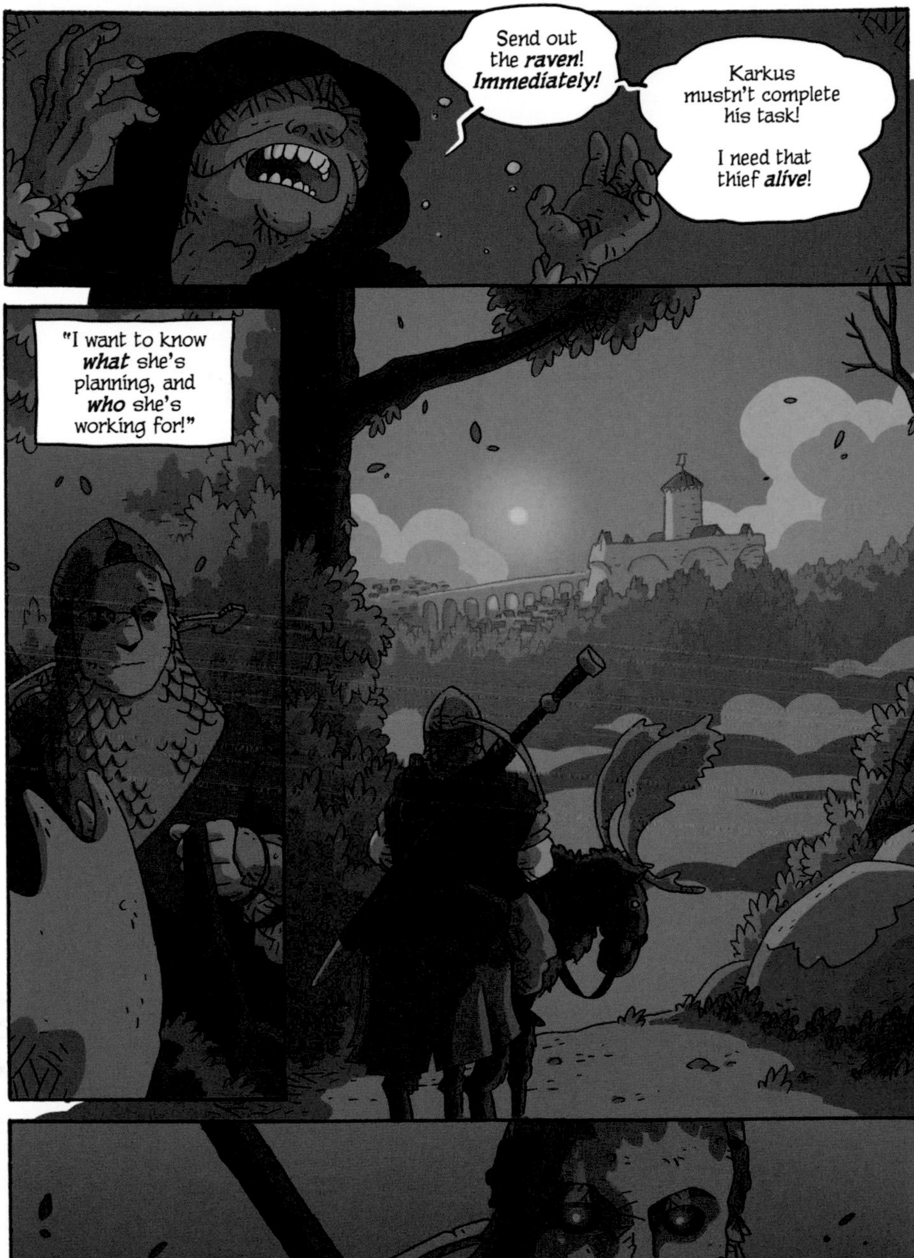

Send out the *raven*! *Immediately!*
Karkus mustn't complete his task!
I need that thief *alive*!
"I want to know *what* she's planning, and *who* she's working for!"

No brightness without darkness,
No darkness without light,
But what lies between them,
Is clamoring and clattering,
Rattling and battling in the night.

The Dead

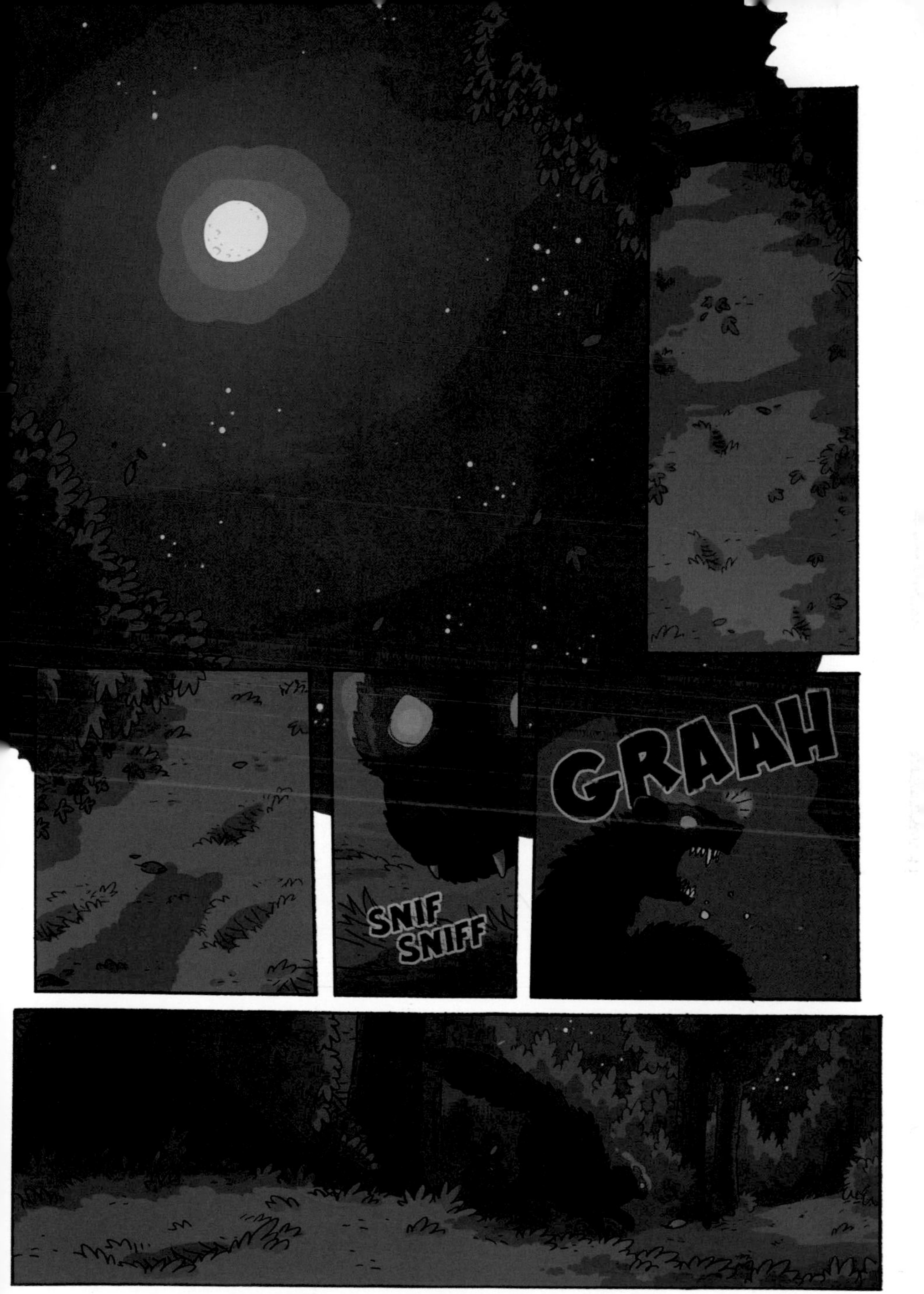
SNIF
SNIFF
GRAAH

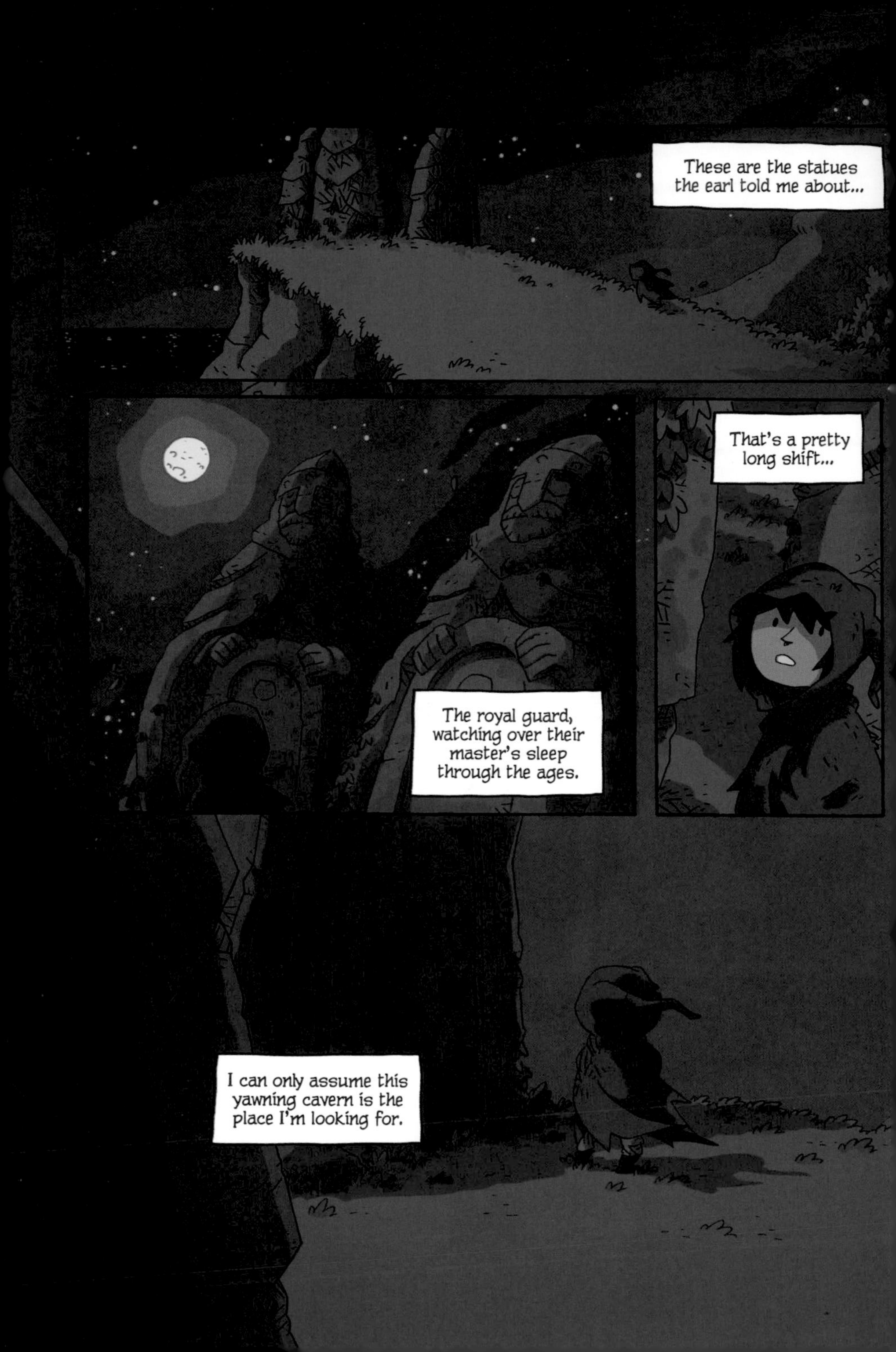
These are the statues the earl told me about...
The royal guard, watching over their master's sleep through the ages.
That's a pretty long shift...
I can only assume this yawning cavern is the place I'm looking for.

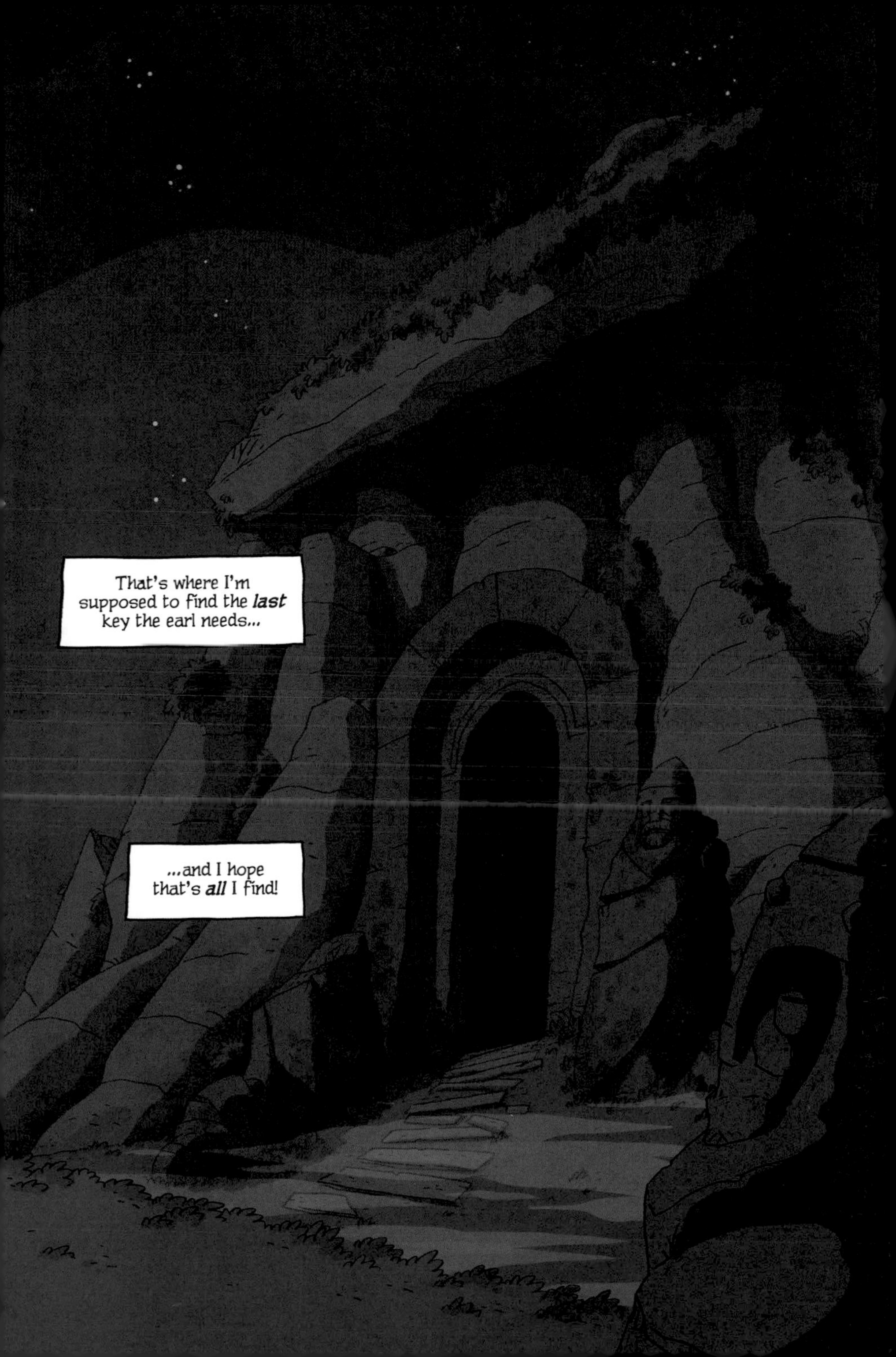
That's where I'm supposed to find the *last* key the earl needs...
...and I hope that's *all* I find!

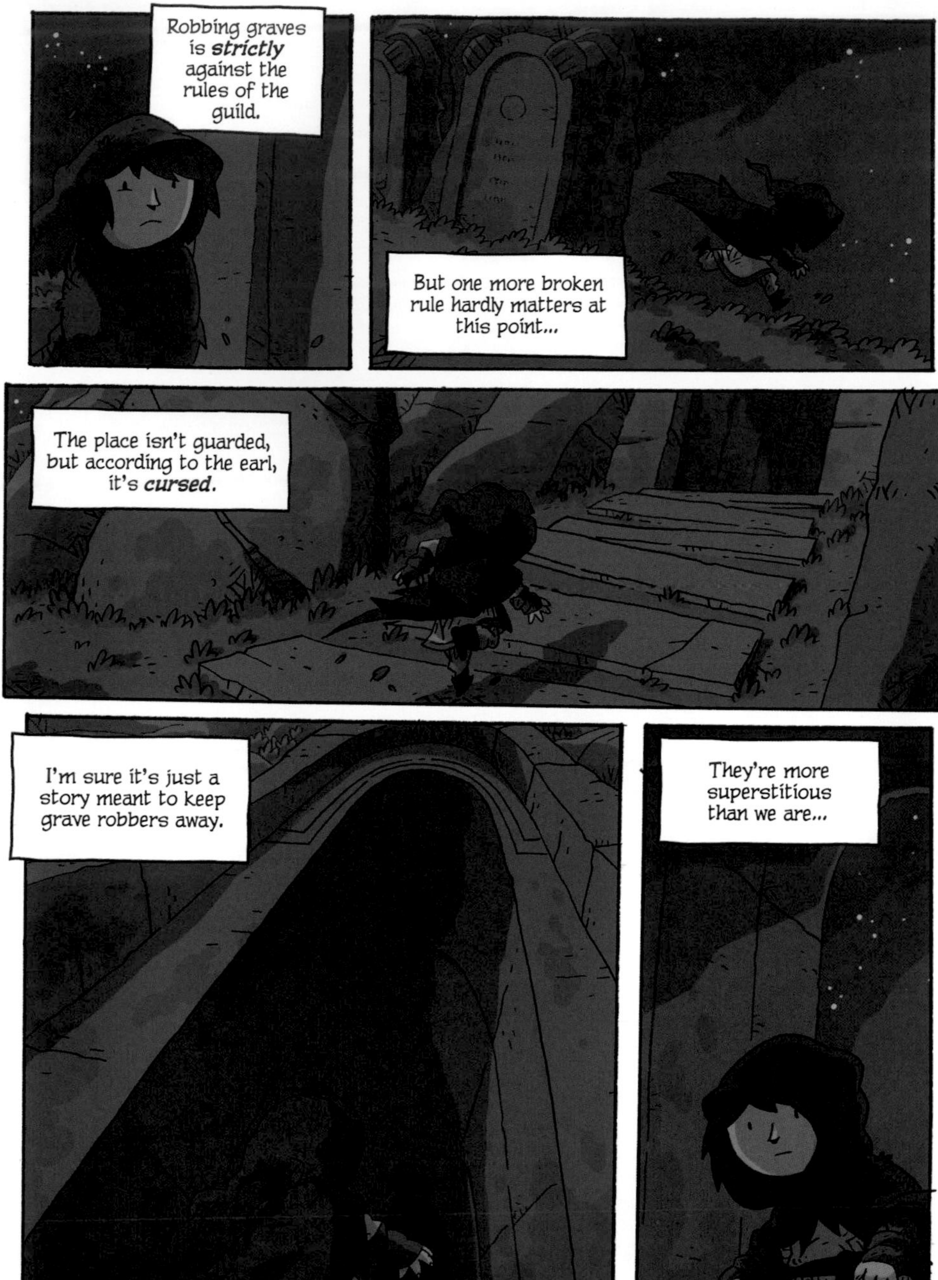
Robbing graves is **strictly** against the rules of the guild.
But one more broken rule hardly matters at this point...
The place isn't guarded, but according to the earl, it's **cursed**.
I'm sure it's just a story meant to keep grave robbers away.
They're more superstitious than we are...

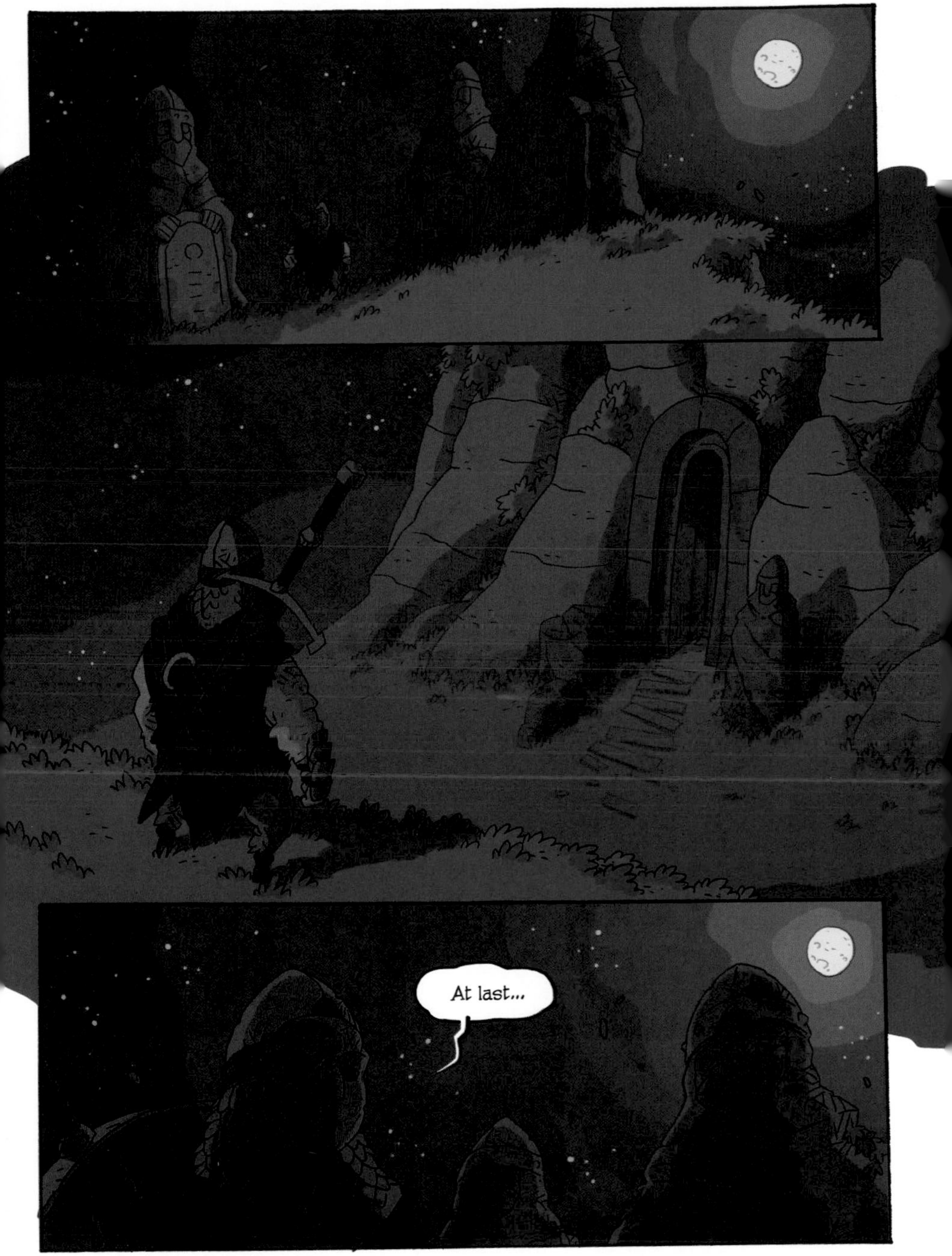
At last...

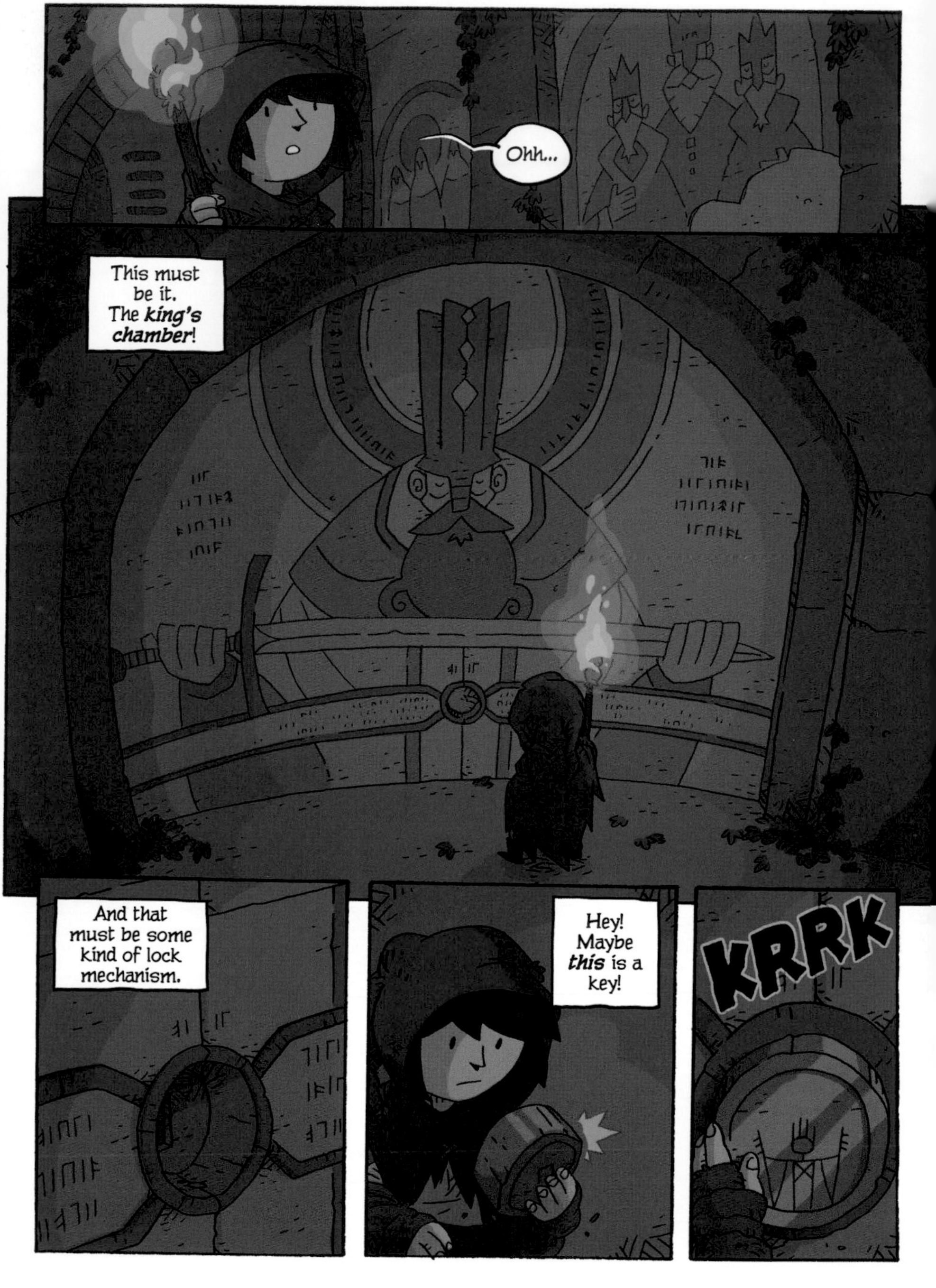
Ohh...
This must be it. The *king's chamber*!
And that must be some kind of lock mechanism.
Hey! Maybe *this* is a key!
KRRK

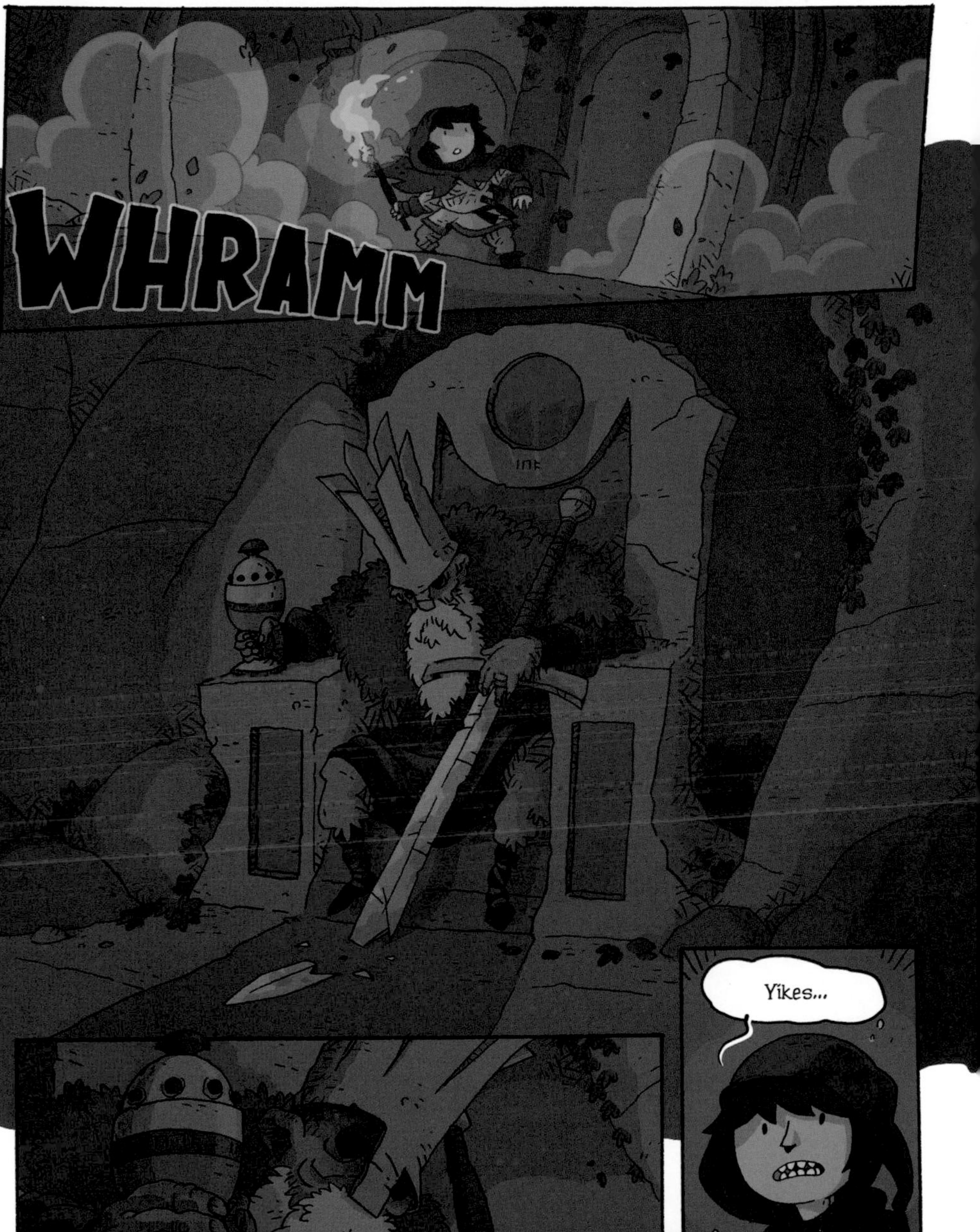
WHRAMM
Yikes...

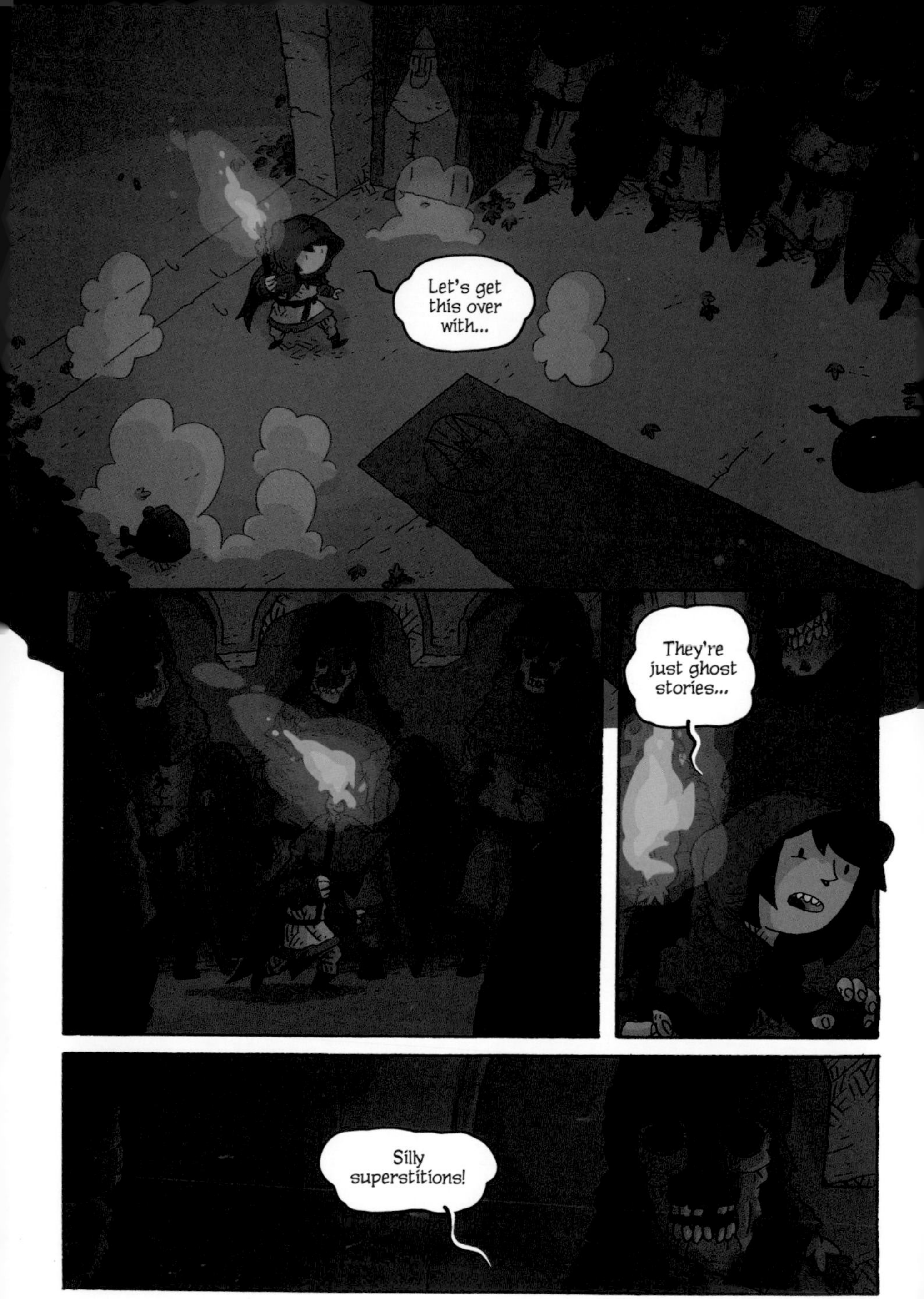
Let's get this over with...
They're just ghost stories...
Silly superstitions!

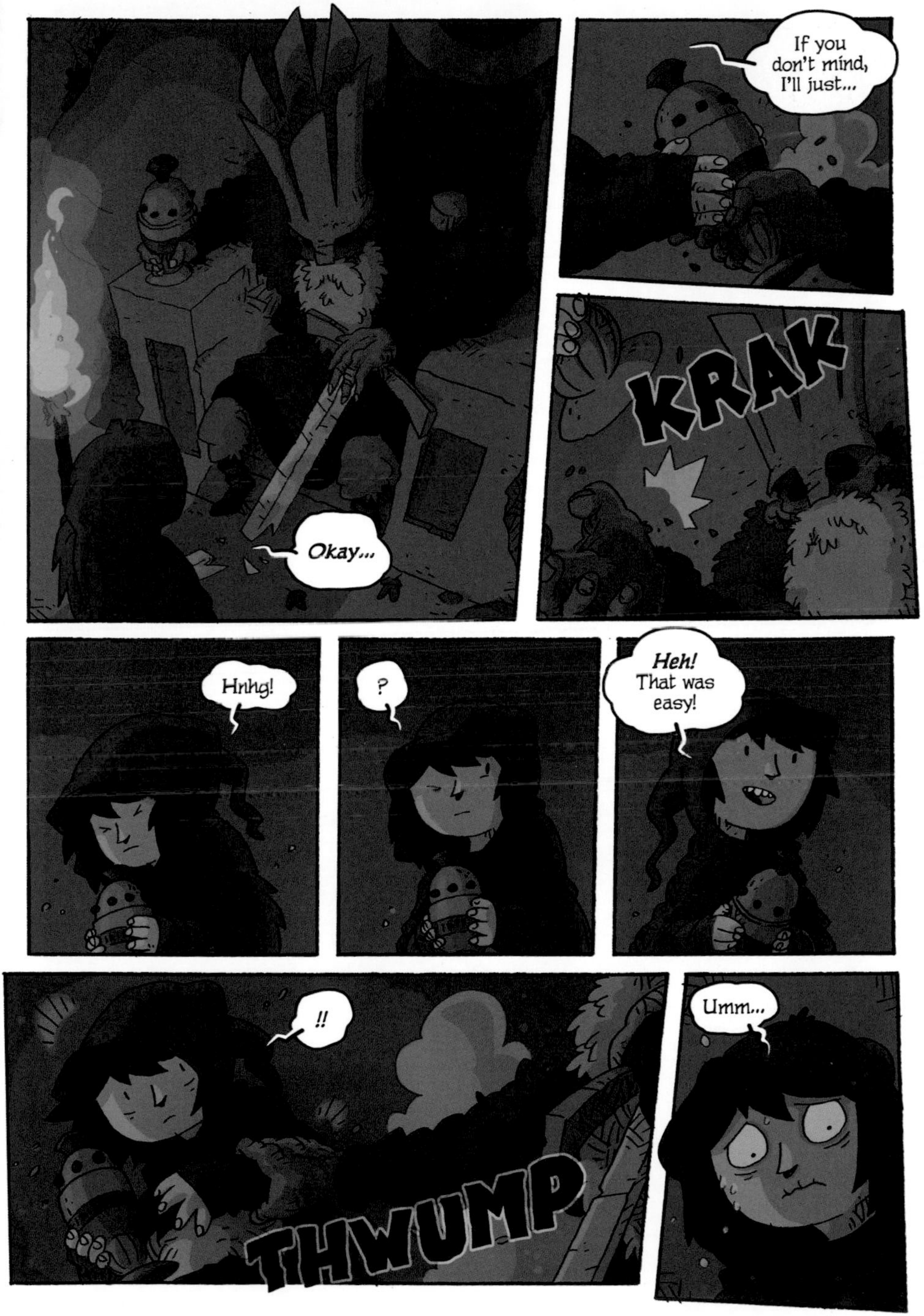
Okay...
If you don't mind, I'll just...
KRAK
Hnhg!
?
Heh! That was easy!
!!
THWUMP
Umm...

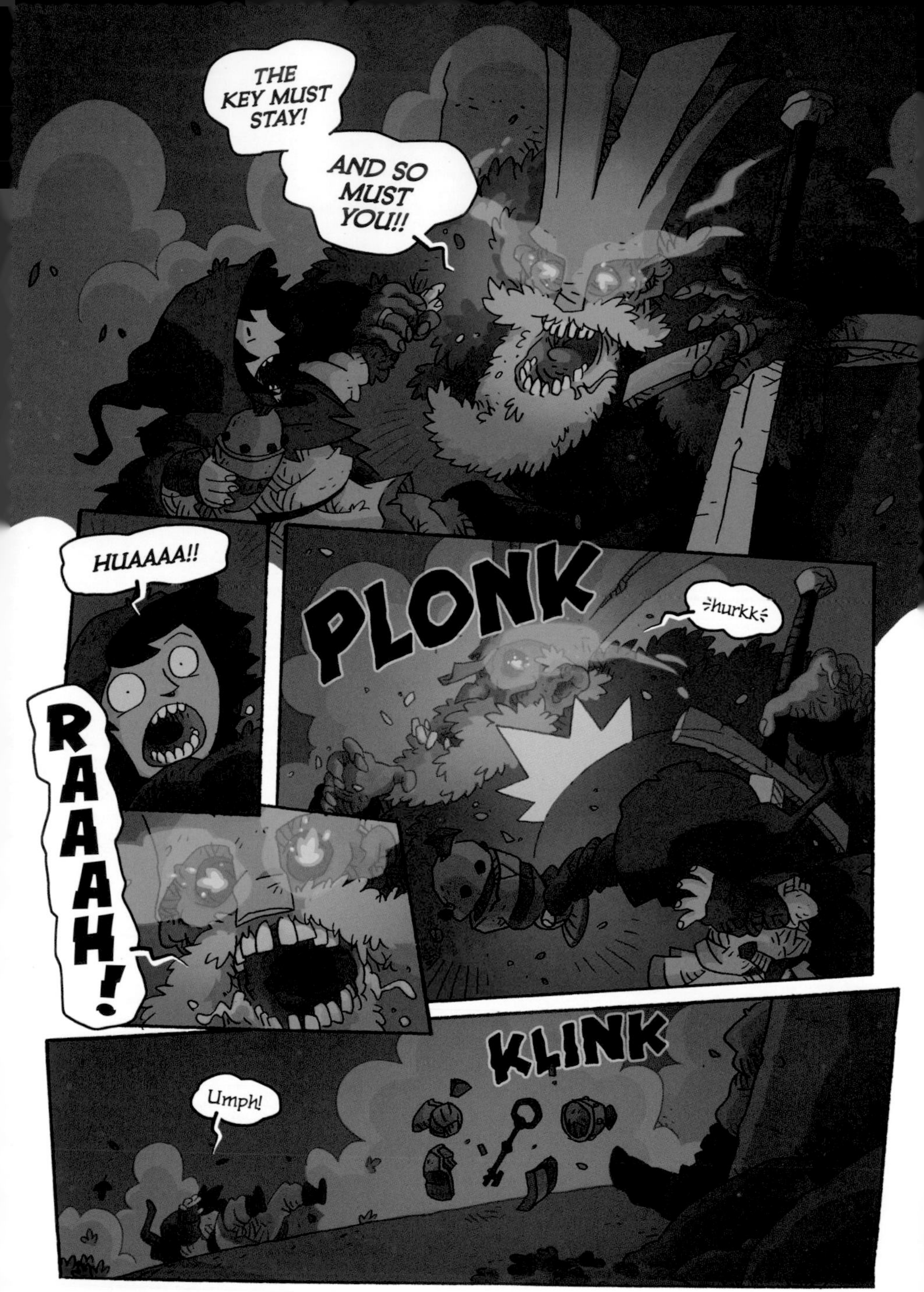
THE KEY MUST STAY!
AND SO MUST YOU!!
HUAAAA!!
RAAAAH!
PLONK
hurkk
KLINK
Umph!

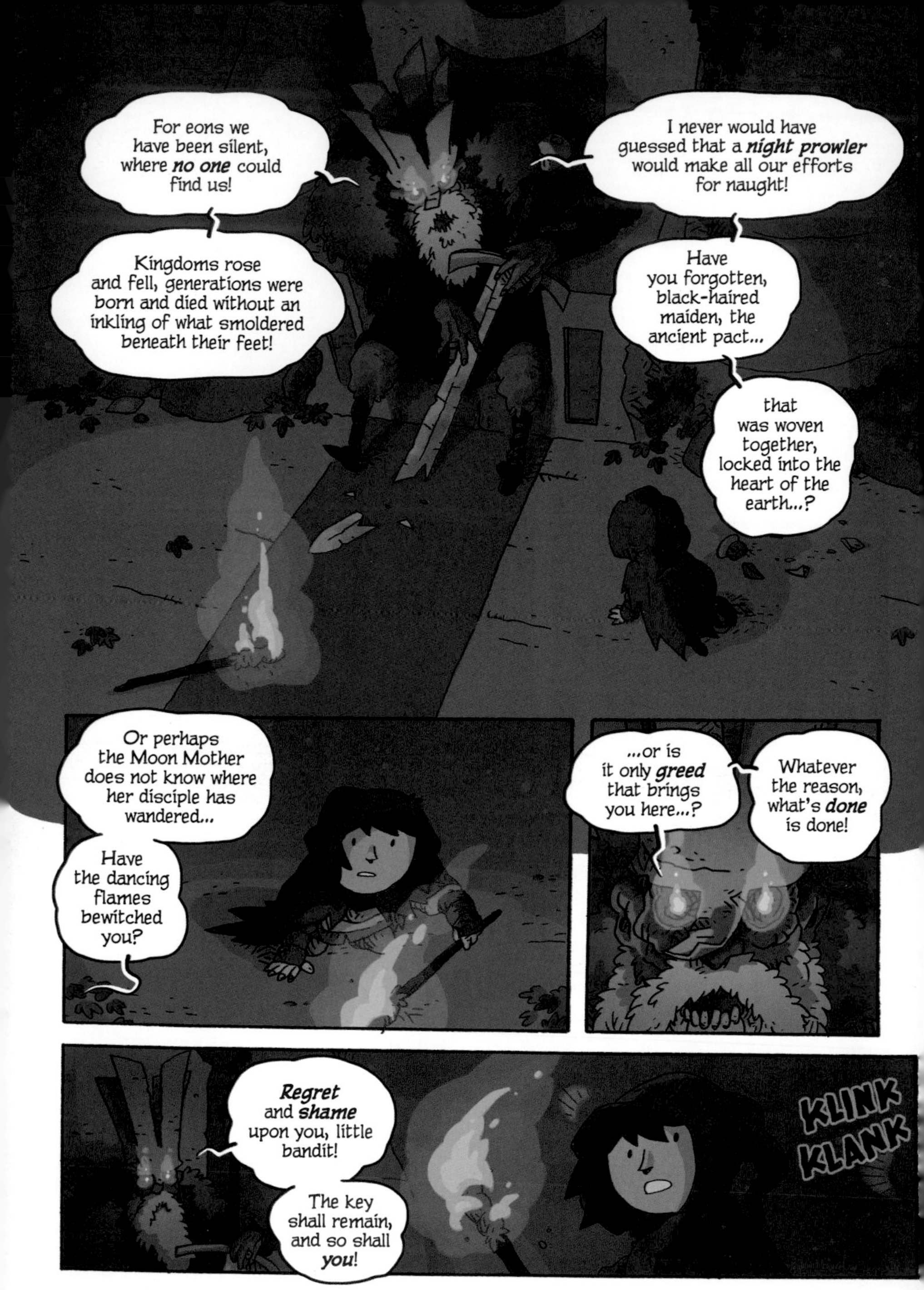
For eons we have been silent, where ***no one*** could find us!
Kingdoms rose and fell, generations were born and died without an inkling of what smoldered beneath their feet!
I never would have guessed that a ***night prowler*** would make all our efforts for naught!
Have you forgotten, black-haired maiden, the ancient pact...
that was woven together, locked into the heart of the earth...?
Or perhaps the Moon Mother does not know where her disciple has wandered...
Have the dancing flames bewitched you?
...or is it only ***greed*** that brings you here...?
Whatever the reason, what's ***done*** is done!
Regret and ***shame*** upon you, little bandit!
The key shall remain, and so shall ***you***!
KLINK KLANK

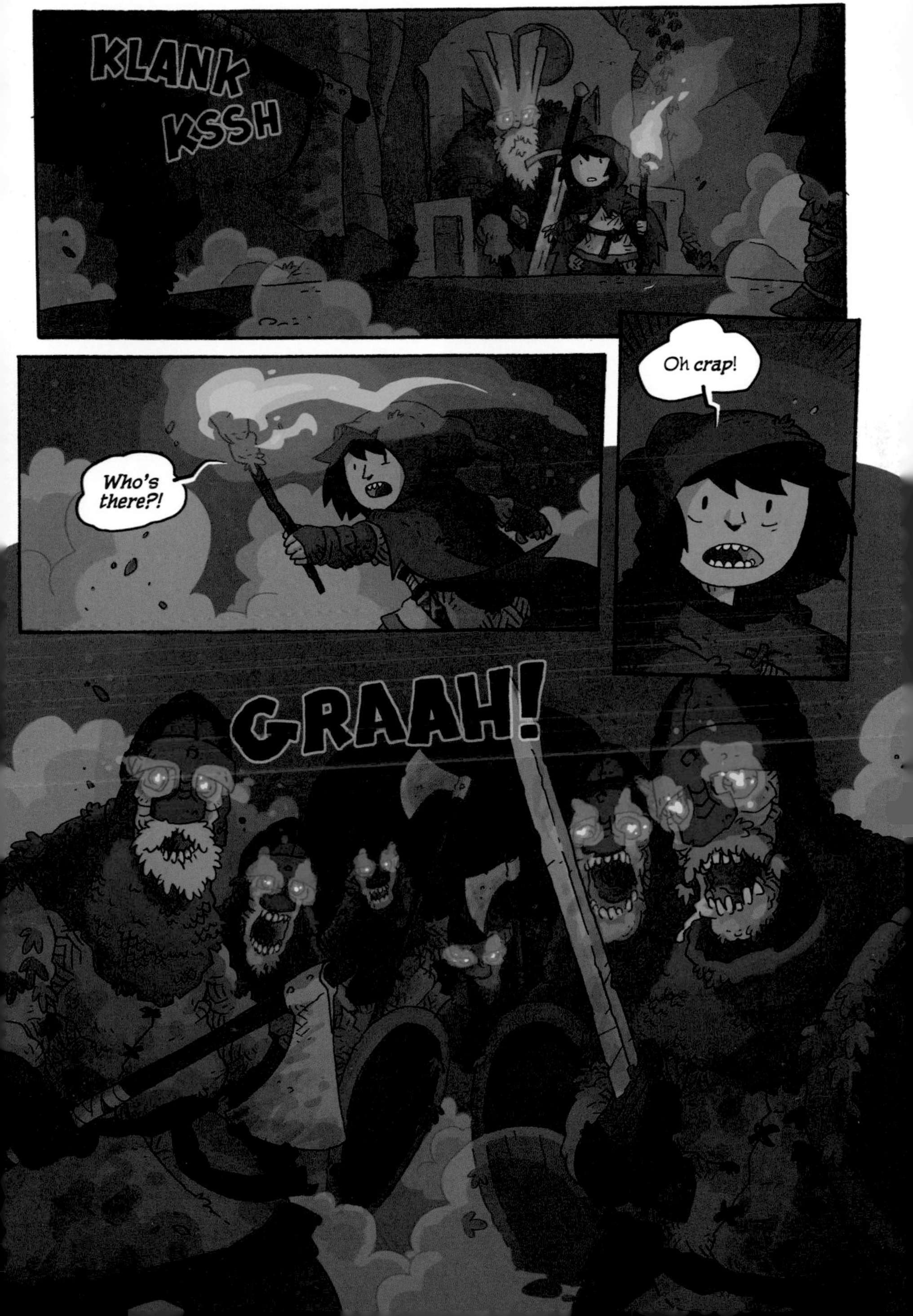
KLANK
KSSH
Who's there?!
Oh crap!
GRAAH!

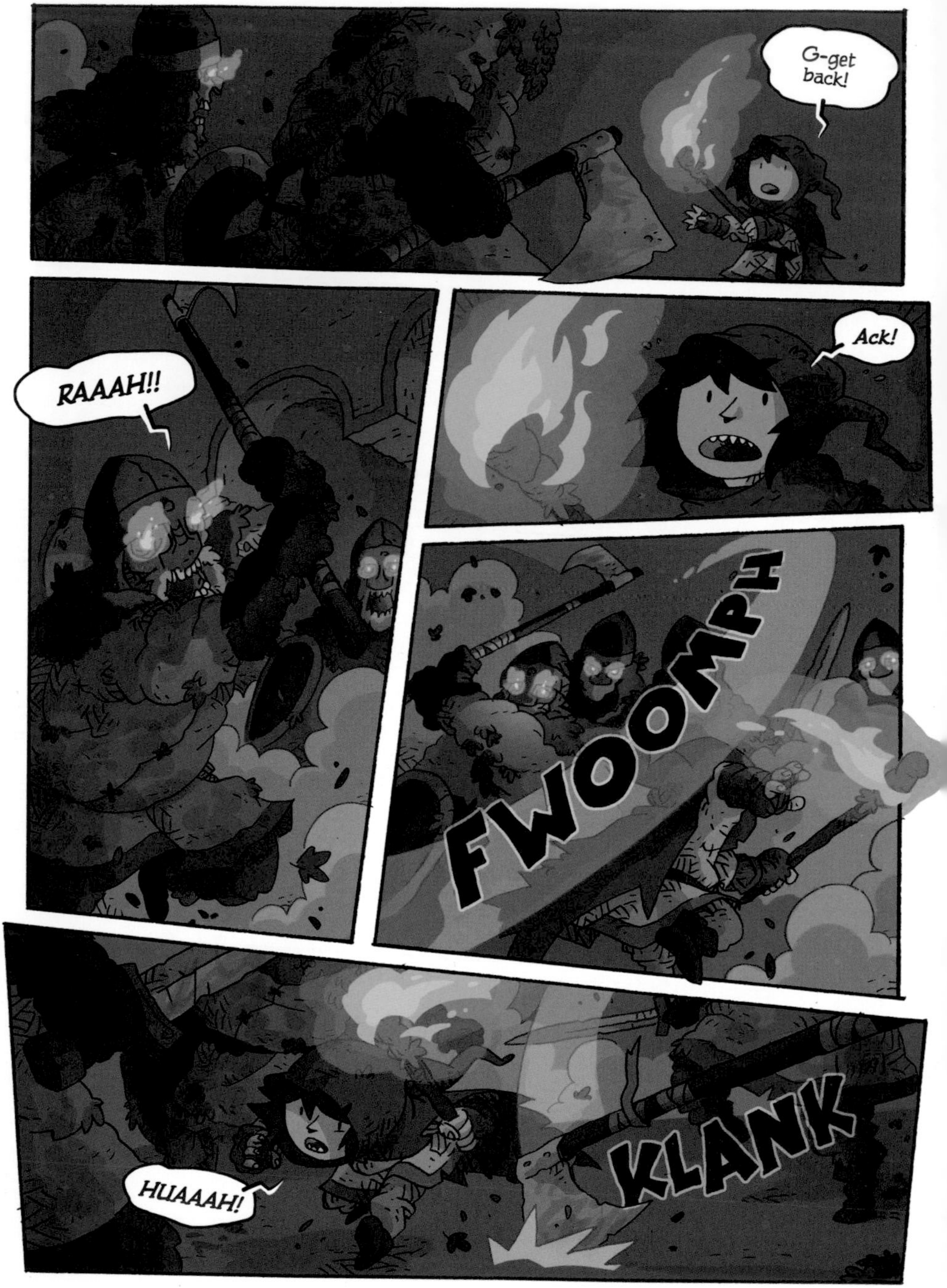
G-get back!
RAAAH!!
Ack!
FWOOMPH
HUAAAH!
KLANK

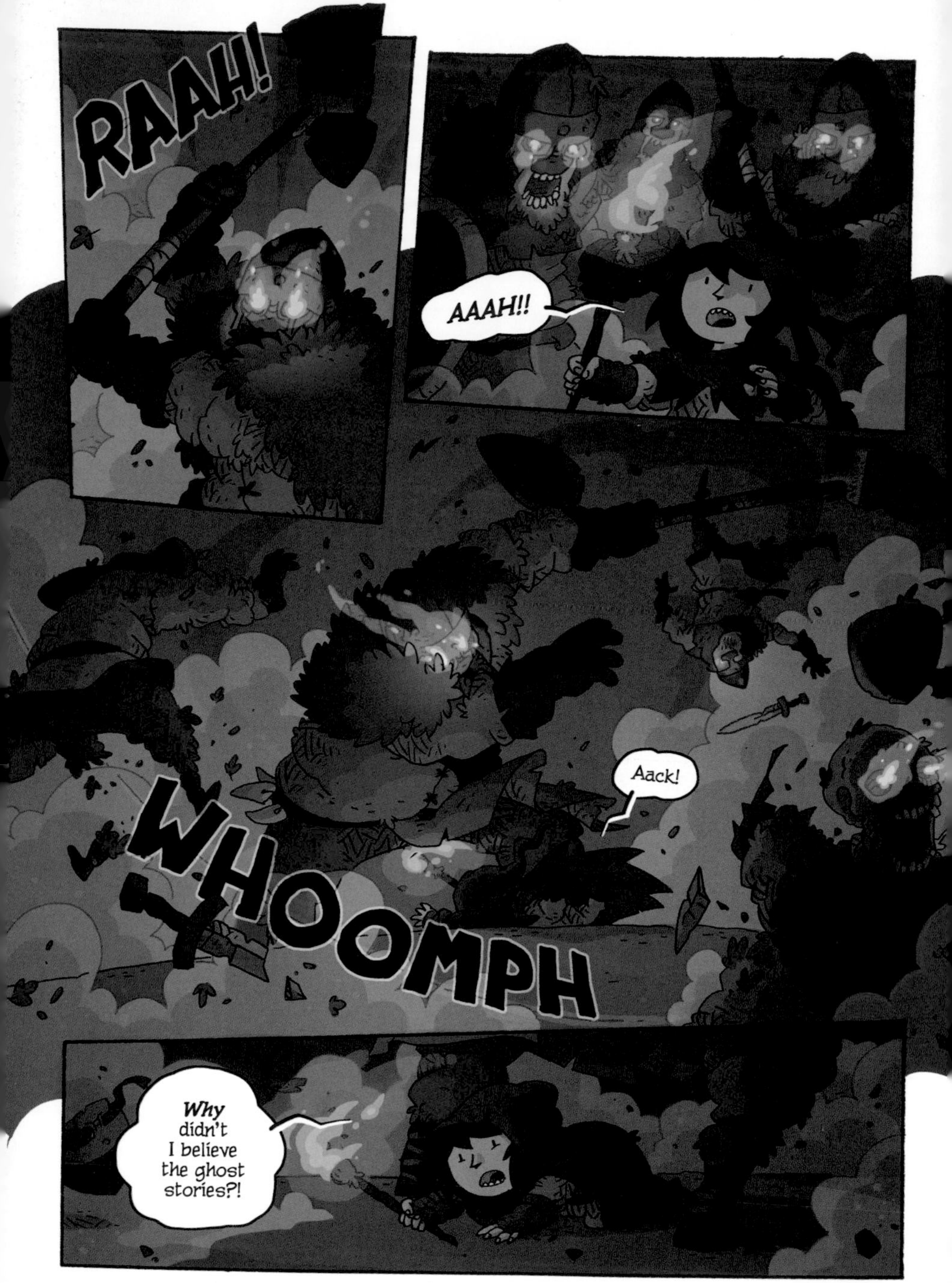
RAAAH!
AAAH!!
WHOOOMPH
Aack!
Why didn't I believe the ghost stories?!

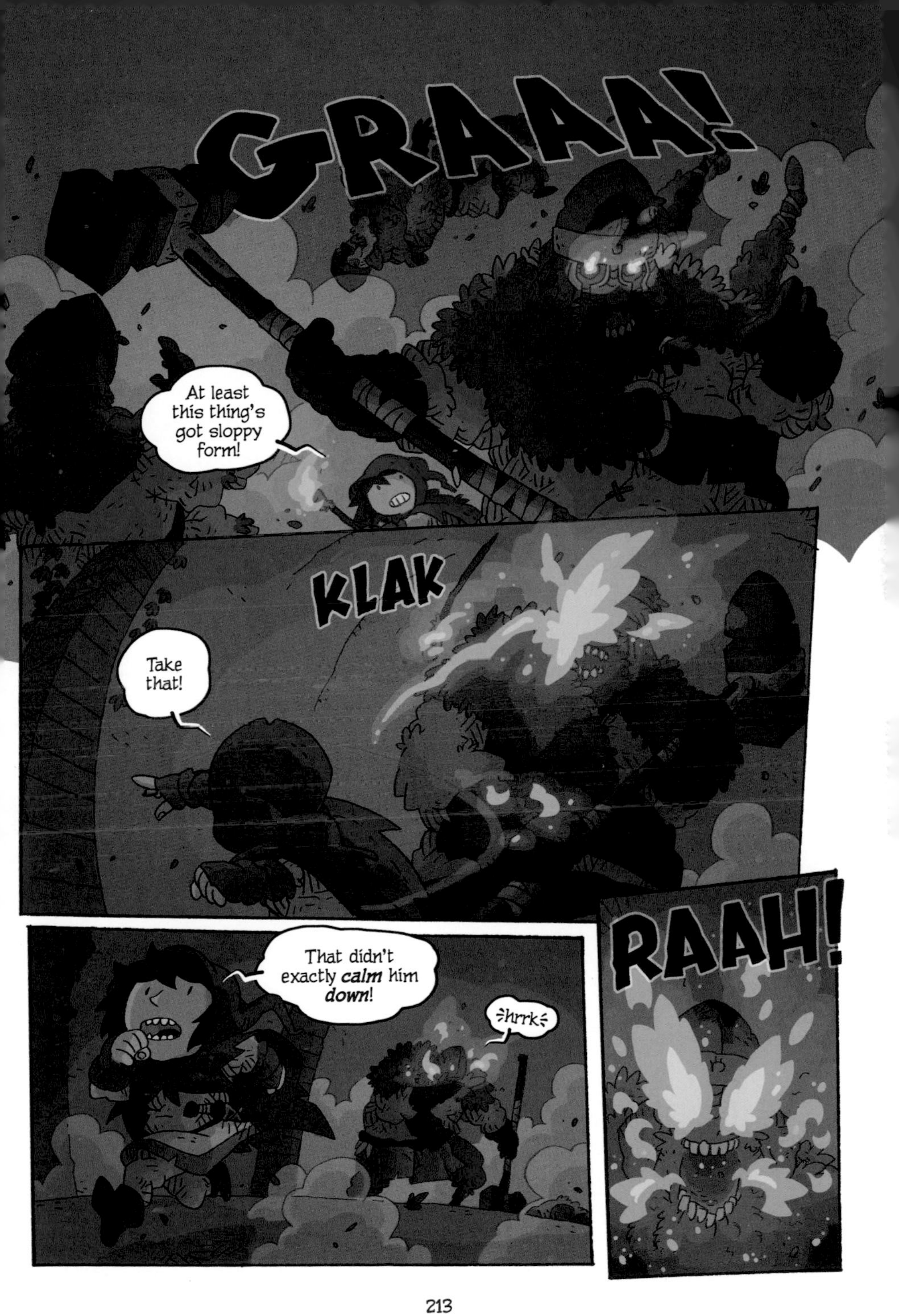
GRAAA!
At least this thing's got sloppy form!
KLAK
Take that!
That didn't exactly *calm* him *down*!
hrrk
RAAH!

215

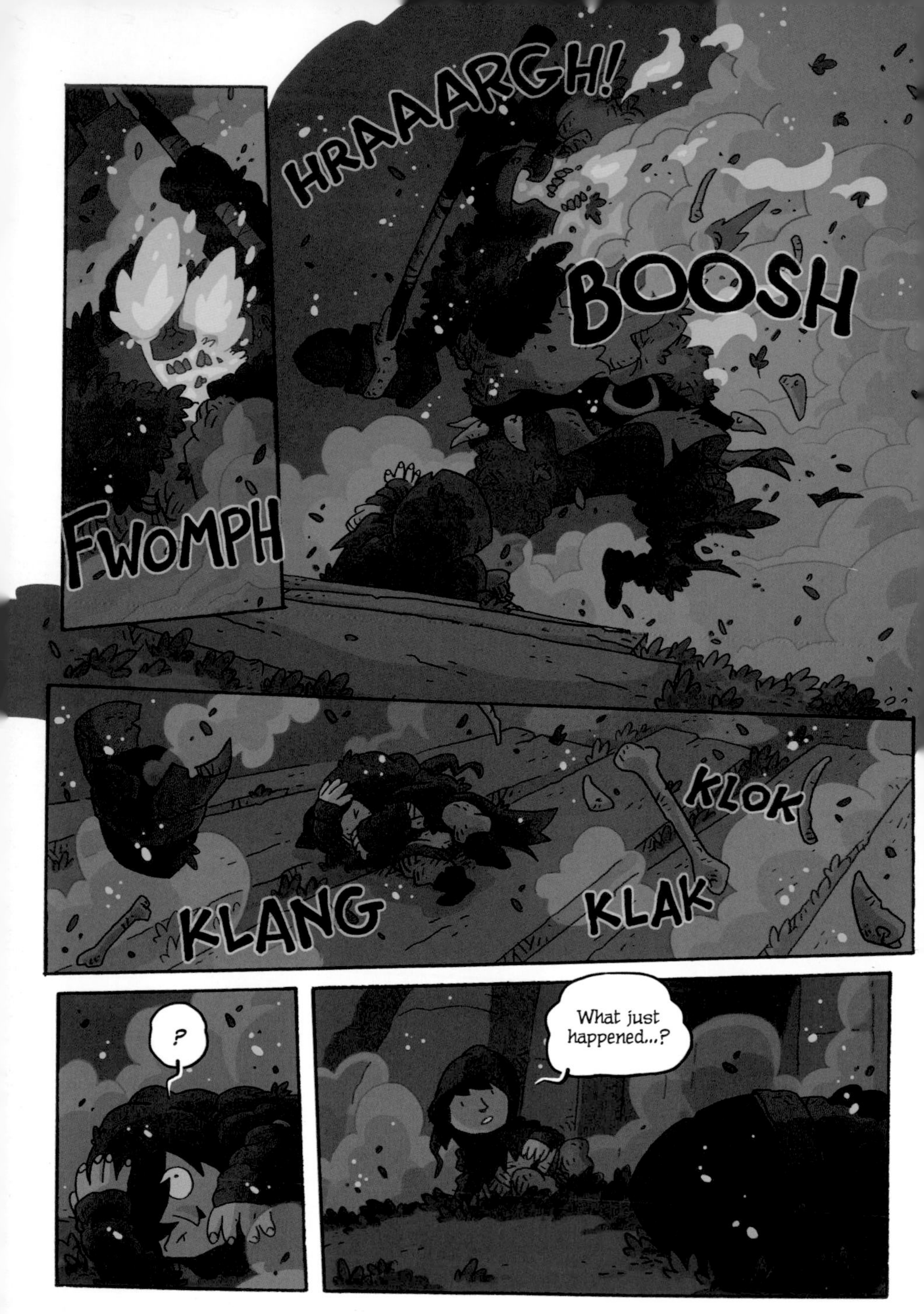
HRAAARGH!
FWOMPH
BOOSH
KLOK
KLANG
KLAK
?
What just happened...?

218

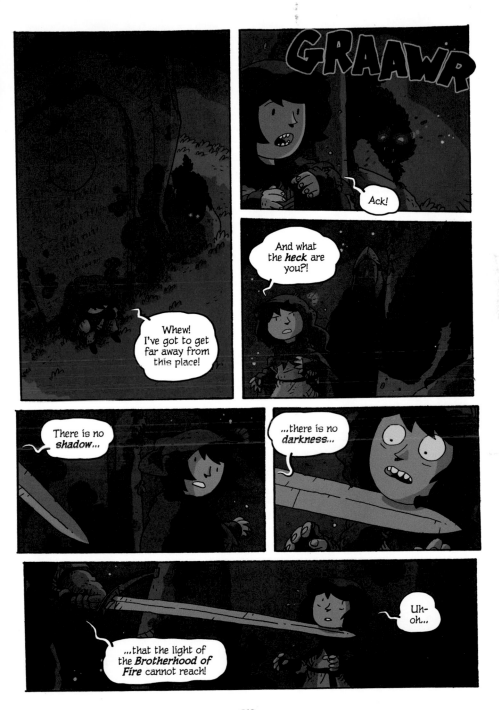

219

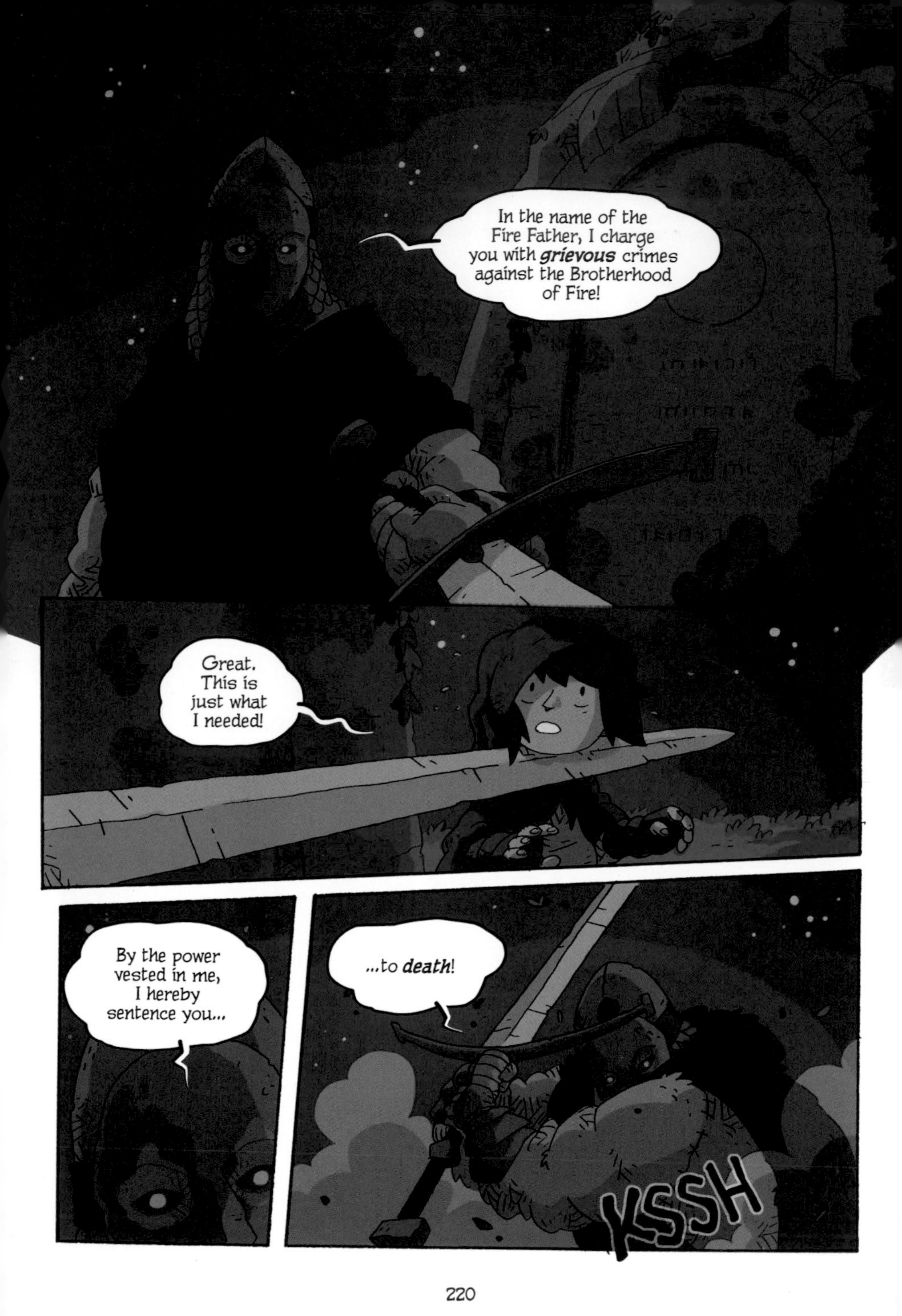
In the name of the Fire Father, I charge you with ***grievous*** crimes against the Brotherhood of Fire!
Great. This is just what I needed!
By the power vested in me, I hereby sentence you...
...to ***death***!
KSSH

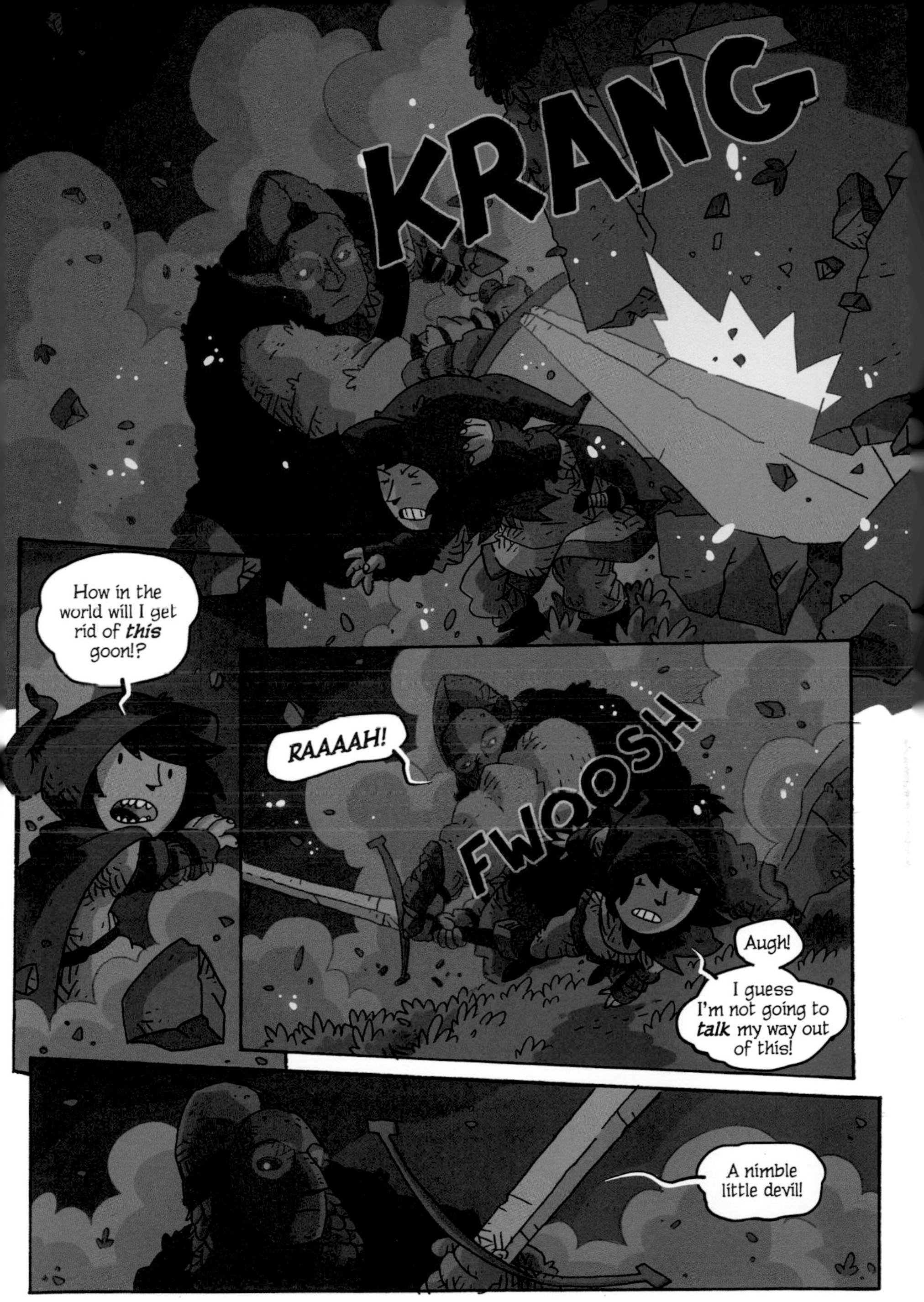
KRANG
How in the world will I get rid of *this* goon!?
RAAAAH!
FWOOSH
Augh!
I guess I'm not going to *talk* my way out of this!
A nimble little devil!

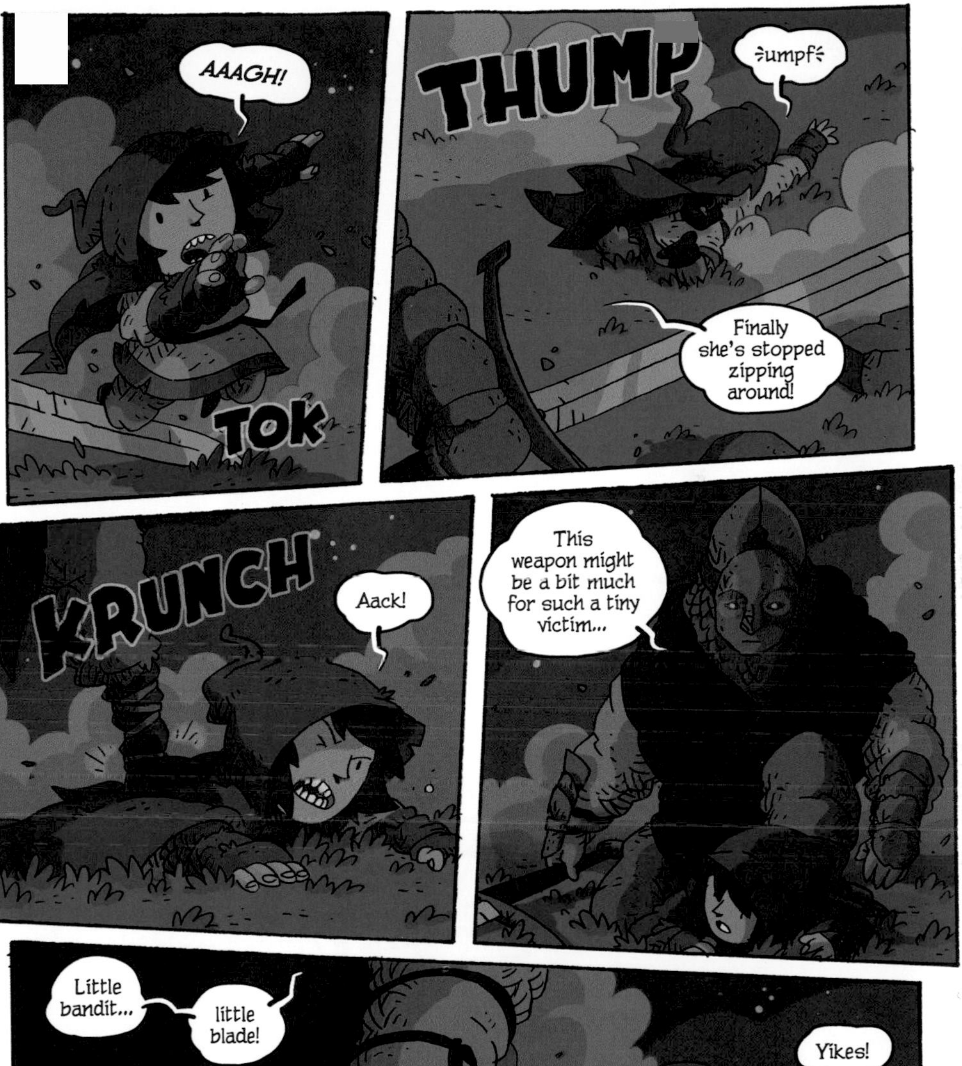
AAAGH!
TOK
THUMP
umpf
Finally she's stopped zipping around!
KRUNCH
Aack!
This weapon might be a bit much for such a tiny victim...
Little bandit...
little blade!
SSHK
Yikes!

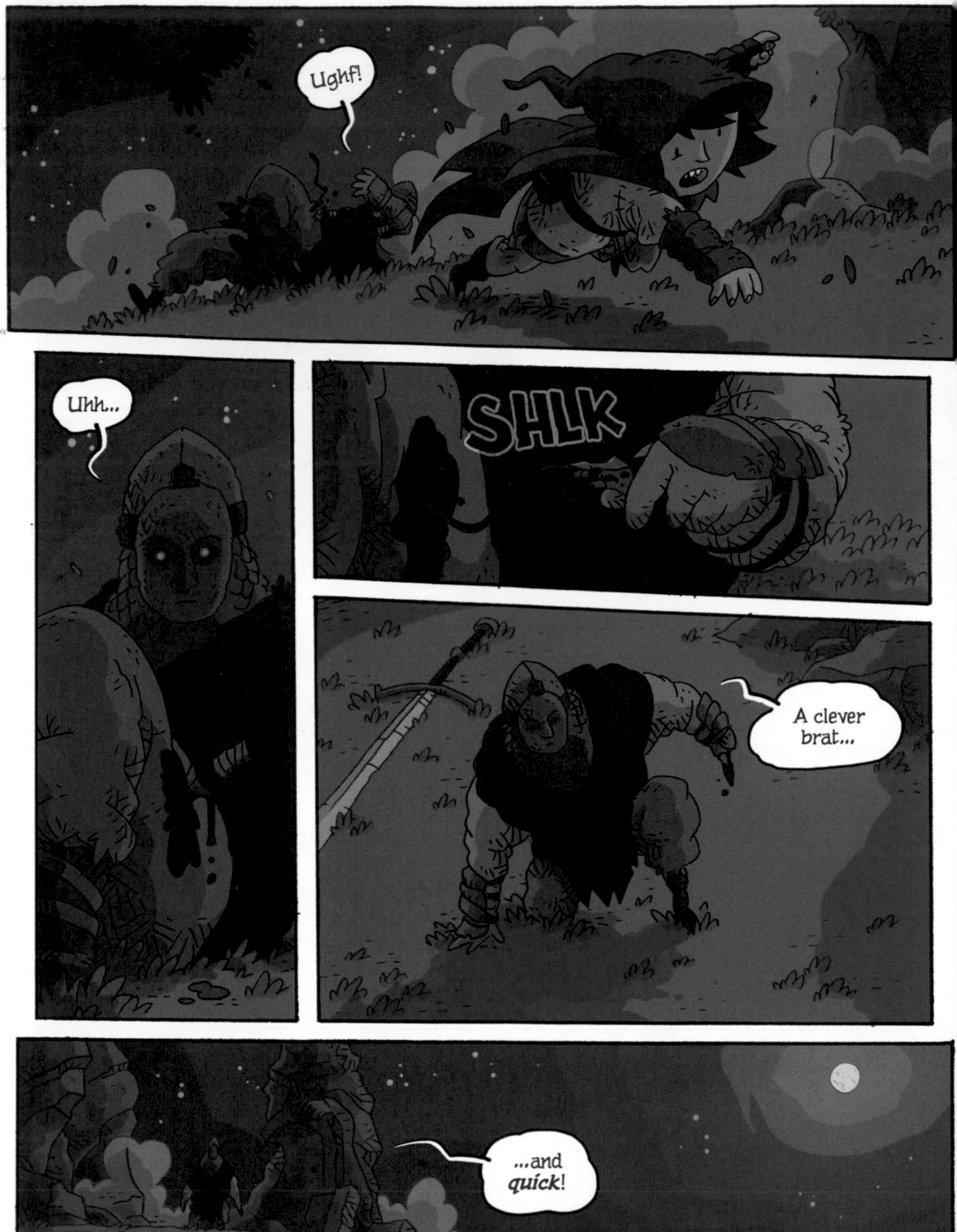
Ughf!
Uhh...
SHLK
A clever brat...
...and quick!

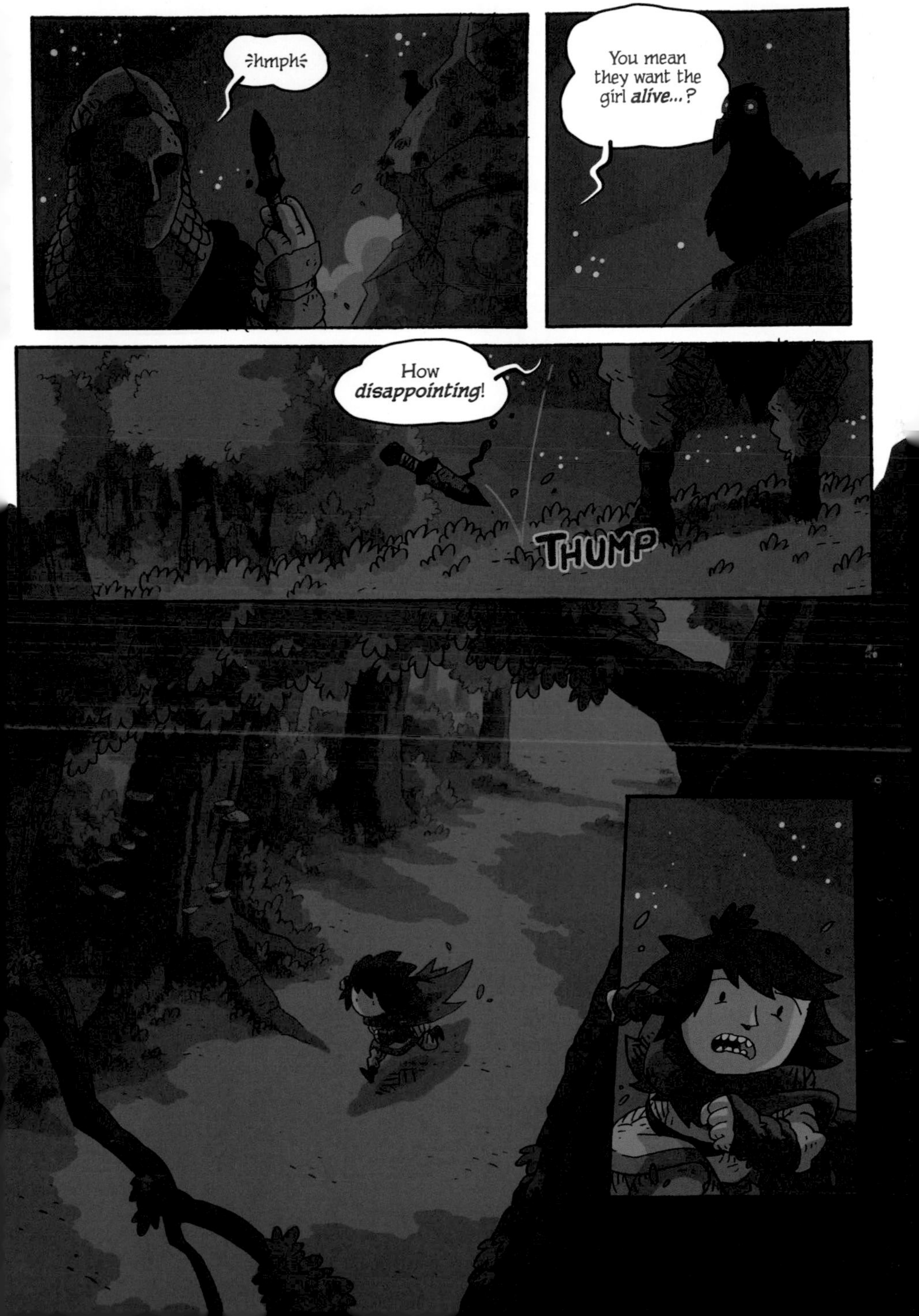

hmph
You mean they want the girl *alive*...?
How *disappointing*!
THUMP

But the day shall come,
When the keys are found,
By a thief who will steal them away,
And Ithiel shall arise,
And many men shall die,
On that fateful day.

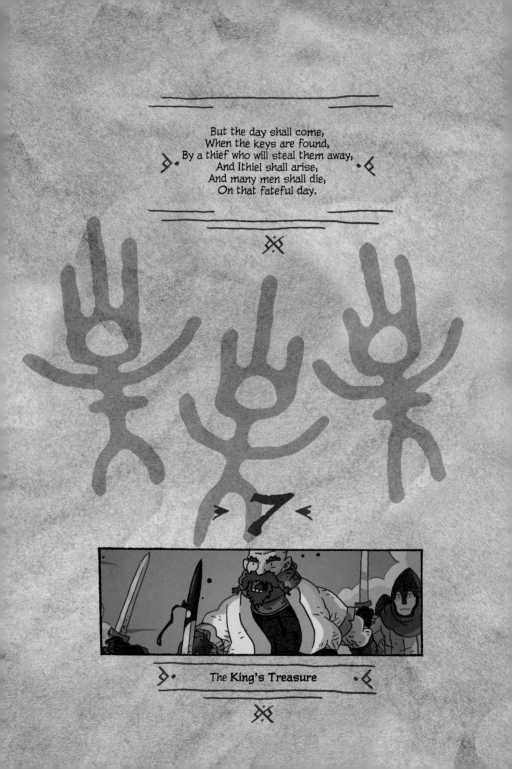

The King's Treasure

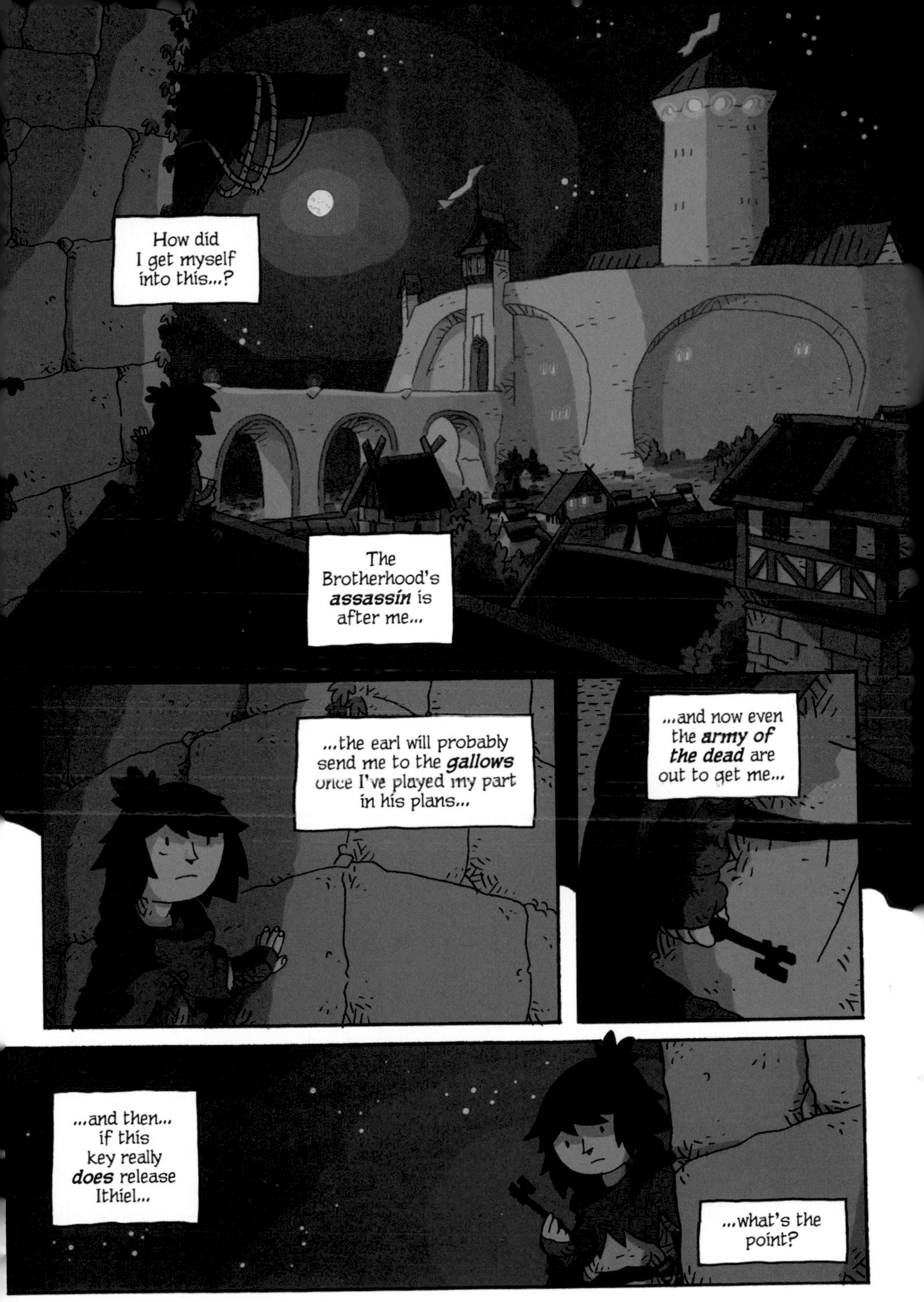
How did I get myself into this...?
The Brotherhood's ***assassin*** is after me...
...the earl will probably send me to the ***gallows*** once I've played my part in his plans...
...and now even the ***army of the dead*** are out to get me...
...and then... if this key really ***does*** release Ithiel...
...what's the point?

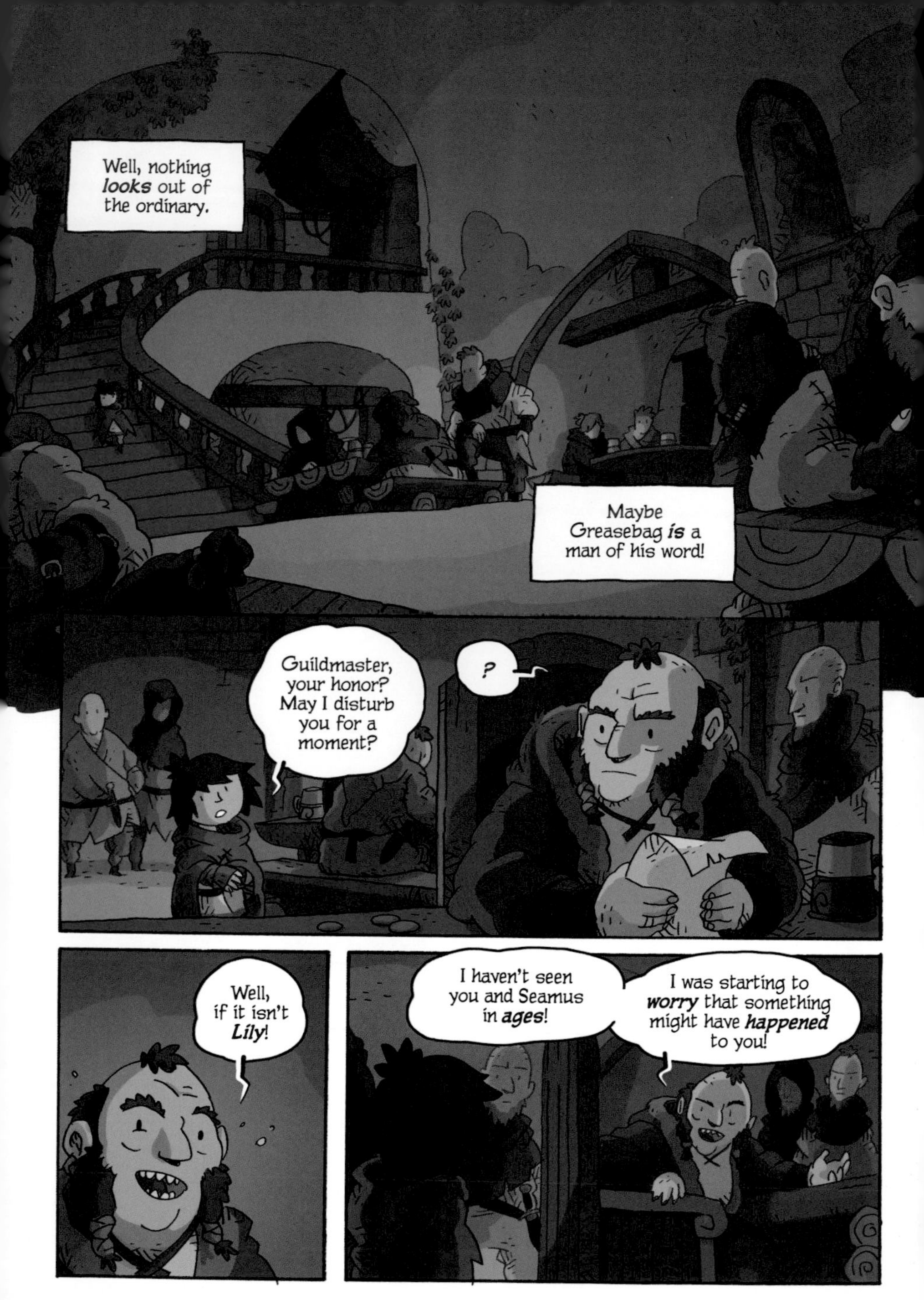
Well, nothing *looks* out of the ordinary.
Maybe Greasebag *is* a man of his word!
Guildmaster, your honor? May I disturb you for a moment?
?
Well, if it isn't *Lily*!
I haven't seen you and Seamus in *ages*!
I was starting to *worry* that something might have *happened* to you!

233

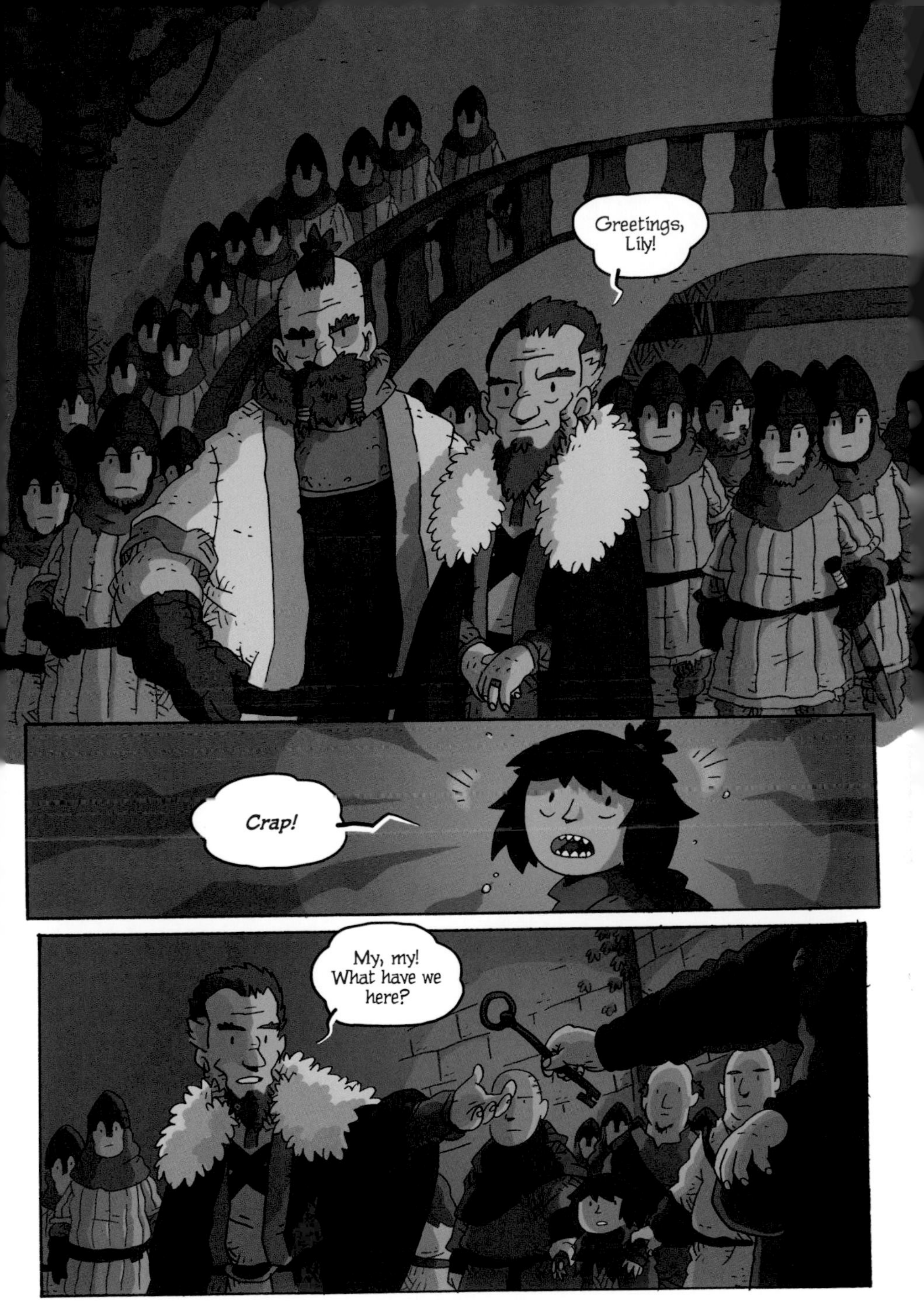
Greetings, Lily!
Crap!
My, my! What have we here?

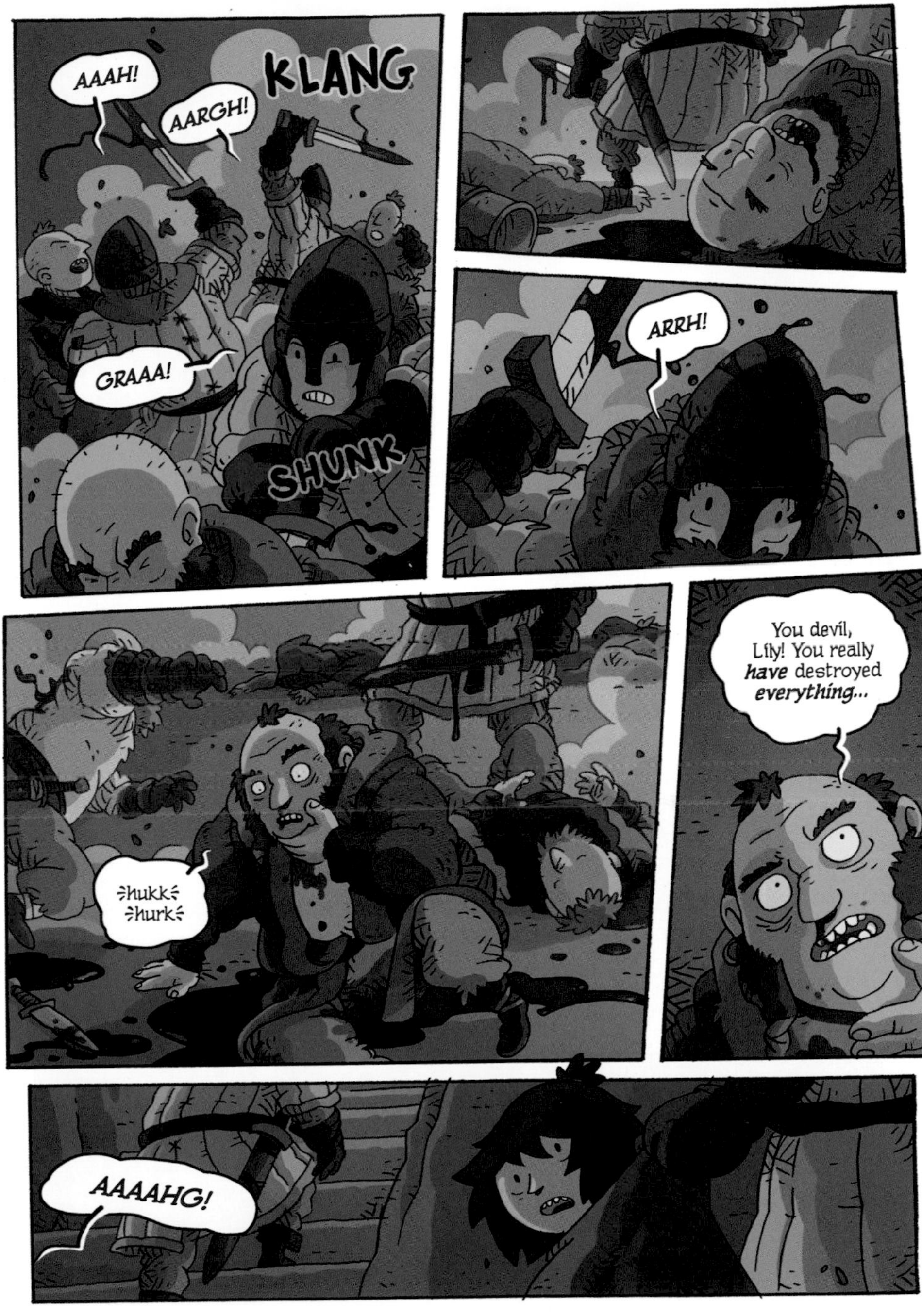

AAAH!
AARGH!
KLANG
GRAAA!
SHUNK
ARRH!
⁼hukk⁼ ⁼hurk⁼
You devil, Lily! You really *have* destroyed *everything*...
AAAAHG!

242

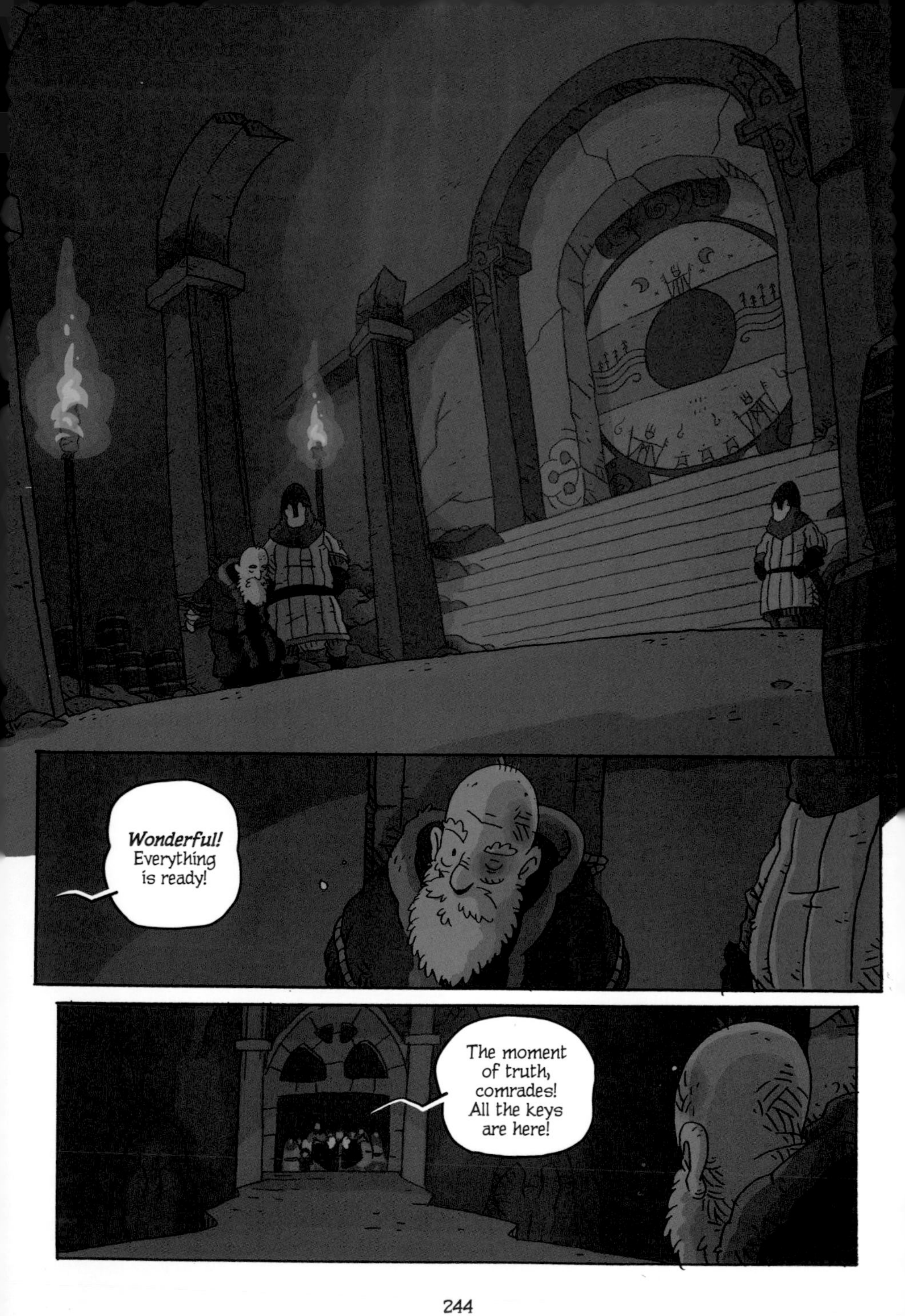

Wonderful! Everything is ready!
The moment of truth, comrades! All the keys are here!

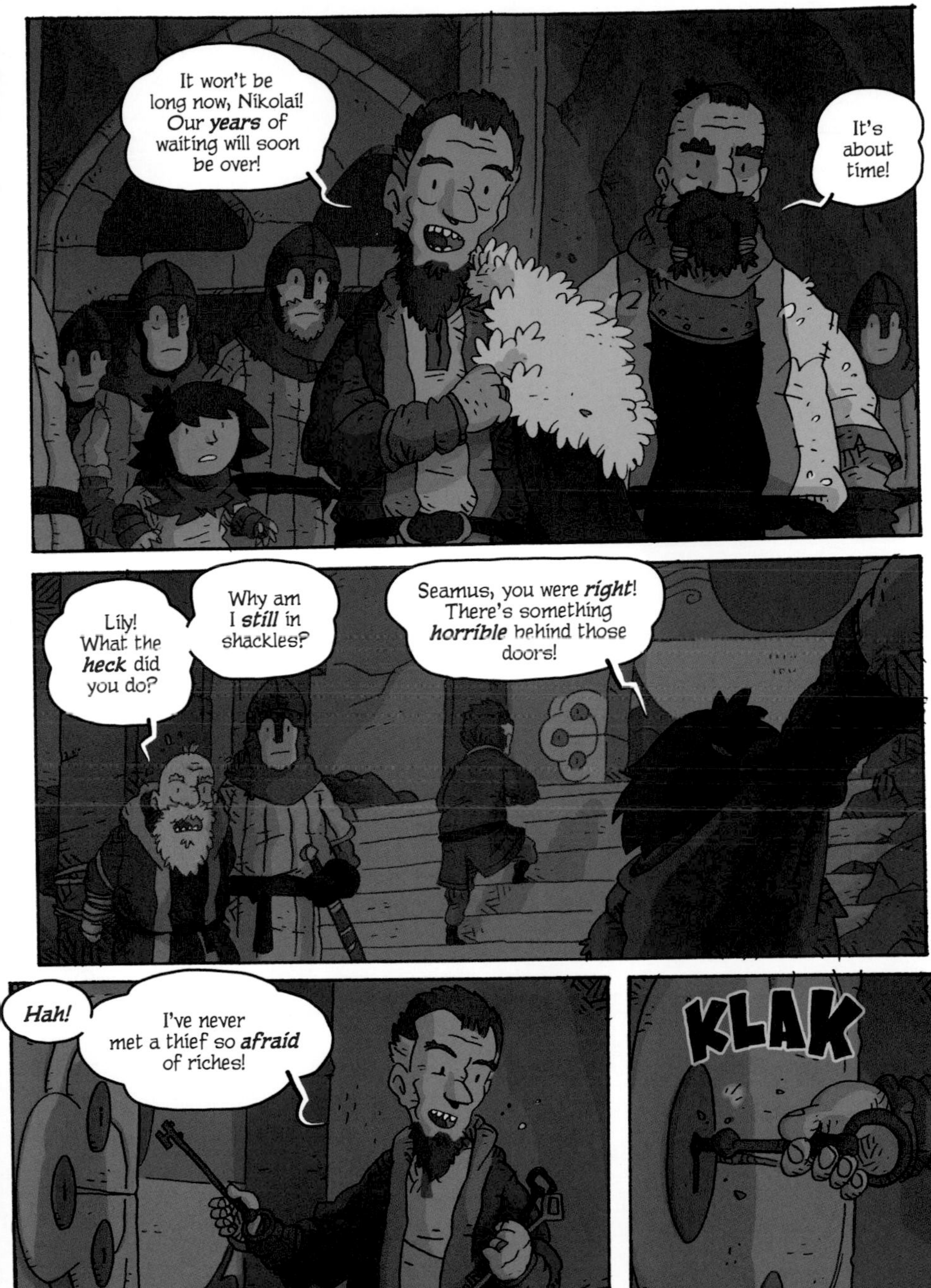
It won't be long now, Nikolai! Our *years* of waiting will soon be over!
It's about time!
Lily! What the *heck* did you do?
Why am I *still* in shackles?
Seamus, you were *right*! There's something *horrible* behind those doors!
Hah!
I've never met a thief so *afraid* of riches!
KLAK

246

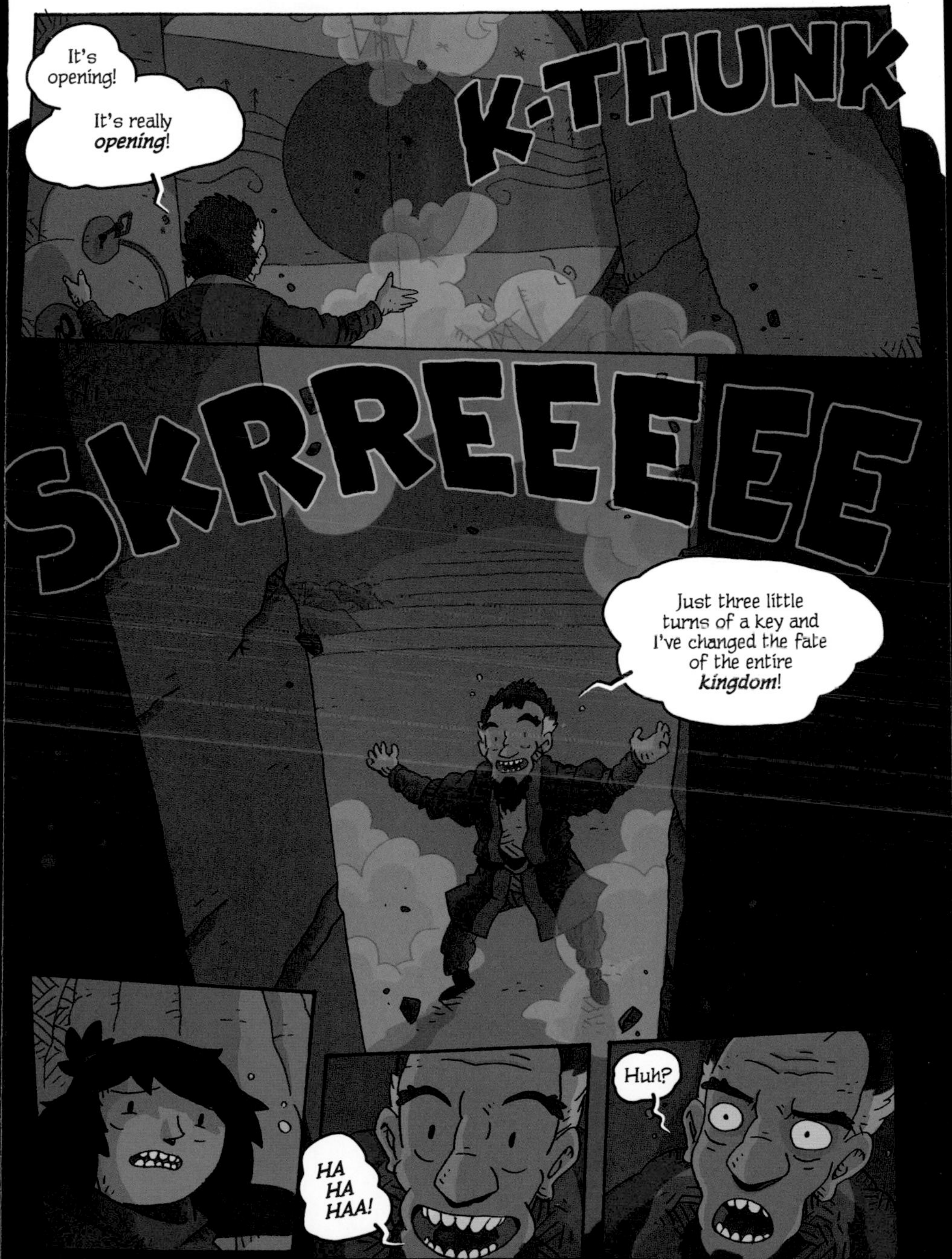
It's opening!
It's really *opening*!
K-THUNK
SKRREEEEEE
Just three little turns of a key and I've changed the fate of the entire *kingdom*!
HA HA HAA!
Huh?

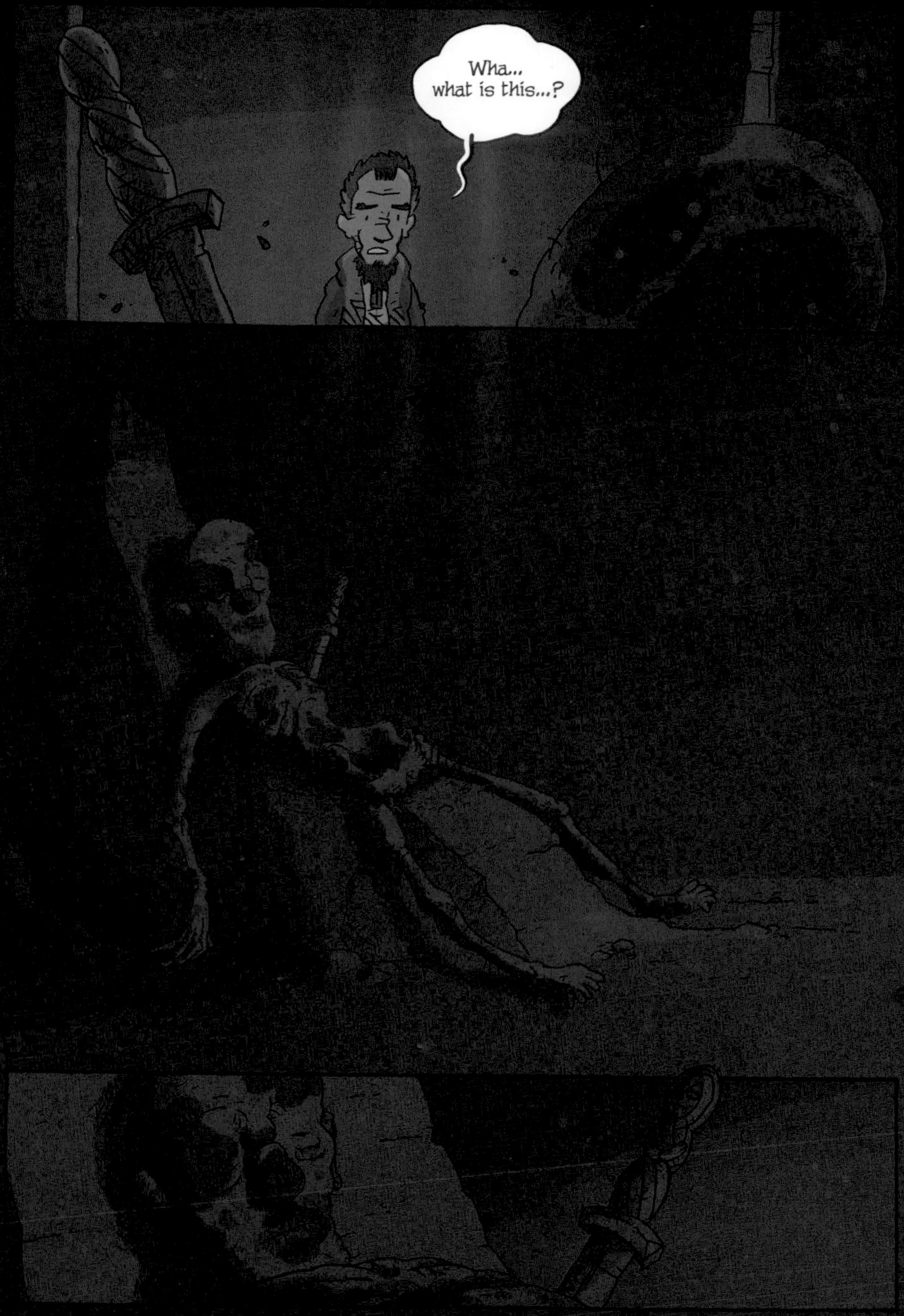
Wha... what is this...?

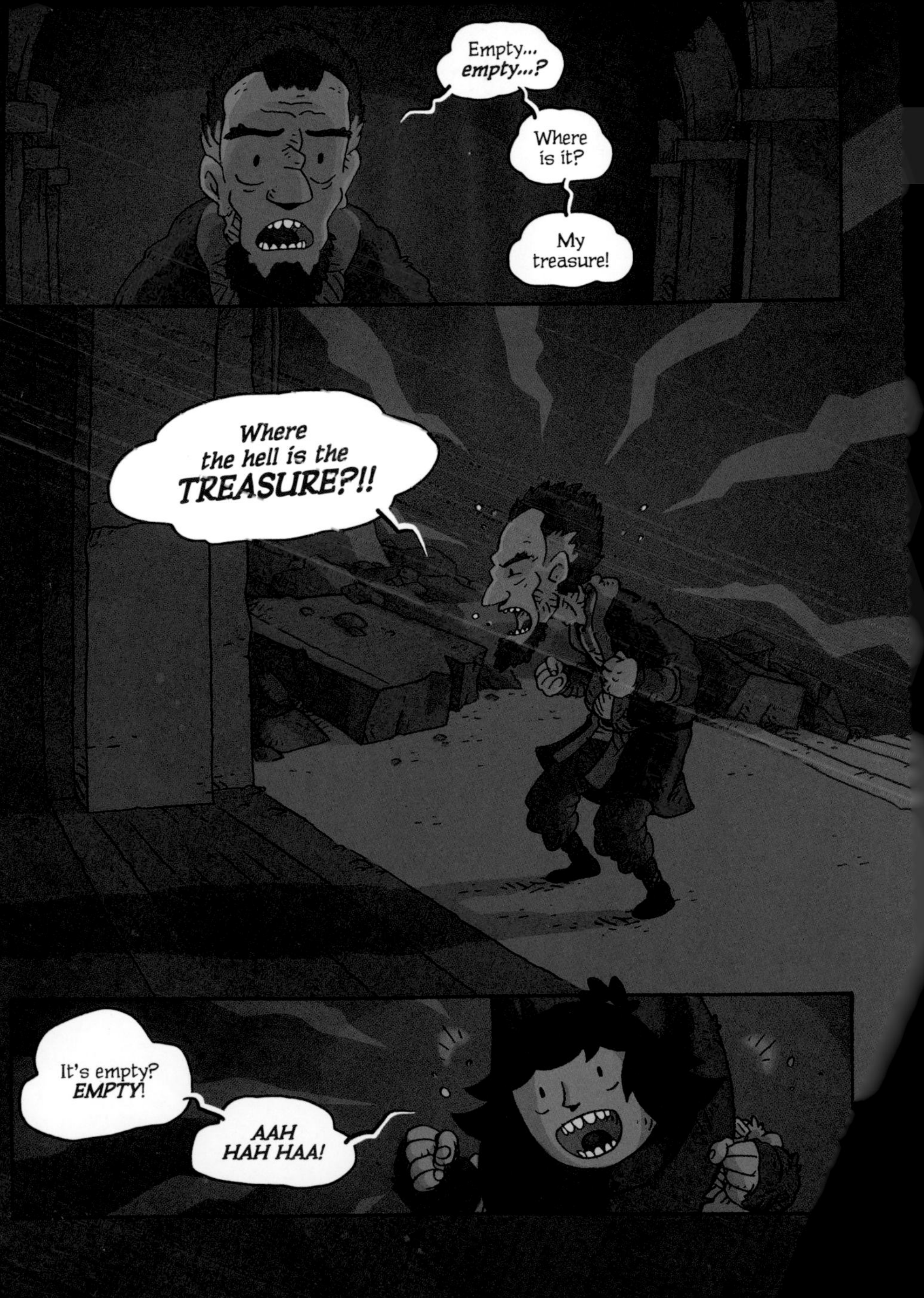
Empty... *empty...?*
Where is it?
My treasure!
*Where the hell is the **TREASURE?!!***
It's empty? ***EMPTY!***
AAH HAH HAA!

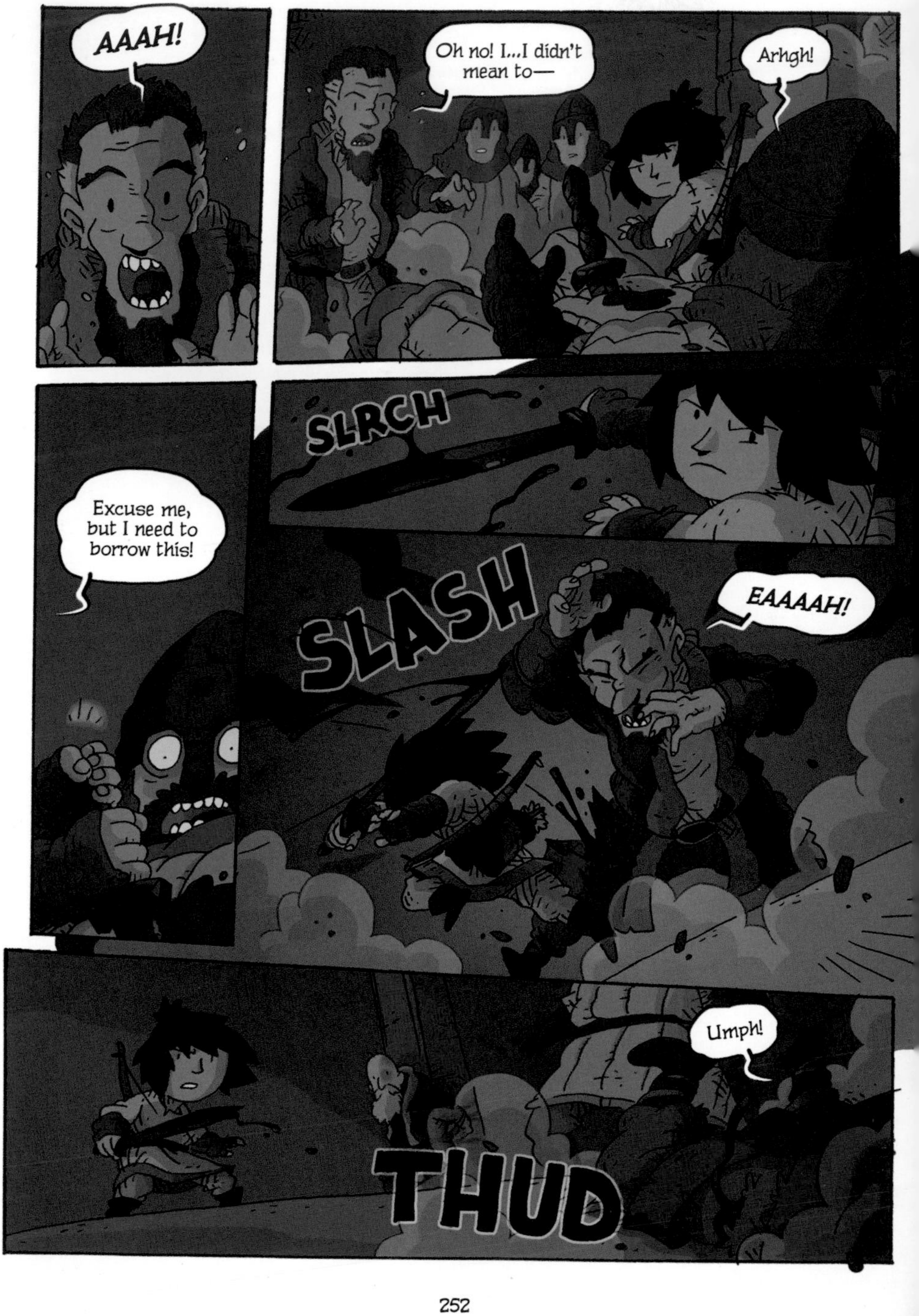
AAAH!
Oh no! I...I didn't mean to—
Arhgh!
SLRCH
Excuse me, but I need to borrow this!
SLASH
EAAAAH!
Umph!
THUD

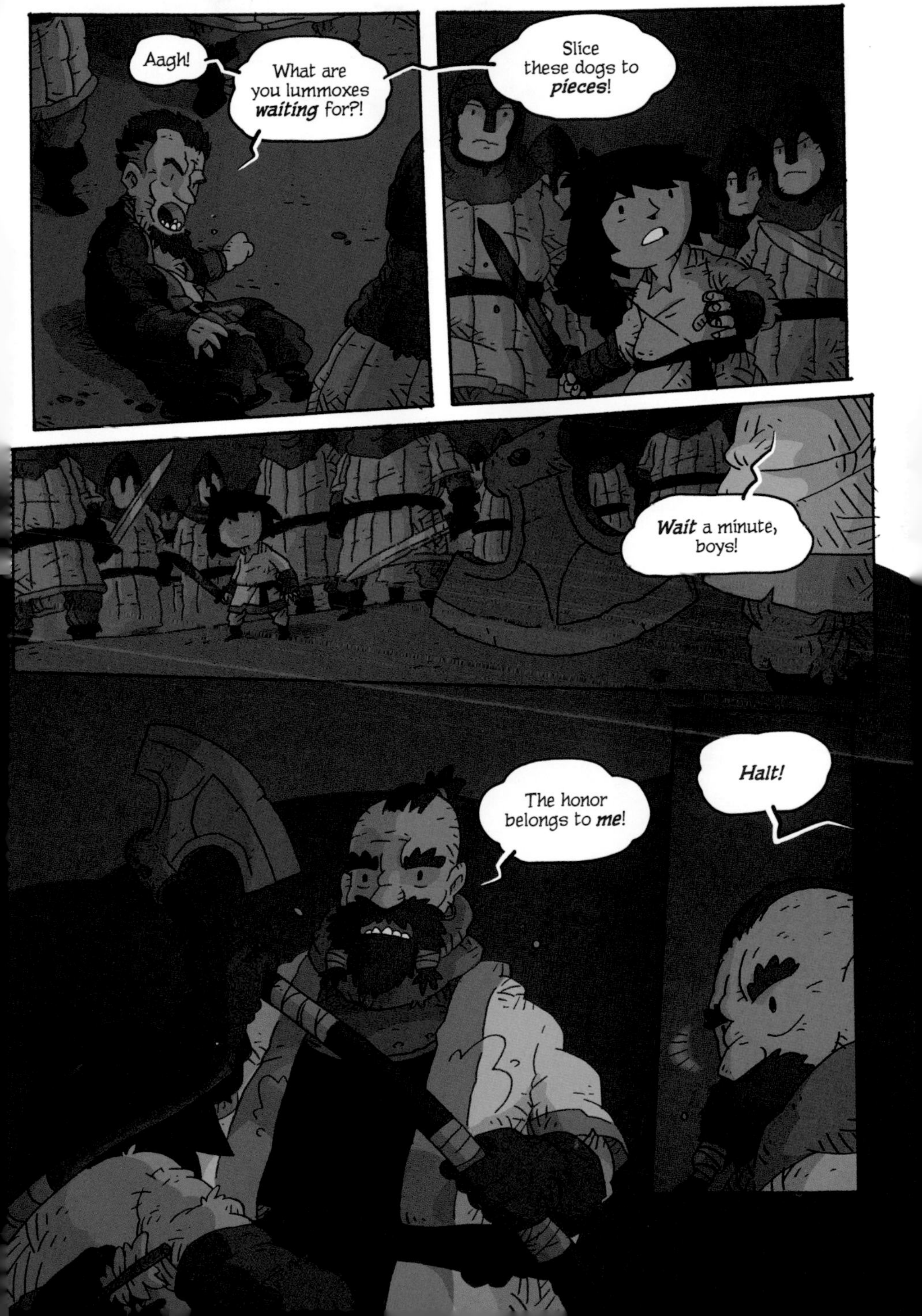
Aagh!
What are you lummoxes *waiting* for?!
Slice these dogs to *pieces*!
Wait a minute, boys!
The honor belongs to *me*!
Halt!

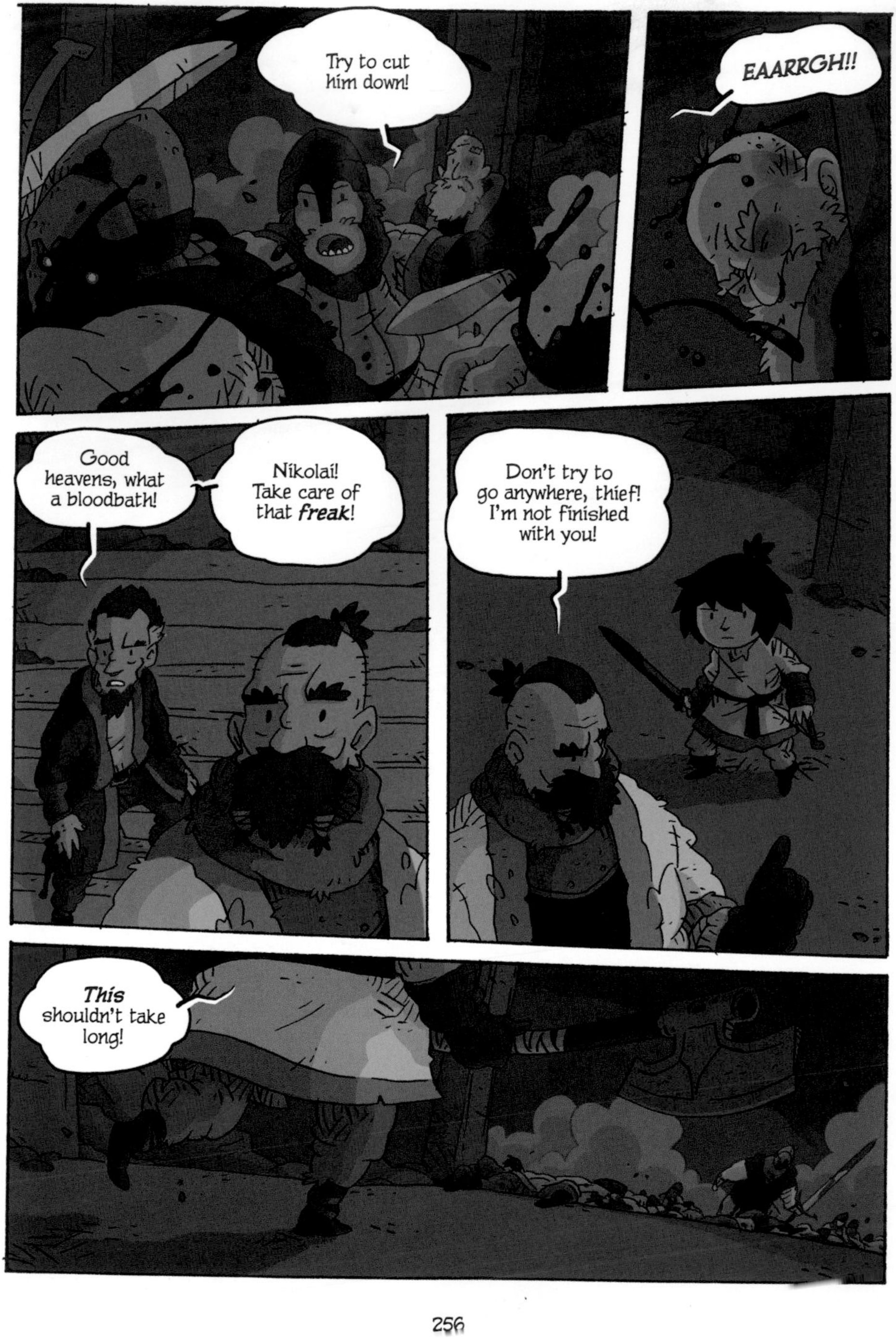

Try to cut him down!
EAARRGH!!
Good heavens, what a bloodbath!
Nikolai! Take care of that *freak*!
Don't try to go anywhere, thief! I'm not finished with you!
This shouldn't take long!

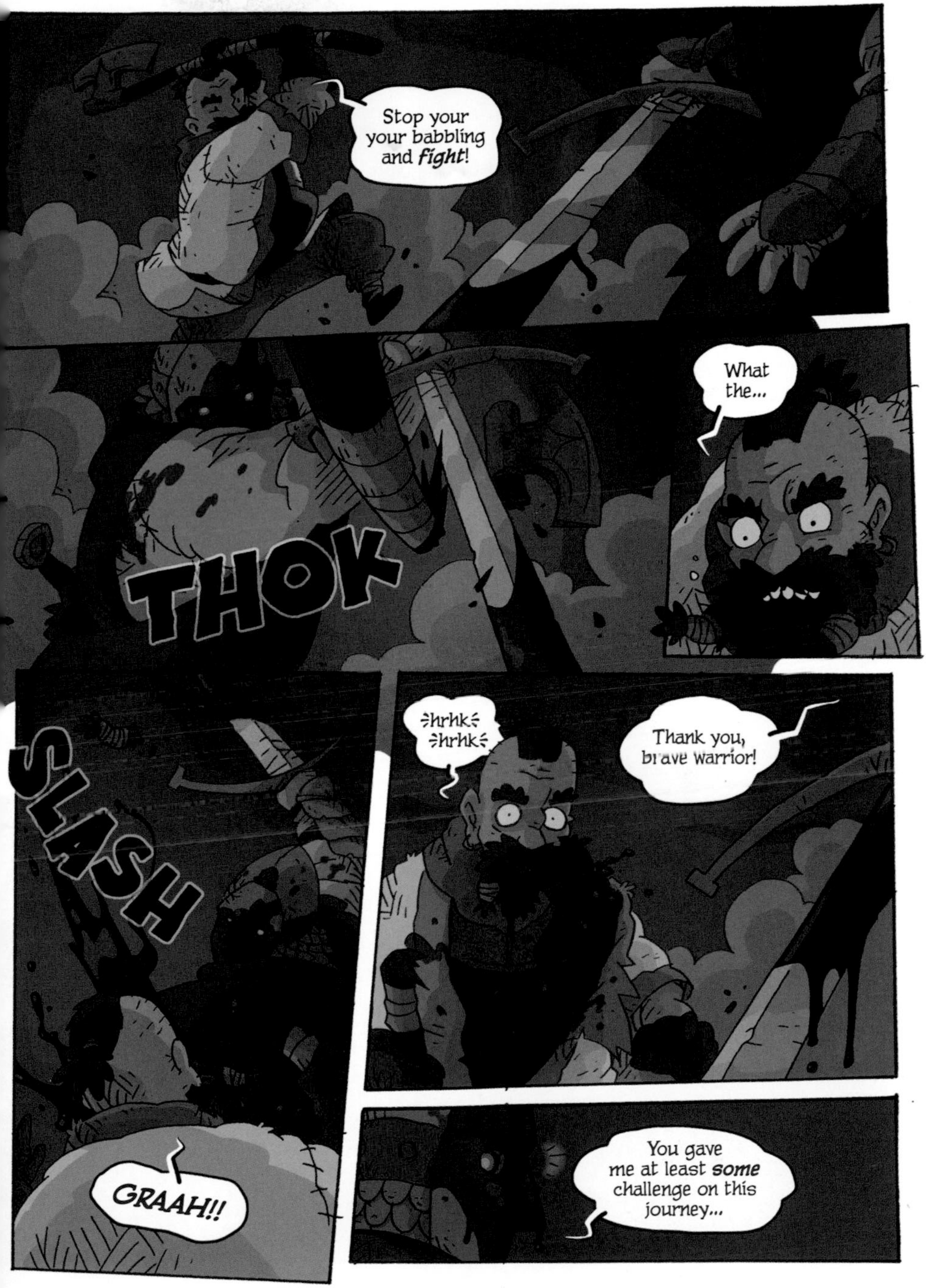

Stop your your babbling and *fight*!
THOK
What the...
SLASH
GRAAH!!
hrhk hrhk
Thank you, brave warrior!
You gave me at least *some* challenge on this journey...

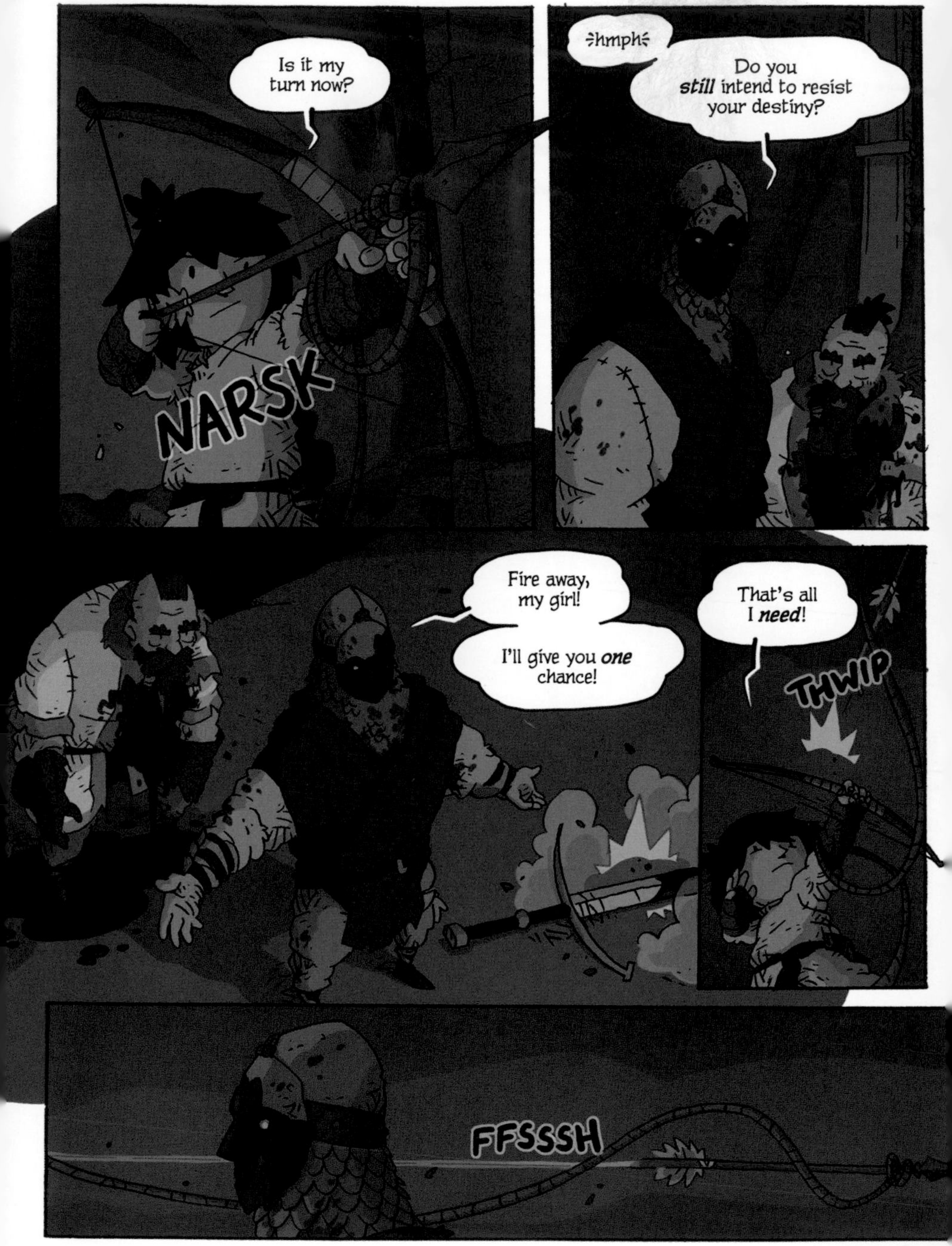
Is it my turn now?
NARSK
⁝hmph⁝
Do you still intend to resist your destiny?
Fire away, my girl!
I'll give you one chance!
That's all I need!
THWIP
FFSSSH

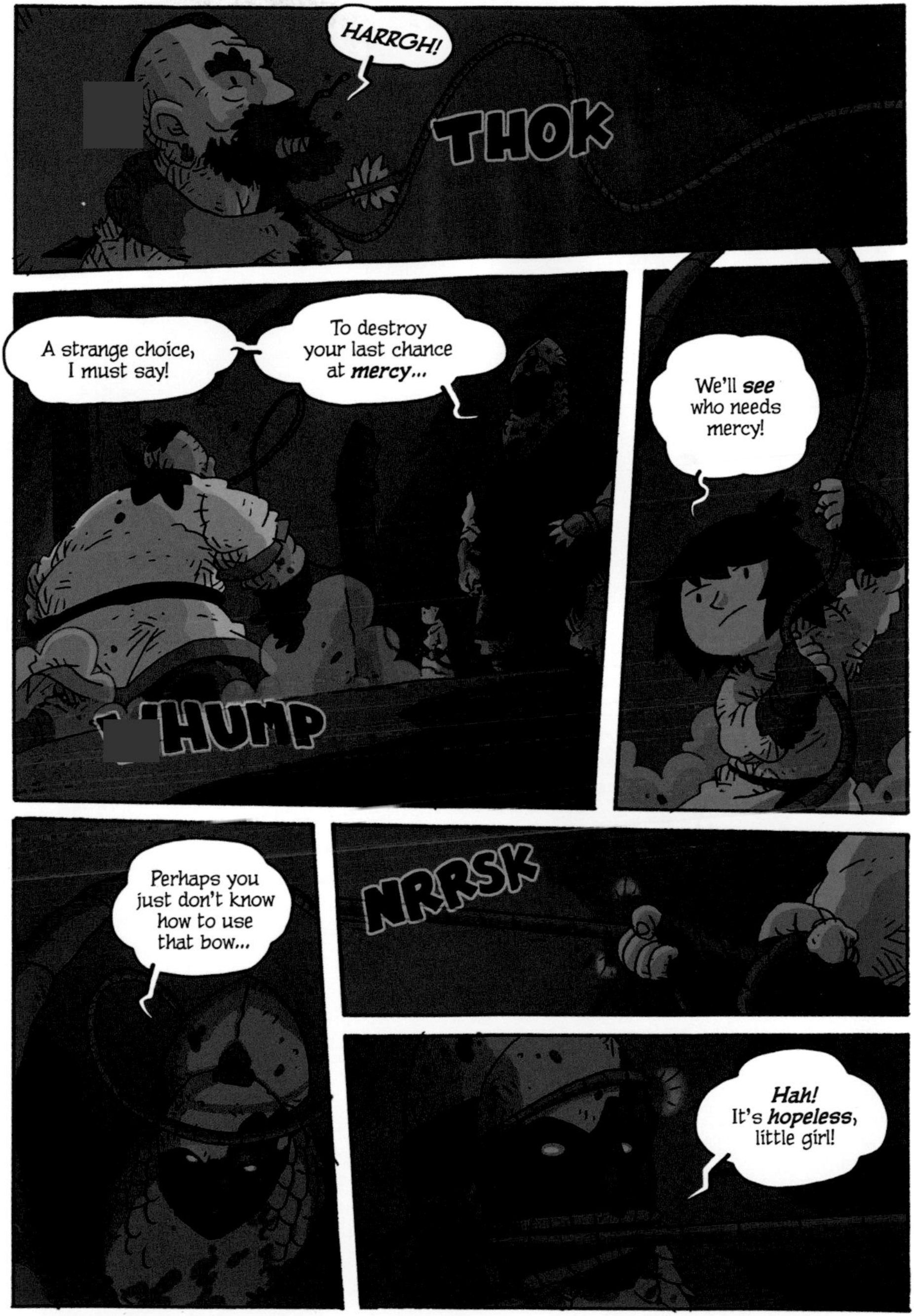
HARRGH!
THOK
A strange choice, I must say!
To destroy your last chance at *mercy*...
[redacted]HUMP
We'll **see** who needs mercy!
Perhaps you just don't know how to use that bow...
NRRSK
Hah! It's ***hopeless***, little girl!

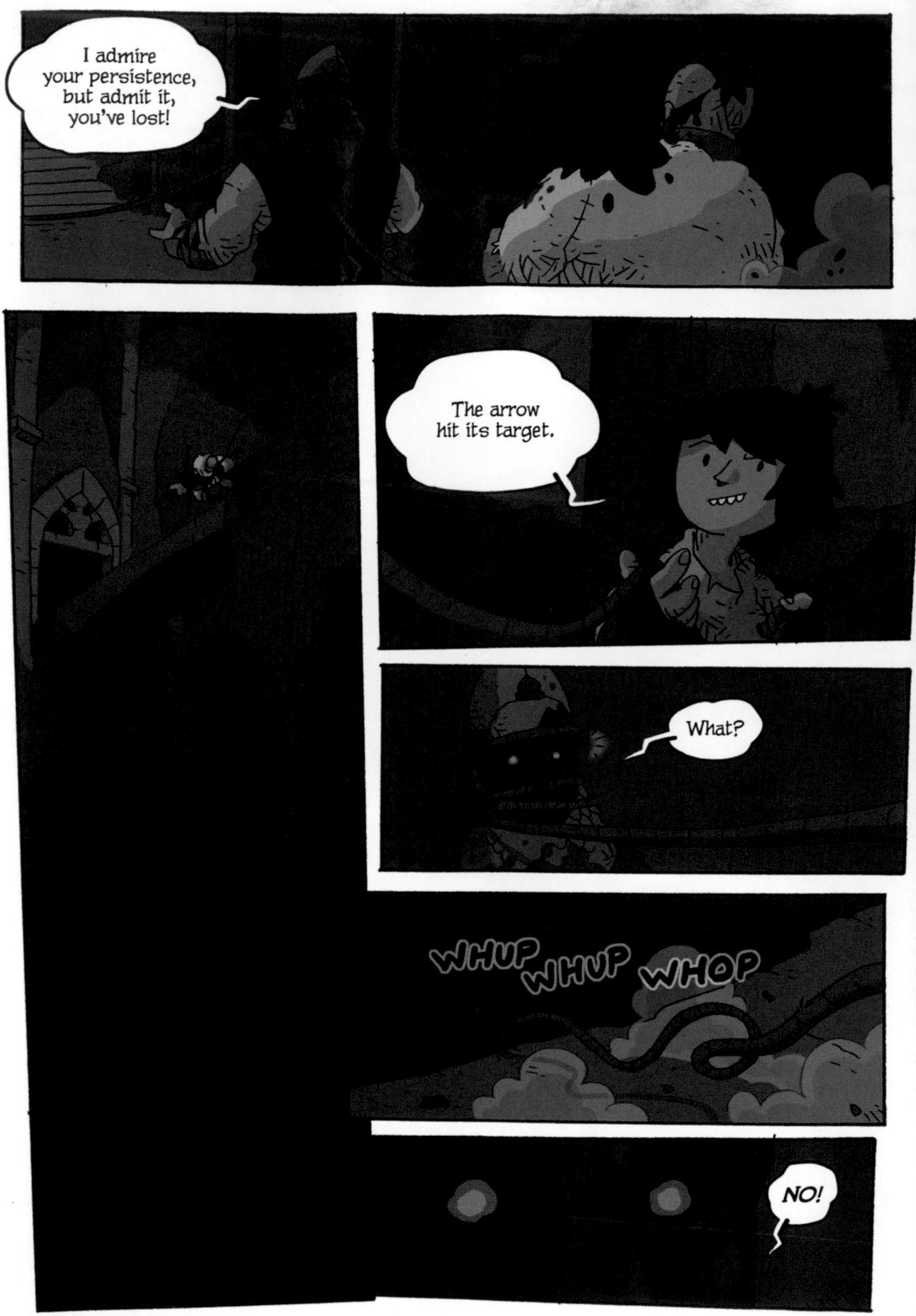
I admire your persistence, but admit it, you've lost!
The arrow hit its target.
What?
WHUP WHUP WHOP
NO!

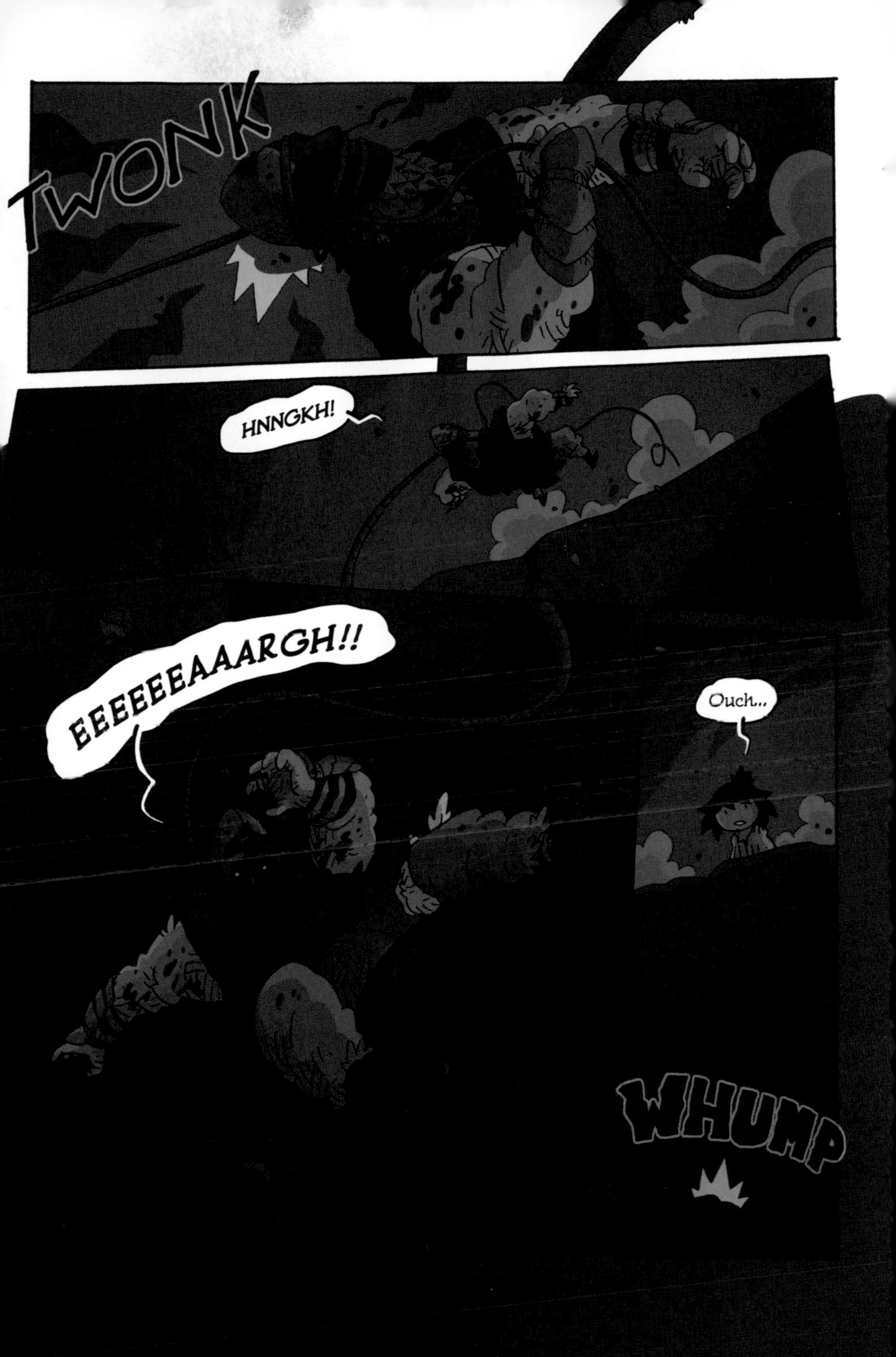
TWONK
HNNGKH!
EEEEEEAAARGH!!
Ouch..
WHUMP

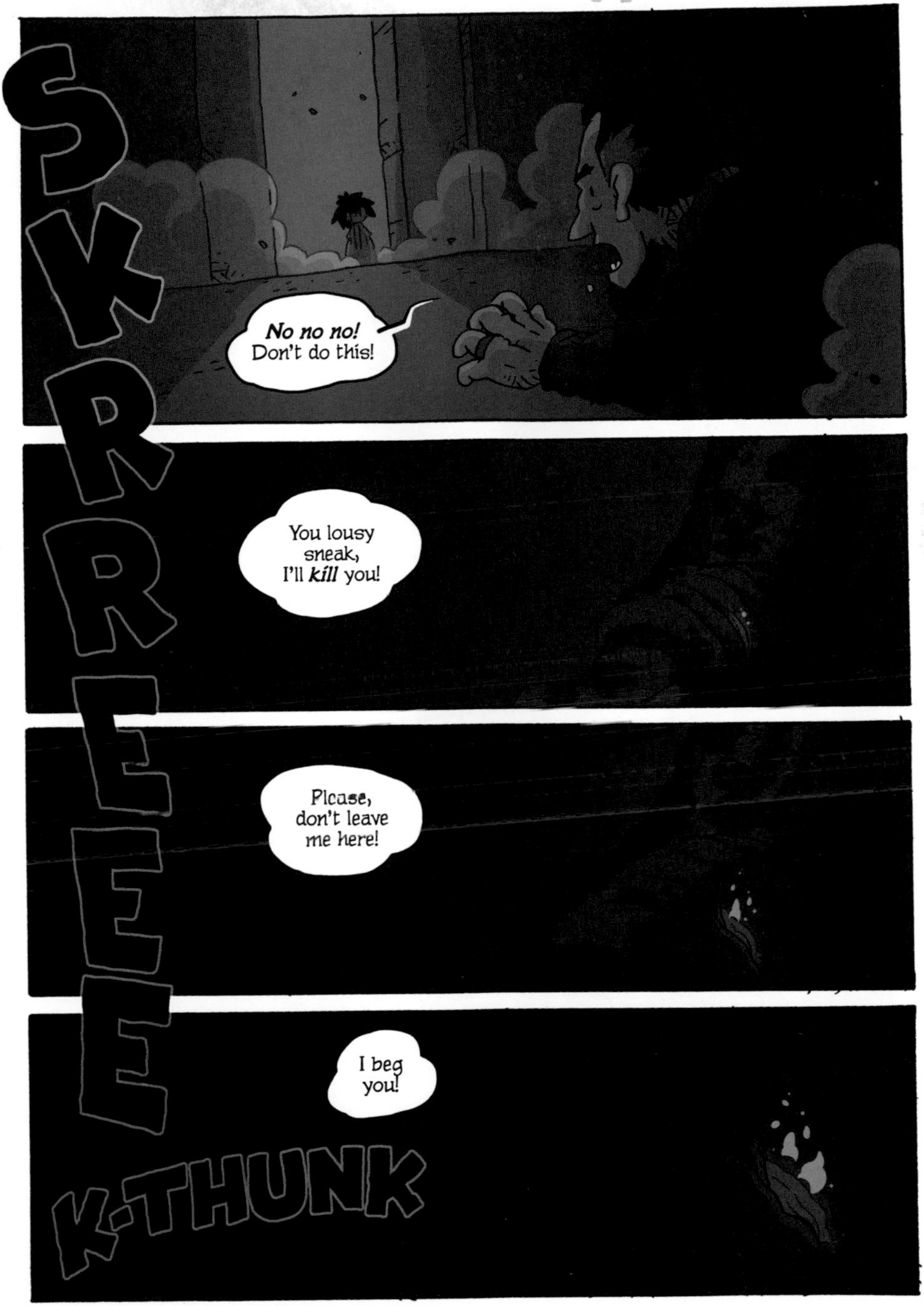
SKRREEEE
No no no! Don't do this!
You lousy sneak, I'll ***kill*** you!
Please, don't leave me here!
I beg you!
K-THUNK

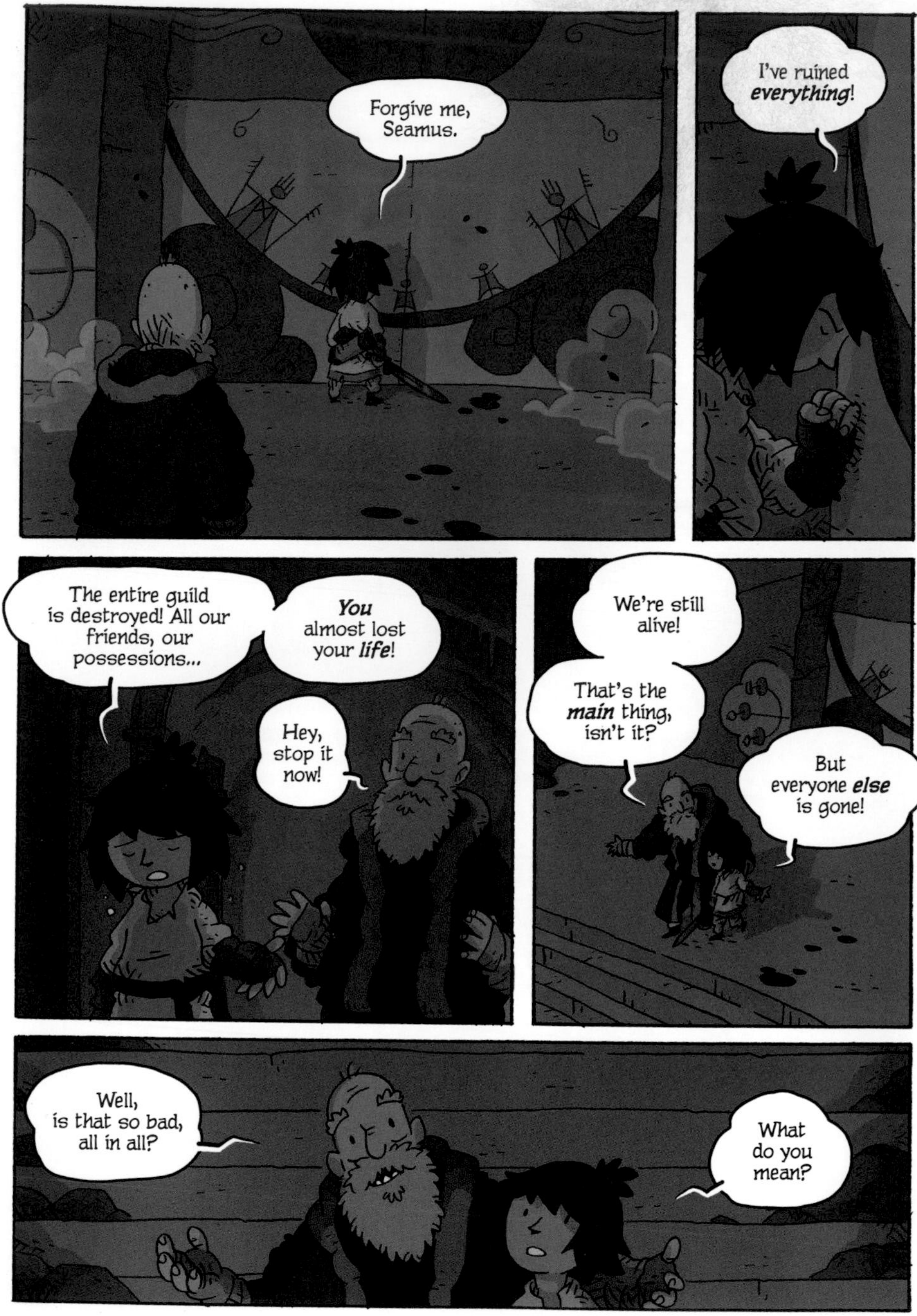
Forgive me, Seamus.
I've ruined *everything*!
The entire guild is destroyed! All our friends, our possessions...
You almost lost your *life*!
Hey, stop it now!
We're still alive!
That's the *main* thing, isn't it?
But everyone *else* is gone!
Well, is that so bad, all in all?
What do you mean?

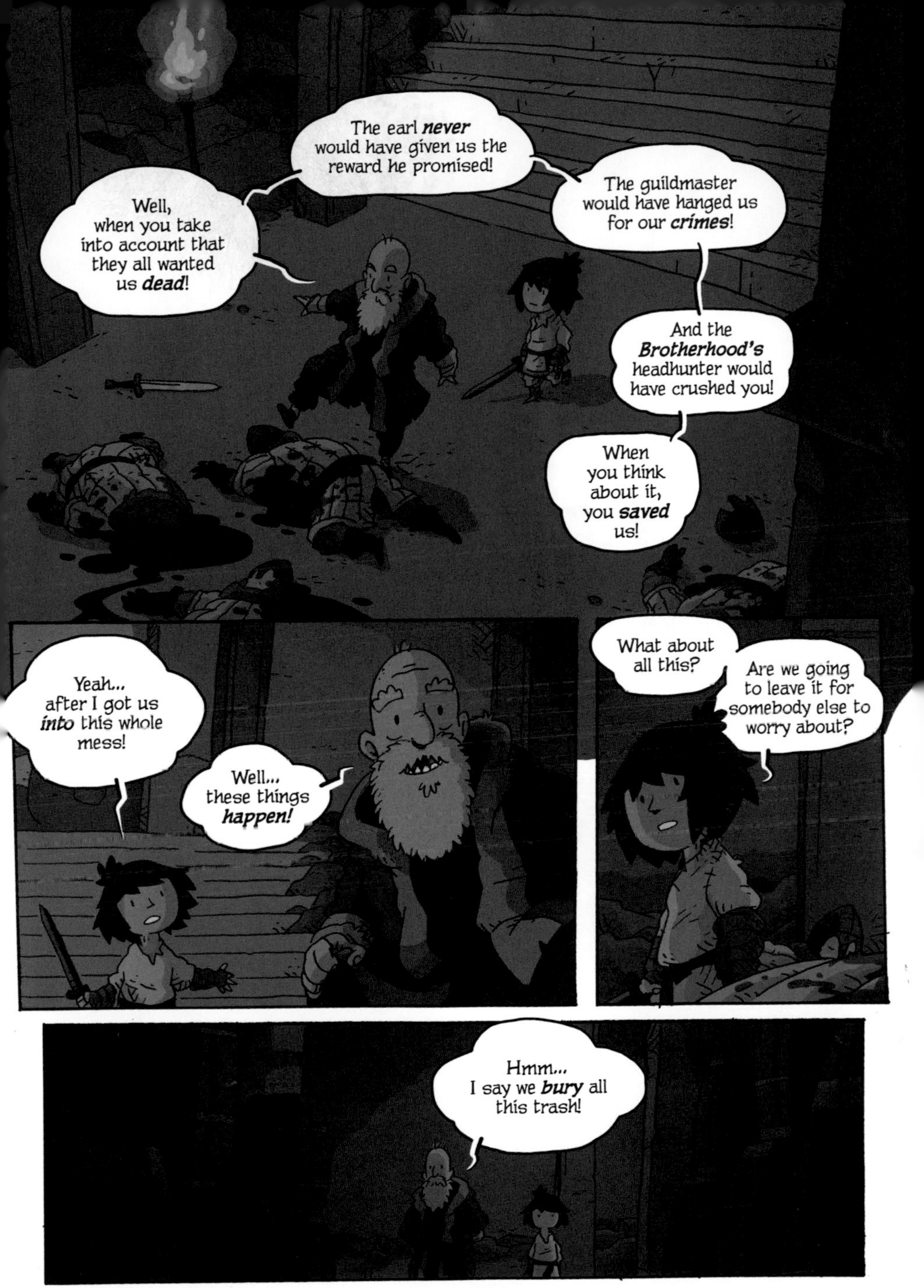
The earl *never* would have given us the reward he promised!
Well, when you take into account that they all wanted us *dead*!
The guildmaster would have hanged us for our *crimes*!
And the *Brotherhood's* headhunter would have crushed you!
When you think about it, you *saved* us!
Yeah... after I got us *into* this whole mess!
Well... these things *happen!*
What about all this?
Are we going to leave it for somebody else to worry about?
Hmm... I say we *bury* all this trash!

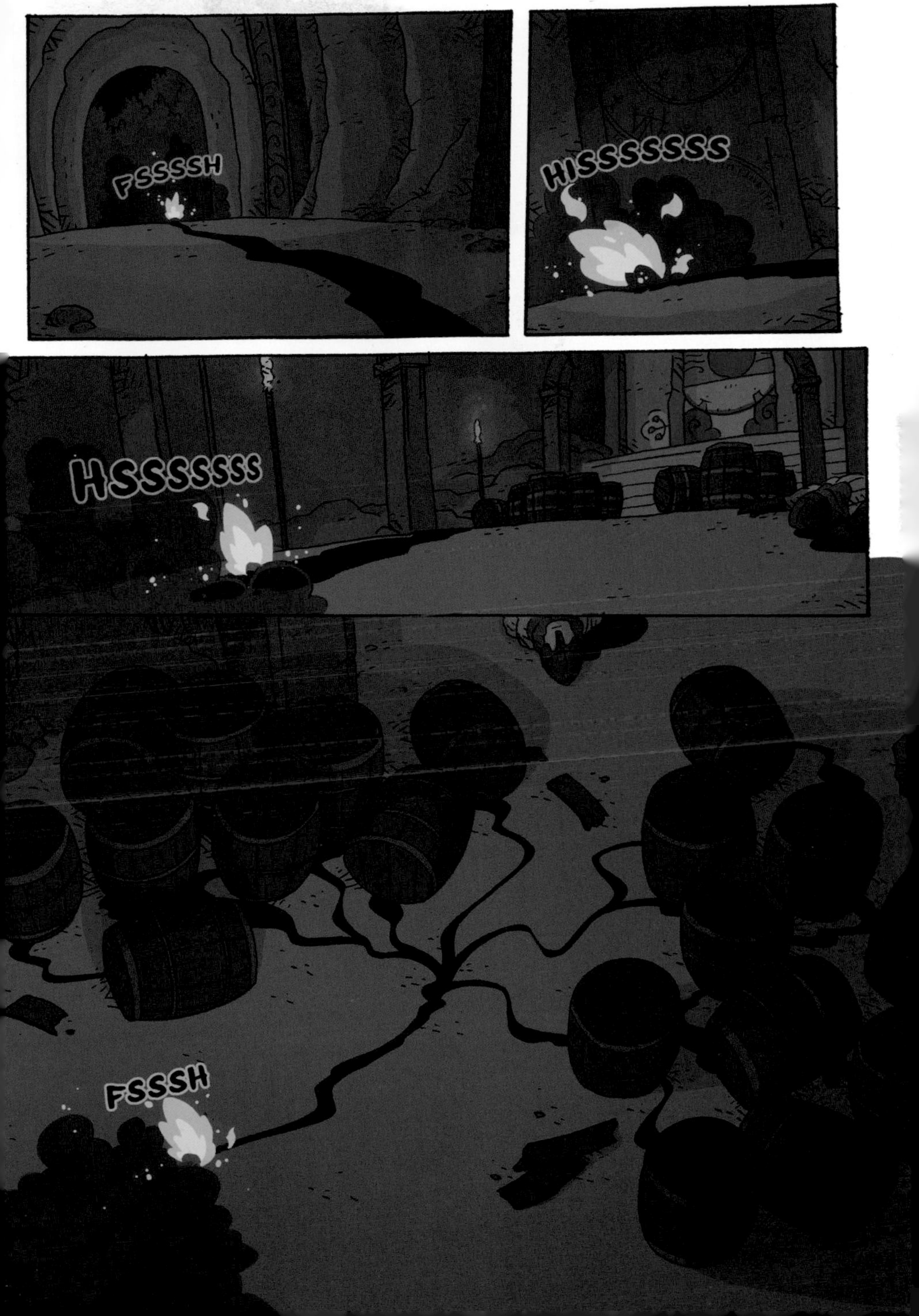
FSSSSH
HISSSSSSS
HSSSSSSS
FSSSH

274

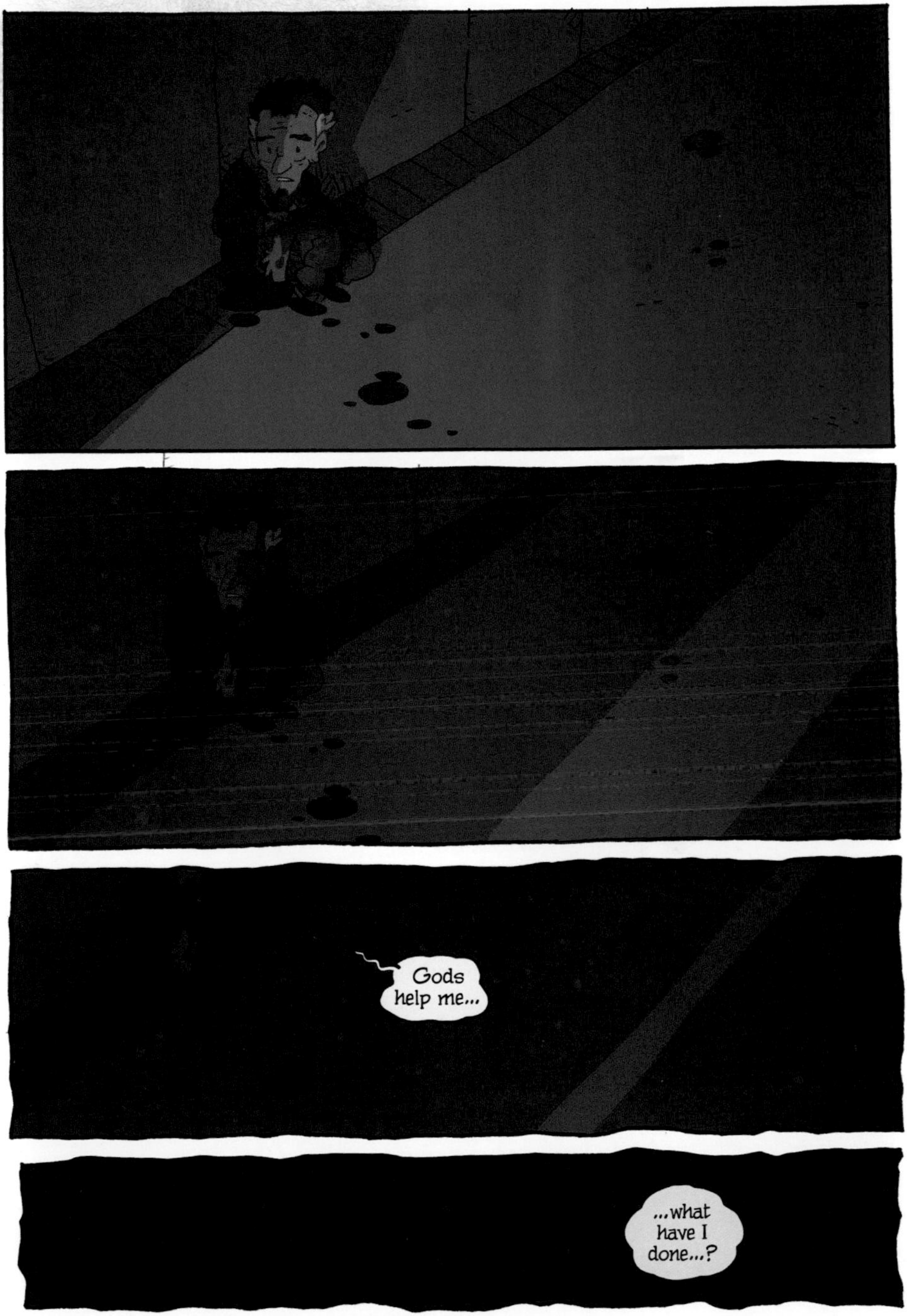
Gods help me...
...what have I done...?

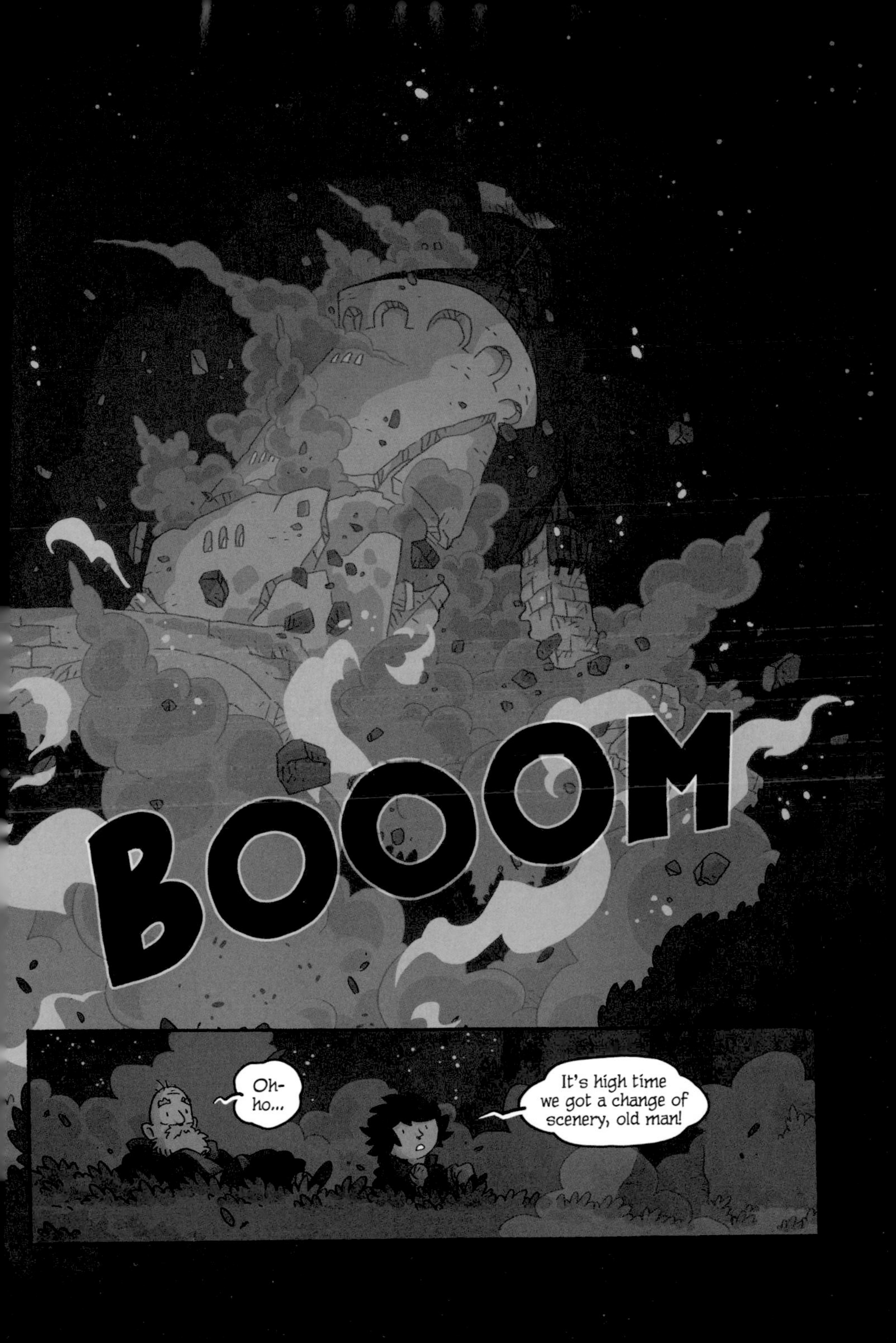
BOOOM
Oh- ho...
It's high time we got a change of scenery, old man!

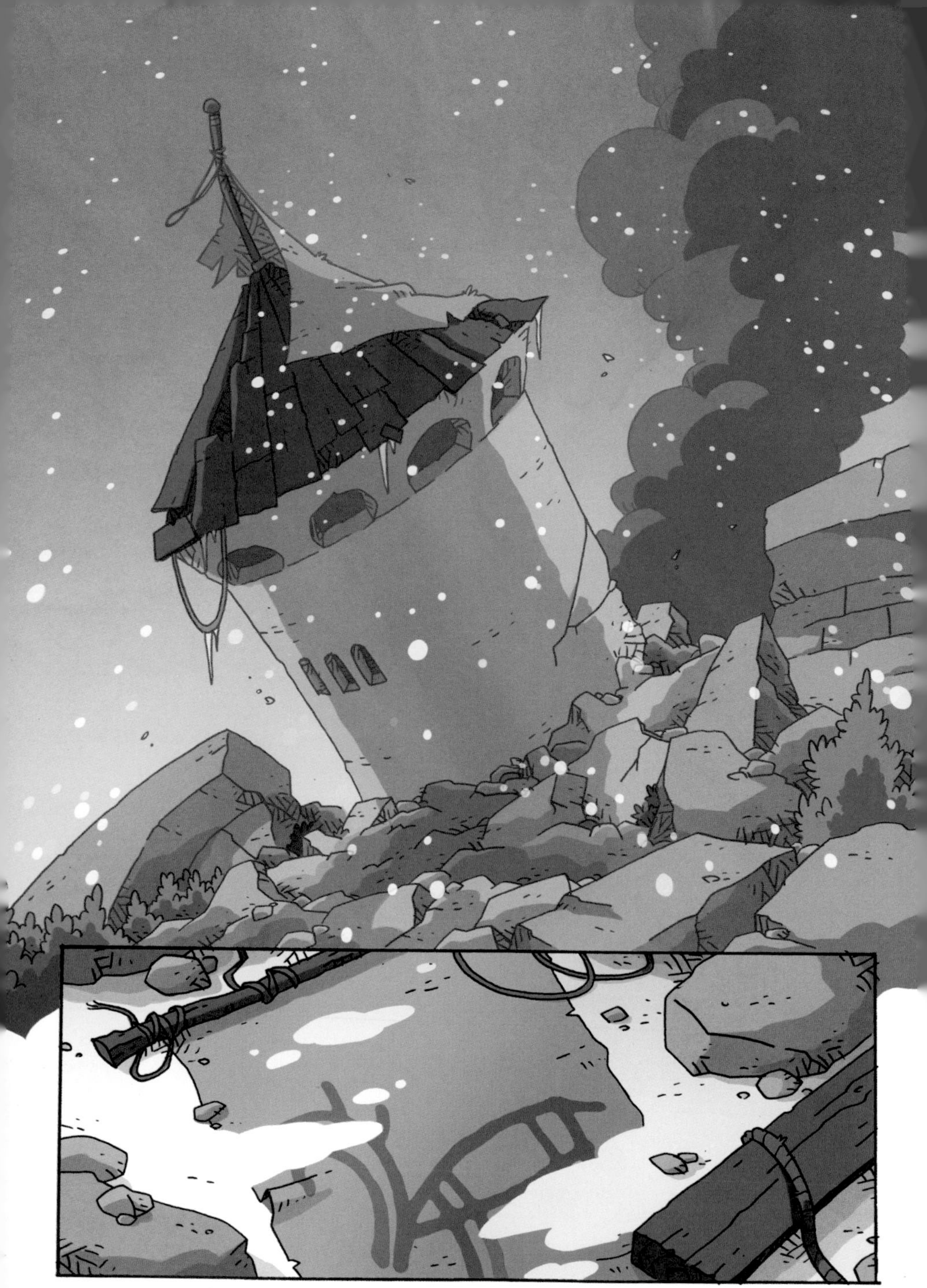

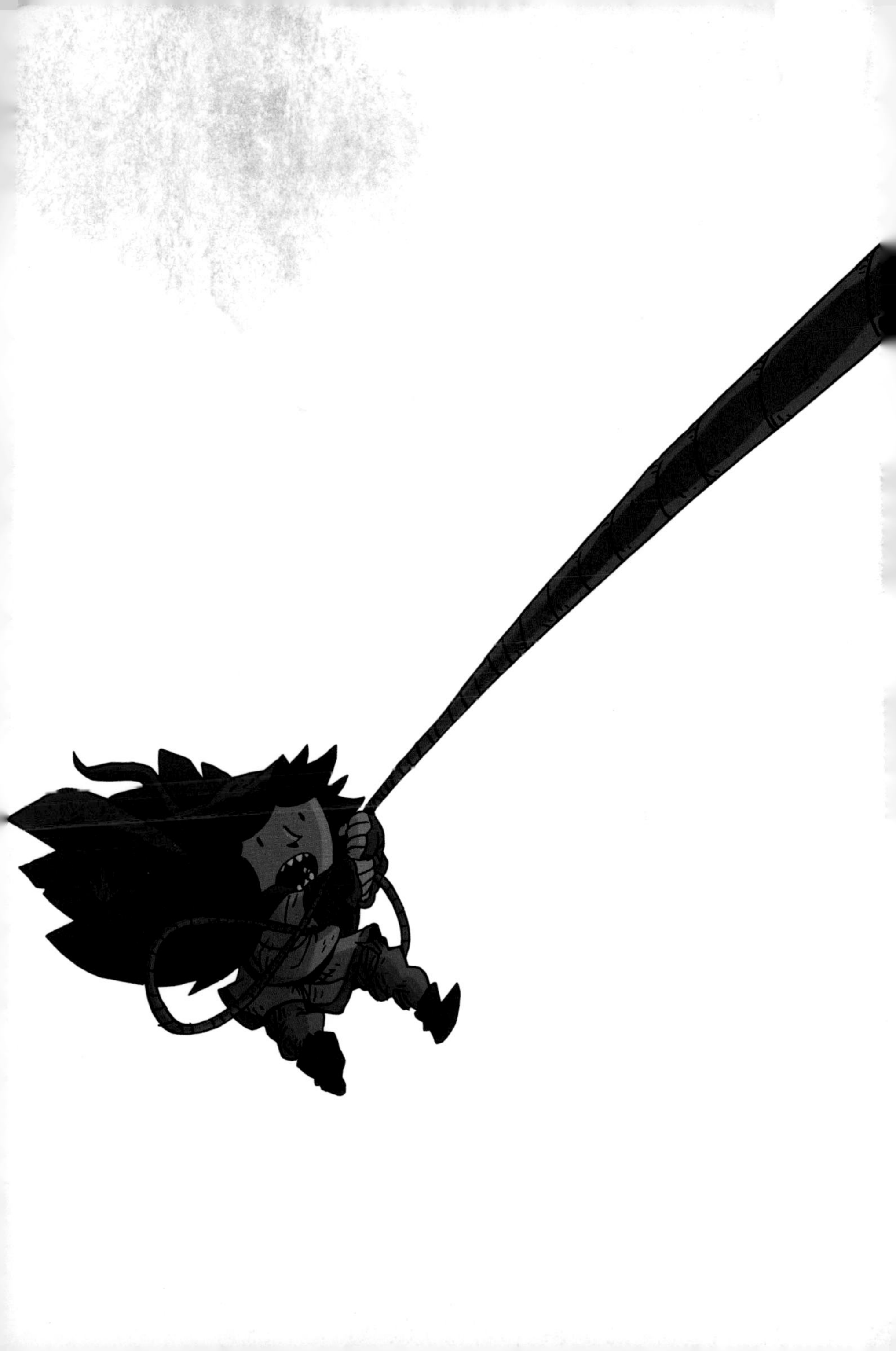

Sketch Gallery

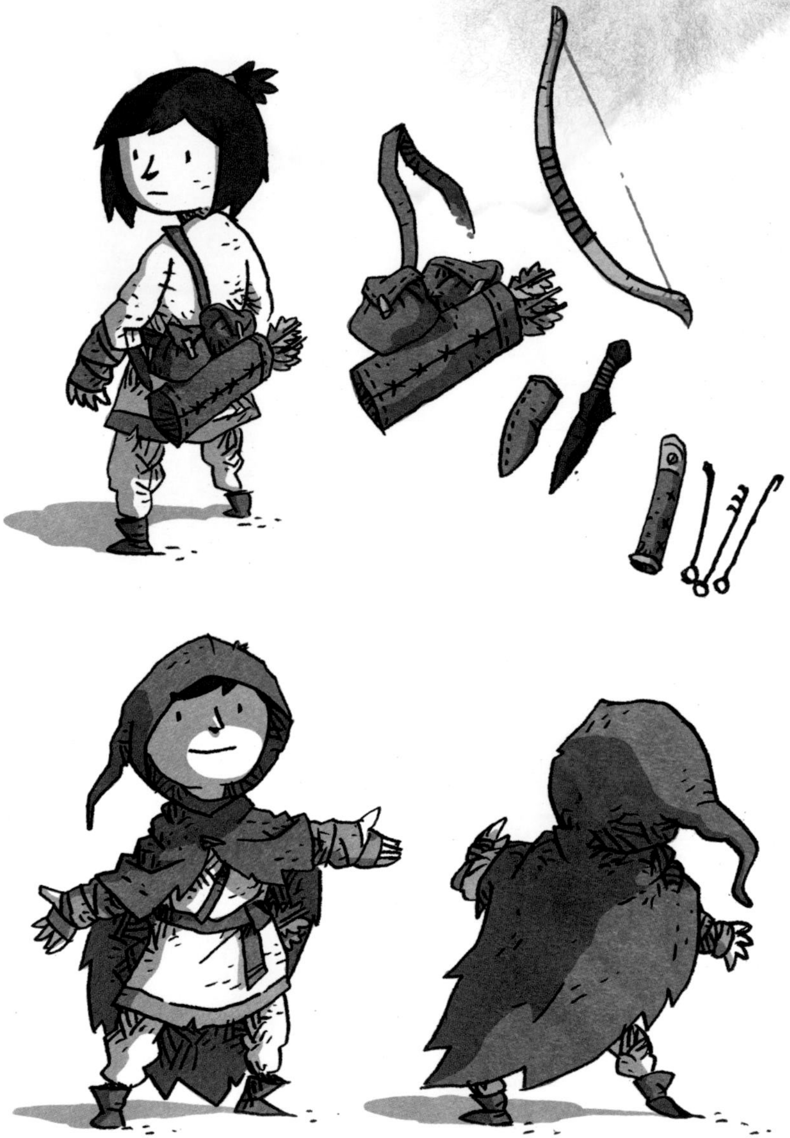

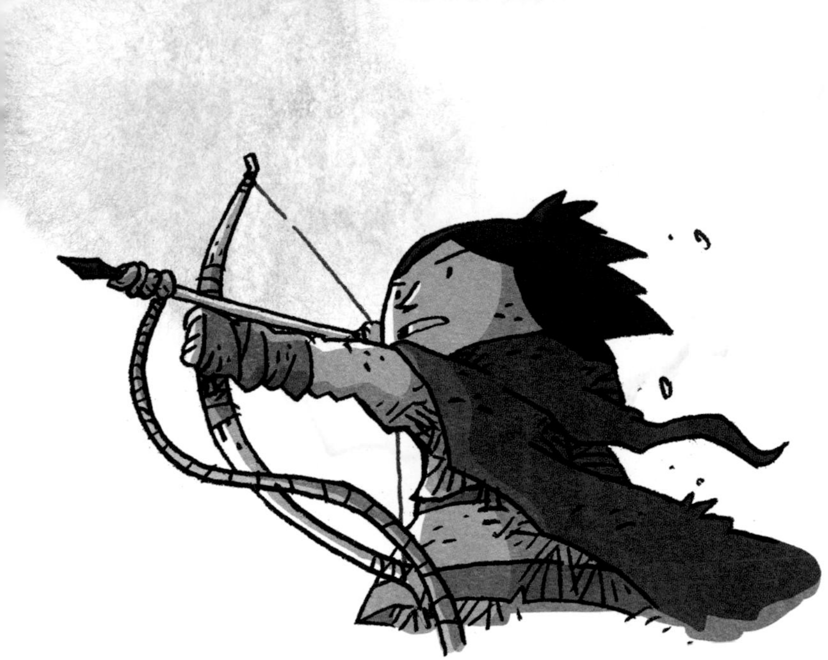

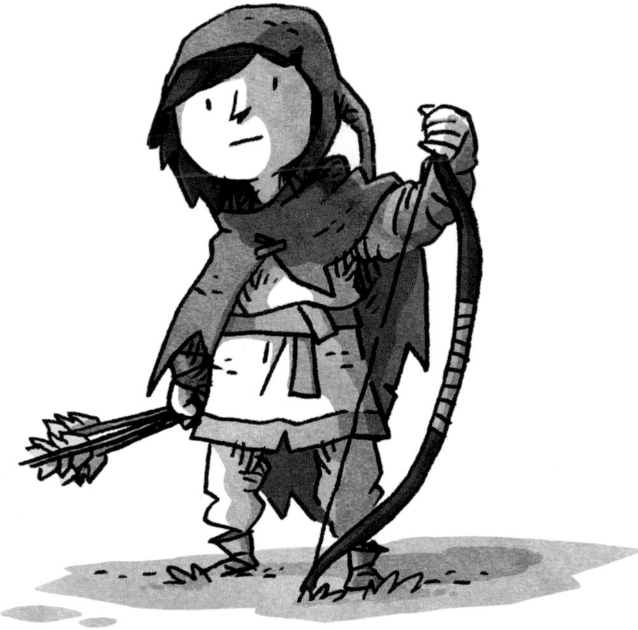

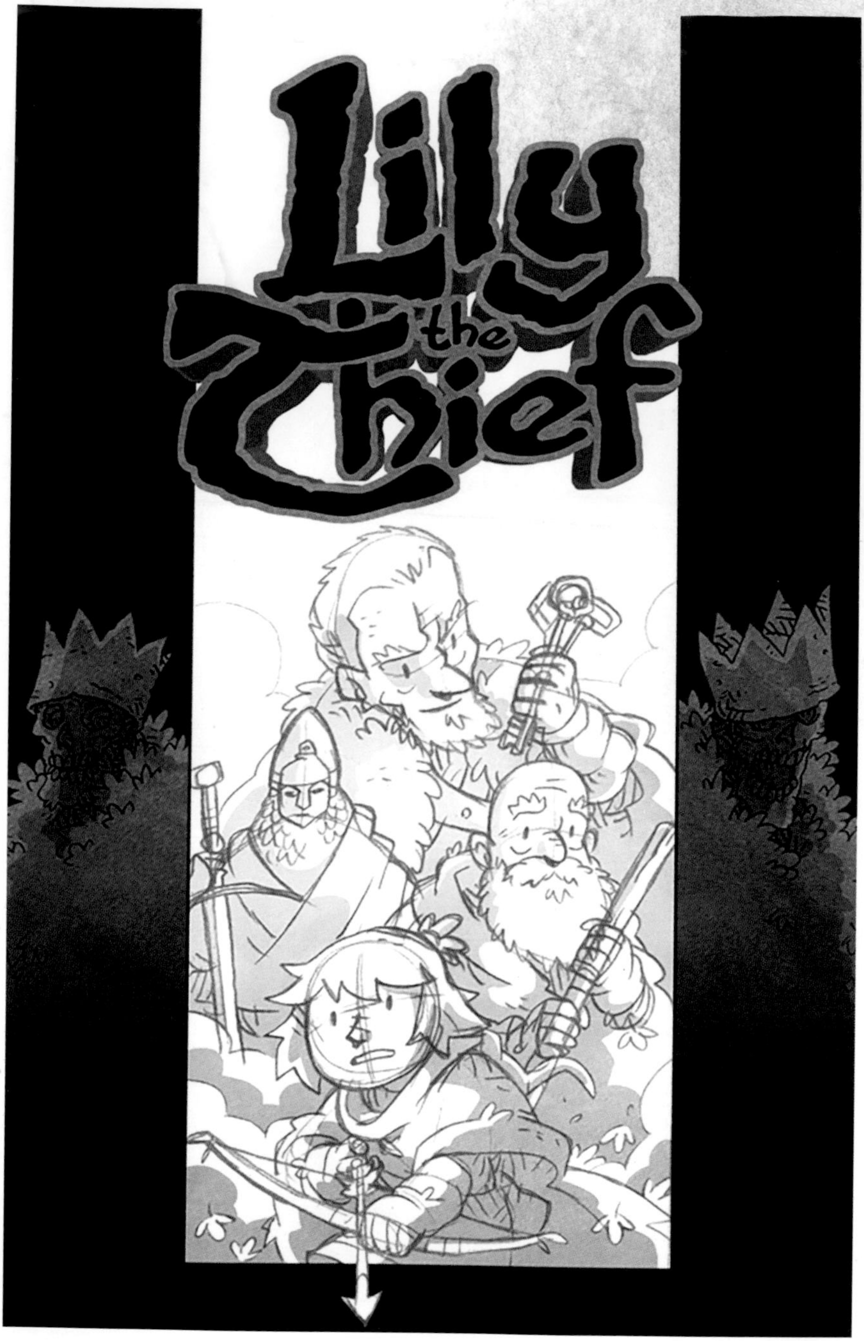
Lily the Thief

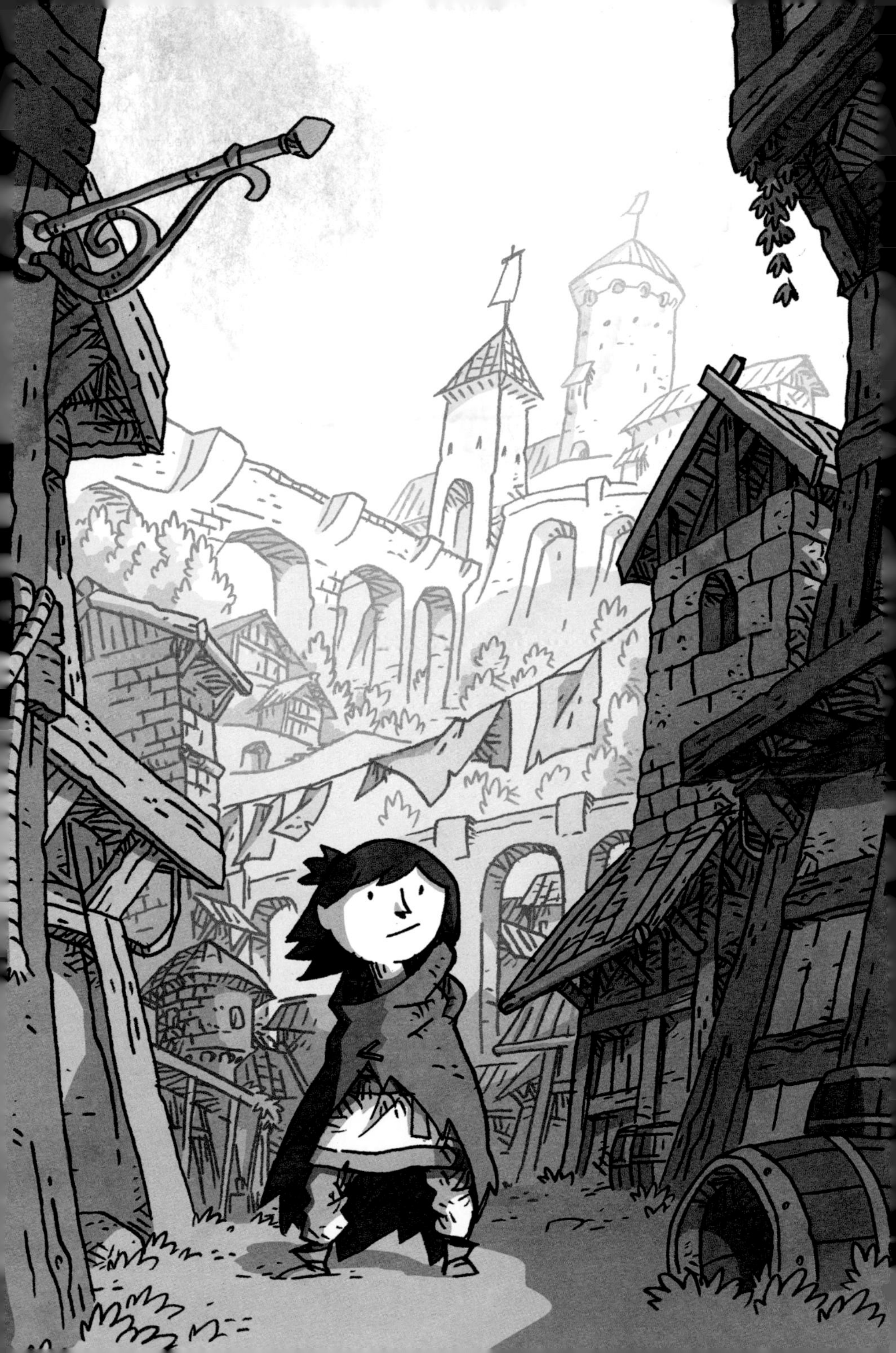

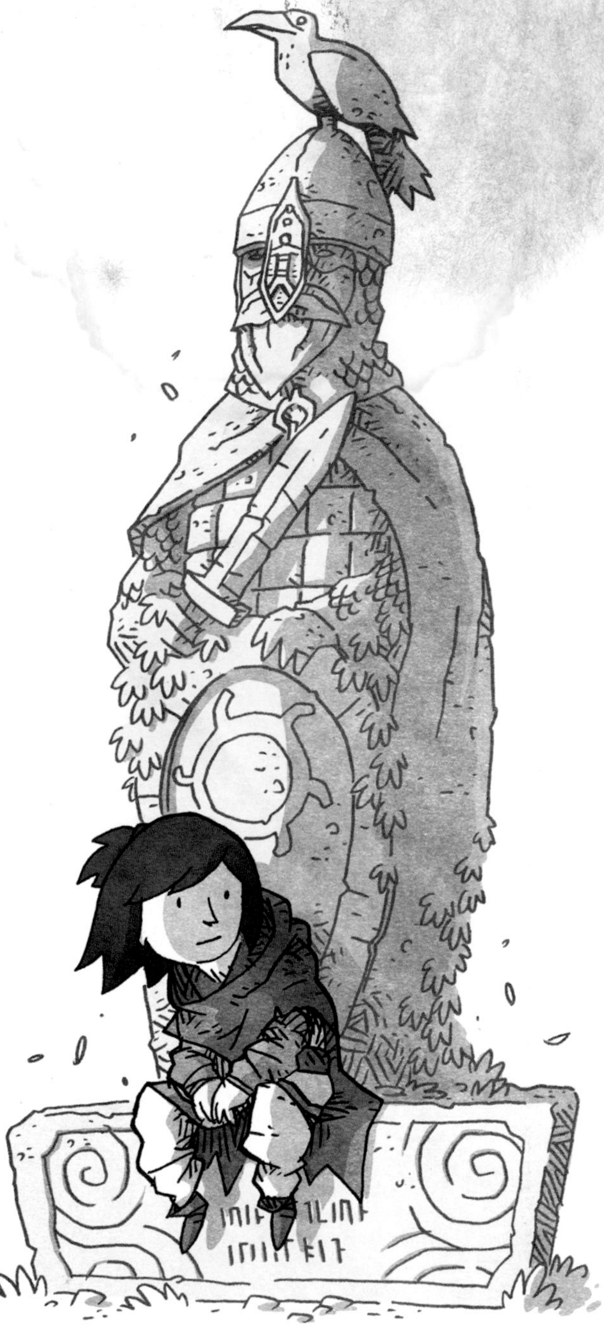

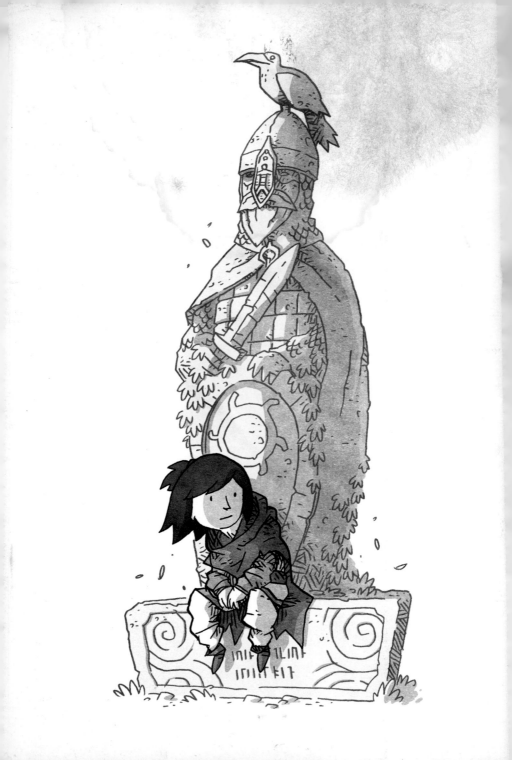

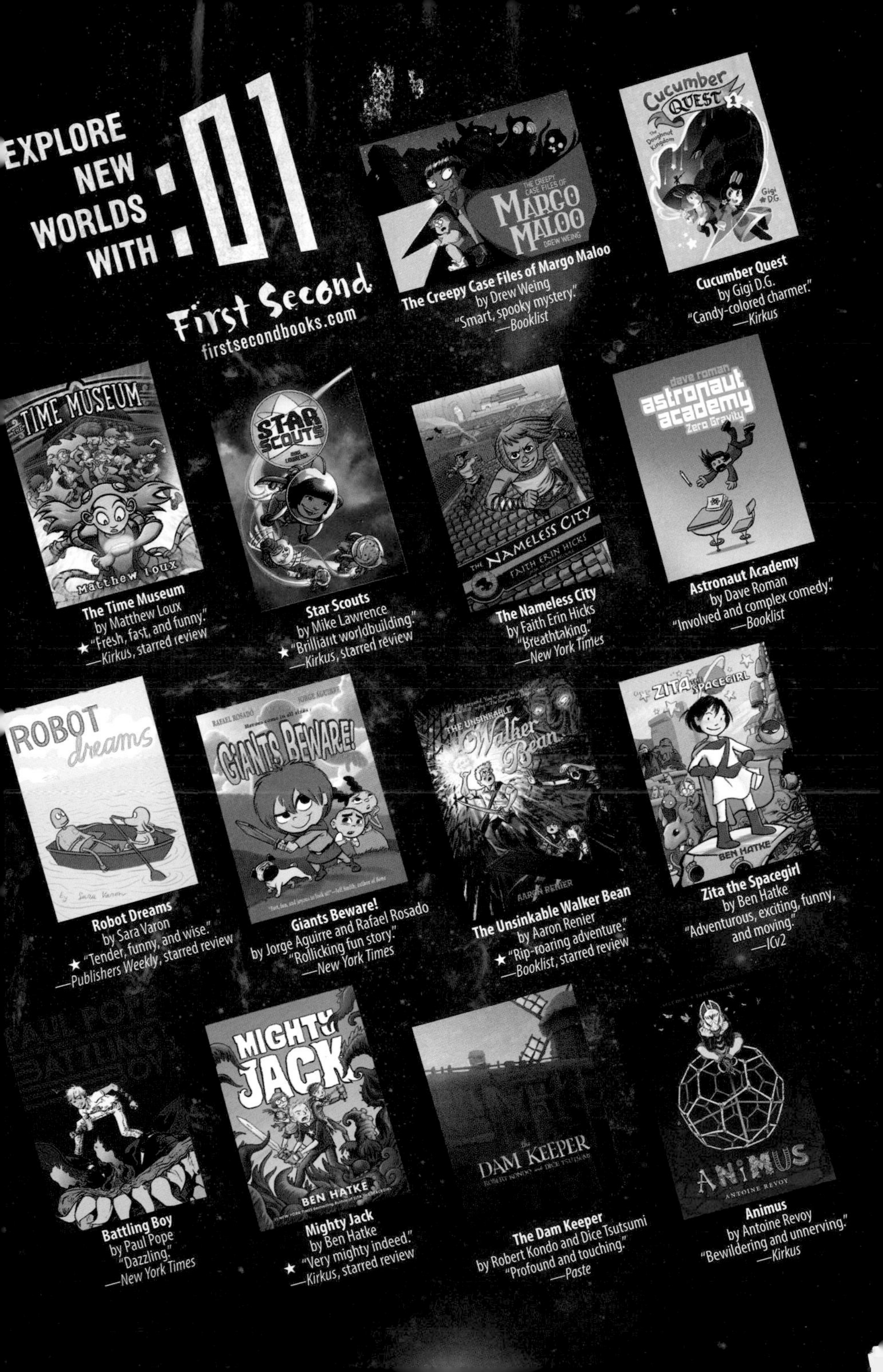
EXPLORE NEW WORLDS WITH :01
First Second
firstsecondbooks.com
The Creepy Case Files of Margo Maloo
by Drew Weing
"Smart, spooky mystery."
—Booklist
Cucumber Quest
by Gigi D.G.
"Candy-colored charmer."
—Kirkus
The Time Museum
by Matthew Loux
★ "Fresh, fast, and funny."
—Kirkus, starred review
Star Scouts
by Mike Lawrence
★ "Brilliant worldbuilding."
—Kirkus, starred review
The Nameless City
by Faith Erin Hicks
"Breathtaking."
—New York Times
Astronaut Academy
by Dave Roman
"Involved and complex comedy."
—Booklist
Robot Dreams
by Sara Varon
★ "Tender, funny, and wise."
—Publishers Weekly, starred review
Giants Beware!
by Jorge Aguirre and Rafael Rosado
"Rollicking fun story."
—New York Times
The Unsinkable Walker Bean
by Aaron Renier
★ "Rip-roaring adventure."
—Booklist, starred review
Zita the Spacegirl
by Ben Hatke
"Adventurous, exciting, funny, and moving."
—ICv2
Battling Boy
by Paul Pope
"Dazzling."
—New York Times
Mighty Jack
by Ben Hatke
★ "Very mighty indeed."
—Kirkus, starred review
The Dam Keeper
by Robert Kondo and Dice Tsutsumi
"Profound and touching."
—Paste
Animus
by Antoine Revoy
"Bewildering and unnerving."
—Kirkus

First Second

English translation by Lola Rogers
English translation copyright © 2019 by Roaring Brook Press

Published by First Second
First Second is an imprint of Roaring Brook Press,
a division of Holtzbrinck Publishing Holdings Limited Partnership
120 Broadway, New York, NY 10271

Don't miss your next favorite book from First Second! For the latest updates go to
firstsecondnewsletter.com and sign up for our enewsletter.

Library of Congress Control Number: 2018953656

Paperback ISBN: 978-1-250-19697-2
Hardcover ISBN: 978-1-250-19355-1

Our books may be purchased in bulk for promotional, educational, or business use.
Please contact your local bookseller or the Macmillan Corporate and Premium Sales Department
at (800) 221-7945 ext. 5442 or by email at MacmillanSpecialMarkets@macmillan.com.

Finnish text and illustrations copyright © 2016 by Janne Kukkonen
Originally published in 2016 in Finnish by Like Kustannus Oy as *Voro*
Coloring by Kévin Bazot copyright © 2019 by Casterman
First American Edition, 2019

Edited by Mark Seigel and Casey Gonzalez
Cover design by Andrew Arnold
Interior book design by Chris Dickey
Printed in China by 1010 Printing International Limited, North Point, Hong Kong

Sketched on a Foldermate sketchbook with a light blue Prismacolor Col-Erase pencil,
finished with Staedtler H pencil. Colored digitally.

Paperback: 10 9 8 7 6 5 4 3 2 1
Hardcover: 10 9 8 7 6 5 4 3 2 1